CORINTHIA FALLS

KIM HUTSON

Outskirts Press, Inc.
Denver, Colorado

Outskirts Press, Inc.
http://www.outskirtspress.com

Paperback ISBN: 978-1-4327-7167-6
Hardback ISBN: 978-1-4327-7169-0

Outskirts Press and the "OP" logo are trademarks belonging to Outskirts Press, Inc.

PRINTED IN THE UNITED STATES OF AMERICA

*To all those who serve and are served by the
Oklahoma United Methodist Circle of Care*

...and to Charles William.

Sarah's & Bill's Family —

Hope you Enjoy this stay
of Faith & Unity.

Join us when the 'Saints
Go Marchin' In!')

Phil 4:13 /

Timber's Story
August

I t was eleven o'clock on Sunday morning in 1981. The bell tower on Corinthia Fall's old church welcomed our local faithful and spiritual, the traditional and established, the dutiful as well as other self-comprised souls. The late morning sun hovering over the small northeastern Oklahoma town was piercing and oppressive. The congregation greeted one another upon entrance with simulated enthusiasm as each proceeded to the simple security of their customary and long recognized seating arrangement. The pianist and organist struggled mightily to play the prelude hymn in unison.

By the way, Timothy Oaks is my Christian name, but only Mom calls me Timothy. Everyone else just knows me as Timber. I'd say I'm fairly handsome, with shaggy-brown hair and of solid build.

I made my way up the stairs of the balcony followed by my teenage entourage. The four of us teens found our special spot where we could observe 'the show' down below. One charismatic group was made up of those who occupied our lower left in the sanctuary. This grouping we nicknamed the Standers. They would stand throughout most of the service, raise hands and shout amens and blessings which I and my young associates thought was some sort of contest in attracting attention.

The assembly was completed by the Setters, seated in the balconies to the lower right. These folks sit stoically during the church service, quiet and almost frozen, standing only when instructed. Their stationary status gave us an impression of disgust toward their counterparts on the left.

"Showtime," announced Anthony Bearkiller, a pocket-sized 4 foot, 8 inch Cherokee lad.

"'Fraid so, Ant," I acknowledged.

Thomas Johnson, the son of the local presiding deacon and only black family in the small community fiddled with his church bulletin. A couple years younger than us, a red-headed, freckled Becky Hooper sat silently behind in the fold-back chairs, adjusting her glasses.

Our church could conveniently seat about 300. From the upstairs, the church was in full view. We could even see the parking area from the clear glass windows surrounding the upper loft. We noticed some late activity occurring outside. I rose and moved to the window on the right side of the balcony. I motioned for Ant and Thomas to join me.

"The Sam's!" exclaimed Anthony. Becky stood at her seat and peered over her glasses at us. We were now a good twenty feet away. Old Doc Pyle looked over the top of his morning sports page with a questioning expression. The rest of the sparse balcony patrons seemed uninterested.

"Shhh," I hushed Ant.

"This is gonna be good," added Thomas, better known as TJ. Doc Pyle nodded affirmatively. Becky's blue eyes seemed to double in size behind her clear rimmed glasses as she covered her mouth with both hands and held her breath.

Sammy Sampson, his brother, Sandy, and their cousin, Gib

Sampson, were scheming outside the east exit door in the adjoining parking lot. Though seldom used, this entrance opened to the front of the church just below the choir loft and pulpit area.

The Sam's were local farm boys always out for a prank. They had with them a leashed billy goat that been coated with red paint. Gib was trying to keep the protesting animal under control while Sandy finished a similar paint job on Sammy. Sammy, barefoot and shirtless, was colored devil red, torso and feet. Gib and Sandy put on the finishing touches by balancing a head from the carcass of a male deer on top of their leader's head. An old pair of red suspenders was added for stabilization by overlapping the antlers of the deer to Sammy's blue jeans.

"Don't forget the pitch fork!" reminded Gib, equipping Sammy with the tool of the devil's choice while all three went delirious with laughter.

The slightly graying black man, Deacon Johnson, entered from the back of the raised platform, approached the pulpit and announced to the semi-full congregation, "Let's all join in our opening hymn on page 327, Nearer My God to Thee." The deacon's wife, Martha, portly yet elegant, stood in front of her small, golden robed choir motioning for all to stand. The Standers on the left were already upright as the reluctant Setters joined them. The Observers from the observation deck stood. Ant, TJ, Becky, Doc and I didn't even pick up hymnals. Our heads leaned forward with great anticipation.

Mrs. Sharp played the introduction on the pipe organ and the singing began:

'Nearer, my God, to thee, nearer to thee!
E'en though it be a cross that raiseth me,
Still all my song shall be,
Nearer, my God...'

The side door bashed opened. The beast-headed red devil in jeans raised his pitch fork in one hand. Leading the restless crimson goat in his other, he busted in to the front of the church of Corinthia Falls.

"Repent, you naughty sinners! Repent!" screamed Satan.

"Maaaaaaaaaaaaaaa, maaaaaaaaaaaa!" cried the goat.

The music stopped. The goat and devil quickly made their way around the pulpit area. The Standers kneeled in front of their pews. The Setters protected their women folk, while the choir made a run for the back door. The widow Fullbright fainted. Those of us in the balcony roared with laughter and applause. The deacon chased the two demonic creatures down the middle aisle of the church waving his Bible.

"Repent! Repent! Or you will turn into a goat! Repent!" repeated the devil.

"Maaaaaaaaaa, Maaaaaaaaa, Maaaaaaaaa!" went the demonic goat rushing the crouching Standers.

"Away with you, Satan!" shouted Deacon Johnson as the intruders made their way to the back of the church and out the front entrance where they piled into the back of an old green Ford truck. With Sampsons and goat in tow, the howling pack of mischief makers sped out of town.

The congregation was in a full state of shock. The Deacon, covered with perspiration, centered himself in front of the pulpit area, looked upward and stared sternly at his son, TJ, who was choking with amusement.

The members gathered themselves. The choir reentered the sanctuary as Doc Pyle made his way down to the Stander's area to attend to the widow Fullbright. Donna Bearkiller, mother to Anthony and a popular member of the Standers, assisted the town doctor.

"Stand back and give her some air," ordered Doc.

"Yep. Better yet, ya'll set down." suggested Emmitt Sharp, the self -appointed leader of the Setters and town mayor. Doc got the 89 year-old fragile lady in a secure sitting-up position. He nodded to an inquisitive Deacon Johnson that she would be fine. The Standers shouted praises. The Setters whispered of retaliations on the impostering intruders. The amused balcony compared notes. Ms. Martha led the choir in Amazing Grace. The Deacon kneeled and prayed for guidance.

Before the service was over, the Corinthia Falls Church had four testimonies of faith, five rededications, and one conversion. Doc Pyle who had rejoined us in the balcony leaned over to us and suggested, "Boys, looks like the Sam's and a goat brought more people to the Lord today than this here church has done on its own in the last ten years."

We followed our usual routine after church service. Our ride was my prized 1969 Chevy pickup, with a baby-blue body, white cab, and custom wheels. The front tag under the grill read 'Saints' and the official Oklahoma tag on the rear: Timber.

TJ and Anthony jumped over the chrome side rails into the bed of the truck. Becky looked over at us from the front of the church lawn. She said nothing but I knew she was waiting for an invitation.

"Coming, Becks?" I said.

She beamed and slid into the cab. The radio was blasting a Creedence Clearwater tune.

The first stop was always at Oak's Corner. Our family had owned and operated 'Oaks' for several generations. The 1980's version consisted of a full line of groceries, fresh meat and produce sections, a deli and grill for whatever any customer desired. Beer, bait and all other necessities any local or tourist might crave on the way to nearby Lake Corinth was all neatly packed into a 6000 square foot building. Two gasoline pumps with a lighted canopy completed the package. The aroma of fresh grilled burgers filled the air for blocks.

The town folk depended on Oaks for their daily requirements. More extensive shopping would require a 25-mile ride to Archer's Grove, the county seat and largest town in Quanapah County. Located at the intersection of two rural highways that connected the rest of the world with the town and the lake, our family had a niche.

I parked way out to the side of the store as was my custom to allow easier parking for our patrons. The Sunday noon rush was on. It was the typical mesh of churchgoers grabbing their end-of-the-weekend groceries combined with sunburned, hung over and worn out lake worshipers returning to their city dwellings.

Dad was at the checkout counter seeming to work both cash registers simultaneously. Mom was in the deli doing the work of three people: grilling burgers, making hoagies and deep frying chicken.

"Hey, Dad!" I said as we all entered through the double glass doors.

"Hey, hey," Dad replied. "TJ, Anthony…"

"Hey, Mr. Oaks," said the always-polite Ant.

"Yo," replied TJ.

"You two boys get the counter. We got a lil' problem out at the pumps." TJ and I took over the checkout area. Like most small town operations, Oak's was family operated with only a minimal amount of help. The Johnson family, the Deacon, Martha and TJ along with Becky filled out the labor force. While TJ and I ran credit cards and punched registers, Ant assisted by sacking groceries, helping us catch up with the surge of summer shoppers.

Dad had made his way out to the fuel pumps where there was a confrontation taking place between a lake visitor in a pickup pulling a pontoon boat and a non-gentleman in a grey Cadillac.

"Check it out!" TJ said, motioning to us.

The much larger owner of the Cadillac was threatening the boat owner with a clenched left fist. His other hand was waving the gas nozzle in the red face of the weekend vacationer.

My father was always the calm hand in many storms. Bill Oaks was well known and respected by the locals as well as the loco. The battle of who got to the fuel pump first was settled with Dad's typical show of mutual respect and pats on the back. The fuel consuming returned to normal status and both men appeared to return to civility.

"Way to go, dad!" I congratulated him, as he reassumed his place behind the checkout counter.

"Yep, Mr.O," added Ant, "I think you saved that pontoon guy from a super unleaded enema."

"Becky!" my mother called out. "Can you give me a little hand back here?" Becky was always eager to help in the deli. Mom had a warmth of personality that was as large as her physique was petite. "Now, wash your hands and throw a couple of birds in the fryer for you and the guys and don't forget to dump in some taters."

Becky got busy while mom worked the grill-full of the legendary over-sized cheese and onion burgers that made Oaks Corner famous. The secret was in the sauce. The store was still crowded and would remain so till the gals finished with the lunch orders. Dad worked the meat market. TJ and I worked the registers. Ant worked at looking busy.

It was almost 1:00 p.m. when Deacon and Martha made it

to work for the second shift. The noon rush hour was dwindling down.

"How'd it go at church today, Deacon?" inquired Dad, looking up from cutting some thick ribeye steaks for the meat display box. Martha scuttled to the back of the store to relieve the ladies in the deli. The boys and I were at full grin waiting to hear Deacon's reply.

"You would not believe it, Bill," the puzzled clergyman responded. "I don't know who worked harder today…this ol' black man, the devil, or God almighty hisself."

"Wha…?" asked Dad.

"Yep," TJ affirmed with a grin as our snickering filled the store. Deacon stared up at his tall, young son as to look right through him. "We'll talk later, son."

The deli crew, Becky, Martha, and mom finished cleaning up after the rush hour. "Thanks for your help, Becky," said mom. "Couldn't've done it without ya, girl."

"You're such a blessing," added Martha as all three embraced in a group hug. "Now girl, get that good smellin' chicken out of here. You and the boys be on your way. Ms. Eunice and I got this covered."

"Need us for anything else, Dad?"

"No Timber, your mom and I are gonna hang around here a little longer then hand it over to Deacon and Martha. Thanks for the help. Have fun at the lake."

On a Sunday afternoon in the hot summer time, my truck knew only one direction. It was off to Turtle Cove, our favorite swimming hole—a place unknown to most tourists. On the way out of town we passed the large old silver water tower proclaiming in worn out blue letters, Corinthia Falls Saints. Halfway up the tower was an attached wooden sign that read, 'Home of the Quanapah Challenge!' Under those words in fresh red paint was '1981 Champion: University of Arkansas.'

Lake Corinth is a canyon style lake, situated in the foothills of the Ozarks, which spills into far northeastern Oklahoma, particularly Quanapah County. The lake is the clearest body of water in the state of Oklahoma. Lake Corinth provides ample opportunity for boating, fishing, scuba diving, water skiing and sailing. The surrounding parks and marinas provide entertaining prospects for families in addition to party seekers. The rocky bluffs that encase the lake are as inviting as they are stunning. Nowhere is the lake area more serene than Turtle Cove.

We drove down the remote dirt road that was concealed by overhanging hickory trees. Before I could stop my truck near the water, Ant and TJ were out of the truck bed, removing jeans and Sunday shirts to reveal their swimming shorts. Typically, lake kids wear swimsuits during the summer instead of underwear. We were always prepared for a trip to the lake. I left the windows down and the ignition on so my favorite FM station out of Tulsa would provide us the proper background music. Becky, still dressed in a yellow summer dress, arranged the chicken dinner on an old wooden picnic table. The chicken was still warm, the fried potatoes medium and the six-pack of Cokes were chilled. A roll of paper towels replaced napkins and plates.

TJ waded out into about six foot of water which only came to his neck. The much shorter Ant swam out to TJ.

"Boost?" asked Ant.

The black youngster elevated the tiny Indian boy up on his shoulders. Using his comrade as a launching pad, Ant executed a perfect back flip into the warm clear water of the cove.

"Lunch," announced Becky.

We ate quickly. Hungry teenagers and Oak's fried chicken make for a quick meal.

Becky tidied up as the boys headed for the water to rinse their lunch off their faces and hands. Becky found a sitting place under a nearby pine to finish off her Coke and scrutinize the boys. Becky would not be swimming. She was much too shy and insecure for bathing suits.

Ant and I did our cliff diving exhibition off the surrounding rock bluffs, and conversation turned to church.

"How 'bout those Sam's today," I started.

"That was hilarious," said TJ. "I thought I was gonna die. Then the old lady passes out and…"

"It was a well presented display of pandemonium," quipped the intellectual Ant.

"I thought they'd never be able to top last winter's stunt of leaving that 100 pound snappin' turtle in the post office. People are still afraid to mail a letter," I added.

"Yo," said TJ, "and they painted 'Eat at Oak's' on its shell," mused TJ.

"My dad's still purty sore about all that. Wonder what they'll try next?" I wondered aloud.

"Leave it to Sammy Sampson. As soon as they're through celebrating, the next plan of attack will commence," said Ant. "That's as soon as they procure all of old man Sampson's moonshine deliveries. They got to keep busy supplying all the hooch for Quanapah County."

"Only one I know ever to go around that way is Doc and he ain't talking," said TJ.

Laughter broke out as Ant and I fell back into the water.

"Well, school starts back in a couple weeks. It's senior year, boys." I said. "Senior year for the class of '82...all five of us."

Ant nodded. "Us and the blest Solomon twins. The lovely and enchanting Sherry and her distinguished brother, Jonathon Bartholomew Solomon III."

"Aww, they're not so bad. Kinda rich, but not so bad," I said.

"We know you're more than a little partial to Sherry, Timber," said Ant. "Can't blame you, though. There is quite a lack of female talent around here. Sorry Becks." Ant looked over to Becky with his apology, and she rolled her eyes as if she was not amused.

"Yes sir, a real lack of lady talent… mainly of the dark variety," smirked TJ. "I guess that goes with the territory."

"Ever made it into the Solomon mansion, Timber?" Ant asked, looking up at me curiously. The Solomon home was the largest and nicest house on the lake, located above Cherokee Creek looking out over of Lake Corinth.

"Naw…, just the backyard."

"Oh, yes, the setting for the optional hole of the infamous Cherokee Creek Country Club." verified Ant with a touch of sarcasm.

"No Ant, numbers six and seven. There are seven holes. Do the math."

"Seven holes and only one green!" retorted Ant.

"What's up for this week?" TJ asked the group.

"We better check with Dad on our work schedule at the store first," I said. "I'd like to get in a little golf. I'm thinkin' Dad might front me to check out the new course over in Tahlequah. If not, it looks like Cherokee Creek," I sighed. "How about you guys?"

"You know, a few hoops over at the old gym. Might catch a fish or two. I might want to go with ya if you're just hanging around Cherokee," said TJ.

"Yes, me too." said Ant. "I'd like to investigate that Solomon backyard for myself. How about you, Becks?"

Becky shrugged her shoulders and smiled, just happy to be included in the conversation.

"Maybe she's goin' to breath holdin' practice," chided TJ.

Becky had developed a habit from early childhood of holding her breath in emotional or stressed situations. It seemed to be a built in protection mechanism. Most of us natives were used to her practice and just accepted it.

"Let's just leave that alone," I warned.

"No, wait," said Ant. "Let's make a contest out of it. Let's see if she can hold her breath longer than two of us put together. As soon as Becks holds her breath one of us goes under water. When he stays under as long as possible, another goes down for as long as he can. Let's see if she has the lung capacity to not breathe through the whole duration? What say, Becks?"

"Uh, okay," said Becky now standing up.

"Alright, who's going under first?" I asked.

"Don't look at me!" said TJ. "Black folks don't go under water. What about Ant? He's already almost underwater."

"Not funny," said Ant. "I'll go first, then Timber. TJ, you go observe Becks and make sure she doesn't cheat."

TJ waded out of the cove where Becky was standing barefoot at the edge of the waterline. A dripping wet TJ pointed at Ant with one hand and Becky with the other. "Game on!"

Becky inhaled deeply till her cheeks puffed. Ant swallowed a mouthful of air and ducked under the water. Standing over Ant, I could see him beneath the placid water. Becky remained composed, gazing slightly upward. TJ watched Becky while swaying his shoulders to the beat of the rock music that was serenading our setting.

Finally, Ant's bubbles began surfacing. I prepared for my part in the competition.

"Ahhhh!" gasped Ant as he broke the surface. Full of Turtle Cove oxygen, I sank underneath. Ant made his way to the edge of the water just several feet from TJ and Becky. He rolled over onto his back and fought for air.

The trick to staying underwater was to remain in a calm state exerting as little energy as possible. As I relaxed in a self-imposed solitude, my thoughts remained on Becky and the contest. Becky was the only child of Sarah Hooper who waitressed over in Archer's Grove and was finishing up her teaching degree at Northeastern State in Tahlequah at night. I always felt sympathy for Becks. Most of the time Becky was left on her own as her mother put in long hours to make ends meet. Our family made an effort to keep her included, sometimes out of compassion, sometimes admiration for her determination.

I could do the gentlemanly thing of letting Becky win, but unfortunately that would be unfair to the spirit of the game. After all, at six foot one and 180 pounds, I was recognized as the best athlete in town even though the small Corinthia Falls school system did not have a sports curriculum. My athletic resume consisted of running for miles through the hills surrounding Lake Corinth, shooting basketball with TJ, and playing golf.

My competitive spirit took over. I was determined to outlast Becky. There was no way I could let her win.

"Hey girl, exclaimed TJ, "your face just turned into one big red freckle! Are you going to explode?"

"More like implode," corrected a now recuperating Ant. "You might want to investigate if Timber has drowned. How much time has expired?"

"I don't know, but the radio is playing its fourth song since this here started. You people are nuts!"

Faced with drowning, I surrendered. The fresh air tasted better than defeat. I crawled my way to the rocky shore and gave Becky a thumbs up.

"Down goes Timber! Down goes Timber!" TJ pointed at me, doing his best Howard Cosell impersonation. "The winner and still champion…Miss Becky Hooper!"

Becky fell to her backside not minding that the yellow dress was now drenched with mud. The expression on her freckled, breathless face was one of satisfaction and contentment. She had not only beaten us, she had humiliated us playing by our own rules. Becky now belonged.

Too exhausted for any further aqua recreation, we spent the next few hours lounging in and around the cove. The talk revolved around breath holding records, school, the Sams, sports, music, girls, cars and finally a recap on last month's Quanapah Challenge, or the QC as the locals referred to the Annual event.

"It's a disgrace the QC in all its wisdom does not give an award for breath holding," said Ant.

The shadows started falling as the summer sun hid behind the western cliffs bordering Turtle Cove. We took a slow ride in the Chevy back to town to start our next week. I found a Creedence song after searching several stations: A bad moon was risin.'

Typically for most Mondays and Tuesdays at Oak's Corner in the summer, TJ and I put in two long days at the store. There was less lake traffic this time of the week. Dad would stay put in the office, TJ's parents, the Johnson's, would check in and out, but the general operation was left to TJ and me. I manned the checkout at the front of the store while my buddy would handle the deli. I took the money, while TJ fed the hungry as well as himself. We put in two long fourteen-hour days. This schedule worked great for us. We were only needed to fill in during busy hours during the rest of the week. We were expected to work some evenings and weekends when school resumed after Labor Day.

On this Tuesday morning a silver Mustang convertible pulled into the drive next to the gas dispenser. Dressed in a blue leisure suit, a tanned, finely groomed man of forty-something began fueling the sports car, taking great pains not to spill any gas on his well polished ride or himself.

"Hey, TJ!" I yelled back at the deli area. "Here's Benny!"

"What's he drivin'?" questioned TJ.

"Mustang convertible, '78?" I guessed. "Quite a looker."

TJ wiped his hands and hurried to the front of the store. He was as anxious to see the car as to see the charismatic salesman, Benjamin Larson. Benny entered the store, pulled out a money clip full of large bills and handed me a Jackson.

"What ya got there, Ben?" I asked knowing his answer would be dramatic.

"Gentlemen, what we got here is a 1978 King Cobra, one out of forty-four ever made. It's equipped with a hood scoop, dual mirrors, and a metric 5.0 engine."

"Bad!" drooled TJ.

Benny was the promoter, owner and fabricator of Larson Motors. His ego was as large as his used car lot west of town. It featured everything from used cars, boats and trucks to washing machines and lawnmowers. He also ran a pawn shop right out of his office. If Benny did not have what you needed in his inventory, he'd find it.

"How much for that baby, Ben?" I knew I wouldn't get a straight answer.

"Not for sale, boys," Benny stated proudly.

TJ and I knew better. Everything Benny had was for sale. There was always another deal, a new promotion and another exaggerated story to enhance the price tag.

Benny was an attention grabbing member of the Standers division at church.

"How about them Sampson boys?" he said. "They nuts or what?"

"More like 'what'," said TJ.

"Let me tell ya something, gentlemen. If you see that brood hanging around my place, let me know? And, uh, keep the change, Timber."

Benny strutted out to his prized Mustang, off for the next deal. I put the extra 75 cents in my pocket.

Wednesday was my day for golf. Dad rejected the idea of playing the Tahlequah course. He wanted me close by in case I was needed at the store. By 9:00 a.m. I had tossed my bag full of Wilson clubs into the bed of my school-colored 'Sainthauler' pickup.

The first stop was to pick up Anthony. The Bearkillers lived just down the block. Ant's parents worked at the hospital in Archer's Grove. Jack Bearkiller was the administrator at the local hospital where Donna, Ant's mother served as a nurse. Ant's older sister, Julie, was a medical student at the University of Oklahoma. All were very intellectually gifted as well as diminutive of physical stature.

We then picked up TJ at the store. He had gone to work with his dad. TJ had a sack of sausage sandwiches and three pints of orange juice ready, a convenient breakfast.

The ride to Cherokee Creek was just a few miles up the north bound two-lane highway. The fine homes nestled above the creek that fed off Lake Corinth offered an exceptional view with the creek down below and the lake to the north.

The first house belonged to Dr. Pyle. It was a modern log-cabin-style home with a two-car garage. Doc allowed us to use his old electric golf cart that he kept for short nature jaunts through the wooded area that led to the creek and on to the lake. Doc kept a spare garage door opener remote in the back of his mailbox. The doctor's front yard served as the starting hole on the Cherokee Creek 'Golf Course.'

There was actually no golf course. In a clearing opposite the creek and to the west of the homes was a small make-shift Bermuda grass green maintained by the homeowner's association, complete with a baby-blue and white flag pin that read 'Saints.' The residents used the green as target practice launching golf balls from their respective properties. Being the only member of the Corinthia Falls High golf team, I was granted a free pass.

We left my truck in Doc's drive. TJ pulled the cart out of the garage, pausing at the truck while I secured my golf bag in the rear. With his knees even with the steering wheel, TJ motioned at Ant to ride in the back of the cart as I walked over to the first tee.

"What it'll be, boss?" asked Ant, my self-appointed caddy.

I studied the hole only 100 yards away.

"Nine iron."

TJ and Ant rarely played. They were just along for the ride. Both friends offered plenty of advice on my game, considering neither knew how to swing a golf club. After a little stretching and a warm-up swing, I hit my first shot onto the green about 25 feet from the flag.

"Do that again," said TJ.

I tossed down another ball and repeated the performance.

This time my ball rested about 10 feet closer to the hole than the first attempt.

"Man! How did you learn how to do that?" asked TJ.

"Watching Jack Nicklaus on TV," I answered handing my iron back to Ant.

"Home course advantage," said Ant.

TJ chauffeured us down beside the lone green as I practiced putting from different locations.

"Keep your head down, Timber," Ant instructed.

"Easy for you to say, Mr. Anthony Bearkiller," said TJ. "You'd make a great putter. Your head is already down."

"There you go again! Another short person insult," pouted Ant.

"You're not short; you're a midget from the only family of Native American midgets in the state of Oklahoma. Consider that a compliment," shot back TJ.

"Compliment, my gluteus minimus!" Ant said in self-defense. "Now pay attention you elongated toothpick. Midget is an unacceptable term referring to a dwarf. Dwarfism is used to describe a physical condition characterized by short stature and disproportionately short arms and legs. I am not disproportionate. Therefore, I am vertically challenged!"

"Whatever…" panned TJ.

"That's enough, you two," I said. "Let's try out the Sharp's place."

The Sharp's was the next house in rotation. Emmitt, the town barber and his wife, Ann, lived in a perfectly trimmed, beautiful ranch style home with finely manicured gardens complete with an American flag waving on a towering pole centered in the front yard.

Both the Sharps were retired military. Ann now taught school.

Emmitt held court at the barber shop, lecturing to the town's male society on God, honor, country and conservative politics.

"Stay off the yard, Timber," warned Ant.

I tossed a couple of Titleists down on the opposite side of the road, respecting Mr. Sharp's well defined directive on reverence to his private property.

"Eight iron," I said and took the club from Ant. The green gained in distance as we continued down the block. I got one shot on and one off the green. We moved on to the next home, leaving the golf balls for later retrieval.

Joyce and Nathan Anderson were a retired couple in their mid sixties. They enjoyed the lake, spending time entertaining grand children at their cozy Victorian two-story home. Joyce served as volunteer secretary at the church.

"Hey, boys!" said Joyce. I saw you fellas pull up at Doc's and fixed you something to drink." Joyce scampered off the front porch, balancing three large foam cups full of iced lemonade.

"Thanks, Mrs. Anderson," said Ant reaching for the refreshment. "You make the best lemonade on the lake!"

"Got that right," said TJ.

The always bubbly, generous lady smiled. "Timber, how's that golf game?"

"Not as good as your lemonade, Joyce. Where's Nate?"

"Oh, he took the grandkids fishin.' Thought he'd better get out there before it got too hot."

"Tell him 'hey' for us," I replied.

"See you in church Sunday, boys."

Everyone liked the Andersons. They were always the first to volunteer for community projects. Never taking sides on town or church politics, Nate and Joyce were admired by everyone. The Andersons stayed in the balcony bleachers with the rest of us

Observers taking their place among the village youth and other non-committals to particular allegiances.

Two six iron stokes later, TJ pulled our cart into the driveway of Matthew and Clara Cox. Mr. Cox was the principal of our nearly defunct small Corinthia Falls School system. He ran the school, taught most of the high school classes, as well as counseling students. Clara taught elementary. Together they made up half of the faculty of Corinthia Falls.

"Here we are, Mr. Anthony," TJ said, smiling at Ant. "The home of your favorite mentors."

Ant was very familiar with the Cox household. As the top scholar in Corinthia Falls, Ant spent many evening hours studying at the Cox's. Matt and Clara were very good friends with Ant's parents. I figured it must be an intellectual thing. The Cox's also stood with the Bearkiller's at church on the Stander's side of the sanctuary.

Now using my five iron, I peppered the green target with several more white balls while TJ and Ant finished their lemonade.

The next tee box was located in the front of Benny's. The flamboyant merchant's bachelor pad conveniently had the three car garage doors all open to display his current toys; a speed boat, a shiny Harley-Davison and a 1975 Blue Cadillac Eldorado.

"Where's he get that stuff?" wondered TJ aloud.

"No where 'round here," I assured him.

"Three iron, Timb?" asked Ant.

"Yep, I think that will be enough." I gauged the distance at about 180 yards. I knocked two balls near the edge of the solitary green.

"We better go pick'em up, TJ. 'Bout out of balls." TJ floored the accelerator.

As I tinkered with chipping and putting the dozen or so balls

I had scattered on and around the green, the guys were admiring the Solomon mansion, our next stop and home of the final two holes.

The recently built Solomon residence was the talk of Corinthia Falls. Built on the high rocky ridge overlooking the water, the 8000 square foot, three storied home provided the perfect view of Lake Corinth.

In the backyard, a native-stone flight of steps led down to Cherokee Creek where the Solomon family's private dock was filled with watercraft for any occasion. Ski boat, fishing boat and a large houseboat: the Sherry John.

On the north side of the house facing the lake was the large swimming pool, complete with a heated whirlpool, all surrounded by a large patio. This setting of the luxury abode was completed with optimum landscaping, appearing more tropical than indigenous.

John Solomon was the president and sole stock owner of the Quanapah State Bank located in Archer's Grove. He inherited the position from his father, Jonathon Bartholomew Solomon I.

Without a local bank, most of Corinthia Falls did their banking at nearby Quanapah State.

The Solomon family, including John's wife, Jacqueline; the benefactor of Corinthia Falls, all sat together on the back pew of the town church in the Setters' area. 'Sir' John sat next to the middle aisle so as not to miss a handshake or a personal greeting.

The Solomon estate provided the final two tee boxes on the course/driving range. The first tee was on the southeast corner of the yard where a professional style, elevated tee area had been constructed. This created the sense of a real golf course. Using my three wood, I prepared to tee up, to the green that was now about 220 yards away, TJ and Ant were still gawking at the enormous structure of the House of Solomon.

Both attempts at reaching the green resulted in two balls about ten yards away on opposite sides of my objective.

"Not bad," said Ant. "Now what are you going to do on the next hole? The par three's are over."

TJ drove us over the circle drive that led to the final hole. The last tee area was located on the edge of the cliffs on the property. We were near the lake side of the house and directly in front of the swimming area.

"Eye candy!" announced Ant.

The stunning, blond Sherry Solomon, attired in a two-piece white bathing suit, was sun tanning in a lounge chair next to the pool. Two yapping tan Pomeranian pups alerted her of our arrival.

"Hello, guys!" Sherry waved while sitting up from her leisure. "Are you playing golf?"

"No, Miss Master, we jist out here pickin' yo cotton," replied TJ just out of Sherry's hearing range. Ant and I choked down our amusement at TJ's ethnic sarcasm.

"Hi, Sherry! Where's your brother?" I asked, trying to return conversation.

"Like you really care," whispered Ant.

"She's out of your league, Timber," added TJ softly.

"Oh, John's working with dad at the bank today," responded Sherry, now walking closer to us while wrapping up in a beach towel.

"Millionaire training?" suggested Ant.

"I heard that, Anthony!" frowned Sherry as Ant's Cherokee complexion added on a shade of red.

"Ready for school?" I asked trying to change subjects.

"Yes! One more year; then we're out of here! Look, I'll see you guys at church. Remember, if you get tired of using Dr. Pyle's cart, dad said you're welcome to use our new one."

"Thanks," I said, as we all watched Sherry gather her tiny pets and lead them into the house.

"I think I just broke one of the Ten Commandments," admitted Ant.

"Which one?" I asked. "Coveting or lust?" Ant nodded with affirmation.

"Why would she want to be 'out of here'?" said TJ. "She gots it made."

"Why would anyone wear makeup and jewelry while sunbathing?" added Ant.

"Let's finish up. It's getting hot," I said.

"What the…" TJ questioned with disbelief as I walked over to the well prepared final tee area. "What is that? Some sort of radar for detecting a Martian attack?"

The large contraption in question did look like something that came right out of NASA. The large, white round-shaped dish apparatus measured nearly 20 feet in diameter and was mounted at an angle pointing just above the southwest horizon of Lake Corinth. It was very impressive.

"That's the latest in communication technology, TJ," said Ant, "More commonly known as a satellite receiver. It receives from an orbiting satellite a digital signal and converts it into an analog format that a standard television can recognize. The Solomons are on the cutting edge. Properly tuned, they can receive around one hundred channels."

"Welcome to the 1980's, TJ," I added.

The last hole was the biggest challenge. Directly in front of the green, just some thirty feet out, was an enormous cottonwood tree that obstructed the view of the green. There was no way to create enough lift with one of my woods to clear the tree and reach the green now 240 yards away. One option was to attempt to hook the ball around the right side of the tree and draw it back to the left. Usually, this resulted in many lost balls to the waters of Lake Corinth. The other alternative was to simply lob the ball over the massive tree with a wedge, which would leave a second shot from the middle of the range. Any way you looked at it, it was impossible to get close. For this reason, number 7 was considered the option hole.

Ant knew the routine and furnished me the pitching wedge. The ball sailed over the tree settling down halfway to the green.

"'Bout all you can do," said TJ. "Go ahead and try to fade one with your driver."

I accepted the challenge as both boys knew I would.

"Here's the big boy," said Ant as he walked over to present me with my driver. "Let her rip!"

Trying to fade a ball to the left from my right-handed stance was a talent I had yet to acquire. As we all expected, my effort resulted in another lost ball to the rock-strewn shoreline of the lake.

"There must be a way of getting it there," urged Ant.

"No way," TJ muttered.

I stood back and observed the entire landscape and the Solomon's new huge satellite receiver just ten yards away to my right.

"Hmmm…" I wondered.

"I think I know where you are going, Timber."

"Uh, huh," acknowledged TJ. "To pick up some golf balls."

"No, no!" said Ant excitedly. "The receiver… centrifugal force!

The moving or directing away from an axis with a gravitational pull as a result of being spun around the object's center."

"Do what?" TJ asked, noticeably confused.

"Okay, look," said Ant. "If Timber could hit a golf ball into the right side of that big bowl that's setting at the perfect angle, the ball should spin out to the left side and thrust toward the green. Speed, height, and position are vital."

With driver still in hand, I lined up the bizarre shot. It was worth a try. TJ looked back at the Solomon's home to make sure no one was watching my assault on their private property.

"Go for it!" TJ demanded.

"Midway and to the far right, Timb," coached Ant.

My drive struck the lower inside of the receiver, slung around and flew back at us, denting Doc's cart.

"Day-yang!" TJ cried out while moving the golf cart to safer sanctuary.

"One more time, Timber," said Ant. "Little higher and to the right. Take a full swing."

As I stood there addressing the ball, I had the sense of the ideal projection of the shot; an outer body intelligence of potential perfection. The ball entered the right side of the large concave contraption, hugging the inner shell and was projected at an extreme velocity out the other. Ant and I rushed to the right side of the big cottonwood as TJ followed in the cart. The ball sailed toward its proper destination, landing several feet short of the green. The momentum of the shot took it nearer and nearer to the hole.

Ant and I were now in a full run as TJ passed us in the cart. The ball continued rolling, stopping two feet from the hole.

"Let's see Jack Nicklaus do that!" exclaimed a now-out-of-breath Ant.

"Money!" screamed TJ.

The three of us stared at the golf ball just admiring the occasion. Without looking in my bag, I pulled out the putter, walked onto the green, and tapped in the short putt. Humbly, in typical golfing manner, I bowed to my audience.

"You just eagled the option hole!" proclaimed TJ.

Golf… it's a great game.

The church was open for business the following Sunday. I found our customary parking spot. My friends noticed several of the men, members of the Setters' Union, posted at each entrance.

"Security is in place," observed Ant.

"Watchin' out for them Sam's," noted TJ as we all exited my truck.

We found our usual seats in the balcony with the rest of the Observers. We saw many of the Corinthia Falls young people and the under thirty crowd gathered, along with other non-members of the partisan groups on the lower floor. Becky sat to the back of us, next to Doc Pyle reading his sports page. I waved over at the Andersons. Joyce and Nate acknowledged my greeting and returned the gesture, both smiling broadly.

Ant walked over to the window to monitor the situation. TJ silently motioned at Ant with palms up and questioning eyes. TJ shook his head as to nix the possibility of a repeat performance by the Sams from last Sunday.

As Ant moved back to join us, Deacon Johnson made his entrance, followed by Ms. Martha and the choir.

"Let's all stand and sing our opening hymn!" invited the Deacon, gesturing with his hands for all to rise.

As we rose and found the correct page in our hymnals, TJ whispered, "I'm on good behavior today. I can't take another lecture from Dad on how my 'conduct in worship is inappropriate for a Christian'."

"Really, then how about those guys down there?" I asked, looking down on the pews below.

The regular casts of characters were in place. The BearKillers and the Coxes swayed to the music as they sang among the other Standers. Benny Larson was winning the hand-raising competition. The widow Fullbright's amens could be heard above the rest of the music.

The Setters stood statuesque, concentrating on the well-known hymn, presenting superior reverence. The finely groomed Solomons, the perfect picture of a family at worship, anchored the back pew. Emmitt Sharp and his wife, Ann, were in their familiar spot up front leading the Setters. Emmitt was glancing to the front and side entrances for possible intruders.

When the music was over, the Deacon waited for the last few shouts of joy coming from the Standers section to begin his announcements.

"As you are well aware, a week from tomorrow is Labor Day," the Deacon began. "Next weekend is a busy one for our community, entertaining the lake visitors for the last holiday of our summer tourist season. It is also that time again for our church's Annual Watermelon Social to be held at the State Park on Saturday evening. This year, again, Brother Lawson is the chairman. Benny, you have anything to add?"

"Oh, Lord spare us," Doc undertoned, preparing for Benny's promotional speech.

"Thank you, Deacon." Benny stood to address the congregation from the middle of the Stander's section. "This year I have arranged for a load of the best watermelons in all of Oklahoma to be delivered right here to Corinthia Falls. I purchased them from a little old couple down south of Sallisaw that have won many awards for their melon crops. After great lengths of contemplation, meditation and quiet prayer, I came to the conclusion that these are the best watermelons on God's green earth! They are crisp, sweet and flavor packed red-fleshed melons with very few seeds. So, come out and enjoy the fellowship at the park next Saturday."

A chorus of halleluiahs came from the Standers while the rest of the church offered polite applause.

"Thanks, Benny, for all your efforts." said the Deacon. "You have this whole church hungry for watermelon."

"Yes, thanks Benny," quietly mimicked Doc.

"On to other business of the church…we received a letter this week from Colonel Armstrong," stated the clergyman, displaying the handwritten letter to the church. As you know, Colonel Armstrong is the Principal Apostle of the Grace in Fellowship of Christian Churches Association to which we belong. The Colonel's ministry connects us to many other small community churches here in the States and abroad."

Deacon Johnson read aloud the correspondence:

"My Brother and Sisters of the Church of Corinthia Falls,

I greet you with the Good News of Jesus Christ who came to us as a man and was shown to be the Son of God when the most powerful raised Him from the dead by way of the Holy Spirit! Let us share in this Good News of the Gospel that we may bring glory to the name of our Lord.

Dear friends of Corinthia Falls, we are among those who have been called to belong to Jesus Christ. Peace and grace be with you from the Father and the Son.

I am writing you from the Church of our Brothers and Sisters we established in Gallay, Mississippi. The people of the Gallay Church send you warm greetings. They have been a blessing in my stay here over the summer.

I have been praying for the opportunity to finally meet you so that we can share the spiritual blessings that will assist your church to grow powerfully in the Lord. I want to dwell among you and experience your good fruits."

"Well then I hope we have some watermelon leftover," inserted Doc softly with his usual dry humor.

The letter continued:

"I should be arriving in the next couple of weeks. The folks here at Gallay will arrange for my transportation. Deacon Johnson and I will discuss my accommodations at that time.

I am also looking forward to hearing about your part in sponsoring the Quanapah Challenge. This event has bought much exposure and publicity to your town.

To God is the glory!
Yours in Christ,
Col. Pavlos Lincoln Armstrong

"Well, isn't this great news!" said the Deacon responding to the announcement of the coming visitation. Let's all prepare our church for the Colonel's arrival and make him welcome during his stay. I understand that Colonel Armstrong travels light, so we will need to make arrangements for his lodging.

Are there anymore announcements at this time?"

"If I may, Deacon?" said Emmitt as he stood and faced the congregation from his front pew position on the Setters' side.

Mr. Sharp was dressed in a short sleeve white shirt and black tie. "There is a problem we need to discuss," he said. "I am referring to the ongoing disruption in our community and our place of worship by the Sampson boys. These young thugs have menaced us for long enough. Since we have no law enforcement here in Corinthia Falls except for the occasional Quanapah County deputy's leisurely appearances, some of the men and I have organized a group to provide protection against these hooligans."

A rumbling of groans was heard from the Standers' section.

"Sounds and looks more like a militia to me, Brother Sharp," said a now upright Matthew Cox from the middle of the Standers.

"Just who gives you this authority and to what extremes will you go to implement it?"

There was a scattering of amens from the Standers.

"May I suggest prayer and counseling as opposed to violence?"

"Hallelujah!" shouted the widow Fullbright now standing with hands high in the air and gazing to Heaven.

Emmitt retorted. "Matthew, if you could get those boys in your classroom maybe then you could counsel them. We are all for prayer, but we must protect our families and our way of life!"

"Yes, with a rear end full of buckshot!" a man's voice from the Setters' side added.

This caused an eruption of accusations. Both sides of the church stood facing each other in an immense argument. The vociferous quarrellings and challenges resembled a prelude to a gang fight.

"People! People!" cried out Deacon Johnson trying to regain control of the contentious assembly. "We are all God's children. This is no way to conduct a worship service!"

"You tell'em, Dad," said TJ almost inaudibly from upstairs.

"Now form a committee…"

"Quit your feuding and let's solve this like Christians," said the Deacon, glancing up at the balcony. "Brother Sharp, Brother Matthew and uh, uh…Joyce Anderson…"Will you meet me in the church office for a committee meeting to help resolve these issues after service?"

With three affirmative nods the near mob scene returned to status.

"Now, let us go to the Lord in prayer…"

September

The following week was spent in preparation for the last fling of the Lake Corinth summer season. TJ, Becky, and I assisted Dad, the Deacon and others preparing Oak's Corner for the tourist invasion of the Labor Day weekend. Extra inventory was required to handle the demand for good food, groceries and fun. Putting it all together was the hard part. The fun part was taking in the money.

By Thursday the store was ready for the onset. Every freezer, refrigerator and walk-in cooler was full. It would be my only day off during the busy week. I decided to sleep a little late and then go for a run before the day became too warm.

Running was right behind golf in my recreational pursuits. The only thing in front of golf and running was breathing and eating. I liked to run.

I liked to start off my jog from our house attired in my light blue Corinthia Falls' gym shorts and my Adidas all-terrain running shoes. Shirtless in the summer, I would run through the neighborhood up to Main Street. From the beginning to the end of town, I pounded the sidewalks, taking in the small business district. I would pass our store. Then, moving further down the boulevard, came the office of Dr. Robert L. Pyle, M.D. Across the street was Sharp's Barber shop with the traditional barber pole on display. The closed down old Comet movie theatre and several empty buildings along the way remained vacant reminiscent of a local economy that was much more abundant in an earlier time.

There was the floral shop and the beauty parlor. The old small brick post office, where Postmaster Chester raised Old Glory, was next to city hall, followed by the hardware store and the single bay carwash. The church was located in the center of town. Its bell tower served as the apex of the community, always within view.

Near the end of town was a well kept historic building that was once the local court house until the county seat was moved to Archer's Grove sometime back in the thirties. The long cement steps surrounded by large granite columns led up to the entrance that still had Quanapah County Court House etched in the masonry over the doors. A conservative sign placed neatly in the well manicured yard read Corinthia Falls Gentlemen's Club. The aged structure's parking lot stretched to the next corner and around the backside.

On the way out of town was our undersized school where the Cox's green Buick Regal was parked out front as the Cox's prepared for the new school year.

My trek would lead out of town to Corinth State Park. The park featured a marina, camping sites, cabins, a boat launching ramp and hiking trails. At seventeen, my well conditioned body was accustomed to the rigors of the lengthy expedition. As I ran under the pine trees shading the unending asphalt roads that interweaved the park, I felt I could run forever. I felt at peace with my surroundings as my mind drifted from the impending weekend, to school, to church and to my future, while trying not to think about Sherry Solomon. The music of Creedence Clearwater rang through my head and off my lips. I felt stronger and stronger, running faster and faster.

"Timber! Wait up!" I slowed down to a brisk walk. Looking

over my left shoulder I saw Johnny Solomon hurrying to catch up. John was fittingly dressed for the lake in swim shorts, a matching Hawaiian shirt, and deck shoes.

"Hey, John. What's goin' on?" I asked in between gasps.

"I just took the speed boat by the marina. Dad wanted me to have it checked out before the weekend. Looks like a big one. The campsites around here are already full and this is just Thursday."

"Yep, it'll be busy, but not as busy as the Fourth or Memorial Day with the 'Challenge' and all." I acknowledge, knowing full well that he was in reality inquiring how large of a deposit my Dad would be making at his father's bank next Tuesday.

"Well, it should be pretty good with this weather," John said. "Ready for school?"

"Gotta be. Say, how's that new satellite TV thing workin' out?" I asked as we were both now down to a very slow walk.

"Well, it was doing great for a while. We were getting all kinds of channels. Then all the sudden last week we were back to just three or four. Dad and I checked out the receiver. It looked like somebody had pelted it with something. The installers are coming back next week."

"Hmm." I swallowed. "Going to the Melon Festival Saturday?"

"If we get off the lake in time," John answered pulling his designer sunglasses down off his blond hair. "You?"

"Sure, if Dad lets us off for awhile. Just have to see how it goes."

"Well, I know TJ and you are going to be busy. Hang in there, sport!" and the future banker slapped me on the shoulder.

"Ok, later." I resumed my original pace.

It was getting hot and a cold lemon-lime Gatorade awaited me at home.

S tarting Friday, it was all hands on deck at the store. My parents, all three Johnsons, Becky and I would work without much of a break throughout the weekend's onslaught of lake goers. The cash registers rang as the throngs of customers emptied the shelves and we separated them from their money.

The gals turned out bundles of prepared meals from the deli's grill, Dad and the Deacon kept the store stocked while TJ and I managed the checkout area.

By late Saturday my Dad looked somewhat tired but pleased.

"Timber, how 'bout you kids headin' on down to the Watermelon Festival?" suggested Dad, wiping his receding brow with a shop cloth. "I think us old folks can handle it for awhile. Besides, we need your representation down there."

"You sure? What about the Deacon?" I asked.

"Things will be fine without me," the Deacon interrupted. "I might run down there a little while later…and after all, we got Benny in charge!"

"Oh, spare me," said dad, rolling his eyes as TJ and I chuckled.

"Hey, Becks! Want some watermelon?" I hollered back toward the deli.

"Sure! Is it okay?" asked Becky, looking at my mom for permission to leave her post.

"You go have fun, girl," reassured Mom as Martha gave Becky a quick hug.

"Let's ride!" said TJ.

We parked in the graveled parking lot next to the covered pavilion located conveniently in the center of the State Park. To the west was the lake, and the sun was starting to go down behind the bluffs. A dozen picnic tables were neatly arranged under the lit canopy where the faithful had gathered for the traditional feast. A hand written sign with bold words 'CHURCH OF CORINTHIA FALLS WATERMELON FESTIVAL...NO ALCOHOL ALLOWED' was nailed to a nearby hickory tree.

The gathering was divided as usual into the different social groups. Standers to the left enjoyed their normal hug fest. Setters in the tables on our right politely occupied their places while the Observers mingled throughout.

Two large livestock water troughs were iced down and full of melons, one in the center of the pavilion where Benny was presiding and another in a farm trailer near the road.

"Hey, you guys made it!" Ant greeted us, as the three of us approached the ensemble.

"Dad had mercy on us," I said.

"Looks like the local mafia is in full force?" inquired TJ as we surveyed Emmitt's men patrolling the grounds.

"Yes, the defenders of righteousness will keep us safe from all harm," said Ant.

"All right, folks," announced Benny. "Let's get this started with a blessing. Brother Bearkiller, if you will...?"

All stood while Ant's father, Jack, raised a hand and blessed the occasion.

"Now form a line right here and get a slice of the best watermelon on the lake. We got plenty, so come back for all you want. How about youngsters first?" said Benny, now fully in charge.

The Solomon family led by the father, did the slicing and serving on paper plates. John Jr. and Sherry served the iced tea while Jacqueline furnished the forks and paper towels.

Becky followed TJ, Ant, and me in the receiving line.

"Timber, how's that golf game going?" inquired Mr. Solomon as he placed a large chunk of melon on my plate.

"Not bad, sir," I responded. "And I appreciate you allowing me to use your front yard to practice."

"No problem, son," the banker replied. "How are the rest you kids?"

"Hi, Timber," Sherry broke in, handing me an iced tea. "You like sugar?"

"You bet he does," whispered TJ.

Ant snickered at the remark. Becky frowned at TJ.

"Sure," I answered. "You and John come and join us when you catch up."

Becky seemed slightly irritated at the invitation.

"Okay, in a bit," said Sherry.

We headed off to join our own age group, gathering at a couple of old tables several yards away from the pavilion, the infamous old green pickup of the Sampson family came speeding through the park. The horn was honking. The tires screeched while navigating the sharp turns. Sammy and Sandy were in the back of the truck waving and gesturing to all of the picnickers as Gib drove.

Everyone stood staring as the noisy old truck vanished out of the park. Several of the delegated men in charge of church security hustled toward the roadside.

"They're up to something'!" remarked Chet Chester looking back at Emmitt Sharp. "Better look around."

"Ominous," stated Ant as Becky held her breath.

People looked under the tables. Parents counted their children. Men surveyed the premises. The widow Fullbright choked on her watermelon.

Doc was leaning on the trailer full of the second round of melons finishing off a cigar.

I walked over to the pot bellied doctor to inquire on his wisdom.

"Got any ideas to what that was all about, Doc?"

"Indeed I do, Timber. Indeed I do," Doc said, looking at me then down at his feet.

The doctor reached down and picked up an empty Mason jar. He brought the open container up to his nose and sniffed. He then tasted several drops of the remaining clear liquid.

"Ahh, good stuff." Doc closed his eyes while stomping out the stogie.

Doc handed me the jar for my inspection.

"Moonshine?" I exclaimed, looking at Doc for verification.

"Shhh." We don't want to entice the masses," said Doc. "Let's take a closer look at these melons."

Trying not to be too noticeable, I reached over the rail of the trailer and retrieved the melon lying on top. I placed it on the outer wheel well for Doc's examination. Together we rolled over the oblong fruit. I could tell Doc was looking for something.

"There it is!" said Doc. "All the evidence I need."

"Wha'?" I asked confusedly.

"Right there, Timber. See that tiny puncture?"

Doc pointed out a very small pin hole that appeared to penetrate the rind of the melon.

"Looks likes the Sampsons injected this batch with some of their pappy's finest, using a veterinary syringe from down on the farm."

"Wow, what a trick!" I said, flabbergasted.

Doc pulled a pocket knife from his trouser pocket and cut into the melon length-wise separating it in halves. He then wedged a large sample out of the heart of the juicy melon with the knife and ate it.

"Watermelon, it's not just for breakfast anymore," Doc mimicked the well-known television commercial.

Doc nodded for Benny to join us at the trailer.

"What's up, doctor?" asked Benny. "Timber, everything all right?"

"Ben, these here melons are a little over ripe," said Doc, offering Benny a taste of melon from the tip of the pocket knife. Curiously, Benny pulled the portion of fruit from Doc's knife and tasted the morsel. Doc joined him in another bite.

"Holy....!" cried out Benny softly.

"Nothin' holy about it, Ben," replied Doc with his mouth full.

"What happened?" asked Benny.

"Sam's," I informed Benny, handing him the Mason jar.

"We'd better keep this quiet," Doc suggested. "These in the trailer are probably the only ones contaminated. If the first batch was juiced we'd have known by now."

"Agreed," said Benny.

I nodded yes to the secret.

"What if we run out of servings?" asked Benny.

"Well, you could save some of this batch for Brother Emmitt's militia," stated Doc somewhat obnoxiously.

Doc and the festival chairman walked backed to the pavilion to mingle with the crowd. It was now getting dark. I rejoined my friends and the other youth.

"What was that about?" asked TJ.

"Over ripe melons." I winked.

"I'm afraid Brother Larson says we must abandon the festival in the honor of safety," proclaimed Emmitt so all could hear. "We know the Sam's are up to something."

"Emmitt, everything is just fine," Benny said. "Is everyone having a good time? How 'bout them watermelons?"

The crowd from the Standers side agreed to progress with the evening. Compliments were given on the quality of the melons.

A round of polite applause was given to Benny and the

Solomon family. The evening continued.

A defeated Emmitt Sharp retreated to huddle with his soldiers. It seems a consensus was made to resume in the festivities, but be alert to caution.

The first load of melons was nearly gone after second and third helpings. The guardians of the social were still on patrol.

Their seriousness created an uneasy ambiance not typical of a church function. Benny could not resist.

"Folk's, how about a hand for Brother Emmitt and his group providing security? Guy's, we still got some more melons over at the trailer and I notice you fellas haven't had a bite."

"Absolutely!" said the cheerful Joyce Anderson among scattered claps of approval. "I insist. Nate, help 'em out."

Mr. Anderson was joined by the Family Solomon as the serving line shifted to the stock trailer. The tailgate of the trailer was the perfect platform for Mr. Solomon to carve the remaining melons. Emmitt and his crew were served. The Solomons, who had been too busy serving, joined the gentlemen for their first taste of the watermelon.

I looked over at Doc with a questioning gesture. Doc, who was now involved in an impromptu version of charades with the adult Standers and Observers, returned my warning sign with shrugged shoulders and a fickle grin.

The trailer melons were being hardily consumed with compliments on the unique quality. The patrolmen became more concerned with conversation than security.

The smaller children were engaged in the lighted playground area. Becky chaperoned the swing set and the slide. Teenagers chatted about the coming school year.

The park was taking on new life as campers returned from a day on the water. The area campgrounds were engulfed by the smell of burgers on nearby grills, clashing music, biting insects and scattered laughter.

Benny began a spontaneous lecture to the women of the Setters group on the therapeutic and medicinal qualities of watermelon. Mayor Emmitt and Chet invited some nearby campers who had wandered over to a slice of melon. The mood was changing.

As the energy level increased, more of the park tourists joined in the gala. A young couple brought in a boom box and entertained with reggae music. A nearby wedding reception joined us, then the Lake Corinthia S.C.U.B.A. Club, followed by the Quanapah Sail Boater's Society. Emmitt danced with the widow Anderson. Chet danced with Jackie Solomon. The picnic tables were pushed to the side to provide more floor space as the reggae fest continued.

"Want to dance, Timber?" asked Sherry with a flirtatious smile.

"Go for it, big fella!" said Ant pushing me toward Sherry.

My blond escort accompanied me to the animated pavilion, now filled with dancing tourists, sailors, divers, local teenagers and the transformed gregarious church congregation. The dressing code ranged from formal gowns and tuxedos to shorts and flip-flops.

It was nearly 11:00 when Deacon with Martha finally arrived to witness the conversion of harmony in his church. Doc welcomed both while lighting a new cigar. He appeared amused and content at the unfolding scene. The Elders of the church gave the impression of astonishment and pride.

"Just look at their joy, Martha!" said the Deacon to his wife observing the intermingling of the various church factions and their new friends.

"Yes, joy," added Doc taking another puff. "And some of them have had a little more Joy than others."

Sherry and I continued in the extroverted reggae dancing display till a limbo stick was introduced to the throng. Keeping to the Caribbean theme, all partook in the Limbo Rock till the local Park officers came to enforce the curfew.

I awoke the following Sunday morning to the sound of rolling thunder. Mom and Dad had left early to open the store. I knew that bad weather could mark the end of the busy holiday weekend. I ran to my truck as the September rain began to fall harder. By the time I got to the store it was a down pour. The lake crowd was making a mass exodus through town putting a halt to the Labor Day celebration.

Trucks pulling boats and campers filled with disappointed tourists surrounded the driveway to top off their gas tanks. The mood was frustrating.

I rushed into the store, totally soaked. TJ was doing his best to collect the gas money from the drenched vacationers hurrying to return to their homes. I jumped in behind the counter and assisted.

Dad let out a long sigh, looking out the glass frontage of our store at the parade exiting Lake Corinth.

"Looks like a wash out, boys. Radio says this has set in for the day."

Instantly lightning lit the premises followed by a clap of thunder that shook the building. The lights blinked. The late summer storm was more reminiscent of the Oklahoma's spring tornado season.

"That was close!" warned TJ.

"Oh boy. Well, it was good while it lasted," said Dad. "We did the best we could. God controls the weather."

Mom was busy in the deli brewing and serving coffee in large to-go cups. Gas and caffeine was in high demand.

"Those poor drenched people. It's so sad this had to happen," said Mom more concerned about others than her own income.

Shortly after 10:00 a.m. the stream of vehicles had come to a halt.

The rush was over but the storm continued. A round of pea-sized hail had temporarily turned the drive and main street white. Lightning chased by thunder was followed by a power outage. The store became dark and quiet. The noise of the refrigeration compressors became silent, leaving only the sound of the wind and rain.

"Geez," grumbled Dad. "What next? Let's get out the flashlights. It might be awhile before Quanapah Electric gets us back on."

Mom joined us at the front of the store. TJ and I broke out the flashlights. Dad surveyed the store, shining his light all over his now dark and vacant marketplace. Pushing his hand over his receding hair line, the forty-year-old shopkeeper came to the conclusion that TJ and I weren't needed. My parents were very dedicated to the business, but were just as devoted to my rearing.

"You boys might as well head on down to church," said Dad. "We can handle it here till the lights come back on. Besides, the Deacon and Martha could probably use your support this morning. I hear the melon festival got a little too festive last night?" added Dad with an inquisitive grin.

"Tell me about..." said TJ.

"You sure everything's alright?" I asked.

"We're fine, Timothy," replied Mom. "You two run on."

The Church of Corinthia Falls was the only church in our town. Those seeking to worship with a particular denomination would have to journey to Archer's Grove or other communities. The church served as the social and spiritual base of the township. The long standing tradition seemed to be one of community pride—what there was left of it. As a citizen, your attendance was part of the locally observed protocol.

The town was powerless and dark as was the church when we arrived. The rain continued to fall. The parking lot was full. The security guards forced inside by the storm, looking more like Leaners than Setters, propped themselves up just inside the entrances. Chet was sitting in a chair at the main entrance hall pretending to be awake. The church was dimly lit by candle light.

Becky and Ant were surprised to see us as TJ and I reached our Observer seats in the balcony.

"Is everything alright?" asked Becky, her red hair still damp.

"Power out just like here," I answered. "Dad sent us on down. Come with us and we'll check on them after the service."

Doc was eased back with eyes closed, snoring in the darkness, with the sports page on his lap.

"This could be very interesting," said Ant motioning toward the congregation below.

The joy of the previous evening had dissipated. It had been replaced by shifting eyes and ominous rumblings from the soggy church members. The reggae music had turned into the sound of a funeral procession. The impression was a cross between a memorial service and a murder trial. There were hints of accusations for unbecoming conduct from the night before as Standers and Setters indulged in an intense staring match. The balcony worshipers leaned forward in anticipation.

"Fasten your seat belts," grinned Ant.

A smiling Deacon Johnson entered the pulpit area followed by Ms. Martha and choir.

"Let me begin by saying what a delight it was to experience the joy we all shared with our church and lake community at the festival last night," stated the black cleric.

Matthew Cox stood and interrupted the Deacon pointing at Emmitt Sharp. "Deacon, that seemed more like drunkenness than joy!"

Deacon's smile turned to a frown as Emmitt stood to retort. "Schoolteacher, don't point your finger at me! Your buddy, Benny, there spiked the melons!"

"I did no such thing!" shouted Benny. "How dare you accuse me for your misbehavior?"

The loud voices woke Doc from his slumber.

"You callin' me a liar, boy?" replied the angered barber.

Both men were now face to face in the middle aisle of the sanctuary. Each side of the church was urging support for the leaders of their own faction. Arguing and allegations erupted. The Observers in the balcony had moved down to the banister in an attempt to referee the disturbance. During the mass hysteria, pushing and shoving led to physical aggression. Benny now had the older Emmitt in a head lock. The Deacon struggled to break up the strangle hold. Chet intervened and was introduced to a whack on the face by the widow Anderson's umbrella. A civil war between Standers and Setters had erupted. The balcony emptied; men wrestled on the floor, women grappled in the pews, children sided with their parents. Anarchy reigned at the Church of Corinthia Falls.

TJ and Ant protected their mothers. Doc, Becky, and I stood at the bottom few steps of the stairway clutching the railing for protection. Becky held her breath.

A bolt of thunder rocked the old church building as lightning through the stained-glass windows illuminated the sanctuary, revealing two terrifying figures on the raised pulpit platform.

The asylum of worshipers gasped in unison. The feuding frenzy came to a halt as all became still. The church was silent as everyone's eyes adjusted to the dim lights reassessing the two ominous silhouettes on display in front of the church. The people cautiously stepped back.

A beast of nature appearing to be a black bear growled. Its teeth were shining white with a long dark tongue that overlapped its awesome chops. The creature stood on four legs with head bent low as if preparing for attack.

The animal stood waist high to the man standing stoically beside it. The mysterious gentleman was a well-tanned Caucasian, tall and approaching sixty with a full head of dripping black wavy hair brushed over his back collar and half way across his ears. His clean face appeared chiseled out of stone with rugged lines accenting his dark eyes and raised cheeks.

He was dressed in all black. Jeans, dress shirt and boots were partially exposed under an open dark grey trench coat. His collar was turned upward around his face. A large old dark green military duffle bag was dangling from his left hand and a thick leather leash affixed to the beast's silver chain choker collar was in his right.

Expressionlessly, he surveyed the congregation till his dark stare rested on Emmitt and Benny. None of us knew how much of the confrontation he had witnessed.

The silence was broken by the baritone barking of the bear-like creature. The widow Anderson fainted. This time the frozen congregation did not rush to her aid.

"Hush, Silas!" ordered the mysterious stranger in a deep voice holding his right hand in front of the bear-dog's face. The woofing ceased.

"Colonel Armstrong!" said the Deacon cautiously approaching the peculiar couple. "We weren't expecting you for another week."

The congregation collectively sighed in the revelation of the stranger's identity. Emmitt stood at attention and saluted the Colonel.

"Deacon, will you please dismiss this throng from the house of the Lord?" the Colonel demanded without a change of expression.

"Uhm. Well, yes, yes. Let's all bow for... never mind. Folks let's just call it a day," said the Deacon, motioning toward the entry way.

While Colonel Pavlos Lincoln Armstrong and his furry companion remained motionless, the humiliated people of the Church of Corinthia Falls exited the premises into the rain.

As we drove to the store the cab of my pickup was hushed. The only sound was the windshield wipers clearing off the rain that had slowed to a sprinkle. TJ, Becky, and I pondered what we had just witnessed. TJ breathed deeply and then exhaled a gust of air and broke the silence.

"Man, that was wild! People duking it out in the church," said TJ shaking his head.

"...and did you see that Bear?" questioned Becky.

"I think it was a dog, Becks," I said.

As we pulled up to the side of the store, the electric power to the downtown area returned. As we entered, Dad and Mom were working quickly with the restored power to ready the store.

"Hey, kids," said Dad, looking up from his routine. "Here a little early? Everything go well at church?"

TJ shook his head. Becky hustled back to the deli to assist Mom where she got a huge hug; the kind of comfort hug one needs when feeling insecure.

"Becky, what is wrong?" asked Mom, pulling Becky back at arm's length.

"You wouldn't believe it," I said loud enough for all to hear. "There was fussin' and fightin' and yellin'…"

"…and a bear," added TJ.

"What in the world are you talking about?" asked Dad.

"Uhh, better let Deacon explain when he gets here," I said.

"Anything to do with last night?" Dad asked.

"Somethin' like that," affirmed TJ.

TJ and I took our normal positions at the cash registers as we prepared for what we expected to be a lackluster Sunday noon hour. Dad resumed his duties managing the store as the gals prepped the deli.

After about 45 minutes Deacon and Martha showed up, accompanied by Colonel Armstrong. The Colonel followed the couple into the store after securing Silas, the bear-dog, to the outside newspaper vending machine.

"Bill, Eunice…we got someone we want you to meet," announced the Deacon.

The five adults gathered in the deli area and exchanged greetings.

"Nice to meet you, Bill," said Colonel Armstrong extending his hand. "Pavlos Armstrong."

"Bill Oaks," said Dad as both men exchanged a firm handshake.

"And this is Eunice."

Mom reached toward Pavlos and gave her customary embrace.

"It's so wonderful to finally meet you! Are you hungry? Sit right down here and let us take care of you," insisted Mom, pointing to one of the only two dining booths in the store located near the deli.

"Thank you, ma'am," Pavlos said in a soft, polite Southern drawl. His personality was now more animated than an hour earlier.

"Bill, we need to talk," said the Deacon as the three men found a seat at the booth.

"Sure sounds like it," replied Dad.

Dad, the Deacon, and Pavlos conferenced for about a half hour while Mom, Becky and Ms. Martha served the Colonel extended helpings from the Oak's Corner menu. TJ and I watched curiously from the checkout counter.

"Timber," Dad called, motioning me to join the table discussion. "I don't think you two have officially met."

"The circumstances were difficult," said Pavlos now standing, putting one hand on my shoulder and clutching my right hand in his other. "Where'd you get the name Timber?"

"He's an Oaks and he's built like a tree," a jovial Deacon answered for me and the three men grinned.

"His mom is the only one that calls him Timothy," added Dad.

"May I address you by your Christian name also?" asked Pavlos as we both sat down with Dad and the Deacon.

"Yes sir. That's just fine," I replied.

"I'm not in the army anymore, Timothy. You can just call me Pavlos…or if it's easier for you, Paul."

"Paul?"

"Yes, with many of my close friends I go by Paul. My father's family was of Greek heritage. To keep up with an ethnic tradition, I was named after my grandfather, Pavlos, which is Greek for Paul."

"What about the Lincoln?" asked Dad curiously.

"My mother's side of the family claimed to be descendants of our beloved President," said Pavlos. "I think that may be more legend than fact, but it went along well with or clan's military legacy."

"Fascinating!" said Dad. "Now Timber, Pavlos is going to be staying in the apartment over our garage. I want you to take him over there and make sure he's comfortable. He's going to be staying for quite awhile working with the church. Obviously, there's a lot of work to be done."

I nodded affirmatively as the three men looked at me intently.

Dad continued. "Pavlos has requested your assistance during his stay. I want you available to give him a hand on anything he needs. Show him around. Help him out."

"What about the store?" I asked

"Don't worry about the store," Dad assured me. "We got the Johnson's and I understand that Joyce and Nate can lend us a hand. Your job is to take care of Pavlos."

"Why me? There's school and…"

"Why not you, Timothy?" interrupted Pavlos. "You are of good stock and come highly recommended."

"Pavlos will work around your school schedule. You might want to get him involved in some golf," said Dad.

"Deal," confirmed Pavlos.

We all stood up. Pavlos formally met Becky and thanked the ladies for the meal. Dad refused to let him pay. The Deacon then introduced him to his son, Thomas, still behind the counter.

"Thomas, I'm Pavlos. How's business?"

"Washed out," said TJ referring to the morning's weather.

Pavlos and I made our way out the door where Silas was attracting much attention. Ant was among the small group of the dumbfounded scrutinizing the strange animal from a distance.

"Don't feed the bears!" quipped Pavlos with an ample smile as he unfastened Silas from the newspaper machine.

"So it is a bear?" asked Ant.

Pavlos and Silas approached Ant as the rest of site seers took several steps back.

"What's your name, son?" asked Pavlos still attached to Silas.

"Anthony Bearkiller," stated the nervous Ant not taking his eyes off the looming beast only a few feet away.

"Seriously now, you're a bear killer?" asked the quick witted Colonel. "Well, Silas here is all dog. Put out your hand."

Ant bravely stuck out his hand to the dog that was twice his size. Silas engulfed his small hand with a large black tongue. Ant pulled back.

"No, go ahead, Anthony. It's okay."

Silas again began to lick Ant's trembling hand. The curious group came closer. The licking turned to face washing, touching, and petting as Silas made the acquaintance of my fascinated buddy. The relieved spectators joined in. Silas welcomed his new friends with dog kisses and waggles.

"See, just a dog," said Pavlos.

After the love fest was over, I led both of my new friends over to my truck. I let down the tailgate as Silas jumped in the back. The Chevy bounced with the impact. The huge now-confirmed dog instantly sprang up placing his front paws on top of the truck's cab balancing his body for the ride. Silas enjoyed the short trip to his new residence with his head high in the air and tongue dangling as we drove through the wet streets of Corinthia

Falls: Paul, Silas and Timothy.

Our house was in the core neighborhood of Corinthia Falls. The house was built in the early '60s just before I was born. The medium-sized three bedroom beige house was surrounded by my mother's flower beds. The front yard of Bermuda grass was well kept and neat.

To the south side of the house was the detached two-car garage. The gravel driveway fronted the garage and a flight of steps on the left side led up to the apartment.

We parked in front of the garage. I was too late to let down the tailgate for Silas who had already departed over the side of the truck. I grabbed Pavlos's large duffle bag as all three of us climbed the stairs. I found the key under the welcome mat and unlocked the door. Handing the key to Pavlos, I welcomed both of our new tenants to their lodging.

"Well, here it is," I said. I placed the bag on the queen-sized bed in the bedroom then walked across the living area to turn on the small window air conditioner.

The apartment was orderly and smart. There was a living area with a sofa with a hideaway bed, a recliner and television with rabbit ears, a small table for dining and a compact fully equipped kitchen.

The bedroom featured a desk and closet with a small bathroom. The windows were trimmed out with curtains Mom made herself. The dwelling was comfortable and efficient.

"This is perfect," said Pavlos as Silas examined his new surroundings.

The presence of the oversized dog made the place feel small. Pavlos removed his trench coat and neatly hung it up in the bedroom closet.

"You have some wonderful parents, Tim," said Pavlos, sitting down on the sofa as his brawny body joints cracked.

"Thank you, sir." I situated myself on the upright recliner, facing him.

"Paul, I noticed the insignia on your bag…Green Berets?" I asked.

"Good observation, Tim. I'm impressed! *De oppresso liber*… To Liberate the Oppressed. From fighting to preaching, my job description has not changed."

"Paul, I'm kind of confused, just what do you do?"

"First of all, Timothy, I am an apostle of the Lord." He now looked squarely into my eyes. "I am not under the command of any human authority. For the last fifteen years my mission has been the Good News of the grace of Jesus Christ. So liberating the oppressed is what I do.

The Grace in Fellowship Association which I founded unites small community churches mainly located throughout the Southern United States as well as some of our missionary churches in foreign countries. I correspond and visit all our member churches assuring them in the Word of God, correcting and encouraging the people in our faith."

"I'm really sorry for what happened at church today. Nothin' quite like that has ever happened before," I said.

"Believe it or not, I've come across worse," said Paul.

I tried to absorb what I was hearing. As I looked into Paul's face I could detect that his dark-brown eyes were not in harmony. Paul perceived my awareness.

"I lost my left eye sometime back. This one is made of glass," said Paul pointing to his simulated eyeball."

"What happened?"

"Let's just say it was a physical affliction and leave it at that for now," Paul continued, "Now what about you, Timothy. You are starting your senior year. You and Thomas are the best athletes in school. You drive a classy pickup. I know you are a good student and help your parents at the family business. You attend church regularly and sit with the so-called Observers in the balcony. Your father tells me you excel at golf?"

I sat up straight surprised at how well he was informed.

"Uh, yes." I gathered myself. "I finished third last year in the Small School State Finals."

"Not bad for a town with no actual golf course and a school without a golf coach. So you finished third in State. Think you can get a scholarship?"

"That's the goal."

Silas joined us, lying down in between Paul and me taking up what was left of the small living room. He rolled comfortably over on his back. His legs extended far enough in the air that our conversation was interrupted. Silas wallowed on the carpet in a show of self contentment. We both bent on one knee and scratched the dog's massive, fur covered under side. Silas encouraged us for more attention.

"Silas was a gift from the church of Phu Quoc, a small island in the Mekong Delta. They gave him to me on my last missionary trip several years ago. The Vietnamese call him a Con Gau Cho which naturally translates 'bear dog.' The breed is very rare. He's some kind of chow. Silas is a loyal companion. He always reflects my attitude and disposition."

"How much does he weigh?" I asked.

"Before or after eating?" Paul cracked and we both laughed.

"Tim, I'm going to be busy settling in here for a couple of days. I have several letters to write to our participating churches and some other connections to make. Tomorrow is Labor Day and I think Tuesday is your first day of school?"

"That right, back to school,"

"Well, why don't you check in with me Tuesday after school? There'll be some things I'll need and some stuff for us to go over." We both stood.

"Sure. Mom said they would be bringing you some groceries over after work. Anything else you need?"

"I'm good for now. Thanks for your help, Timothy."

Silas rose on all fours. Balancing on his back legs he placed his massive paws on my shoulders. I almost lost my footing and was somewhat startled as he looked down at me with a large doggy grin.

"Looks like you got a new friend, Tim!"

I t was the first day of the 1981-82 school year at Corinthia Falls. Mom fixed me a big breakfast. She encouraged me to make my senior year 'the best year.'

I had washed and waxed my baby-blue pickup the day before, making it ready for a fine presentation. I picked up TJ at the store, where he was helping his parents with the breakfast crowd.

We parked at my long-established spot. The Solomon twins pulled in beside us in a brand new red Z28 Camaro. Sherry rushed up to me and grabbed me by the arm.

"Timber!" said the stunning blond. "Are we all ready for this?"

"Sherry, John," I said very comfortable with the attention I was receiving from Sherry. "Nice ride, John!"

"Thanks," said John in his customary suave manner. "What ya say, TJ?"

"I say we get this over with," muttered our tall black friend.

TJ was referring the routine we all knew very well; traditional first day assembly. We enter the side door of the old gym/cafeteria/

assembly hall. About fifty students from K-12 had gathered on the folding chairs lined up on the front half of the gymnasium floor facing the stage. The enthused youngest were accompanied by mothers.

Ant had reserved five seats on the front row. The ritual was senior class to the front backed by the junior class and so on all the way back to kindergarten.

"Down here," Ant waved at the four of us. Sherry remained snuggled next to me as we took our seats. The senior class of 1982 was intact and in position.

Becky was two rows back of us on the sophomore row. Looking over my left shoulder, I gave her a smile. She returned my gesture with a small nod and slight smirk, alert to Sherry's flirtations.

Principal Matthew Cox approached the microphone at the center of the stage. The American flag was to his far right and the State of Oklahoma flag to his left. His wife, Clara, took a seat at the old upright piano on the floor just to the lower right of the stage. The Cox's were in their late thirties. My dad often referred to their appearance as 'a cleaned up version of the 1960s. Mr. Cox began.

"Let's all stand for prayer and the Pledge of Allegiance."

After Mr. Cox blessed the assembly and we saluted the flag, the principal announced enthusiastically,

"Now let's all sing our school song!"

As corny as it was, the old hymn was sacred in all the hearts of the Corinthia Falls Saints. It was the first song we learned as children and united us in spirit and pride. We sang it joyfully and fanatically.

Mrs. Cox played the first stanza. Clapping in time, we all joined in:

Oh when the Saints... go marching in
When the Saints go marching in...in Corinthia Falls!
Oh lord I want to be in that number
When the Saints go marching in...in Corinthia Falls!

We are traveling in the footsteps
Of those who've gone before
But if we all stand united
Then a new world is in store!

Oh when the Saints... go marching in
When the Saints go marching in...in Corinthia Falls!
Oh lord I want to be in that number
When the Saints go marching in...in Corinthia Falls!

Our rendition was followed by applause, foot stomping and cheers. Sherry, the closest thing we had to a cheerleader, turned and faced the enlivened assembly rotating two fists up in the air as if to simulate the waving of pom-poms.

"Well, that was just great!" said Mr. Cox. "Now if you will all be seated I'd like to introduce this year's faculty and staff."

"This won't take long," whispered TJ.

Clara Cox joined her husband, walking up the short stairway onto the stage followed by the remaining school personnel. Ant, TJ, and I were surprised to see Becky's mom, Sarah, join them. I turned around to see Becky beaming.

"Anthony Bearkiller, will you please join us?" asked Mr. Cox, looking down at his prize pupil.

TJ opened his right hand palm up. Ant slapped his friend's hand, accepting his congratulations and joined the others.

"Well, first of all you know that we will be handling the junior high and high school students," reaffirmed Mr. Cox with his hand on his wife's shoulder. "Then we have Mrs. Sharp leading our elementary."

Mrs. Sharp was well known for her strict disciplinary tactics. The staunch posture of the barber's wife suggested this year would be no different.

"Then we have our new addition...Ms. Hooper. Ms. Hooper will be instructing kindergarten, first and second grade."

Sarah Hooper received polite applause from the older students and the adults in attendance that appreciated her accomplishment. Sarah, with red hair and light complexion, was a thirty-five year old version of her daughter.

"Again this year we have Mr. and Mrs. Hummingbird returning."

Mr. Hummingbird was the long time school custodian and bus driver. His wife was the school cook. The older, plump Cherokee couple stepped forward.

"...and Mrs. Benson, our receptionist."

The white-haired lady who was Mr. Cox's office assistant, secretary and school gossip smiled pleasantly at her boss.

Then Mr. Cox approached Ant at the end of the lineup and laid a hand on our small friend's back. Before he began to introduce Ant, a large white goose waddled onto the rear stage from behind the drawn curtains. Unbeknownst to those on stage, the gander shuffled closer to the front, gawking curiously between the school workers and an audience that was now erupting with laughter. The big bird inched closer, tilting its long neck with an inquisitive motion. Hysteria broke loose.

"There is nothing funny about Anthony!" scolded Mr. Cox.

"This talented young man will be assisting the staff this year."

The goose toddled closer finding another opening to peek

through between the principal and Ant.

TJ was bent over laughing so hard I thought he was going to cry. Ant shrugged his shoulders in embarrassment. We stood and pointed at the goose with his cocked head almost touching Mr. Cox's thigh. Ant thought we were pointing at him as he checked the zipper on his jeans.

Another goose wandered onto the scene from back stage. The spectators roared. The new goose joined his friend.

"Behind you!" I screamed, still pointing.

The confused group turned in accord. The birds were as startled as the staff. The geese began honking.

"Onk!-onk!-onk!" exclaimed the alarmed geese.

A shocked Mrs. Sharp screamed and fled for safety. The geese, with feathers flying in an act of retribution, attacked the lady teacher nipping at her buttocks. The assembly was engrossed as the custodian and principal tried to corral the misplaced feathered refugees.

"Sam's!" said TJ and I together in unison, suspecting the perpetrators.

The senior class ran together, following TJ's lead to the parking lot. In the near distance, the Sam's were departing town in the old green truck. Sammy Sampson stood in the back of the getaway vehicle, removed his ball cap and took a bow.

TJ shook his head. "Wait till the barber hears what happened to his wife at School today."

Joyce Anderson was her usual vibrant self, working the checkout counter at Oak's Corner. She displayed the energy and enthusiasm of a school girl.

"Look boys what I've learned to do!" said Joyce proudly as TJ and I entered the store. "I know how to punch all these here buttons and work all this stuff!"

TJ joined her for his evening shift behind the counter.

"Looks like she gots it all down, Timb," confirmed TJ.

I reached out and gave her a high-five.

"Yes!" Joyce exclaimed. "I love this!"

Dad, the Deacon, and the Colonel were gathered at the back booth in the deli. Paul was dressed in his traditional black with his dress shirt cuffs rolled up just below his elbows.

"Here comes your protégé, Colonel," said the Deacon as I joined them in the discussion. I sat down next to Paul as the three men welcomed me.

"We hear you had some excitement at school today?" said Dad.

"Yep. The goose got loose," I answered, knowing full well the three had already been briefed on the assembly episode. News travels fast in a small town.

As I filled in the details, all three adults were trying to suppress their laughter. Dad's smile became so tight that tears started to form in his eyes. The Deacon bowed his head, struggling to hide his amusement. Paul calmly smiled. Finally, the laughter broke loose.

We all tried to compose ourselves. The silence was broken when the Deacon looked up at my dad and the belly laughing began again. Pavlos and I joined in the contagious uproar.

"Okay, okay now," said Deacon, trying to catch his breath while Dad wiped the tears from his eyes with a napkin. "Was it Sams?"

"Yes, it was Sams…another Sam attack," I confirmed as Paul put an arm around my back and patted my shoulder.

Mom was not amused. She had been listening to us while

cleaning the deli in preparation for the evening's business.

"Well, if you ask me, those Sampson boys are starved for attention. They just need someone to love them."

"Eunice is right. Timber, what do you say you and I pay the Sampsons a visit?" announced Paul to our surprise.

"You can't be serious!" said Mom, changing her tone. "Bill, you can't let Timothy and the Colonel go out there unprotected and unannounced. That old Demas Sampson is a crazy man!"

"Colonel, are you sure this is a wise move?" asked Dad.

I was very apprehensive. In fact, I was scared to death. I found myself praying that Paul would listen to my parent's counsel.

"Bill, I wouldn't put your son in any harmful situation," said Paul, knowing his reputation preceded him. "I have been in many situations of conflict. I find that in this type of circumstance it is best to develop a relationship with the worst of the crowd first. You know the way, Tim?"

I reluctantly nodded. The Deacon raised both of his hands with his elbows still resting on the table. We followed his example. My mother joined in standing at the front of the booth as all five engaged in the joining of hands.

The Deacon asked for God's blessings and protection for our mission. "...and all God's people said...Amen."

Paul noticed my nervousness as we drove over the secluded gravel roads with Silas in tow. The late afternoon sun was in our eyes as we traveled west. The Samuel's place was located about five miles from town and even farther from Lake Corinth. The meager land in the rolling hills grew more rocks than grass.

"You know these boys very well?" asked Paul, breaking the silent tension.

"Somewhat, " I said. "They were in and out of school a lot. Neither has been back since Sammy and I were in seventh grade. Haven't talked to them since. I think Sammy is actually a year older than I am and Sandy should be about a year younger. I don't know anything about this cousin, Gib, that's been hanging around. One thing…as wild as they are, they are not stupid."

"Now, what do you know about their father?" asked Paul.

"Demas Sampson? Well, he's one bad dude—a loner. Most folks who come out this way are moonshine customers. The deputy sheriff leaves him alone. Don't know whatever happened to his wife, but there are plenty of rumors. We need to be careful. Just what are we trying to accomplish with all this?" I asked with a touch of despair.

"A little harmony, Timothy. Just a little harmony. So the boys are raising themselves?" inquired Paul.

"Appears so," I said as we approached the long, dirt driveway that led to a wire-meshed fence that enclosed the property.

A metal gate with a 'keep out' sign stopped our progression. A small old native stone house with a withered deck was about 100 feet directly in front of us. An old windmill slowly twirled between the house and the galvanized, rusty steel barn to our right. The familiar green Ford pickup was parked by the barn.

A vegetable garden behind the barn had surrendered to a long, hot summer. Several head of cattle, some goats and chickens completed the farm yard. A small pond about a hundred yards away was occupied by a couple of familiar geese.

Paul and I cautiously exited my truck. Silas bounced out of the back with his nose in the air as if to smell the uneasiness.

A small, thin balding man with a beard probably in his forties and dressed only in denim coveralls stepped out on the deck of the old farm house with a shot gun hanging down on his right side.

"State your bid'ness," demanded Demas Sampson slightly raising the gun with his left hand.

Paul raised two open hands chest high. Petrified, I duplicated his action.

"It's alright, Pa! I got it," said Sammy hustling out from the barn, gesturing at his father with his right hand. Sammy was followed by a brown pit bull that headed straight for Silas and an impending confrontation.

"Better put that thing inside your truck before I open this gate!" warned the leader of the Sams, pointing at Silas. "Banjo here is a trained killer!"

"This 'thing' is a trained peacemaker," said Paul, confidently lowering his raised hands. "Let's let them get to know each other."

Sandy and Gib, now alert to the commotion, rushed out of the barn, eagerly anticipating the conflict. Demas stepped down off the porch to get a closer view.

"I gave you fair warning," said Sammy with a portentous grin, swinging open the large gate to allow us entry.

Silas sauntered into the barnyard. Twenty feet away the pit bull began his charge. The trained, muscle-bound assassin ran low to the ground at Silas with a wide open mouth full of teeth and a growl that signaled his intent.

Just before Banjo could launch at his victim and place a death grip with his powerful jaws, Silas stood up on his back legs and assumed his bear-like qualities. The bear-dog stood tall, balancing himself with his massive front paws. Silas returned the bulldog's glare with a fierce, deafening roar.

Banjo instantly stopped his assault. The killer's death barking turned in to the whimpering of a puppy. He rolled over on his back just below the towering Silas wiggling in the dirt, making the canine gesture of surrender.

Silas returned his front paws to the ground and inspected the submitting dog's underside with his huge black nose. Banjo playfully licked Silas's face. A friendship was born.

"Woooow!" said Sammy with his mouth nearly touching the ground.

Pavlos put an arm around me as we entered the once-protected property. My heart began to beat again. I was just as surprised as the Sam's and their old man.

Sandy just stared and shook his head. Gib lit a cigarette with a flip of his Zippo lighter. The doggy odd couple inspected the grounds in an engaging form of recreation.

"Mutts," muttered Demas entering his house.

"Never seen nothin' like that," said a still bewildered Sammy.

"Mind if we join you?" asked Paul.

"Why not?" offered Sammy directing us to the barn where the other two boys had returned.

The wide retracting overhead door was open. Off to one corner was an old John Deere green and yellow tractor. Hay bales filled the left side of the barn. Several other bales were strategically located in the absence of furniture.

A small black and white television set on a small stool connected to an antenna mounted on the side of the barn. An old white Frigidaire was next to the TV. Both appliances were connected to long extension cords that went through the wall, connecting to the electric meter that serviced both house and barn.

The hay-covered, dirt floor as well as the rest of the shelter was coated with bird droppings from the barn swallows that made their summer homes in the rafters. A green water hose connected to a ground faucet appeared to be the only water supply for the barn dwellers. Several stalls available for livestock looked as if they were make-shift bedrooms. A slight smell of manure filled the air.

All three young men wore jeans. Gib, in a white muscle shirt, leaned his back against a stall finishing his cigarette. Sammy wore a grey t-shirt. Sandy sat on a hay bale in the center of the barn dressed in a red Oklahoma Sooners football jersey and faded blue Lake Corinth ball cap while he plucked at a brown and tan Gibson guitar. I contrasted the threesome in my pleated Levis and baby-blue golf shirt.

The Sampsons were thin and all of average build. The family resemblance was evident. All were tan with unkempt brown curly hair. Sammy and Sandy had the beginnings of youthful beards.

"Well, Timber Oaks," said Sammy turning and inspecting me as Paul and I entered the barn with him.

"Sam," I acknowledged. "Sandy."

I nodded toward Sandy as he briefly looked up from his guitar and silently returned a greeting gesture.

"And uh…" I started to address Gib pretending not to know his name.

"Gib," he said, stomping out his Marlboro.

"Gib's our cousin. Been hanging out with us this summer. He comes from over in Cherokee County," Sammy informed us.

I knew better than to inquire into anymore background. The boy's attention turned to Paul.

"Uh, guys, this is Colonel Pavlos Lincoln Armstrong."

"Is it true you're a real live Southern Colonel?" asked Sammy, apparently already aware of who Paul was and his credentials.

"Except I don't fry chicken," Paul remarked cleverly.

Most of the remaining tension was broken with laughter.

"So, what brings Elvis, Boy Wonder and the dancing bear out here?" the curious Sammy asked.

Sammy walked over and opened the old refrigerator.

"Beer?" he offered.

Paul and I shook him off.

"I forgot, preacher men don't drink."

"I've had my share," admitted Paul.

Sammy opened his can of Budweiser and set down on the hay next to his brother. Paul and I joined them on a nearby bale. Gib remained leaning on the stall, studying the scene.

I was startled when a fading light-red goat dashed from behind the tractor through the gathering and out in to the barnyard.

"Friend of yours, Timber?" grinned Sandy, looking at me.

"A brief acquaintance," I replied dryly as all three boys laughed.

A white and gray mourning dove flew through the open barn door perching on the lower exposed roof beam just above us. A couple of chickens and a small pig joined the red goat outside.

"Bacon and eggs," said Gib.

"May I take a look at your Gibson?" Paul asked Sandy, reaching out his hands.

"Sure." Sandy offered his guitar to Paul.

The Colonel strapped on Sandy's prized possession and ran through the progression of several chords. The Sams and I were mildly surprised at the revelation of Paul's talent.

"Know any Creedence?" I asked, somewhat embarrassed after I spoke.

Paul shifted keys and began a slowed down blues version of 'Proud Mary.' His rhythmic baritone voice gave evidence of a trained musician as he sang.

Sammy and I were bobbing our heads in time as Sandy pulled out his harmonica and echoed Paul's deliberate measured beat. Sammy and I fell in on the chorus about rolling on a river.

It dawned on me that Paul had ironically found the connection, better yet the harmony he was trying to accomplish.

"All right! Not bad," complimented Sammy. "Where did you pick that up?"

"It's a gift," replied Paul, returning the Gibson to Sandy.

Sandy smiled as he took back the guitar and shook his new fellow musician's strong hand.

Our visiting dove began cooing in admiration. The atmosphere became more relaxed.

"I bet playin' music and preachin' and hangin' out with religious people is not as dangerous as fighting commies," stated Sammy.

"Word is you were a Green Beret?"

"Correct."

"Where all have you been? How many people have you killed?" asked Sammy, itching for a war story.

"Vietnam, Cambodia, Laos," answered Paul. "Other assignments and places, as well as my procedures, are still classified."

"Does that mean if you told us you'd have to kill us?" asked Sandy, light heartedly breaking his silence.

"My killing days are over, boys," said Pavlos.

"See! He did kill commies!" validated Sammy.

Paul looked squarely at the Sampson brothers. "You asked me if preaching is safer than war," Paul said in his serious southern drawl.

"This is the only scar I received serving my country."

The former Green Beret held out the bottom side of his right forearm to expose a healed gash.

"And this…"

Paul began unbuttoning his black dress shirt. He tossed the shirt to the side and pulled off a black undershirt revealing an upper torso covered with scars.

His burly back was disfigured from what appeared to be lashes from a flogging. The whip marks were too numerous to count. The blemishes and wounds on his hairless chest and upper arms were visibly the result of a burning instrument. A large skin graft covered his right rib cage. Across his chest was the raised tissue where a knife engraved the word 'DEVIL.'

Sam, Sandy, and I stood in shock. Gib came closer to inspect the butchered body of the Colonel. Sandy reached out a finger to touch a scar on the Colonel's back as if to make sure they were real. Paul slowly rotated to expose his distorted physical condition.

"Man, who did that to you?" asked Sammy still in awe and taking a step back.

"…this is what I got from hanging out with religious people," said Paul finishing his testimonial.

"So, church people did that to you?" asked Gib, as if almost to confirm his own question.

"Religious people," corrected Paul.

Paul sat down and leisurely redressed. Gib joined us on the hay bales, removing a double-edged black handled knife that had been implanted in the hay. The boy's cousin fiddled with the knife in a way that suggested retribution for the injustice inflicted on Paul.

"Why did they do that to you?" asked Sandy.

"They were afraid of the truth. Afraid I was trying to interfere with their way of life. In the late sixties in the South, integration and race came into play. In other countries, it was also rebellion against long standing man-made customs."

Silas and Banjo joined us, lying down to convalesce from their barnyard romp. Sammy joined me in rubbing their heads.

"Religious people are all hypocrites just like those people at that church in town," said Sammy as the rest of the Sams gave a nod in agreement.

"Sammy, it might surprise you that I agree. These scars are evidence of that," confirmed Paul, gathering the boys' attention and mine.

"The wicked folks that did this to me were well aware of God. They can clearly see the earth He created for us. The truth about God is known to them instinctively through his invisible qualities, divine power and eternal nature.

"The religious tend to develop their own ideas of what God is like and become confused. They think they are wise by following man-made traditions and rituals. They end up worshiping their own possessions and the things that God made rather the Creator himself. Religious people defend their beliefs by rejecting others who proclaim the Good News of Jesus Christ."

"But you're religious!" said Sammy, challenging the Colonel.

"Sam, religion is people acting on set ceremonies and procedures to gain God's attention or favor. In contrast, Christianity is God designing a way to get our attention. So…I'm not religious. I am an apostle of Jesus Christ; God's instrument to get our attention."

"You're saying Christians are good and everyone else is bad. Heard it all before, preacher," said Sammy defending himself from condemnation.

"No son, everyone is bad. If you think about it, we are all guilty of doing the same things the hypocrites you talk about do. We are boastful and proud. We all gossip, fight, and deceive. All of us are unforgiving and heartless.

"God, being a fair judge, will punish anyone for doing such things. Do you think God will punish the evil and not us, when we keep on inventing new ways of sinning just like them?"

"Sin?" asked Sandy. "What is and what isn't a sin?"

Paul leaned back and looked around. He stood and walked over to a nearby wooden support beam about 25 feet away. Tucking in his shirt tail he turned and addressed Gib.

"You pretty good with that blade?"

Both Sammy and Sandy backed up Gib's capability.

"Let's see if you're accurate enough to hit this spot."

Paul pointed at a two inch round knot hole in the beam about chest high.

Gib stood and flipped the knife in his hand with an air of cockiness. Holding the end of the blade between thumb and forefinger, he took careful aim. Raising it over his shoulder, Gib released the knife with a flick of his arm. The blade stuck in the wood about one inch away from the target.

"Not bad. Not bad at all," commented the Colonel as Sammy reached over and congratulated Gib with a slap on his open hand.

"But, as good as that was, you missed the mark," said Paul pulling the imbedded knife out of the wood and walking over beside Gib.

"By definition you just sinned, Gib...you missed the mark. That's what sin is. When we miss the mark that God has set for us, we sin.

Paul patted Gib on the shoulder and continued.

"Just like Gib here, we have all sinned and have missed God's target, but through belief in Jesus, God declares our aim accurate and true. We hit the bull's-eye when, through faith and not religion, we accept that Christ shed his blood for us so that we may be made right with God."

Paul quickly turned toward the missed target and underhandedly hurled the knife into the center of the knot hole.

"So God removes sin," said the former Green Beret as the four of as gaped at the protruding knife.

"Then what?" asked Gib, still staring at the perfectly thrown knife.

"Freedom!" exclaimed Paul. "And eternal life! Tim, will you go get the Bible I left on your dash?"

The Sams all looked down to the ground and started groaning. I went out to my truck to fetch the Colonel's gift.

"Here we go. He's bringing in a Bible," pouted Sammy.

"It won't work, preacher. I can't ever get past the Flood."

I rushed back to the barn handing Pavlos the new Bible.

"Well, this time, try starting here," suggested Paul opening to the Gospel of John and handing the Bible over to Sammy.

Paul leaned over to Sandy and whispered something in his ear. Sandy nodded his head.

"Thanks," said Sandy softly.

We traded handshakes with the Sampsons. Silas seemed to know the meeting was over and jumped into the back of my pickup. Banjo attempted to join his new companion but could not make it over the tailgate.

"How's the golf game, Timber?" hollered Sammy at me while Paul and I climbed in the truck.

"Not bad," I said, "But I'm hitting too many sins."

The next day was Wednesday and Paul decided to take me up on the round of golf that was promised. I had checked with Sherry Solomon at school to confirm if it was still alright to check out her father's new golf cart in an effort to impress the Colonel.

Ant got word of the pending golf match, and I invited him to join us at the proverbial Cherokee Creek neighborhood golf course.

"Well, here it is guys," said Sherry, who already had the custom made golf cart ready for us in the circle drive of the Solomon mansion. "Nice to meet you, sir."

"Pavlos," returned the Colonel, gently shaking Sherry's hand.

"Okay. Well, you fellas have fun and just leave the cart in the garage when you're done."

The fancy cart had a front and back seat, head lights and built-in radio. The plush, baby-blue golf sedan was the essence of style and class.

"Incredible!" said Ant admiring the cart.

"Very nice," added Paul.

Paul, still dressed in his customary black, wore a black sports shirt and a pair of old-fashioned black high top basketball shoes. I was in my jeans and golf shirt. Ant wore shorts and a visor.

Ant loaded the golf bag on the back of the four-seater cart as I changed into my golf shoes. Ant took a seat in the back.

"Nice. I don't have to stand in the back this time," my small friend said gratefully.

As Paul stepped into the front seat of the comfortable cart on the passenger side, Silas jumped in the back practically covering the whole backseat as well as Ant. Ant sat frozen as Silas began licking his face.

"Looks like your relationship with Silas is continuing to develop," I said as Paul and I shared a laugh.

"I'm just a little intimidated by dogs over twice my size," said Ant, working a hand free to grudgingly pat Silas's massive head. "Are we doing the option hole?"

Since we were at the end of the block we would play the seven holes in reverse. I drove our cart over to the option hole with the big cottonwood staring us in the face, blocking out the green.

"Option hole?" questioned Paul.

"Paul, this is the so-called option hole. Normally it is last but we're doing things backwards today. As you can see, this is a tough one," I said, pointing to the enormous tree.

I stepped out of the cart and put on my single golf glove. Ant wedged himself out from under Silas and handed me my pitching wedge.

"Well show me how it's done," urged Paul.

I loosened up, took a couple practice swings and hit a perfectly lofted shot over the tree. I tossed down another ball and repeated the performance.

"Your turn," I said to Paul in a mild challenge.

Pavlos got out of the cart, stretched and observed the landscape. He noticed the giant satellite receiver overlooking the lake. Curious, he walked over to examine the unique contraption.

"I've been reading about these things…interesting," said Paul, still examining the receiver.

"Are you familiar with digital analog communications?" asked Ant.

"Yes, but not in a domestic situation," Paul replied while rubbing his fingers over two small indentations on the inside of the receiver.

Pavlos looked back at me in the tee box area in which I was still standing. He seemed to be measuring the distance with his eyes. Ant and I suspected he had detected our guilt.

"Hmmm…" Paul removed his perceptive fingers from the two dimples.

I showed no response, trying to act innocent. Ant changed the focus by asking Paul which of my clubs he wanted.

"Three wood and tee, Anthony."

Paul walked over next to me and teed up his ball. Without taking a practice swing, the gifted gentleman lined up the shot.

The golf ball went sailing over the cliff of no return then hooked to the left. The perfect hook shot rolled onto the green from the right hand side.

"The perfect draw!" cried out Ant. "You need to teach Timber that one."

"I see you've played this game before," I added. "I can't make that shot."

"Sure you can, Tim," said Paul. "Just start with your usual alignment. Adjust your feet to aim to the right of your target. Try 10 to 15 degrees to the right. Aim the club face direct at your target and use your normal grip. Here, you try it."

Paul handed me the three wood and I followed his instructions. My first attempt eluded the water but was way right and short of the green.

"Again!" demanded Pavlos, tossing down another ball at my feet.

My next try curved faultlessly around the cottonwood and came to rest on the fringe of the green.

"Nice," said Ant.

"That felt good. Thanks, Paul."

"Yes," added Paul, "and it's a lot better than denting up satellite receivers."

My embarrassment was obvious. Paul slapped me on the back as we walked over to the Solomon's next tee box.

Silas jumped out of the back of the cart. Joining in on the fun, he dashed to the green. I had never seen an animal cover more than two hundred yards so quickly. He returned just as fast with two golf balls in his immense mouth and offered them to Paul.

"I think he's part retriever, too," said Paul. "That's enough, Silas. Now go and play."

Silas took off in a romp of excitement, covering the huge

clearing. He scrutinized the complete golf course area. By the end of our golf outing Silas had retrieved several chewed up golf balls, an old rusted five iron, three empty pop bottles and a possum.

We continued our golf game with Paul matching me shot for shot. As we moved from house to house, Paul inquired about Benny, the Coxes, the Andersons and especially the Sharps and Doc Pyle.

After we had completed pelting the lone target with our whole supply of golf balls, we traveled out to the green to take turns putting and chipping.

"So, Anthony, what's your buddy Thomas up to today?" asked Paul looking over at Ant from the putting surface.

"Wednesday is TJ's gym day," replied Ant, leaning against the golf cart. "Too bad we don't have a team for him to play on. The guy is made for hoops."

"So I've heard," said Paul eyeballing another putt with his only good eye.

"What else have you heard, Pavlos?" asked Ant.

"Paul—just call me Paul, Anthony."

I winked at Ant. "He reserves that for his good friends."

"Well, let's see…" started Paul as we gathered back at the cart, "Thomas and the two of you are best of friends. Anthony, you're the smartest student in school and even assist the teachers. You're expecting to receive a scholarship to the University of Oklahoma to pursue a career in medicine. Timothy is very bright and the best athlete in the school. He helps in the family business. He wants to go to college on a golf scholarship. Thomas is the son of a preacher man and the only African-American boy in town. Deacon is loyal to Tim's dad for moving them to Corinthia Falls and assisting them in difficult times, but it has deprived Thomas of his passion for basketball. Each of you is blessed with wonderful parents. The three of you attend church regularly and sit together in the so-called Observers section. The threesome collectively made confessions of faith together in the seventh grade, were baptized by Thomas's father at Turtle Cove, and made a pact of unity for life."

"Sounds like you have been attending classes at Oaks Corner, Paul," said Anthony very impressed.

"Yes, he has," I confirmed.

Silas piled into the back of the cart with Ant as we rode back in the direction of the Solomons. Ant had a conversation with Paul on mathematics and sociology which was over my head. With golf clubs and Silas loaded in the back of my truck, we returned to town.

"What's next?" I asked Paul, who was sitting between Ant and me in the cab with his arms draping both our shoulders.

"Next Wednesday, let's do basketball with Thomas," he suggested. "Tomorrow after school, we start work on the church. Here's a list of things I need you to pick up at the hardware store, Tim. Your father assured me the church has a charge account there. Would you like to be of assistance, Anthony?"

"I can do that," said Ant, "But you forgot one thing."

"What's that, son?"

"TJ, Timber, and I all like watermelon."

After school the next day, Ant and I stopped by Corinthia Hardware to collect the supplies on Paul's list. Most of the items were related to painting: several brushes and rollers, sand paper, several gallons of different colors of paint, thinner, putty knives and all the extras that suggested we would be sprucing up the old church.

We weren't sure why he wanted the two five-foot chains, the padlocks and rope. Ant suggested it might be used for Emmitt's men to secure the Sams.

"How was school, boys?" asked Paul, looking down at us from a ladder balanced over the church entryway.

I smiled up at him. "No geese today. Where do you want all this stuff?"

"Why don't we just put it in the men's room," said Paul climbing down the ladder where he'd been scraping off the old, peeling paint from the trim that separated the red brick from roof.

"We will be doing some touch-up around here. The pay's lousy but the works plenty!"

Ant and I unloaded the supplies from the back of my truck. Silas was taking a nap in the foyer. He woke from his slumber and accompanied us for several trips back and forth.

Joyce met us in the hallway exiting the small church office. As usual, she was cheerful and full of enthusiasm.

"Timber and Anthony!" she greeted us. "Are you boys helping out the Colonel?"

"That's our orders," I answered as she followed us to the men's room where we relieved ourselves of another load of supplies.

Silas inspected the brown paper sacks for any edible goods.

"I came down to print off the bulletins for church Sunday," said Joyce to me softly, "but Col. Armstrong said it wouldn't be necessary."

"We're learning the man has a diverse style," stated Ant.

"Well, Nate and I are getting to run the store tonight. Wish me luck!"

"Good luck and God's blessings," said Paul who must have overheard much of the conversation.

"Thank you, Colonel!" Joyce smiled and stopped for a quick hug. "See ya, boys!"

The rest of the evening as well as the next, Ant and I gave a long-needed grooming to the old building. All the outside trim and window framings were painted as well as the office and the two restrooms. The alter railing was sanded and given a new gloss of varnish.

While we labored, Paul instructed us on the importance of work:

"When we work we earn a wage that we deserve. Those who work are not a burden to others. But the worker is made blameless by God through their faith."

"Show me a person of true faith in Christ," said Paul, "and I'll show you a good worker—no matter the task."

Late Friday evening we had finished. Our last job was cleaning the stained-glass windows. Tired but satisfied, we locked up and headed for my truck.

"Tim, Anthony, there's one more chore for which I'd like your help in the morning. Meet me down here sometime after breakfast. It won't take long."

Saturday morning the church was unlocked. A ten pound bag of Purina was slit open in front of the covered entrance where Silas was enjoying breakfast. The hungry dog seemed uninterested in Ant and me.

We found Paul in the sanctuary tying off the stairway to the balcony section with the rope from the hardware store. Across the rope was taped a hand written sign that said 'STOP'.

"Morning, gentleman!" a refreshed Paul greeted us. "I could use some assistance in moving these pews."

Paul directed us to move the wooden pews to the back of the church, setting some on top of the others. After the pews were carefully arranged, the dark green carpeted sanctuary floor looked empty and barren. We located a vacuum in a closet and took turns sweeping the floor. The pews remained stacked, leaving an open floor area.

"That's about it," said Paul. "Grab those last two sacks in the men's room."

Ant and I followed Paul out the side door of the church. Paul reached into the heavy sack I was holding and pulled out the weighty linked chain. He fastened the chain through the outside handle and threaded it to the adjoining metal clasp. Pulling the chain tautly, Paul secured the two ends with a padlock. On the door was a red and black sign duct-taped that read: 'CLOSED.'

The three of us walked around to the front of the church and climbed the steps to the main entrance. Silas was done with his meal. I cleaned up the empty bag of dog food

Paul repeated the process with the second chain and padlock. Removing the hardware from the sack Ant was toting, he draped the chain through the two large door handles and snapped the padlock. He finished securing the site with an even larger 'CLOSED' sign.

"Does the Deacon know about these signs?" I asked Paul.

"…and your father," confirmed Paul.

"Thanks for your help, boys. Silas and I are going for a walk," said the satisfied church official.

Colonel Pavlos Lincoln Armstrong strode merrily toward downtown with his companion.

"See you tomorrow morning," said Paul, looking back over his shoulder at our bewilderment. "It's Sunday, you know."

"Confirmatory," said Ant. "The man has a diverse style."

S unday morning came. It was an established tradition that Oak's Corner would not be open for business till after church services on Sunday mornings following Labor Day, and would not be open on Sunday mornings till Memorial Day weekend. The summer season of Lake Corinth was over. This would be the first Sunday back to church for my parents since last spring.

As was also a custom on the first Sunday after the holiday, my friends and their families were invited to our house for breakfast before worship service. By 9:00 the Bearkillers, the Johnsons and the Hoopers, both Becky and her mom Sarah, had joined the house of Oak's for our traditional brunch.

Mom had been up early preparing the morning meal. There were homemade biscuits and gravy, scrambled eggs with green onions, pork chops, blueberry waffles, country fried potatoes, iced cinnamon rolls, fresh squeezed orange juice and a large pot of hot coffee.

The ladies helped Mom put on the finishing touches. The feast was lined up buffet style on the kitchen counter. Our dining room table was just big enough to get eleven people around.

The menfolks gathered in the living room. The talk started out on football which is a male's main focus of conversation in Oklahoma during the autumn months. Jack Bearkiller changed the topic.

"Deacon, what is the closed sign on the church all about?"

TJ, Ant and I looked over at the Deacon sipping his coffee. We were eager for an answer. Dad and the Deacon had been very tight lipped since yesterday morning. Rumors coming through the store on Saturday ranged from general maintenance to lack of funding.

"I think we'll find out this morning," said the Deacon as my father nodded. "Anyway, the Colonel is in charge for now. I know everyone is somewhat apprehensive after last Sunday's fiasco."

"Time to eat, boys!" declared Ms. Martha.

Shortly before 11:00, our caravan arrived at the church. Kids in my truck, Sarah Hooper rode with the Deacon and Martha while the Bearkiller's passengered with my parents. Most of the congregation had assembled on the bottom steps of the church entrance, with others backed up to the sidewalk.

Silas, sitting on his haunches, was bonded with his leash to the still padlocked front doors. A mound of fist-sized stones had been positioned on the lawn just off the walkway.

The church membership was divided as usual. The Setters gathered to the right, opposite the Standers, with the Observers intermingling throughout. Our group found our proper positions in the assemblage of would-be worshipers. Silas rose on all fours, excited to see his friends.

The Deacon made his way through the cluster and climbed the steps followed by my father. They turned and faced a disturbed throng with anxious questions and accusations.

"What's in God's name is going on here, Deacon?"

"Unlock those doors!"

"Are we being shut out of our own church?"

"Never in my life!"

The grumbling continued.

"Do something, Bill Oaks!"

"I already have," announced Emmitt Sharp sounding very authoritative.

Just as the mayor was scaling the steps, a Quanapah County Sheriff's patrol car with lights flashing pulled up in front of the church. A young , slight-of-build uniformed deputy stepped out of the vehicle. Practicing proper procedure, the officer observed the situation, noting the closed sign on the chained doors and peered perplexed at the large black animal guarding the entrance.

The serious lawman rested his hands on his gun belt and questioned Emmitt.

"What seems to be the problem here, Mayor?"

"Jimmy, we need this church opened and returned to its rightful owners," said Emmitt.

"…and just who would that be?" came the familiar low southern voice from behind the crowd.

The people parted as the Colonel seemed to appear out of nowhere. His usual all black attire was topped off with another dress shirt complete with silver cuff links. Paul's demeanor was more soft and gentle than usual. He had a self assured smile as he approached the deputy halfway up the steps. The Deacon, Emmitt, and Dad stepped down and joined the congregation to witness the unusual confrontation.

"Can I help you, officer?" asked Paul politely.

"And who are you?" asked the deputy sternly, looking up at the much larger man.

"I am Colonel Pavlos Lincoln Armstrong."

The deputy cocked his head. "Are you responsible for this?" he asked, motioning at the locked doors and Silas.

"I am," replied Paul calmly.

The assembly of witnesses gasped and mumbled.

"Then I order you, sir, to unlock these doors and remove that… that an…ani…"

"Dog," offered Paul to the stuttering deputy.

Paul went up to the top platform unleashing Silas.

"You want him? Take him!"

Silas stared at the nervous officer. The huge bear-dog bent his head down sounding a fierce, rumbling growl. His thick, black fur stood on end. Silas edged his way slowly down the steps in an obvious attack mode.

Jimmy, the deputy, retreated down to the sidewalk as Silas edged closer, now even more threatening. The crowd stepped back. Becky held her breath. The widow Fullbright almost fainted.

The panicking law enforcer reached for his pistol, too nervous to draw it out of his buckled holster. Visibly frightened, the fidgety and insecure Deputy Jimmy withdrew to the protection of the inside of the patrol car. Silas made chase as the deputy raced down the block and out of town.

TJ, Ant, and I snickered among ourselves at the way Paul and Silas handled the authority. Emmitt looked embarrassed. All was silent except for the distant, powerful barking of Silas.

Paul scanned the group, now totally in charge of the situation. He was confident but not pompous. He smiled broadly as everyone moved closer, eager to hear his response.

Paul walked down the cement steps and stopped at the pile of rocks. Reaching down, the Colonel picked out two of the stones. He held them both outward, one in each hand, giving everyone a close look. He then banged the rocks together making a sharp, solid noise that echoed through the streets of Corinthia Falls.

"Dear people, these things are hard," Paul pointed out, clashing the stones together again. "Timothy, pass out some rocks," he directed as he remounted the lower steps.

Ant and TJ helped me distribute a rock to everyone in the crowd. As we finished, I undetectably motioned Paul with my eyes to the two figures hiding in the shadows a block away at the post office. With a slight bob of his chin, Paul confirmed to me that he was aware of Sammy and Sandy Sampson watching from a distance, unnoticed.

"In the times of Christ," Paul began, "stoning was the common punishment for breaking God's law. You know folks, these things would hurt."

Paul pounded his two rocks together a couple more times.

"I think I would rather be taken out with a gun than to be encircled by a mob equipped with these. These rocks are lethal!

Imagine being pelted with these things one at time by your relatives, neighbors and, might I add, church members—being stoned and bloodied by your own brothers and sisters till you succumb to death.

"Remember the story of the Pharisees who brought the woman accused of adultery to Jesus in the temple? God's law said to stone her. How did Christ handle this?

"Now, I don't know where the man was that was involved in this sin nor do I know why the Pharisees were in such a place to witness it. God's law says the man is just as guilty as the woman and deserves the same punishment. It would be easy for us to respond 'No man, no crime.'

"But our Lord took another path. He said 'all right, you just go right ahead and stone her, but let those without sin cast the first stone.' Don't you see? Christ was the only one without sin.

"To execute someone by stoning, it took two witnesses, usually the victim of the crime and someone else who observed transgression. Jesus said 'I am one witness and God is the other.'

"What are Christ's two great commandments?" asked Paul to the gathering, each still holding a rock.

The Deacon stepped forward and boldly announced, "To love God with all your heart, mind, soul and strength!"

"And…" said Paul.

"To love your neighbor as yourself," I added

"Dear brothers and sisters of the Church of Corinthia Falls, last Sunday there was no such love present. Neither was there any joy in your worship. But God is your judge, not me. Christ is the witness qualified to throw the first stone for our disobedience. But what did he do with these stones?"

Paul held the large rocks out at arm's length to present them one last time. He then slowly ascended the rest of the steps. Turning to face the congregation, he stood in the position of the crucified Savior hanging from a cross with his arms and hands extended outward; he let loose of the rocks.

The stones tumbled down the steps coming to a rest at the feet of the crowd.

"Now go and sin no more."

Emmitt was the first to drop his rock. Benny was next to toss his down. The two leaders of the fighting church factions met together in the front of the gathering and embraced to the blunt sounds of rocks hitting the sidewalk and the church grounds.

Tears trickled down faces. Forgiveness was in the air. Hugs turned into laughter. The joy in the Church of Corinthia Falls was returning.

Over the next couple of days, the talk of the town and at school was about Paul's sermon of reconciliation and forgiveness delivered from the church steps. The Colonel's reputation was growing as an evangelist.

Everyone was inquiring and debating as to when Paul would reopen the church. With people realizing I was Paul's appointed assistant, many people prodded me for information. I was as clueless as anyone.

The next Wednesday was Paul's day to visit the school. Principal Cox gave him a thorough review of the facilities. Ant accompanied Paul throughout the day.

The highly educated former soldier participated in the various curriculums. Paul assisted Mrs. Sharp and Mrs. Hooper as they tutored the younger students in their grammar, math, and geography. The elementary students became very fond of Paul. His storytelling ability made learning fun.

At lunch time, Paul helped Mrs. Hummingbird serve lunch. All of us got a laugh at the pink hair net he had to wear over his bushy hair.

In the afternoon, Paul took over the junior high Spanish lesson. He then moved on to a discussion about history and philosophy with the older students.

Seventh hour was the high school's physical education time or what we called 'whatever class.' We could go for a jog, goof off in the gym, study, or just whatever. On many days I was allowed to leave early and practice golf, but today was Wednesday and that meant TJ would be shooting hoops in the old gym.

By the time Paul, Ant, and I got to the gym, TJ was already in his rolled up grey sweats working his game. There was only a lone goal remaining, located opposite the stage. The backboard was white metal and the game was half court.

In the distant past, Corinthia Falls had been a Class A basketball powerhouse. The old gym housed many former state championship teams. The last one was in 1957. The old timers often reminisced and reminded us about the glory days, especially the '57 team led by all-star guard, Emmitt Sharp.

In the 60s all competitive athletics were eliminated due to declining school enrollment. My golf was the only exception.

Paul had changed into his black t-shirt and high tops. I remained in jeans and my custom tennies. Ant was outfitted up in an old basketball uniform with a jersey that almost swallowed him alive.

Several balls were available in a rack on the far side of the gym next to the old wooden bleachers. TJ already had the newest old ball. Ant ran over and distributed the basketballs.

TJ looked the part: 6' 5", lean and agile, with long limbs. He took the sport seriously. If he'd attended school anywhere else, he would be a star.

"Hey, TJ! Let me dunk one!" said Ant dribbling his ball out to join his foot-and-a half-taller friend.

"Not again," TJ sighed.

TJ and Ant repeated their routine from Turtle Creek. Tom gave Ant a boost. Ant stood on TJ's lofty shoulders. With his head now above the rim, Ant slammed the ball through the net. The basketball bounced off TJ's head.

"Man, that feels good!" exclaimed Ant.

"Not so good for Thomas," said Paul, starting to dribble his ball.

TJ tossed down the little guy. Landing on his feet, Ant made TJ a challenge.

"Show the Colonel that thing you can do!"

"Okay, but this is it. I'm here to play ball," warned TJ.

I stood next to Paul, fully aware of what was coming next. TJ took several steps back from the goal. He leaped and grabbed the rim and pulled himself up. Placing a knee on the stiff old rim, he climbed to the top of the backboard and sat down.

"Agility," said Paul, looking up at TJ. "How's the view?"

"Now are we done?" asked TJ, looking down at Ant and returning to the gym floor.

Several high school students trickled into the gym for seventh hour. Most took to the bleachers. Becky was the first one there.

The four of us took turns practicing our jump shots. The Colonel displayed classic form. Becky went under the basket to rebound for us.

"So, old man, you got game?" asked TJ, addressing Paul cocky and playful.

"Probly so," I replied for Paul. "He's good at everything else."

"Well, let's find out," said TJ, eager for some competition. "What say Timber and I take on all comers?"

"So the two best athletes in the school, huh?" considered Paul aloud. "Okay, I'll take Anthony and…Becky here."

Becks, the tomboy at heart was eager to join the fray. She quickly rolled up her jeans to just below her knees and kicked off her shoes. Reaching into her pocket, she took out a rubber band and pulled her red hair back in a ponytail.

"First one to ten. Baskets are worth one point each," said TJ passing the ball to Ant. "Your first out."

The two on three match had caught the attention of those in the gym. The principal and his wife, Clara, entered the old building, along with Sherry Solomon.

"Wow! A basketball game," proclaimed the blond would-be cheerleader excitedly. "Go, Saints!"

TJ guarded Paul under the basket. It was my job to take on the two small ones out front. As Paul and TJ struggled for position, I denied Ant the ball, leaving Becky all alone with a twenty-five foot shot.

"Take it, lady!" urged Paul.

Becky's high arching shot swished through the net. Her mom, Sarah, made it to gym with several of the elementary students just in time to witness her daughter's accomplishment.

"Got to get on her, Timb!" instructed TJ.

I knew this game was all about getting the ball to TJ under the goal. I lobbed him a pass that he quickly dunked over the Colonel's head. The student and staff spectators were getting into the game.

The Colonel got the ball, blocked out TJ with an elbow and executed a perfect layup. The crowd started to chant.

"Colonel! Colonel! Colonel!"

TJ dazzled us with his ball handling, I hit a couple jumpers, but the Colonel's squad matched us point for point.

The aged gym was filled with more enthusiasm than it had been in twenty years, as Sherry led the cheering for both teams.

It was 9-9 after TJ slammed another basket. Gushing sweat, all five of us were winded and bent over, grasping at our knees. Becky inbounded the ball to Paul.

Paul faked and pivoted to the basket only to be rejected by TJ as the impact on the blocked shot brought both of them to the ground. The ball trickled out to me.

With only Becky guarding me, the game was mine to win. A short set shot over the outreached hands of a girl was all that was needed for victory. My shot was almost halfway down the basket when it rimmed out and eluded TJ and Paul, still struggling to get back to their feet.

Ant picked up the rolling ball. All alone and too far away for me to guard, the little Cherokee scholar made his only score of the game.

The old gymnasium went wild. Ant made several victory laps while TJ demanded a rematch.

"Not today," said the exhausted Colonel.

After the ballgame, Paul invited our whole group to the garage apartment for dinner. He enticed us with a promise of his Cajun catfish recipe. Becky volunteered to assist him prepare the meal.

I dropped Paul, Becky and Silas off at the apartment. After

checking in at the store with Mom and Dad for a couple hours, I rounded up Ant and TJ.

The boys and I could smell the aroma of fried meat as soon as we got out of the truck. Silas met us at the door. Becky was busy in the small kitchen. Paul was fixing iced tea.

"I hope that stuff tastes as good as it smells," said Ant trying to wrestle himself free from Silas who had him playfully pinned on the small living room floor."

"Nate Anderson supplied the catfish," stated Paul as he helped Becky remove the last of some golden brown fried potatoes from a large frying pan. "The secret is peanuts: peanut oil, peanut breading and peanuts in the hushpuppies. I picked it up from one of our pastors from a small parish in Louisiana."

TJ settled in the recliner, pretending to be interested in the evening news. The small TV's volume was turned down low as President Reagan was discussing the economy. TJ was still rather depressed about the afternoon's loss.

"All right, here is yours," Paul informed the hungry dog, holding up a large bowl of scraps and dog food. Silas's bowl was empty before Paul could get through saying grace.

"Kids, just help yourselves and find a place to sit. I'm going to get Silas a drink of water."

Paul went through the small bedroom and turned the bath water on in the bathroom. Silas straddled the side of the tub with two paws in the water and began to gulp.

Becky, Ant, and I filled our plates and sat at the undersized dining table. Paul joined TJ in the living room. After handing TJ a loaded plate of fish and fixings, he sat with him on the sofa.

"Gulp, gulp, gulp...." came the sound from the bathroom.

"Thomas, you have quite a talent for roundball," said Paul.

TJ looked up at Paul with his supper plate balanced on his lap and gave a half hearted, "Thanks."

"Gulp, gulp, gulp," continued the thirsty hound.

"I have a friend who's the assistant basketball coach at Georgia." stated Paul. "I would like to see if we could get the two of you together. How would you like to be a Georgia Bulldog?"

TJ sat up in the recliner, almost choking on his dinner.

"Uh, a…you mean for real?" said the wide-eyed teenager.

"Yes, son. I think you have a good chance. I'll try to set something up before he gets too busy during the regular season."

"Way to go, TJ!" said Ant.

"Gulp, gulp, gulp," went Silas.

TJ and I both rose and approached each other, connecting with a high five. TJ's mood livened up as we finished dinner.

"This is delicious," said Ant, now on his second plate.

"Soul food," added TJ.

"Compliments to the chefs!" I chimed in as we lifted our glasses of iced tea to Paul and Becky.

As we began cleaning up after dinner, Silas finally reentered the living room with bathtub water dripping from his muzzle and front paws. Paul returned to the bathroom and turned off the running water to the tub. Silas let out a belch that sounded like something an elephant might make.

"Better let him out for awhile, Timothy," suggested Paul.

We washed dishes and cleaned up the kitchen. Paul wrapped the leftovers in aluminum foil and placed them in the oven.

"I'm saving this for a visitor that should be arriving soon," Paul explained to us.

"Who's that?" I asked, shutting the door behind Silas.

"Someone who is lost," said Paul as we gathered in the living room area. Becky, Ant, and I took up the sofa; TJ sat down on his favored recliner while Paul remained standing.

"A mystery guest?" suggested Ant.

"If someone is lost, how do you know they will find you?" softly inquired Becky.

"Uh yeah, how do you know they're coming?" asked TJ.

Paul smiled confidently. "Let's just say a little bird told me."

The conversation turned to optimistic talk about the future, centering on a potential NBA all-star, a professional golfer, and the world's next great cardio-vascular surgeon. Paul encouraged us to imagine the possibilities.

"I just hope we can make it happen," said TJ.

"Let's pray God can make it happen," Becky corrected. "Then I'd have three famous friends."

"That's true, Becky," said Paul. "It's important to dream… we can achieve anything with the power of Christ."

Let's all get in here," urged Ant as we formed a huddle, each extending a hand to the center of the circle. Paul placed his other husky hand on top.

"On three," said TJ. "1-2-3…Saints!" we proclaimed in unison.

Silas was still outside. His deep, repeated barks sounded a call to alert.

"Must be our visitor," said Paul

Becky opened the door. Looking down the stairway that led up to the apartment, she gasped at the sight of Silas greeting the stranger. She quickly reentered and slammed the door.

"Sams!" said Becky as she covered her mouth and drew in her breath.

I reopened the door. In the shade of the evening at the foot of the stairs was a crumpled up body that could barely stand. The male figure's head was down. A guitar was strapped to his back. He held a muddy blanket in his arms in place of a travel case.

As a beaten face slowly looked up at me, I realized it was Sandy Sampson.

I cautiously hurried down the stairs. Putting an arm around Sandy to brace him, I glanced around to see whether he was alone.

The rest of the gang peered down at us anxiously from the top platform of the wooden steps. As I relieved him of his blanket full of belongings, I saw his battered face. One eye was swollen shut. His lower lip was bloodied and inflated. Tears and mucus covered his face. Sandy was helpless.

"Give me a hand!" I said, looking to the top of the stairs for help.

TJ joined me in helping Sandy climb the steps. We made it into the apartment. Ant secured his guitar as we sat him on the sofa.

"Man, what happened to you?" asked TJ looking down at the youngest Samuel brother, not really expecting an answer.

Becky instinctively wet a clean dish towel with warm water. As she gently cleaned his facial wounds, Paul sat down beside him.

"Bring Sandy some water," ordered Paul.

Paul had seen the results of domestic abuse before. The rest of us being parented in good homes did not recognize the situation. Paul sought to comfort the battered youngster.

"My Pa didn't think much of that Bible you left with me, Colonel. I thought I might take you up on that offer," said Sandy, still trembling slightly but regaining some composure.

"You are safe now, son," said Paul. "Care to tell us what happened?"

"Well, I guess you could say I really got to thinking about those things you said the other day. The life Sammy and I live has not been very good since mom left us.

I know you saw us listenin' in at the church last Sunday. I'm just so tired of all the hating. Pa got drunk this afternoon and caught me readin' that Bible out in the barn. I was checking out that John stuff.

Pa took the Bible away and started cussin' big time. Sam got in a big fight with him. Gib didn't want nothing else to do with any of it and left. I don't know where Sam went. Pa was so mad he took it all out on me.

Colonel, I just want all of this stuff to stop and start over. Is it true that I can be born again?"

"Call me Paul, and yes it is true."

"Then that's what I want. I want Jesus. I want forgiveness and I want a redo!"

Paul motioned for the rest of us to gather around Sandy. TJ and I knelt beside him. Ant and Becky came closer. As Paul laid a hand on Sandy, he encouraged us to do the same.

"Sandy, the first thing you have to do is invite Jesus into your heart. Then you must confess with your lips. Do you understand?"

Sandy nodded.

"Sandy, do you acknowledge in the presence of these witnesses that Jesus Christ is your Lord and Savior?"

"Yes, yes. Jesus," said Sandy with his swollen eyes closed.

"Do you admit that you're a sinner and repent of your sins?"

"I do repent, Jesus. I've missed the mark. Please forgive me?" pleaded Sandy, with tears dripping off his cheeks.

"Do you accept His gift of salvation?"

"I do! I do!"

"Then, Sandy, open your eyes and meet your new family in Christ."

Sandy's tears turned to joy as he opened his eyes. His previously dulled face took on a gleam. The first to embrace him was Becky.

While hugging Becky, Sandy asked, "You mean Timber Oaks is my brother?"

We all laughed, we cried, and rejoiced together. We took turns welcoming the new believer.

"I never thought I would be hugging a Sam," said Becky.

"Let's get him some supper," said Paul, referring to the leftovers in the oven.

We prepared the best meal Sandy had probably had in quite awhile. He sat at the dinette table and was treated as an honored guest. As he gobbled down the fish, the laughter and encouragement continued.

"You know what's next, Sandy? Baptism!" TJ said.

"That's right!" said Ant looking over at Paul. "Can we do it tonight?"

"Would that be okay with you, Sandy?" asked Paul. "Baptism is a demonstration of your new faith in Jesus Christ and the washing away of your sins."

"We can do it at Turtle Cove!" I urged.

"Let's get wet!" said Sandy, standing to the occasion with his mouth still full of fish.

"What are we waiting for?" said Ant.

We all hurried down the steps to my pickup where Silas was still lingering, putting his mark on all four tires. Paul joined me in the cab. TJ, Ant, and Becky jumped in the back. I backed out of the drive so quickly that Silas didn't have a chance to load.

"Stop by the store," Paul told me. "Let's get some more witnesses."

We breezed through the streets of Corinthia Falls with Silas hot on our heels. I pulled up to the door at Oak's Corner, unconcerned in my excitement about blocking the drive. As I honked on the horn, TJ hopped the rail and bolted inside.

"Dad!" said TJ to his father behind the counter. "We're going to Turtle Cove. The Colonel is going to baptize Sandy Sampson!"

The Deacon dashed to the glass door to see with his eyes what his faith was denying. Paul, with his arm around Sandy, motioned for him to join us just as the massive Silas managed to catch up with us and jump into the bed of the now swaying truck, decking Ant.

"Glory halleluiah!" cried out the Deacon looking up as if to heaven. "Bill, Eunice! They're baptizing Sandy Sampson!"

My father ran out from his office and Mom hurried out from the deli to the front of the store.

"It's true, honey. They got that Sam's boy in Timothy's pickup," said Mom. "Praise the Lord!"

"What do we do Bill?" asked the Deacon.

"Quick, lock this baby up," said Dad taking command. "You go pick up Martha. I'll call the Anderson's. We'll meet you there!"

TJ helped his father close down the store as Dad placed the phone call. Benny Larson pulled up on his Harley and got caught up in all the commotion.

"What in the world's going on here, Deacon?" asked Benny.

The Deacon pointed out at my pickup as he locked the register money in the safe.

"Sam! Baptize! Turtle Cove! Now! Colonel! Glory!"

Benny stared at my crew in the pickup in disbelief. Mom and Dad escorted Benny out of the store; TJ set the alarm as the Deacon fidgeted with his keys, nervously trying to lock the door.

Benny put it all together. "Jump on!" he said to TJ, handing him the spare passenger helmet. TJ jumped on the back of the powerful bike as Benny stomped his foot and throttled up.

"Let's ride!" Benny screamed over the sound of the motorcycle

"We'll follow you," Dad yelled at me.

"Y'all wait till we get there," added the Deacon.

As we arrived at the dirt road leading to Turtle Cove, Joyce and Nate Anderson were waiting for us and fell in line with the motorcade. We parked the cars and lone motorcycle under the pines. We left our lights on to illuminate the still waters of the cove as it was now almost dark.

Paul took Sandy over to the side of the water away from the rest of us. Facing him with both hands on his shoulders, Paul whispered in his low voice answering Sandy's questions and giving some last minute instructions.

The Johnson's family car pulled alongside my pick up and added more lights to the serene setting. Martha rushed to Joyce as both women embraced. Rising up and down on their toes as to simulate leaps of joy, the two ladies rejoiced silently.

The Deacon joined Paul and Sandy by the water's edge. Benny stood with an arm around Nate at the side of his bike. Silas sat motionless at Benny's feet.

TJ, Ant, Becky and I had removed our shoes. We were almost knee deep in the water, desiring to be close to the ceremony and show our support. We held hands as Paul, Deacon and Sandy removed their shoes and entered the warm September waters of Lake Corinth.

The only sound that night was the cooing of a dove from the upper branches of a pine tree till Martha began to sing at a very slow and reverent tempo. The deliberate slow pace of her hymn gave a fresh meaning to our favorite song as the clergymen and Sandy waded out waist deep in the lake.

"When ~ the ~ Saints, go ~ marching ~ in…

Oh Lord, ~ I ~ want ~ to ~ be ~ in ~ that ~ number…"

Her song continued as teardrops pierced the placid waters of the cove.

The Deacon stood behind Sandy for balance. Paul stepped up to Sandy's side, laying one hand on his shoulder as his other reached up to the night sky. Paul began as Martha finished the old spiritual.

"We are all children of God through faith in Jesus Christ. We have not been saved by our deeds but through his mercy.

Christ washes away our sins through His death on the cross and reunites us with Him through His resurrection."

As the two men slowly began to dip Sandy backward into the cleansing waters, Paul declared, "I baptize you, Alexander Simon Sampson, in the name of the Father, the Son and the Holy Spirit."

On Wednesday night, September 16, 1981, Sandy Sampson went under for the Lord.

The next morning, I gave Paul, Sandy and, of course, Silas a ride to the store. The plan was to get Sandy a good breakfast. TJ was busy working his regular pre-school shift at the checkout counter. Ms. Martha was handling the deli. The Deacon greeted us and ushered us to our customary meeting booth.

"There you fellas are," said Martha as she finished helping a customer with coffee and a danish. "How'd you sleep last night, Sandy?"

"My first time in a real bed in a long time, ma'am," said Sandy.

Paul sat down with Sandy and the Deacon in the booth. I walked behind the deli counter and helped myself to my usual orange juice and breakfast sandwich and assisted Martha with the morning patrons as she prepared two large plates of biscuits and gravy for Paul and Sandy.

"Well, I know you two have a lot to go over," said the Deacon to Paul and his new roommate. "Those new to the faith have so many questions. Just listen to the Colonel, son, and let the Holy Spirit guide you."

Martha served Sandy with a loaded plate as the Deacon continued.

"We know you are concerned about your family, son. Let me assure you that we will be praying God sheds His grace on them just as he has you."

Martha served up Paul's breakfast and informed Sandy.

"Young man, as soon as you get through with that, I'm gonna do some measuring. Some of us gals in our ladies' group are going to Archer's Grove this afternoon to get you some presentable clothes."

"Thank ya so much, ma'am," said Sandy.

"Now you just call me Ms. Martha. Ms. Martha's my name. How old are you anyways?"

Sandy's face still looked very sore. His worn out jeans and the rest of his unwashed clothes had seen better days.

"Sixteen, Ms. Martha," answered Sandy the best he could with a mouthful of biscuits.

"Tim, can you meet us after school over at Dr. Pyle's?" asked Paul looking back at me behind the deli. "We need to have the doctor give this boy the once over."

We all gave a little shake of the head. We suspected that Sandy might have other unnoticeable wounds.

"I'll be there," I assured him.

As soon as TJ and I got to school we were bombarded by students and teachers alike with questions about Sandy Sampson and the previous evening's event. Sarah Hooper and Becky had gotten the ball rolling based on Becky's account of the baptism. Ant spent much of his time that day in the office with school secretary, Mrs. Benson, squashing rumors, from gunshot wounds to a robbery at Oak's Corner.

By the time I got to Doc Pyle's after school, the talk of the reformed member of the Sams' clan was all over town. The numerous spottings of the Colonel and Sandy together gave way to much speculation.

The little bell above the door jingled as I entered. Paul was busy using a towel to dust the doctor's office furniture.

"This place is a mess!" said Paul, acknowledging my arrival.

The waiting room was a familiar site for the citizens of Corinthia Falls. There were two old beige sofas and a small table of outdated magazines. Some Norman Rockwell prints hung on the green walls along with the doctor's framed degrees and licenses. Some dangled crooked, and all were covered with dust.

The large desk sitting to the left side served as the office. The Wall Street Journal and the morning's sports page covered the old rotary black telephone, and there were scattered folders and files. A half smoked cigar was smoldering in a metal ashtray.

Doc did not employ a receptionist or any type of staff. He claimed to be too old for such things.

The short and rotund town doctor's dishevelment was a sharp contrast to the more formal ex-Green Beret and southern gentleman. Paul continued his volunteer housekeeping as Doc walked out of his lone examination room with Sandy.

"Mr. Timber," Doc greeted me.

"How's the patient?" asked Paul.

"He's a little banged up, alright," confirmed Doc with a hand on Sandy's shoulder. "But he's not too badly damaged. Nothin' broken. Nothin' that won't cure itself."

Doc reached over to his desk and relit his half-burnt stogie.

"Here's a little something for the pain and swelling," said Doc handing a small bottle of pills to Paul.

"Now Colonel, I'd like to invite you to be our guest and speaker at the Gentlemen's Club Saturday night. We meet the third Saturday evening of each month at seven p.m."

I was shocked that Doc would ask a preacher to the Gentleman's Club. The Deacon and my father were not a part of the organization, though many of the men of the church were. I had never been in there, but I had heard some things.

"How about Timothy? Can he come along?" asked Paul.

"Well, Timber is not twenty-one. But if that is a prerequisite, I imagine we can break a few rules..."

"I hear you're pretty good at that, Dr. Pyle," said Paul with a smile and a wink. "Saturday night it is."

"Excellent!" Doc said. "By the way...no charge, today."

"What's next?" I asked Paul, as Sandy and I followed his lead crossing down Main Street. Silas, waiting outside, joined us and gave Sandy a full body sniff.

"This boy needs a haircut."

Paul opened the glass door to Sharp's Barber shop as the three of us entered and Silas waited outside. Two men sat on the couch passing the time as well as a gentleman sitting in the lone barber chair draped in a grooming bib. They were startled when they recognized Sandy Sampson. Instantly, the trio bolted past us out the door as if in fear for their lives.

"Looks like we're bad for business, mayor," said Paul.

Emmitt gathered himself and stood at semi-attention in Paul's presence.

"Colonel," said the barber, giving Paul his total respect.

"At ease, soldier," returned Paul. "This young man needs some fixing up."

Paul motioned Sandy to the barber chair as I took a seat on the couch. Emmitt covered Sandy in a fresh white apron and pulled a comb through his shaggy, matted brown hair.

"Pavlos, looks like this is gonna take some work," said the barber, studying Sandy's scalp.

"Colonel Armstrong to you," said Paul.

Sandy snickered and I covered my face with one hand, choking down a chuckle. Emmitt seemed intimidated at Paul's pulling rank.

"Relax, Emmitt," Paul said. "Pavlos is just fine. I was only kidding."

Paul studied the barber shop as the more relaxed barber resumed his task. The small shop was neat, organized, and very masculine. The floor was tiled in a white and black pattern. A long mirror stretched above the sink and working area. A white and red antique barber chair provided flair and style.

The white walls were adorned with several mounted trophy-sized fish, a nicely displayed full size American flag, a signed framed picture of President Reagan and an eloquent glass casing that exhibited Emmitt's Congressional Medal of Honor.

Paul studied the medal. Underneath was the inscription:

'Second Lieutenant Emmitt H. Sharp'

'United States Marine Corps'

"Marines," said Paul

Emmitt turned on his electric clippers. "Fourth Marines, Third Division, Korea and Nam."

"Congratulations on your service," said Paul respectfully.

"And to yours, Colonel…uhh, Pavlos."

"I'm sure you thought about what you would do when Demas Sampson comes looking for this boy?" said Emmitt in a questioning manner.

"I have," said Paul. "Emmitt, you are a leader in this community and of the church. Soldier to soldier, I must ask you to stand down."

"Yes sir," Emmitt said, disappointed that Paul did not require his assistance. "But if I'm needed…"

Sandy was uneasy with the direction of the conversation. Paul noticed his discomfort and remarked on the evolving haircut.

"Let's take some of that stubble off his chin."

Emmitt finished up the trimming, removed the apron and spun the barber chair around for Sandy to admire his new look.

His hair was now tapered with a part down the right side. His facial hair was gone. Sandy seemed content with his fresh appearance.

"Looks like the barber gave you an Anthony Bearkiller," said Paul.

As we all laughed, Sandy observed, "Well, I think that works better on me than a TJ."

As I worked on my golf skills at Cherokee Creek the following Saturday, I could not disregard what the evening might bring. The Gentlemen's Club was popular, but secretive. Except for the organization's sponsorship of the Quanapah Challenge held annually on Memorial Day weekend, the inner activities of the club were very guarded.

My parents were very apprehensive of my participation. Mom reminded me to act appropriately and remember my upbringing.

Paul left Silas at the apartment with Sandy and a Bible assignment. He had worked the last two days with the new believer, giving him "a solid foundation for his faith."

I dressed up a little. Instead of jeans, I wore my white slacks with my baby-blue golf shirt. Paul was dressed in his customary black.

Paul could sense my nervousness as we rode to the Gentlemen's club.

"Just relax and be yourself, Tim. Nobody there is going to devour you."

"Paul, I guess you're going to make a speech. What are you going to tell them?"

"I'm not sure," said Paul. "I'll be given the words."

A couple dozen cars and pickups were parked in the parking lot of the old courthouse.

"Looks like they're waiting for us," said Paul.

We were met at the entrance way by Emmitt Sharp. This made sense. Who else for a sergeant at arms than Emmitt?

"Welcome, gentlemen: Pavlos, Timber." Emmitt said with extra firm handshakes. "Make yourselves at home."

Emmitt escorted us across the marble-tiled foyer that led directly into the old courtroom. The elaborate aged courtroom was well preserved. The mahogany woodwork lining the spectator area, the judge's bench and witness stand area, along with the jury box were polished and well maintained.

A large hand-painted mural depicting the history of Quanapah County, including Chief Quanapah himself, adorned the front wall. The wooden floor was cleared of any unnecessary furniture except for several rows of padded folding chairs in the spectator vicinity.

The room was lightly filled with smoke circulated by several slow turning original overhead fans. There were no signs of liquor although a slight tinge of bourbon filtered throughout. It looked like about thirty men were in attendance, all familiar faces.

On the left side of the historic room opposite the jury box, a group of musicians entertained the gathering as they conversed about weather, football and politics while balancing paper plates full of hors d'oeuvres.

Benny Larson was playing the sax. Matthew Cox was on clarinet. Nate Anderson, trumpet. The banker, John Solomon, was enjoying himself on trombone. Mr. Hummingbird was located behind them on drums. Music flowing from such an odd combination of personalities sounded like a cross between amateur jazz and an October fest band.

Doc Pyle, cigar in one hand and glass of refreshment in the other, rushed down the aisle to greet us.

"Here's our guest of honor," said Emmitt to Doc, talking just above the music. "Can I get you two anything?"

Paul looked at me, then suggested a couple Cokes.

"Two Cokes on the rocks coming right up."

"Colonel, Timber, let me show you around." Doc took over as our host and we moseyed through the courtroom, receiving a courteous reception and welcoming handshakes. As Doc led us by the band, Benny stopped playing long enough to ask me if I was playing any golf.

"A little," I said, loud enough for him to hear. "Know any CCR?"

"No!" shouted Benny with a big smile. "They don't play our music and we don't play theirs."

"Come on over here, fellas," said Doc, signaling to the band to play something a little softer.

"This is our hall of fame."

Doc motioned to the display of 8x10 pictures on the wall that were neatly framed and labeled. I had seen some of the same photos at school in the trophy case. Paul took to the particular shot of the 1957 Corinthia Falls Saints' Class A State Basketball Championship team with a young Emmitt Sharp hoisting the trophy.

As Emmitt rejoined us with our colas, Doc announced, "Here's our hero now!"

Emmitt had a proud look of satisfaction as we studied the picture of the Corinthia Fall glory days. I remember wishing I could have had the opportunity to bring such pride to our town.

"You looked pretty good there, mayor," said Paul.

"That was many years ago," added Emmitt.

Further down the wall was a collection of more recent color photos of the winning teams of the Quanapah Challenge. The pictures were as interesting as they were unusual.

"We started up the QC, as we refer to it, back in '69," began Doc. "Timber can probably remember the first one.

"It started out as a simple fund raiser—a way to bring some money into the town. It's now become Corinthia Fall's principal source of revenue. It also helps out the merchants and provides some nice publicity."

Paul nodded as Doc continued.

"Colonel, we decided on a competition commemorating Chief Quanapah's legendary journey through the hills to warn the people of Corinthia Falls of impending doom. The town was just a small trading post back then. Most of it is Indian folklore. We don't know for sure what the impending doom was all about. Most say it was some sort of attack."

"Probably an attack from those hillbillies up at Archer's Grove," added Emmitt. "They could very well still be planning to invade."

Paul laughed and Doc puffed comfortably on his King Edward.

Doc Pyle carried on his history lesson, pointing to a large framed description of the annual event. Across the top it read: Quanapah Challenge. Bellow it was a short passage from a poem by an author unknown:

'He swam the river,
He soared on paws
And climbed the cliffs
To Corinthia Falls.'

Underneath the poem was a revised version of the four stages of the relay race:

Swim across Lake Corinth
Ascend Rock Hill on a beast
Climb Eagle Cliffs
Then dash to the East.

Doc held forth enthusiastically. "As the story goes, Quanapah was a young Cherokee scout. He had to swim across the river. He then rode an ox over a hill and had to climb some cliffs before he then ran quite some distance to alert the town folks.

"We decided it was a lot safer to make this a relay for safety sake as well as encouraging more participation. One individual would just get too exhausted. Our biggest concern is safety.

"There's no river anymore. The Corp of Engineers took care of that back in the forties giving us Corinth Lake. So we start it out at Boulder Ridge Marina. That's just up the road from Turtle Cove. It makes a good starting point."

Doc spotted the marina on the map next to the posted rules that traced the route of the contest.

"The first leg of the QC is to swim across the lake, almost a half mile. The next leg and the most controversial is the ascension, or so we call it, of Rock Hill. The hill's base begins right at the end of the swim. As the legend suggest and the rules state, you've got to do it on an animal. The trick is not to lose your mount.

As you can see, Colonel, in this progression of photos through the years, the mule has evolved as the preferred choice. Mules seem to have the strength and intelligence to scale the hill faster than a horse or an ox, although we have seen everything attempted from a buffalo and an elk to a Clydesdale furnished for a team by a Muskogee beer distributor."

"Don't forget the razorback hog that group from Little Rock used," said Emmitt. "That was hysterical! Or the guy that showed up with the grizzly bear from Kentucky!"

"That was not allowed," said Doc. "We had to change the rules to animals indigenous to this region. We don't need any elephants or camels 'round here."

"Amazing," said Paul.

"At the top of Rock Hill is Eagle Cliffs. You can easily spot it from across the lake. It's right next to the Falls. Young folks like to dive off the cliffs in the summer. If a climber misses his footing, he simply falls into the lake. At the summit of the cliffs is the east side of the State Park."

Doc showed Paul the location on the diagram.

"That begins the final leg—a two mile run through the park

over the dam, on the highway and on into town."

"So, the University of Arkansas covered it in thirty nine minutes and twenty-eight seconds last year?" asked Paul, reading the inscription under the picture of last year's champions and their mule.

"That was a record," said Emmitt. "The times are affected by the weather conditions. When we began this thing, no one took it very seriously. The crowd and competing teams just laughed their way through it. Over the years it has become much more sophisticated and refined. Now teams are coming from colleges, local universities, and athletic clubs. We're getting some world class runners and swimmers, professional mountain climbers and some pretty well trained animals and professional jockeys."

"I catch up a little on this every year and have followed it with great interest, knowing I would one day come here," said Paul. "It always gets a mention on the national news on television, just not enough to fully understand it with the mule race and all."

"That's all about to change this year," said Doc confidently poking Paul lightly in the chest. "I'm making a big announcement tonight."

Benny and the guys broke into a jazzy version of Saints Marching In. All the men set down their drinks and snacks. The membership gathered around the band, singing and clapping in time.

"That signals the meeting is about to start," Emmitt informed us.

Doc took his place at the judge's bench and urged the men on as they celebrated the Corinthia Falls theme song.

"Catchy tune," said Paul as we joined in the fun.

"We claimed the tune before that football team in New Orleans," Emmitt informed Paul over the loud music.

The music continued as the men broke ranks, moving to their seat assignments. Most took a seat in the spectator's area. Postmaster Chester led a group of eleven others into the jury box. Doc motioned at Paul to sit up front next to him in the witness stand.

Doc stopped the music and brought the meeting to order with several strikes of a gavel. The musicians and I found a seat in the back.

"I bring this meeting of the Corinthia Falls Gentlemen's Club to order," said Doc who was obviously the presiding officer.

We began with prayer offered by Benny and were led in a flag salute by Emmitt. Minutes from the previous meeting were read, detailing the success of the last Quanapah Challenge.

"Tonight gentlemen," began Doc, "We're going to be short on new business. I know we're all anxious to hear from the Colonel, but before that I have great news.

"As you know, the last several years the QC has been receiving increased media attention. The newspapers and several local televisions stations have been boosting our coverage. There have even been some clips that have made the national news.

"Well, this afternoon I got a call from the ABC News sports division. The network has decided to cover the QC live on their Wide World of Sports!"

The old courtroom erupted with cheers and a standing ovation. The men were stomping feet and congratulating each other. Paul and I joined in the enthusiastic response. Doc struck his gavel several times to bring things back to order.

"Now, we know we have a lot of work ahead of us getting ready for ABC and what will be the biggest Quanapah Challenge so far. I know you are all excited about the increased exposure for our town, but it's not too early to start on the preparations. In our exuberance, let's get our various committees busy at the task ahead. Eight months go by quickly.

Gentlemen, we have several honored guests with us tonight."

I'd never heard the word gentlemen used so frequently. It must have had to do with the protocol of the situation.

"Everyone knows our resident golfer and young friend, Timber Oaks. Timber, stand up and be seen."

I'm sure I appeared a little embarrassed as I stood to polite applause.

"Our special guest tonight is Colonel Pavlos Lincoln Armstrong. The Colonel is the principle Apostle of the Grace in Fellowship of Christian Churches Association. Did I say all that correctly, Colonel?"

There was some chuckling as Paul confirmed his title.

"The Colonel will be residing in town for awhile. He will be working actively with our local church, which is a member in a network of small town churches he created and administers."

"Colonel," Doc addressed Paul with last minute instructions. "As you can see we're in an old courtroom setting. As is the custom of this body, we invite your testimony from our witness stand. The jury has been seated and you have our complete attention."

As Paul stood in the confined witness stand, there was a courteous round of applause. The audience became solemn and intent.

"Gentlemen of Corinthia Falls…" Paul spoke clearly and with ease.

He was very aware of his audience and their manner. Paul gestured with his hands in a non-defensive manner.

"I have never been surrounded by an assembly of such mediocrity…but then I digress."

Doc Pyle leaned back in the judge's chair and let go a belly laugh. The room was filled with laughter at the satire of Paul's opening statement. Doc sounded his gavel as Paul resumed.

"I grew up in a military family. I was educated at some of the finest prep schools in the East. I am fluent in five languages. I have degrees in philosophy, science and law.

"After graduating first in my class at West Point, I applied for and was accepted into the United States Army Airborne, better known to you gentlemen as the Green Berets, where I achieved the rank of Colonel.

I led a small group of superior soldiers that specialized in filtering out small bands of enemy soldiers that took refuge in rural areas and villages. Our mission was to flush out the enemy and purge them from the local citizenry. Our missions were so classified that I cannot tell you today of our locations except that they were carried out in the Southeast Asia region.

My name became notorious among enemy guerilla camps. The name Pavlos was feared by villagers and opposing combatants alike. All were frightened even speculating of my presence. When I showed up, it meant bloodshed.

"Our adversaries would shed their uniforms and blend in with the natives. Our techniques for distinguishing the enemy from the citizenry involved intimidation and threats which sometimes led to skirmishes. Many innocent were killed in an eruption of gunfire. Peaceful villages that tried to hide from war were often left destroyed.

Family members would betray one another to avoid capture. Though we were sent to free the oppressed, the oppressed valued their lives more than their freedom. They faced two enemies: their oppressors and me. So is the shadowy side of war."

The men in the courtroom were consumed with Paul's story. I was amazed at the confession of his past life. Paul rested his hands on the rail in front of the witness stand, gathered his breath and continued keeping tight eye contact with the men in the jury box.

"We were on a jungle road en route to another small community of grass huts to rescue the people from an enemy infiltration. The driver of my jeep was Sgt. Mark Barnabas. Mark was a good soldier of great faith. I was not a true believer. However, my decision to keep Mark close was based more on superstition than anything else.

"A couple miles from our destination, we hit a road mine. Our vehicle overturned. Sergeant Barnabas was uninjured. I was thrown out. I think it was the intense light from the explosion, maybe it was the sun, but I lay blinded on the roadside. That is how I ended up with this glass eye."

Paul flicked his left eye with his forefinger to demonstrate it was artificial.

"I heard a voice so loud and resonating. The voice said 'Pavlos! Pavlos! Why are you not pursuing me?'

'Who are you, Sir?' I asked.

'I am Jesus, the one you refuse to pursue! Now go back to your base and I will give you a new mission.'

"The sergeant and the rest of my unit were astounded. They had heard a voice, but saw no one.

"Our assignment was cancelled. My men took me back to base camp where I remained in the sickbay. Mark Barnabas never left my side, continuing to pray and lay hands on me.

"Pavlos," said Mark after three days, "it is time for your healing and for your baptism. The Lord has given you a new mission. You are to be His instrument to take His message to small communities all over the world—small towns and villages just like the ones you persecuted."

I knew this was true for I had received the same communication.

Coming from a face to face encounter with the risen Lord and Savior, I was convinced of His authenticity and truth.

As Mark baptized me in a nearby stream, my vision was restored to my right eye. I could sense God's Holy Spirit dwelling within me.

"Shortly thereafter, I accepted a medical discharge from the Army. I returned to the states to begin my ministry. Mark Barnabas was instrumental in helping me set a solid foundation to start the Grace in Fellowship Association. He is now a pastor of a church in South Carolina.

I began by networking small churches across the South. With their support I have taken the Gospel to some of the small villages overseas that I once helped destroy. I have suffered much physical abuse for my endeavors, but I know I can achieve anything with the power of Christ.

So, here I am, gentlemen of Corinthia Falls: the worst of all sinners. I am a retired decorated veteran, a war hero and defender of freedom with innocent blood on my hands. I have no defense except for the fact that the blood of Jesus Christ washes away all sin."

As Paul sat down, the group remained motionless and stunned by his remarks. Some wept openly; many just stared at the floor. Doc looked down at his desk, shaking his head, then addressed the jury.

"Gentlemen, have you reached a verdict?" asked Doc.

"Yes, we have," replied Mr. Chester. "We find Colonel Pavlos Lincoln Armstrong...not guilty!"

When we got back to Paul's apartment, the hum of the small air conditioner was replaced by a breeze wafting through the open windows. The only sounds were Sandy's guitar and Silas' munching of a large beef bone that Dad had sent over. Both were waiting for us with some buttered popcorn and apple cider.

We sat and talked late into the night. Paul talked of the many churches he had visited and some that he helped establish. He let us know that compared to the many hardships he had endured, Corinthia Falls was a pleasant challenge.

I asked him why God allowed him to suffer so much. He said, "If we are to share in his glory, we might also have to share in His suffering."

I was becoming more fascinated with this man and his story. A soldier God salvaged from war, sending him on a mission of peace.

I was learning that Paul was not only a preacher and a missionary, but a teacher as well. Sandy shared in the discussion with intelligent questions and insight. In the past three days he had soaked up Paul's lessons on scripture and Biblical doctrine like a mop.

"Sandy's starting school Monday," said Paul. "Think you and Anthony could give him a hand?"

"Hey, that's great! Ant will have him up to snuff in no time," I assured them both. "So, what about tomorrow? The men at the club and everyone else wants to know if we're having church."

"You been working on the songs?" Paul asked Sandy.

"Yes sir!" You want to hear 'em?" replied Sandy grabbing his guitar.

"It's getting late. Let's just save it for tomorrow morning."

I slept later than usual on Sunday morning. I woke to the smell of bacon and fresh coffee. My parents were just as curious as everyone in town of what Paul had planned for church.

"That closed sign is still on the church," said my mother. "Are you taking the Colonel and Sandy to church, Timber?" asked Dad.

"No," I answered, finishing off my scrambled eggs. "Paul said just go about my business as usual. I'll pick up TJ and Ant. I guess we'll just meet you there."

When we got to the church, Sandy was sitting halfway up the entrance steps with his guitar on his lap. He was wearing the new clothes that the ladies had purchased for him. His facial wounds were nearly healed. He looked comfortable in his fresh appearance.

Most of the church membership had already gathered at the foot of the steps and out onto the lawn. The entry remained chained and locked.

Paul and Silas worked the crowd. The man in black was smiling as he welcomed the curious congregation, exchanging hugs and handshakes. Silas, with whom the town folks had become much more content, circulated through the gathering, looking for attention.

Paul's disposition was one of joy; it lent a glow to the overcast morning. Paul found Becky and grabbed her by the hand. He led her to the middle of the steps and they sat down by Sandy with Paul in the middle.

Paul motioned for TJ, Ant, and me to join them. We sat directly behind the three, not knowing what was up.

"We need the rest of the youngsters up here," said Paul, waving a persuasive hand. "That's right! Even you little ones."

The Deacon and Martha helped the small children to the steps. Paul whispered for us to smile so the children would not feel threatened.

Parents nudged the smaller kids to come forward. The older youth sat to the back, with the youngest settling in front of Paul. Sherry Solomon found a spot next to me. Paul reached out and placed a reluctant toddler on his lap.

Paul nodded at Sandy to begin. The chords were simple but crisp. The tune was familiar to all.

'Jesus loves the little children…all the children of the world…'

Paul moved his free hand to conduct the music and to promote participation. The adults moved closer to the steps as all united in the simple song. Some of the youngest children stood and sang raucously, demonstrating their talent while parents beamed with pride.

'…Jesus loves the little children of the world!'

As the song came to an end, Silas was not to be outdone. He let loose with a deep howl that was almost on key.

"Arhh – ahrr, awrrr – awrr, arr-arrr arrrrrr.'

Everyone laughed and applauded. Some of the little ones hugged the canine scene stealer. Paul stood and petted Silas on the head, joining in with the rest of the massive dog's admirers.

"Colonel, can we go into our church now?" came an adult female voice from the group.

Paul, still standing, smiled and looked over his shoulder at the padlocked doors.

"Come nearer," he said.

The people gathered closer as the children remained seated on the steps, eager to hear Paul's words.

"The only thing that can break those chains is the power of love!" announced Paul, pointing at the church doors.

Paul winked at Sandy who very softly and slowly began to play: This Little Light of Mine. Paul began his message with the melody in the background

"I can speak in many foreign languages: Yeshua ohev otcha... Chua yeu bang...Lesus tu amat. Jesus te ama...Jesus loves you. But without love in my heart, it's all just a bunch of insignificant clamor.

Paul continued to quote First Corinthians 13: "If I could preach the most compelling sermons on spirituality and prophecy, but had no love for you, my words would be worthless.

If my faith was so powerful it could make miracles happen, without love my faith would be useless.

If I gave all my wealth to the poor, but did not do it out of love, my generosity is of little value.

Love is tolerant and thoughtful. Love is not arrogant, envious, and swollen with pride nor impolite.

Love does not have predetermined conditions. Love is not short-tempered and has no list of grievances. It is never pleased about discrimination, but celebrates the virtuous.

Love never surrenders or lacks confidence. It is optimistic and is tolerant forever.

Faith and trust will last throughout eternity, but love is the grandest of all!"

The people gathered around Paul. He stretched out his arms, embracing the crowd. The church gathered into a huddled mass of tears and joy.

Sandy's guitar rang louder as Ms. Martha and her scattered choir sang:

"This little light of mine, I'm gonna let it shine...let it shine, let it shine, let it shine…"

S andy rode to the store with TJ and me after his first day of school. He was loaded down with books and lessons. It was Monday and TJ's evening behind the counter.

Joyce was ending her day shift as TJ relieved her. Paul, the Deacon, and my father were conferencing in the deli. Sandy and I joined them to report in.

"Well, how'd the new scholar do?" asked Dad.

"Real good," I said as Sandy smiled. "Ant and Mr. Cox got him working in the sophomore class."

"Not bad for a guy that's been out of school for several years," said the Deacon patting Sandy on the shoulder.

I reached behind the heated display box and got Sandy and me a burrito.

"What's next, boss?" I asked, looking over at Paul who sat in the booth.

"I'll tell you what's next!" said Joyce, making her way back to the deli area. "The ladies' bible study group meets at my house Wednesday night and the Colonel is our guest. You come along too, Timber."

"Better you than me, son," Dad assured dryly.

"Bill, these two guys are goin' places we've never been before," the Deacon pointed out.

"That's just fine," assured Joyce. "They will be well taken care of. And Colonel, please bring Silas."

"Fed or on an empty stomach?" asked Dad as we all laughed.

The drive to Cherokee Creek on Wednesday evening gave Paul and me a chance to talk.

"You've about made all the rounds after this," I said. "School, the men's club, about every business in town and now the ladies. Is this all part of your plan?"

"God's plan, Tim," said Paul. "He's just making sure all the doors are open."

"All the doors except those on the church?"

The sun was going down on Lake Corinth when we arrived at the Anderson home. Silas was the first one out of my pickup as we cleared our way through the crowded driveway of cars and to the front door of the well-lit home.

"There you are!" said Joyce opening her door before we had a chance to knock. "And good evening to you, Mr. Silas."

The living room was filled with a couple dozen women, all familiar. Becky was busy in the kitchen with Ms. Martha, laying out all the desserts: cookies, pies, cakes and other snacks of the feminine venue. Mrs. Benson from school was preparing some pink punch in a large serving bowl while keeping those interested up on the local gossip.

Paul greeted each woman with hugs and pleasantries. I did the same, but was a little embarrassed when I got to my mom. I could see Becky in the kitchen giggle at me when I was getting a kiss from the widow Fullbright.

Silas worked his way through the petting strokes to the display of pastries on the kitchen table. He was tall enough to look down on the table while inspecting the menu.

"Looks pretty good, doesn't it ol' boy? I wonder what the rest of us are going to eat," Paul said to Silas, amusing the ladies.

"Well, let's have grace and then we can get started," said Joyce. "Ms. Martha, if you will?"

After Martha's blessing, Paul and I were pushed to the front of the line. Donna Bearkiller made sure we tried one of everything. Joyce led Silas to the back hallway, enticing him with a large serving tray full of scraps, dog treats, and left over pie dough.

"Just find a seat wherever you like," instructed Joyce.

Paul sat on one of three couches between Ann Sharp and Mrs. Hummingbird. I balanced my plate on my lap in a nearby chair that was off to the side. Becky sat down beside me. Sensing my discomfort, she gave me a playful nudge with her elbow.

While we were enjoying Joyce's hospitality, Jackie Solomon gave a presentation on the mating routine of the bald eagles that inhabit Lake Corinth. Then Martha led the group in a pleasant but reverent version of the Corinthia Falls theme song. After we got the Saints marched in, Paul commented on how frequently he had heard the song since arriving in town.

Paul stood and addressed the room of ladies that encircled around him.

"Does everyone know the scripture that song is based on?"

"Colonel, doesn't it come from the Book of Revelation?" asked Clara Cox.

"That's right, Clara, the Revelation of Jesus Christ to the Apostle John. Everyone turn their bibles to Revelation twenty-two, fourteen."

Paul took control of the study group while those with Bibles flipped to the back of the book.

"You got it, Sarah?" Paul asked Becky's mom.

Sarah stood up and read, "Blessed are those who wash their robes so they can enter through the gates of the city and eat the fruit from the tree of life."

"God's people, or Saints," said Paul, "will march into the New Earth to eat from the 'tree of life' signifying everlasting life because their sins have been removed by Jesus' death and resurrection.

Just as your town's song suggests victory in competition, so does the original theme imply victory over death. For all of God's children and creatures..."

Silas pranced into the room joining his master as if queued. Paul rubbed God's big bear of a dog on the ears.

"... Yes, all of God's creation waits the day when it will join all of the Saints to celebrate freedom from death.

What can I say about something so wonderful? What could ever undo Christ's love? Nothing...nothing could! Nothing in this world or the next!

Not the future we agonize about or Satan himself can undo God's love. No matter where we are in this world, nothing can separate us from the love of God that is made known through the grace of Jesus. So, just like your favorite song, we march to victory through Christ."

October

S aturday morning and it was time for my weekly run. Paul decided that he would join me, along with Sandy and Silas. We
started at the house and stopped at the store for a cup of inspiration: coffee for Paul, Sandy and I settled for orange juice, while
Silas helped himself to a gallon of water from the outside water
spigot.

The weather was slowing as we merged from summer to fall.
The warm humid Oklahoma air was now cooler and crisp. The
leaves were starting to display a hint of yellows and reds.

I kept it down to a slow jog, not knowing if my new running
companions could keep up. The leisurely pace through town allowed for some chat as we acknowledged folks along the way. Silas
paused to address nearly every sign post and telephone pole in our
path, effortlessly catching back up with us.

Sandy was sporting a white t-shirt, shorts and athletic shoes
from his new wardrobe. Paul was in his black high-tops, black
shorts and sweat shirt. For the first time I got a look at the scarred
tissue on his muscular lower legs.

As we came halfway through our trot at the state park, Paul
mentioned that he heard I was a runner, not a plodder. I recognized his challenge.

"You doin' alright?" I asked Sandy, who was starting to fall
behind.

"Sure," said Sandy, short of breath.

Our tempo was increasing. Sandy could not keep up with our longer strides. The game was on! I would not let this man three times my age outrun me.

"First one to the church!" shouted Paul.

It was two miles back to the church. The pace quickened. Silas bolted out ahead of us as if he knew our destination, but this race was between Paul and me.

By the time we were crossing to the dam on the highway back into town, Paul was a few strides back matching every attempt I made to pull away. Sandy was struggling at least a city block behind us.

With less than a mile to go, I was running the familiar path faster than ever before. My heart was racing as fast as my legs. Still, Paul did not yield, staying just a step back.

As the town came into view, it was a full out sprint. It took all I had to keep ahead of Paul. I could hear the old soldier's knees and joints crackle as we both pushed forward.

When we hit the sidewalks of Corinthia Falls, I had about a ten foot lead. I could sense Paul falling back as the church came into sight where Silas was waiting for us.

"Go, Timothy! Go! Go! Go!" Paul shouted encouragement.

I crossed an imaginary line at the foot of the church steps. I collapsed on the lawn fighting for my breath. Paul finished just seconds behind. The old warrior bent over grasping his legs in obvious agony, fighting back the pain. We were both covered with sweat.

After several minutes of recuperating, I made it to my feet, wondering who really won—the young athlete or his seasoned mentor?

"I've never run so hard in my life," I told Paul, between breaths.

"Me either," said Paul, stretching his arms in the air to catch some wind. "I knew you would not let an old man beat you. Tim, I also knew I could not outrun you, but I could push you and make you better. That about sums up my job description: to make people better."

We sat on the church steps while Silas licked the perspiration off our arms. Sandy finally made it. He had settled down to just a fast walk.

"Glad you could join us," Paul said playfully.

Paul stood up and removed a key from his pocket.

"How about some water?"

Sandy and I followed Paul up the steps. He unlocked and removed the padlocked chains from the doors and ripped away the closed sign. We went inside, taking turns drinking from the water fountain just inside the foyer.

Paul took the sign and chains to the office and returned with a large white construction paper sign and some thumb tacks. We walked back outside and watched Paul attach the notice written in black magic marker to the front doors:

'MEET AT THE SCHOOL YARD 10:30 SUNDAY MORNING'

"What's that all about?" I asked Paul.

Sandy smiled and tilted his head back as if he knew something I didn't.

"Just be there." ordered Paul. "And Tim, bring your three wood."

"Where ya goin'?" Sandy asked Paul.

"To get a haircut...

"Somethin's up," said TJ as he slid into my pickup.

"Yes, I detect an unidentified ambiance settling in," added Ant.

Anthony had spent the night at the Johnson's home. I picked them up on the way to the school meeting Paul had set for Sunday morning.

"My parents were all excited and stuff this morning. They left the house about an hour ago," TJ said.

I let the guys know that the situation was very similar at my house. By 9:00 that morning, Mom and Dad had left with Paul and Sandy. Silas wasn't anywhere around.

"I don't know what's goin' on. I was just told to bring my three-wood."

I nodded to the back of the cab where the golf club was lying. TJ and Ant looked even more confused.

The school parking lot was already full, so we parked on the side of the street. The whole town had showed up. Joyce was passing out helium-filled blue balloons to everyone in the crowd.

Doc Pyle was in the driver's seat of a converted white Volkswagen dune buggy with an open top. Baby-blue crepe paper and balloons decorated his newest toy. The widow Fullbright sat next to Doc in the front seat holding her balloon. Two other elderly couples were stuffed into the back seat.

The mood was festive, resembling more a carnival than a church service. The setting felt like an old fashioned pep rally with noise makers, merriment and optimism.

TJ, Ant, and I got out of the truck without a clue. We received shouts of approval from the assembled merrymakers as Joyce handed us our balloons.

"Looks like party time?" asked TJ.

"Timber, the Colonel needs your golf club," Joyce informed

me. "We're just about to get started!"

Joyce hurried off to the gym with my club. As anticipation built, our bewilderment built more.

From out of the gymnasium doors Mr. Hummingbird appeared with a snare drum strapped to his shoulders. Sounding a military beat, Benny, Mr. Cox, Nate and Mr. Solomon marched behind holding their instruments. The band from the Gentlemen's Club was joined by Sandy, clutching his harmonica. All marched in step out to the street.

The musicians lined up across the street as the cadence of the drum methodically continued. Becky and her mom trailed them, supporting a long blue and white banner from opposite ends that read in large letters 'Corinthia Falls Saints.' They positioned the banner in front of the band across the road.

Next, Sherry Solomon jogged to the front dressed in a white pant suit, shaking two large baby-blue pom-poms. Tagging along behind her were two grade school girls in blue twirler outfits with their batons.

The parking lot spectators cheered as Sherry and her helpers found their places and struck a pose just behind the band. The anxious crowd pushed closer to the street while cameras flashed.

Ms. Martha summoned her church choir all robed in babyblue to gather behind the band. Doc eased his decorated dune buggy to the middle of the street behind the choral group.

Mr. Hummingbird's drum came to a stop. Colonel Pavlos Lincoln Armstrong appeared in the gym doorway. He was dressed in olive-colored military fatigues with his trousers tucked into near knee-high army boots. The signature green beret that dipped near to his right eye had a gold crucifix in front in place of a traditional insignia.

Paul's brushed-back wavy black hair had been replaced with

a military buzz cut. He held a silver whistle in his teeth. The base of the 3-wood rested in his right hand as the shaft rested on his forearm just as a drum major would carry his baton.

With a ringing blow on his whistle, all the assembled came to attention. Strutting to the back of the pageantry, Paul marched through the participants with his head leaned way back and chest high in the air stepping quicker with every pace. Our leader made his way to the front of the pack, stood at attention while raising the golf club baton high in the air and blew on the shrill whistle three times. The music began and the parade was on.

"Dude sure knows how to make an entrance," said TJ.

With the help of Sandy, the gentlemen's club went once again into the Corinthia Falls theme song. The crowd of churchgoers cheered as Doc honked his horn repeatedly. The procession began down Main Street.

Paul marched from side to side of the road in the fashion of a polished drum major. His gait was in rhythm as he pumped the golf club to the beat. The choir started to sing as the parade began its march.

"When the Saints, Go marchin' in…"

Those of us remaining joined in the parade. The guys and I brought up the rear. The music and the singing became louder and more animated.

"Oh Lord, I want to be in that number, When the Saints go marching in…"

Following that line, the students would pump their fists upward echoing, "…in Corinthia Falls!"

Benny and the band swaggered, pumping their instruments in various directions. Paul continued his impersonation of Professor Harold Hill from the Music Man movie. The little twirlers improvised while Sherry led cheers as joy rang out in Corinthia Falls.

Paul led the celebration to the steps of the church where the Deacon and Silas were waiting with both doors wide open. On October 4, 1981…The Saints went marching in.

The music, singing, and celebration continued as the congregation was reunited with their church. A huge banner hung from the cathedral ceiling welcoming home the Saints. The pews were still stacked in the back of the church and the balcony was still roped off.

Benny and the new worship band joined Ms. Martha and the choir on the podium. The assembly stood throughout the service singing one praise hymn after another. The open arrangement of no seating was of little concern. There was no preaching, but somewhere between 'Onward Christian Soldiers' and 'I Love to Tell the Story', the Deacon led us in a prayer of reunification followed by Paul reciting some lines from Psalm 96.

With his arms stretched out and beret removed, the old soldier bellowed out to the revival celebration as if shouting to the angels.

"Sing a new song to the Lord!

Sing to the Lord; bless his name…

Let the heavens be glad, and let the earth rejoice!"

And with those words, the praise of God coming from the restored Church of Corinthia Falls continued till mid-afternoon.

A new energy was in the air. Throughout the town and school there was a sense of anticipation. There was a feeling of unity in Corinthia Falls—a restored hope.

Paul met with TJ and me on Wednesday in the gym after school. TJ was working on his jump shot.

Paul told us about Coach Jorell Aquila. Coach Aquila was

driving all the way from Athens, Georgia to 'give Thomas a look.' The tryout would be the next day at the gym.

"JL, I mean Coach Aquila," said Paul, "is the assistant coach at Georgia and is also in charge of recruiting."

"Right here at this ol' gym with just one goal?" asked TJ, swallowing deeply.

"Think about it, son. Wouldn't you be more comfortable on your home court? Anyway, Coach said this would work out fine."

Paul went on to tell us about his relationship with Coach Aquila. The coach was a former Green Beret that served under Paul on many missions. They got back together when Paul started his ministry. Coach Aquila now volunteers with the Grace in Fellowship Association giving motivation lectures to students throughout the South.

"One more thing, boys," added Paul. "Jorell wants Tim to workout with you, Thomas. He needs someone to bounce off you. Anyhow, Tim, it's important for you to compete hard and push Thomas."

"All right!" said TJ slapping me some skin.

"Tomorrow at this time, gentlemen," ordered Paul. "Thomas, try and get some sleep…if you can!"

The word had circulated through school and all of Corinthia Falls of TJ's 'try out.' Never in the history of the school had anyone received an athletic scholarship to a major university.

TJ's parents were sitting in the old wooden bleachers beside Emmitt. Mayor Sharp came to "represent the old guys." Ant sat next to Becky just below them.

Most of the students, as well as all the staff, were in attendance. John Solomon sat by Sandy while Sherry sat up in front of the stage to lead the cheering.

TJ and I came out of the old locker room dressed in the

throw back baby-blue uniforms of the Saint's glory days. Everyone stood and shouted approval. Immediately, Benny and the Gentlemen's Club band appeared on the open stage playing our theme song. TJ and I were somewhat embarrassed yet excited by the enthusiasm.

As the band played on and Sherry began leading cheers, Paul, Principal Cox, and Coach Aquila entered the gym together.

Jorrell Aquila was an African American in his mid-thirties. He was a little taller than Paul, thin and in great shape. His hair was neatly groomed and parted on the right with a thin, perfectly trimmed moustache.

He wore a bright red Georgia Bulldog sport shirt and black dress pants. A referee whistle hung from his neck. The coach demonstrated an air of confidence with his stature and infectious smile.

As the three men walked out to center court, Coach Aquila handed Paul a clipboard to free his hands to applaud the reception.

"I love it! This is what it's all about," said the coach loud enough for all to hear.

Mr. Cox motioned for TJ and me to join them. We hustled over and the introductions began.

"Thomas," Paul began, "this is Coach Aquila."

The two shook hands. TJ, for one of the first times in his life, looked humbled.

"I've been hearing a lot about you, Thomas," said the coach. "How are your grades?"

"TJ has a 3.1 grade average," Mr. Cox answered for TJ.

"Excellent!" replied Coach Aquila. "So, you got game?"

"I hope so," said TJ.

"Well, you've sure got a lot of support around here. And this is…"

"Timber Oaks, sir," I responded, shaking his hand.

"Thanks for helping us out, Timber."

Coach Aquila instructed us that we would begin with some agility drills. He would be checking our speed and quickness and basic athletic ability.

We started off running sprints from baseline to baseline. We ran forward, backwards, sideways and repeated each drill dribbling a ball. Then an obstacle course of folding chairs was set up on the court for us to maneuver around.

Each routine started and ended on the coach's whistle. He would then check his stop watch and have Paul enter the times on his clip board.

The younger students attending thought this was a competition between TJ and me. They cheered me on as I beat TJ in most all the drills. This discouraged TJ and those that understood what was at stake.

"Very good, gentlemen. Catch your breath and then we'll check out your verticals," said the coach, tossing us a towel to wipe off sweat.

Everyone was glad to hear this. No one can out-jump TJ. Finally, something he could beat me in.

"Timber, let's start with you," ordered the coach. "I want you to start at the free throw line and run up and touch the backboard as high as you can."

I knew I could touch rim, but not much more. I slapped my hand on the old metal backboard a few inches higher than the rim.

"Your turn, Thomas."

Thomas took off and thrust his outstretched palm against the very top of the backboard which was more than two feet higher than the goal. The crowd was wowed. The coach almost swallowed his whistle.

"Son, can you do that again?"

TJ gained an air of confidence as I smiled and gave him the thumbs up. This time he ran up and grabbed the very top of the backboard and just hung there on one arm.

"Told ya!" said Paul to the astonished coach.

Sherry led the spectators in cheers that ended in a standing ovation. The rest of the afternoon focused on the game. We took turns shooting the ball. Coach Aquila would stop things to give TJ some pointers and help him with his form.

We then played one-on-one. No matter how hard I tried to compete with TJ, he totally dominated me. His natural skill was on display. From the outside or under that basket, I was no match for my friend. When coach blew the final whistle, we were exhausted.

"Great work, men!" said the coach. "Get you a shower. Mr. Cox, can I borrow your office phone?"

Ant joined us in the old locker room to congratulate TJ.

"Well, what do ya think?" asked TJ of both of us.

"He didn't say no," answered a positive Ant.

We cleaned up and reentered the gym, where most of the students and spectators had left. We waited for what seemed like forever with the Deacon and Martha. Emmitt, Becky, Paul and Mr. Cox stayed with us.

Coach Aquila finally returned holding a white Georgia t-shirt and a red ball cap. Approaching TJ, he put one hand up on his shoulder, offering him the garments.

"Thomas, how would you like to be a Bulldog?" asked the coach trying to hide a smile.

"Praise God!" exclaimed Martha.

"Yes!" shouted TJ with delight.

Becky held her breath and jumped up and down. The Deacon

beamed with pride as the rest of us took turns congratulating and hugging his son.

"I knew you could do it!" said Emmitt.

Paul and Mr. Cox stood off to the side admiring the scene of jubilation.

"Thomas, I've got some papers for you and your parents to sign in Mr. Cox's office. The rest of you can join us," offered the Georgia coach.

We all stood behind the desk where the coach, TJ and his parents signed the official papers for Thomas Johnson to attend the University of Georgia. Mr. Cox was busy taking pictures that would appear in the Quanapah Times county newspaper the next week.

After our little ceremony was breaking up, the Deacon asked Coach Aquila when he knew he would be offering TJ a scholarship.

"Was it when he hung from the top of the backboard?"

"No sir," replied the coach. "I knew your son would be a Georgia Bulldog as soon as I got the call from the Colonel.

TJ enjoyed his celebrity status for the next few days.

A reporter from the Tulsa World called to arrange an interview with the new Corinthia Falls icon. The Oklahoma sports world was shocked that a young man who'd never played organized sports received a basketball scholarship from a Division I university.

Paul requested help in rearranging the church pews for Sunday morning service. I rounded up my two buddies on Saturday morning. We met Paul, Sandy and Silas at the church.

Silas gave Ant his customary greeting as we entered the church sanctuary. As Ant got up off the floor from underneath Silas, he wiped his face and announced, "Here's the superstar!"

"Has he come down any yet?" asked Paul, referring to TJ.

"About as far down as the town water tower and his head is just as big," I replied.

TJ just smiled as he walked over to Sandy and slapped his hand.

Paul instructed us on the new seating arrangement. The pews were still stacked in the back of the church. Paul wanted the pews assembled in a three-quarter circle three deep leaving a gap at the front near the raised platform area. A wide area was left open in the center.

As Paul explained, he wanted the congregation to see the altar and choir, leaving the center of the floor open for preaching and witnessing. It was also pointed out that this new arrangement for 'church in the round' should eliminate the segregation of any left-over factions in the church.

When we were finished with the new alignment, we moved around to different pews to check on the view. TJ took to the center of the circle and did his best impersonation of his father, the Deacon, delivering a sermon.

"Can you see me now, little person?" asked TJ in his best preacher's voice.

"Very amusing," answered Ant dryly. "I can see you and your big head from anywhere in the church."

Paul was laughing as he moved to the front pew and sat down. Sandy and Silas rested on the steps of the altar. Ant, TJ and I sat across from Paul.

"Boys, let's make sure we know the difference between pride and self respect," Paul said looking at TJ. "Pride is the ignorance of God. Self respect is presenting yourself worthy for God's purpose.

The Bible teaches that the Lord despises pride but honors the humble."

TJ nodded his head modestly.

"By the way," added Paul, "Jorell will be giving the message tomorrow morning. Make sure all the young people are here. He's a very good speaker."

"That's cool! Where's he at now?" asked TJ.

"Still hot on the recruiting trail looking for some future teammates for you," replied Paul with a smile.

The streets and sidewalks of Corinthia Falls were littered with the falling brown and yellow leaves of October. The cool Sunday morning brought out some of the first long sleeves, coats and jackets of autumn.

The Deacon was outside of the front doors of the church welcoming his congregation. Joyce was with him, making sure everyone received a bulletin and a hug. Silas helped in the greetings, giving everyone a chance to pet his head.

The flock was gathering a little earlier than normal. The mood was upbeat in anticipation of the service. The word was out that Jorell Aquila, the basketball specialist from afar, would be addressing the church.

When Ant, TJ and I entered the foyer, Paul was dressed in his usual black attire introducing the worshipers to Coach Aquila. The coach was dressed perfectly in a fashionable dark suit with a red shirt and black tie.

People were in line to shake his hand. The quick conversations were jovial as the confident and relaxed coach exchanged talk about basketball and TJ.

"There he is!" said Coach Aquila, noticing TJ.

Ant and I let TJ be the first to greet his new mentor. TJ seemed humbled in admiration of the coach as the two exchanged greetings.

"Timber!" said the handsome young coach. "Got a sec?"

I followed Jorell and Paul back to the church office.

"Son, I never got the chance to really thank you for your help last Thursday," said Jorell shaking my hand. "You're some kind of athlete—not necessarily a basketball player; but still you got abilities."

"Thanks, coach," I said as Paul shook his head in agreement.

"Your times on those agility drills were off the chart!" continued Jorell. "Do you play any sports?"

"He's a golfer, JL," answered Paul for me. "He has a lot of potential."

"Golf?" said the coach, somewhat surprised. "Who's your coach?"

"Jack Nicklaus," I replied. "I read his book."

Both men broke out in laughter. Jorell put a hand on my shoulder as a thought crossed his mind.

"Wait a minute," said the coach, pulling out his wallet. He fumbled through a list of business cards looking for one in particular as the organ music began in the sanctuary.

"Here it is," said the coach handing Paul the card.

"Colonel, you remember George Apollos? I ran into him at a Christian coaches' meeting last summer. He's now the golf coach at TU in Tulsa."

"Apollos? Christian? Golf coach?" asked Paul dumbfounded.

"He's come a long ways from his days with us in the cruel jungle."

"True," confirmed the coach.

"Hmmm…" said Paul. "Time for church."

The congregation seemed pleased with the new seating arrangement. Paul was correct as usual. The oval positioning of the pews eliminated the division of Setters and Standers. The Observers were still roped off from the balcony. The young people were encouraged to sit in the front of the circle.

The guys saved a seat for me up front. I sat down between TJ and Ant. Becky was to the left of TJ and the Solomon twins were to the right of Ant. Sherry leaned down to give me a wink.

"What was that all 'bout back there?" asked TJ.

"Golf," I replied.

"Naturally," said Ant.

The service took on a more contemporary flavor. The music was buoyant as was Ms. Martha's choir. The Deacon handled all the preliminaries from inside the circle.

A special instrumental music presentation was performed by Benny on his sax accompanied by Sandy on guitar. The duet was followed by polite applause that seemed mostly directed toward Sandy.

Paul introduced Coach Aquila, giving a brief history of Jorell's athletic career and their association together in the military. The charismatic coach stepped down to the center of the church from the altar area where he had been singing with the choir.

The contagious speaking style of Jorell was inspiring to old and young alike. He was very professional and personable. He rotated about the interior of church, very comfortable with 'church in the round.'

For me, it wasn't about who he was, but what he had. He was a man confident in his direction yet modest in his abilities—both positive and intelligent.

The coach preached to us that, just like in sports, it was important in life to have focus. He talked about how the Colonel was the most focused man he ever met.

"The best way to get your life focused is through Jesus Christ."

Jorell then went on to tell about his involvement in the Grace in Fellowship Association founded by Paul's ministry. He told how Paul's mission was to network small churches all across the world similar to the way our church pews were now arranged: a 'circle of care'.

"By building new churches in small communities and connecting them together with those presently existing, we can create a circle of care worthy of our faith.

"Faith without action is of little use, but, by serving one another, the lost will witness our Faith. So feed the hungry, clothe the needy, encourage the hopeless, spread the Gospel and extend our Circle of Care throughout the World! Amen."

The next week was the perfect weather for golf. I spent most of my time hitting balls out at Cherokee Creek. I was inspired by TJ's success. I knew the idea of my getting a chance to play college golf on a scholarship was a long shot, but with the way things were going since Paul's arrival, anything seemed possible.

With a little encouragement from Paul, my father gave the two of us the go-ahead to play at the new course at Tahlequah on Friday. The opportunity to get back on a real course was overdue.

We decided to walk the course instead of renting a cart. This would save enough money to treat ourselves to a chicken fried steak dinner on the way home on Dad's cash.

I was hoping that Paul would open up about this golf coach at Tulsa that Jorell had mentioned. By the twelfth hole, I couldn't take it any longer.

"So, what do you know about this Apollos guy at T.U.?" I asked Paul.

"What do you know about golf at Tulsa, Tim?"

Paul seemed to be deliberately waiting for me to start this conversation. I obliged him with my knowledge.

"They've turned out some good golfers up there…Nancy Lopez…Ron Streck. They play in the Missouri Valley Conference. I know they get to practice some at Southern Hills and that's about as good as it gets."

"Well, let's see," said Paul pushing his hand through his wavy black hair. "Crazy George, as the guys called him, or George of the Jungle… Not the kind of soldier you would want a whole platoon of, but a couple were always nice.

"George Apollos was the type that knew no fear; a *John Wayne*. He was a ready, fire, then aim type of guy. It was if the enemy could not see him in their sights. It was like he knew he could not get hurt and we knew it, too. God protected him for some special reason and now he's a believer and coaching at Tulsa University. I knew he loved golf, but he thought the game should be played by opposing teams in football uniforms: a type of field hockey on a golf course. There just wasn't enough violence in the game for George.

Corporal Apollos kept an old eight iron on hand. He used it for everything: a sword, a club, a good luck charm…whatever. He called it his Moses staff.

Once we were ambushed. We lost our vehicles and most of our weapons. We were bogged down in a small ravine. The enemy had the advantage from a farm house up on a hill. We were defenseless.

"Tim, that farm house was a hundred yards away. No one could throw a baseball that far, much less a grenade. George jumped up out of the ravine and smacked a grenade. While under fire, with that eight iron of his, he hit the greatest golf shot I have ever seen. Jorell and a dozen other good men owe our lives to George Apollos.

"Wow! Now that's a war story!" I said, almost in disbelief.

"No Tim. That's a real golf story."

The following Sunday the Church of Corinthia Falls was fuller than the last. More young adults were in attendance with their children. The worship style and reputation of the former Green Beret was bringing out the curious and the seeking.

The Deacon announced during the service that Wednesday evening would be the Fall meeting of the church administration. Anyone interested in the future business of the church was urged to attend.

Paul enlisted me to join him at the administration meeting. My father informed me that usually only five or six attend. Dad, the Deacon and Ms. Martha and Joyce, the church secretary, were the regulars at handling church affairs. This left TJ and my mother to run the store that evening.

Dad rode with Paul and me to the meeting in my pickup. When we got to the church, the parking lot was nearly half full. The Deacon stood in the inner circle of the sanctuary using a music stand to organize his agenda. I guessed there were around fifty members scattered in the pews.

"This might be a bad sign," whispered my father.

Dad had let me know that usually only those with complaints attended administration meetings. However, everyone seemed content and harmonious.

After an opening prayer led by Ms. Martha and the usual

meeting preliminaries, Sarah Hooper addressed the need for a nursery since more young families were showing an interest in attending worship service regularly.

Sarah pointed out that the old utility room could be cleaned out. She volunteered Becky and herself to coordinate the nursery. A motion was unanimously approved. Donations of toys and children's furniture were offered.

Matthew Cox suggested a community Thanksgiving Dinner be held at the school cafeteria the following month sponsored by the church. The focus would be on the needy of our area. This idea was enthusiastically accepted. Dad donated a dozen smoked turkeys from the store.

The need for Christian education was brought up. Jack and Donna Bearkiller volunteered to head the new Sunday school committee.

Joyce stopped from taking the minutes long enough to talk about Halloween, coming up the next Saturday evening. Benny and I were volunteered to accompany the trick or treaters around town together in one group using our pickups. It was suggested that the children could be dressed as Biblical characters as it would be educational as well as fun. Ann Sharp and Clara Cox would help with the costumes.

"I now have an important announcement to make," said the Deacon. "It seems like the Colonel and Coach Aquila's talks on a Circle of Care and community service is catching fire.

"We have received a substantial anonymous donation. This gift includes the title deed to the old Miller Department Store downtown that has been vacant for many years and an endowment of money to be used specifically for the creation of an outreach mission. The mission would be used to supply clothing and essentials to poor and disadvantaged families in the surrounding communities."

Those attending the meeting were astonished at the Deacon's announcement. Paul's eyes gleamed. He was obviously already aware of the donation. There was a standing ovation and tears in many eyes.

Jonathon Solomon made a motion to accept the gift and conditions. The banker offered his family's services to conduct the business of the Mission of Corinthia Falls.

It was always suspected that the money and idea came from John and Jackie Solomon. The motion passed. The emotion continued.

Paul stood up from our front row seat. He walked over and embraced Jackie and John. He then hugged the Deacon in the center of the circle of pews. Wiping a tear, he addressed the meeting.

"Our first action of the reunification of this church was your rededication to each other and the Lord for whatever direction He gave you. Now you have been called to excel in the gracious ministry of giving. Generosity is how we prove our love is real.

You should carry out these projects to completion just as enthusiastically as you are beginning them. Give what you can afford with what resources you have."

Doc Pyle stood to make a statement. "Speaking of resources, Colonel…" Doc had been sitting patiently with Emmitt and Benny in the back row. The three had been quietly conversing during the meeting. The portly doctor strode to the center of the church and stood with Paul and the Deacon.

"Some of the men of the Gentlemen's Club and I have been discussing the possibility of converting the old court house into a home for disadvantaged young men, much like our friend, Sandy Sampson. We certainly have enough office space to be turned into bedrooms. We already have a fully equipped kitchen. We think we might be able to facilitate two dozen boys."

Emmitt and Benny joined Doc in the hub of the pews. Paul

and the Deacon sat down as Emmitt took over.

"We have several major obstacles," said the mayor. "The first is to get licensed by the state of Oklahoma. The Department of Human Services requires an inspection of the property and certified counselors. There are some other hoops to jump through but all are within our capabilities.

The other problem to consider is continual funding for the day to day operations of the residence. If this is to be a church-run facility, we would not qualify for state funding."

Mathew Cox stood and interrupted Emmitt.

"But I'm assuming these boys will attend our school. By increasing the enrollment we can receive more funding for our school system that we desperately need."

"Correct!" added Benny taking his turn. "Now get the big picture. We would be providing care for young men, say ages thirteen through high school that are experiencing problems which prevent them from living at home or in foster care. This would include physical or sexual abuse, drugs or alcohol and other behavioral problems.

Our area is full of boys like Sandy Sampson. Bill Oaks, you know that we're walking a thin line with Sandy staying at your place. It's just a matter of time before ol' Demas comes looking for his son.

The meeting erupted. Everyone began talking at once. The mayor, Doc and Benny were overwhelmed with questions of how and when and who.

Paul stood, raising his hands chest high, motioning the gathering to sit and come to order. The man in black's confident style calmed the disturbance. Paul smiled, laying a hand on Benny's shoulder.

"Well done, Gentlemen's Club," said Paul. "This is what the Circle of Care is all about. Through the Grace in Fellowship

Association we, and I mean all churches belonging to the Association, fund the Circle of Care Foundation through our gifts and offerings.

This is a perfect project for our foundation. You have established a need for the ministry. We have in place support groups that can assist in the remodeling of the building. Although a great deal of the funding will have to come from this community, there is financial support through the Circle of Care.

As a matter of fact, we already have boys' and girls' homes in several of our churches' areas. Ahh, here's a picture of the Gallay Youth Home we just established."

Paul thumbed through his wallet, finding the photo of himself and some others in front of an impressive building. He passed it around for all to see.

"I'm sure the folks of Gallay, Mississippi would be honored to help us jump through those hoops Emmitt was talking about. They could assist us in the legal matters and probably send some folks to help on the building."

Everyone was heartened by the Colonel's words. Doubt turned into hope.

"What do we need to do to get started," asked Benny excitedly.

"Well, the first thing that will have to be done is to deed the courthouse to the Circle of Care," said Paul. "Is that doable?"

"Yes!" said Emmitt.

"Then the next thing to do is give praise to God," said the Deacon standing with outstretched hands. "He has revived our church and is rebuilding our town!"

On Friday Paul met with the leaders of the Gentlemen's Club. By a unanimous vote, the old courthouse was deeded to the Circle of Care. It was also decided my father would co-chair the committee to oversee the transformation of the Gentlemen's Club to a boys' home. Paul advised that it would be good to have someone on board that was not a member of the club for reasons of transparency and to purge any old habits. I sat by Dad during the meeting. It was asked what name should be given to the boys' home. After many suggestions my father stood and asked, "Why not just leave it as the Gentlemen's Club? Isn't that what we're trying to accomplish here; making young men gentlemen?"

With that suggestion, Bill Oaks assumed the leadership of the team to convert the courthouse.

John Solomon had already begun the renovation of the Miller Department Store. He hired a construction crew from Archer's Grove to remodel the old store into the mission. The Solomon's family project would be completed for the holiday season.

I woke up Saturday morning to a banging on the back door of our house. It was Sandy accompanied by Silas.

"Paul said for you to meet him out at Cherokee Creek."

"What's it all about?" I asked, wiping the sleep from my eyes.

"Don't know, but you 'spose to bring your clubs."

It was Halloween morning. It certainly was not a good morning for golf. The thermometer on the back porch read forty nine degrees. The sky was overcast. The wind was gusting hard enough to blow the remaining brown leaves off the trees.

I skipped breakfast, threw on my regular attire of white slacks and golf shirt, and grabbed my blue windbreaker.

I tossed my golf bag into the back of my pickup, now full of leaves that had rained down during the night. Silas hopped in, not to be denied the chance of a golf outing.

When Silas and I arrived at Cherokee Creek, Paul was standing with a man in Doc Pyle's front yard. A late model spotless silver Jeep pickup with a Tulsa Hurricane front license plate was parked in the drive. The truck had a gun rack in the rear window that carried a single golf club.

Paul wore a grey jacket over his regular black outfit. His black hair was being tossed by the wind. As I stepped out of my pickup, he motioned for me to come over.

The man with Paul was a little short but in excellent shape dressed in a gold golf shirt and tight fitting jeans. He looked to be about forty and appeared like one solid muscle. His forearms were as big as his calves.

He had a dark tan and brown, crew-cut hair. Without a jacket, he seemed oblivious to the weather. The golf coach from Tulsa resembled more of a drill sergeant than a man of golf.

"Timothy Oaks, this is George Apollos."

Coach Apollos' handshake grip was so firm that it hurt. So, I thought to myself, this is Crazy George of the Jungle.

"Timber, isn't it?" said the coach, looking up at me. "And this animal must be Silas. We could have used him in Nam, Colonel!"

Paul nodded in agreement. Silas gave Coach Apollos his traditional greeting by sticking his head in the short man's protruding chest.

"Nice to meet you, sir," I offered politely. I pointed to the golf club in the Jeep window. "Is that the eight iron?"

"What all have you been telling this lad about me, Colonel? Yes, that's the Moses rod. I prefer to call it Destiny. Like to take a look?"

For the first time, Paul looked a little embarrassed. Crazy George stepped over to his truck to retrieve the famous old golf club. He handed it to me to examine.

The old eight iron was rusted and tarnished. Its nicks and scars did resemble more of a weapon than a golfing instrument. On the bottom of the club facing, the word Destiny had been etched in. If this thing could talk, I thought to myself…

"Let's hit a few, Timber," said the coach, taking back his prized possession.

I got my bag out of the pickup and propped it up on the stand. After zipping up my windbreaker, I tossed out some golf balls in Doc's yard. Before I could get my golf glove on, Coach was hitting his first shot at the green using the Moses rod. Even through the gusting wind, his swing was fluid and effortless, landing his ball on the center green from a hundred yards away.

"Your turn," demanded Coach.

I was very nervous, not knowing what all this was leading to. The wind was swirling hard enough off Lake Corinth that I knew it would take a few shots to get my range.

After a warm up swing, my nine iron shot was caught by the north wind landing ten yards past the hole.

"Again!" ordered Coach taking on a much more serious tone. "But this time, use this."

The Tulsa coach handed me the Moses rod. I was confused. The old club felt very awkward. The grip was different and so was the weight and length. Paul looked on encouragingly.

My swing felt different. The ball projected much lower than my previous attempt. It landed on the front fringe of the green, rolling up to kiss Coach Apollos' ball.

"Let's walk," said Coach, not nearly as impressed as Paul and I were with my shot. "Just bring your putter."

The three of us walked to the green with Silas following us. The big dog seemed confused that more golf balls were not flying through the air for him to retrieve.

When we reached the green, Coach turned and addressed me. His eyes pierced through mine as if he was looking into my soul. Fearful and needing comfort, I stood close to Paul.

"Well, I see you have the swing," said Coach. "Been reading Jack's book?"

"Yes sir."

"So has everyone else," Coach continued, now pacing back and forth just several feet away, persisting in his stare.

"Many young men have the dream of playing college golf then turning pro and making millions of dollars. That is a dream.

"Take, for instance, that boy that beat you in the state finals last year. I know all about him. He's better than you. He's played at his daddy's country club since he could walk. He takes the lessons and uses the finest equipment. He's been groomed for golf all his life. Son, those kind are a dime a dozen!"

The coach continued his speech with more intensity.

"It's fine to have a dream, son. But dreams are achieved through destiny. What's your destiny, Timber? And don't tell me its golf! This ain't about golf!" shouted the coach.

I could feel my knees shaking as the wind tossed my hair. I searched for an answer that I had never considered. No, I had never thought of golf as my destiny. It was just what I liked to do.

I looked at Paul for help in my response, but he, too, had a questioning look.

I was not interested in taking over the family business. Nor had riches and fame ever crossed my mind. From deep inside came a spiritual reply.

"To be a disciple of Jesus Christ."

Paul placed his hand on my shoulder and smiled his approval.

"All right then, I've got one scholarship left for next year," said Coach, reaching over to pick up the two golf balls off the green.

He tossed Paul one ball and stepped off twelve feet from the hole. He wiped off the golf ball with a small rag from his pocket and placed it on the green. Then he pulled the flag from the hole and laid it to the side.

"One twelve-foot putt for all the marbles…one chance for a four year scholarship to play golf at the University of Tulsa."

I looked at Paul as if to ask if this Crazy George Apollos guy was serious. Paul winked and pushed me toward the ball.

I could feel my heart hammering. My palms were sweating as I lined up the putt; the same twelve-foot putt that I had made so many times on this green now looked thirty feet away.

"Think about it, son. Can you feel the pressure? How will all this wind affect your putt? This green hasn't been mowed in two weeks." The coach tormented me while walking across the line of the putt.

Paul walked over to me and tried to calm my nerves.

"He's just trying to get into your head. It's old army stuff. Just trust in yourself."

"This is about destiny, Timber!" yelled Coach.

I took a deep breath and dried my hands on my pants. The autumn leaves trickled on and off the green as a dove tried to balance itself in the wind on the horizontal flag stick.

I played the shot a little more to the right compensating for the wind. It would all come down to touch; the speed of the ball.

As I took a practice stroke, I wondered if they could hear my whisper.

"I am capable of anything through God who gives me power."

The ball skipped on the unkempt green bouncing to the right of my target. I just knew it was going to the right of the hole and short when a large gust of wind pushed it to the left. Just as the ball was losing its momentum it dropped in the cup.

"George, looks like you found your man of destiny!" said Paul proudly.

"Yes 'we' have!" confirmed the coach.

I was so excited to get to the store and tell my parents about what had just happened that I forgot my golf bag. I went back to Cherokee Creek where Paul was waiting with Coach Apollos, expecting my return.

"Forget something?" asked Paul with a grin.

Paul put my clubs in the back of my pickup as Silas flew over the tailgate not to be left behind. I thanked Coach again and again.

"Tell your parents we will have a little signing ceremony in a few weeks," Coach informed me. "I'll be sending you some paperwork to fill out."

Silas enjoyed a fast ride to town. I could not get to the store fast enough to tell Dad, Mom, and TJ. I ran into the store after parking the truck. Silas must have thought it was a game of chase as he followed me in.

The huge dog beat me to the checkout counter where TJ was handling the front. Silas propped his front paws on the counter in a standing position and began barking as if he wanted to be the first to make the big announcement.

"Whoa, there big fella!" said TJ backing away from the counter.

Two customers grabbed their groceries and backed away from the counter. Another ran out the door, terrified.

"What's up, my man? Haven't seen you this excited since you knocked that ball on the green off the satellite receiver."

"Teej! Scholarship! Tulsa! Golf! I got it, I got it, I got it!" I shouted as I joined TJ behind the counter.

"For real? You gonna be playin' golf at T.U.?"

"Yes!"

Silas continued his reverberating barks while TJ and I broke into a simulated dance, exchanging high fives. Bewildered customers stood, bewildered and ignored. Mom and Becky hurried out from behind the deli to see what the commotion was about.

"What in Heaven's name?" said Mom, witnessing the unusual scene at the front of the store.

"It's all about Heaven, Mrs. Oaks!" said TJ continuing his dance routine. "Your baby boy is goin' to the University of Tulsa to play golf!"

I leaped over the checkout counter to embrace my mother. Becky's eyes grew wide as she covered her mouth to hold her breath while I explained to Mom about Coach Apollos and Paul at Cherokee Creek.

TJ phoned his parents and demanded that they come down to the store quickly. Mom ran to the back office to get Dad.

"Bill! Bill, Timber got a golf scholarship to Tulsa!"

Mom told Dad the news as they both rushed back to the front of the store together. Dad gave me a look as if to ask, 'Is it true?'

Dad gave me a bear hug while announcing to the store full of waiting customers, "My son is going to Tulsa on a golf scholarship!"

Applause broke out from the enlightened shoppers. Dad repeated the announcement on the drive where several people couldn't figure out why the gas pumps were not coming on.

In the middle of all the emotion, celebration and well wishing, Becky seemed to come out of nowhere. The redheaded tomboy stood on her tiptoes as she put her arms around my neck. Our lips met as Becks delivered a kiss that I would not forget for a lifetime.

It was unexpected but real.

"Oh, my gosh!" I could hear TJ giggle while pounding his fist on the counter. Silas sounded his approval.

I backed off, just a little embarrassed. Maybe it was because of the public display or maybe the realization that I had just kissed one of my buddies. Becky blushed and backed away. My eyes remained on her as I realized my life and relationships were changing fast.

Most of the town made an appearance at the store that afternoon as the word spread that the party was on at Oak's Corner. There were free cheeseburgers and fountain drinks for all.

The yellow marquee sign with the arrow on top in front of the store read on both sides:

SAINTS!

Through all the excitement I had almost forgotten that it was Halloween night. With the celebration coming to an end at Oak's Corner, Ant, TJ, Becky and I headed for the church to help with the trick or treaters or as it was now being referred to: Blessings and Graces.

Benny was in the church parking lot with a refurbished El Camino that he borrowed from his used car lot. Mrs. Sharp and Mrs. Cox were busy in the church hallway costuming all the excited elementary students as various biblical characters.

We divided up in two groups. Hauling close to a dozen children each, TJ would ride in the back of Benny's vintage truck to supervise. Ant, dressed as King David, rode in the back of my truck to do the same.

Silas naturally had to ride with Ant which thrilled all of the kids. Clara Cox made the town's favorite dog a Goliath costume complete with breast plate and a long plastic sword strapped to his rib cage.

Becky rode up front with me. She sat close to the passenger door, leaving plenty of room between us.

"Where to first?" I asked

"We're going to do Cherokee Creek first, then work our way back through town and the neighborhoods," said Becky, looking straight ahead to avoid eye contact.

Benny gave me a thumbs up as both vehicles eased out of the parking lot. Ant and TJ had both loads settled. The ride would be slow to protect our cargo. After several moments of silence, Becky finally spoke.

"Timber, I'm sorry about this afternoon. It's just…just…well I was just so happy for you."

There's nothing to be sorry about, Becks," I said. "I liked it a lot better than the one the widow Fullbright laid on me with her mouth still full of cheeseburger."

Becky playfully punched me on the arm. I returned the favor by poking her in the ribs. The jabbing exchange continued with her getting the best of me while I was trying to watch the road. The tension was eased as I caught her hand and pulled her close to my side.

"Better?" I asked.

"Better," she sighed with relief.

The routine throughout the evening was the same with every house we approached. The children took turns informing the home owners which person from the scriptures they were portraying and gave a Bible verse that went along with their character.

We had Moses, Abraham, Noah, Samuel, Joshua and most all the apostles. There was Rachel, Sarah, Ruth, Esther, Martha and all the Marys.

So went the Blessings and the Graces. By the end of the night, everyone had a grace basket filled with goodies.

The finale at each doorstep was the portrayal of David and Goliath. Silas would rear up on his hind legs exposing his armor and letting out an intimidating roar. Ant, dressed as the Shepherd boy would pull out a dime store slingshot and slay the giant with large marshmallows.

Ant got the glory, but Silas got the marshmallows. That Halloween we went through five bags of Jet-Puffs.

November

The following Sunday morning was euphoric. My life had a new meaning. The destiny that Coach Apollos talked about had become a reality.

I picked up TJ at the store. Ant and Silas joined us in the church parking lot, still dressed as King David and Goliath. To the thrill of the congregation, the children were also still in costume.

The church foyer was crowded as people were waiting in lines to add their names to the sign-up sheets volunteering labor and furniture donations for the boys' home and the mission.

"Guess we know where we'll be spending our spare time for awhile," I informed my friends.

I waved to Becky and her mom. They had the new nursery mostly under control. Silas joined the six toddlers present to offer any assistance in a quest for more marshmallows.

The service started late. There was much excitement and conversation about the new church ventures.

"Sounds like too many chiefs and not enough Indians," said Ant, tongue in cheek.

After a couple opening hymns of praise, the Deacon welcomed Principal Cox to address the church. Matthew was proud and motivated as he asked Ant, TJ, and me to the center of the sanctuary.

We stood together, embarrassed yet gratified. The three childhood friends; one tall and dark, another short and brown, one lanky and tan. We represented a picture of contrast and diversity. Mr. Cox began the introduction.

"I'm sure you all know our King David, here."

Ant pulled out his sling shot and did his Goliath-slaying impersonation. Polite laughter and applause ensued.

Anthony Bearkiller will be our school's valedictorian this year. He's the best student I've ever taught. Anthony will be attending the University of Oklahoma. The paper work on his scholarship is now complete."

Ant took a bow as his parents beamed. Some stood to their feet and clapped. Mr. Cox continued.

"Now there has been a lot of excitement over these other two young men. As you know, next year Thomas Johnson will be playing basketball at University of Georgia and Timber Oaks will be taking his golf game to T.U.!"

Sherry Solomon jumped up and broke into her cheerleading routine. A standing ovation followed with cheers of 'Go Saints!'

"Not bad, Matthew, for a school with no athletic program!" yelled Emmitt.

Just imagine what we could do with a real gym and a golf course!" shouted Benny.

Mrs. Sharp on the piano and Sandy on harmonica broke into the Corinthia Falls fight song. When the impromptu pep rally was over, I addressed the church.

"The three of us would like to thank all of you for your support. We are very proud of our school and especially our church. We would also like to thank Colonel Armstrong for the change he has made in our lives and this community. Go Saints!"

We pumped our fists in the air. The congregation stood once

again, clapping in time and singing one more round of our theme song.

After all were finally seated, Paul stood to speak.

"Catchy tune!" said Paul.

Paul used most of his time discussing the reformation of the Gentlemen's Club. He went in to detail on how the Circle of Care operated. He answered many questions of the enthusiastic audience and sorted out much confusion.

Emmitt reported on the boys' home state licensing requirements and procedures. John Solomon followed with an update on the Corinthia Falls Mission.

The three men, along with my father, were able to organize the inspired congregation into committees and task forces. The ladies' study group, not to be outdone by the Gentlemen's Club members, would handle the finer details such as furnishings and decorating for both projects.

"I want to remind you in your enthusiasm that Satan is not very happy with us now," Paul said.

"I do not know any other way to say this than we have really been kicking his butt lately and he is not happy about it. Be on guard! This is spiritual warfare.

"Focus on the mission at hand. Remember the vision statement for the Circle of Care. 'To make disciples of Christ by assisting those in need.'"

The Church of Corinthia Falls had a record-setting offering that Sunday.

During the month of November, downtown Corinthia Falls resembled a construction zone. Busy volunteers piled on the sidewalks unneeded fixtures that had been removed from the old department store and courthouse. Pickups full of plumbing supplies and electric parts were parked daily in front of the entrances.

The retired folks worked mostly the weekdays. Those with jobs and students worked in the evenings and Saturdays. My father kept up a very frantic schedule managing the store and overseeing the courthouse renovation.

John Solomon and family finished with the construction company in just two weeks at the mission site. A canvas awning hung over the glass front of the building. The inviting front had blue lettering painted across the four full horizontal windows... Corinthia Falls Mission. The goal of John Solomon of having the new mission open for the holiday season appeared on schedule.

In mid-November a van full of volunteers arrived from the church of Gallay, Mississippi. They would assist for the next ten days and celebrate the community Thanksgiving Dinner with us.

The leader of the missionaries from Gallay was Senator Jeremiah James. At seventy years of age, the former United States Senator from Mississippi was tall and silver haired. His cordial personality was only exceeded by his statesmanship.

Jerry, as we came to know him, had expertise and experience with the licensing and certification of foster care agencies like the boys' home. He worked extensively with Mayor Sharp to expedite the procedure through the various state agencies.

Jerry had attained much wit and wisdom through his political career. I first got to meet him while I was helping out at the courthouse. Paul was taking him around to become acquainted with the locals.

"Young man, why are you working here?" asked the distinguished former lawmaker.

I stumbled in my answer, blurting out that 'it's just the right thing to do'.

"I want you remember something, son," he said looking at me through his pale blue eyes of experience. "Those that know how, work for those that know why."

I never forgot that advice for the rest of my life.

On Saturday night, November 21, TJ, Ant, and myself saw the course of our lives change forever. We had finished a full day's work at the new Gentlemen's Club. Paul asked us to remain after the other volunteers left.

Paul had labored just as hard, if not more so, than all the workers. His time was spent between the two projects and answering large stacks of letters that he received every day. The incoming mail for Paul was so vast that Postmaster Chester had to arrange for his own post office drawer.

"Well gentlemen, what do you think?" asked Paul with his black clothes covered in saw dust.

We walked through the corridors and hallways admiring all the work that had been done to the court house in a few short weeks. Old office space had been transformed into bedrooms complete with beds and desks.

The kitchen was upgraded to handle the demand of the appetites of a future cast of hungry teenagers. A special living quarters was created for the prospective house parents, complete with den and private bath.

There was a laundry room added with several donated washing machines and dryers. A nearby utility closet stored all the janitorial supplies.

The old courtroom maintained its original décor and fixed

furnishings with the mural of Chief Quanapah and the picture displays of the Quanapah Challenge still intact.

This area would be used for a lounge and study for the boys. Several long tables replaced the rows of chairs. Recliners and sofas were added for comfort. Shelves with donated books began the creation of a library.

A large family style television was hooked up to a newly installed antenna. A stereo system with a variety of cassette tapes rested next to the television. I made sure that there was a little Creedence on hand.

"Very accommodating," said Ant sitting at the judge's bench, barely able to see over the desk. "If someone becomes an irritant, we can conduct a trial."

We followed Paul back into the kitchen area. We found Silas supervising the snacks and lunches that the ladies' group had been preparing for the volunteers. Paul filled some paper cups with ice from the freezer and we finished off the last pitcher of orange Kool-Aid.

"Boys, I want to show you something," said Paul.

We sat at the adjacent dining room table. Paul unrolled a map across the large table. Ant stood to get a better view.

"This map highlights all the various locations of the churches in the Grace in Fellowship Association," Paul explained.

"Man, looks like you've been busy!" said the wide-eyed TJ.

Penciled in on the map of the southeast quadrant of the U.S. were all the churches belonging to Paul's ministry. Virginia to Florida from Alabama to southeast Texas and as far north as Missouri and Kentucky, were the names of about fifty small towns that we did not recognize and had difficulty pronouncing.

"Corinthia Falls is your only church in Oklahoma?" I asked.

"For now, but we are pushing to the north and west," answered Paul.

Paul flipped the map over.

"These are our churches in Southeast Asia."

A dozen locations were marked from Thailand, Indonesia, and Vietnam.

"This is the missionary work. These churches are also in small towns. It's a place where things can get pretty sticky."

"Why always small towns?" asked Ant.

Paul stood and looked down at each of us, taking some time to consider his answer.

"The homes of Christians in small communities are where the Church got its start. Unlike larger cities, small towns establish with their faith the structure of their society.

Smaller churches from rural areas cling to the basic composition of faith, family and community. By founding a ministry that unites and networks small congregations together, we can set a solid foundation for all churches whether big, medium or small to pursue and participate. This is particularly true of our Circle of Care."

"So looky here," said TJ, "out of all the small towns and churches, what brought you to Corinthia Falls?"

"Thomas, I think by now you boys know where I get my orders from," said Paul sitting back down at the table and leaning back in his chair.

"Your father was the Lord's instrument. Through my correspondence with the Deacon over the last couple of years, your church took up membership in the Grace in Fellowship Association. I make every effort to visit all new churches of our organization. Although with our growing numbers, it is becoming increasingly difficult.

Corinthia Falls is actually not much different from any other small town where I have been involved. Often the local church has dissolved into a power struggle over personalities and worship styles.

Well meaning believers forget that our purpose is to be the body of Christ and to bring hope to the lost through the Gospel message.

Making soldiers for Christ is much like training soldiers for the Army; you got to break them down and then build them back up."

"But you have experienced violence," said Ant.

"Yes, I bear those scars," acknowledged Paul.

"Well, we don't have that trouble 'round here," said TJ.

"Not so far," said Paul.

The guys and I looked at each other. We were puzzled at Paul's last statement.

"Gentlemen, I will have to move on before too long. But before I do, we have something very important to discuss."

Paul stood again and gathered his thoughts. He smiled, rolling up the map on the table.

"Thomas, you asked why I'm here. I have already discussed why I am here in Corinthia Falls. There is another reason. What I have to say now is confidential."

"Top secret like army intelligence?" asked Ant.

"Something like that," began Paul.

"I'm about to turn sixty years old. I have always remained faithful to the ministry God appointed me to. My race is not over, but my mission will get increasingly dangerous.

"When learning about Corinthia Falls from the Deacon before I came here, I learned about the three of you. I learned of your faith, your upbringing, and friendship as well as your small town experience.

I was very excited to meet the three young men that would one day lead the Grace in Fellowship Association into the future.

"Say, wha?" asked TJ. "You askin' us to take over your ministry!"

"I'm not asking, son. I am informing you of a decision that comes from far beyond me. An assessment I reckon was made a long time ago. However, I rejoice in God's wisdom."

We were all astounded. Nothing had prepared any of us for such a revelation. I stood and addressed Paul with the same doubt I knew TJ and Ant were both feeling.

"Paul, we're honored, but we don't know nothin' of missionary work and what all you do. We just want to go to college! Why us?"

"Why not you, Timothy?" Paul asked as I slowly sat back down with my baffled friends.

"You will most certainly go on to college. That's been in the works all along. Your education and careers will aid you in developing the ministry. Continue your passions with great zeal: golf, basketball and medicine. Your journey is just beginning. Your destiny awaits you."

"There's that word again...destiny," I said. "Hey wait a minute. Does Coach Apollos know anything about this?"

"And Coach Aquila," Paul assured TJ and me.

"Anthony, you will also be in good hands. It's important for all of you to make good decisions. Surround yourself with believers and choose your mates wisely. Let the Lord be your Shepherd and may God's Holy Spirit guide you."

"What about you, Paul?" asked Ant.

"I will remain in contact for as long as possible. In the coming years there will be tremendous advancements in technology.

All of you will be updated with the advancement of the

association. The groundwork has been set for our Circle of Care; a ministry that will change the world!"

The trio of us sat mesmerized staring at Paul. TJ asked one more question.

"Anything else, boss?"

"Just one more thing, coach," replied Paul.

"What's with the coach stuff?" asked TJ.

Paul flashed his confident smile without answering.

"Timothy, my son, you will be the leader. Join with me, brothers."

Paul led us in prayer while Ant and TJ joined with him in laying hands on me.

"Lord, keep our brother Timothy faithful to what he has been taught and what he will learn. May he trust in your Word which comes from believing in the salvation that comes from Jesus Christ alone. Amen."

The perception of my future granted me little sleep Saturday night. Opportunity had opened its doors. Commitment entered my soul. Doubt darkened my path.

Ant rode with me to church the next Sunday morning. He looked as tired as me.

"Couldn't sleep either?" I asked.

"Not much," he said. "Up most of the night talking with my parents. Timb, there are some big changes coming down."

"Boy, I know," I agreed.

"Not just all that with the Colonel yesterday," Ant went on.

"Mom and Dad are quitting their jobs at the hospital."

"What?" I asked. "You didn't tell 'em about what Paul said, did you? Paul made it clear to us that none of our parents were aware of our future with the association, nor was anyone else in town."

"Nope, I think they will be telling you about it themselves."

Senator James was the guest speaker that Sunday. He gave the history of the Circle of Care. We were amused by the Senator's anecdotes and awed by his eloquence.

At the end of his presentation, Paul joined his old friend to make a special announcement. The two men invited the Bearkiller family to join them in the center of the congregation.

"Here it comes," whispered Ant as he joined his parents.

The diminutive Native American family was arm-in-arm with Ant standing in the middle. Each had an expression of acceptance combined with determination. Paul put his arm around Jack Bearkiller and the senator did the same at the other end of the lineup with Donna. Paul began his declaration.

"People of Corinthia Falls, I would like for you to meet the new house parents for the Gentlemen's Club."

TJ and I along with the rest of the church were taken aback. The hesitation grew into applause and shouts of approval as Donna smiled broadly and shook her head to let us know it was true.

"Jack and Donna are making a major commitment," continued Paul. "They are leaving the security of their home and careers at the hospital to provide leadership and counsel for the young men that will be joining this community.

Jack with his administrative experience will be the director of the boys' home. Since Donna's a nurse, she will provide full time medical assistance, not to mention the fact that she's done an outstanding job raising two children. Together Jack and Donna will make up our compensated staff."

Jack took his turn while Ant looked on and his mother fought back tears.

"I'd like to remind everyone that there are still plenty of volunteer positions to fill. They don't pay anything but the job security is great!

"We may need some help moving in because, with the help of the good senator and his group from Gallay we hope to have the new Corinthia Fall's Gentlemen's Club up and running by Christmas!"

As the church celebrated once again with our favorite song, I could see God's handwork in the Bearkillers' appointment to the Gentlemen's Club. The transformation of our town continued as I received a glimpse of my future.

A cool weather trend set in near the end of November. A seemingly unending light mist covered northeast Oklahoma. Deer hunters made their usual invasion on Thanksgiving weekend to the Lake Corinth area in search of a prize white-tail buck.

The State Park cabins and campgrounds were full. Outdoor sportsmen dressed in orange fluorescent hunting caps and vest made a steady stream through Oak's Corner.

Thursday the 26th was Thanksgiving Day. The community dinner sponsored by the church was that afternoon. Flyers, posters and newspaper ads had been advertising the free dinner for the past two weeks. A large turnout was expected.

Becky and TJ volunteered to work the store while the rest of us assisted in the dinner held at the school. TJ always liked working Thanksgiving. Local folks felt sorry for him having to work and would bring plate after plate of turkey and ham piled with the rest of the traditional provisions. TJ felt like he was getting paid to eat.

Becky worked the deli serving turkey and swiss hoagies to the soggy hunters. The influx of holiday travelers and hunting season always had a positive impact on the family business.

The school gym was decorated in customary holiday style. Tables of various sizes were covered with yellow and gold table cloths with center piece cornucopias filled with dried vegetables and colorful autumn leaves, neatly arranged.

Senator James and his group from Gallay were the guests of honor. The missionaries had a special table up front with thank you notes scattered across their table.

A row of long tables lined the wall next to the kitchen, covered with my father's hickory smoked turkeys, Mrs. Hummingbird's pineapple glazed country hams and Jackie Solomon's smothered roast beef.

Ms. Martha and Clara Cox were in charge of the kitchen and assisted by the rest of the ladies of the church. Continuous platters of sweet potatoes, mashed potatoes, green beans and yeast rolls filled the buffet.

Large roaster pans full of giblet gravy and Martha's walnut turkey dressing was followed by endless rows of pecan and pumpkin pies.

At the end of the line, the Deacon served iced tea, coffee, and hot-spiced apple cider.

Doc Pyle presided over the smoked turkeys with a carving technique reserved for a master surgeon. Teenagers bussed the tables, keeping them cleared and cleaned off for the next group of holiday diners.

The church served many that day. People of all economic means enjoyed the hospitality of the Church of Corinthia Falls. The underprivileged from the surrounding area were encouraged to take home extra helpings. Everyone was fed and everyone was thankful.

Benny Larson, Sandy and the Corinthia Falls band kept the Thanksgiving attenders entertained on the stage. The music was festive—sometimes on key, sometimes not.

Those of us serving took turns eating. Paul visited at each table and offered grace for their friends and family. Silas patrolled the gym, making sure any spilled food was demolished.

I spent the afternoon eating, washing dishes, and answering questions about golf. By later in the afternoon, Ant and I finally caught up with Paul.

"Colonel, so far Timber and I have washed three hundred sixty one plates," reported Ant.

"Yes, things have been going quite well," said Paul. "But things are not quite over."

Paul fixed his good eye upon Sandy on the stage playing guitar. The young musician appeared happy and in his element, far removed from his previous predicament.

Ant and I recognized Paul's look and the tone of his voice. Something was going to happen and he knew it.

"Trouble?" I asked.

The man in black stood stoically surveying the old gymnasium as would a director of a play or a leader of soldiers, ensuring all participants were in place.

"Let's just call it a heartfelt reunion."

Within minutes, the side gym door opened. A young man clutched a trembling middle-aged woman, both staring down toward the floor. Both were drenched and cold from the outside elements. They were dressed in jeans and sweat shirts. The woman was wearing an over-sized green jacket.

She was fragile. Her drawn up wet face and premature long, silver hair marred what once must have been a beautiful blond.

The expressions on their faces were hollow and hopeless. Each

of them was thin and emaciated. Sammy Sampson raised his face
and looked over toward Paul as he tried to balance his mother.

Everything became quiet as the eating and the music stopped.
The only sound came from Sandy on the stage as he stood and
stared at his family in disbelief.

"Momma? Momma?"

Sandy's questioning voice sounded more like that of a small
child as he jumped off the front of the stage in tears, rushing to
his mother and older brother. Sammy let go of his mother long
enough for the two to embrace and then joined them.

The astonished gathering of guest and servers remained motionless till Martha, Joyce, and my mother came to their assistance.
It was a situation that called for the ladies' touch.

"Oh, you poor things!" said Mom.

Martha and Joyce escorted the three to a nearby vacant table.
Mom pulled out the chairs while the mother assured her youngest
son of her identity.

"You must be freezing!" said Joyce as some of the women
brought out some towels from the kitchen.

Doc pulled off his white serving apron and did all the routine
examinations. He took pulse, heartbeat, reflexes and temperature
using only his hands as the sobbing continued.

"They're dehydrated and exhausted and suffering from shock.
Bring 'em some water!" demanded the old doctor.

"Been a long time, Doc," said the woman, looking up at her
old friend.

"Yes, that it has Phoebe. Now I want the two of you to drink
and have something to eat. Then you need some rest."

"You've grown so," said Phoebe, turning toward Sandy and
combing her hand through his short brown hair. "And you are so
handsome, just like Sammy.

I tried to come back and make things right with your father. I thought things might have changed. I missed you two boys so much! I just made things worse."

"No mom, you're making things better!" said Sandy.

Sammy nodded his head in agreement, still not saying a word.

"Well now, we have nowhere else to go…" Phoebe's voiced cracked hopelessly, looking at all those surrounding her.

Benny began playing a poignant, soft version of Auld Lang Syne on his saxophone from the stage. The Thanksgiving social returned to normal with the clatter of silverware and conversation.

The Sampson family was served a hearty dinner. Sam went through three plates and dessert. Tears broke into smiles.

In the far corner of the gym, Emmitt was huddling with Ant's parents. I was standing next to Sam trying to draw out some conversation when Jack Bearkiller motioned for Paul, Ant, and me to join them.

"Think Emmitt wants to have Sammy arrested?" I asked Ant as the three of us walked across the gym.

"Incarceration would be safer than cohabitating with his father," replied Ant.

"Colonel," said Emmitt with a soft smile as we approached. "I think the Sampson's will be the first three new residents of the Gentlemen's Club."

The following Friday was moving day. The men of the church assisted the Bearkiller's, transporting their furnishings and belongings to their new residence at the Gentlemen's Club.

The Sampson boys were lodged in a room together while the ladies of the church fixed up the perfect private room for Phoebe next to Sammy and Sandy. Clothes and other accessories were donated for Sammy and Phoebe.

Emmitt Sharp and Jack Bearkiller arranged a special allowance from the state to board the Sampson family before the final inspection and licensing. It was hoped that Sammy could start school at the beginning of the next semester. Paul suggested a meeting with the Sampsons to discuss their new status as residents of the Gentlemen's Club but wanted to wait till they had time to settle in.

By Saturday, the damp weather had cleared for the last weekend of deer hunting season. Paul sent me over to the new mission that morning to help the Solomon's. Much progress had been made as they prepped for their opening in time for the Christmas season.

The Solomon twins were busy as I walked into the refurbished department store for the first time. Sherry was dressed in a pink turtle-neck sweater working in the front of the shop. John Jr.was bringing out boxes of donated inventory from the back storage room. His orange polo shirt was indicative of his future alma mater.

Sherry saw me first.

"Timber! You come to help?" asked the bubbly blond.

John rose up from his merchandise inspection and headed for the front.

"Hey, buddy! What do you think?" asked John, slightly pompous.

The old Miller Department Store had been gutted. New lighting was added to accent the newly painted walls of light blue, yellow and white. Freshly stained wood covered the floors.

The front half of the far wall of the mission was lined with new toys for Christmas. Several aisles of clothing hung properly on hangers ran to the back of the building. On the opposite side was shelving full of canned foods and dry goods.

The look on my face must have impressed John.

"And this is just the showroom…you ought to see all the stuff we have in back! There's lawn mowers, furniture, appliances…you name it!"

Sherry pushed herself up on the custom built checkout counter that caddy-cornered near the front door. She sat on the center of the counter smiling at me, while dangling her feet in a flirtatious fashion.

"No cash register," said Sherry. "Dad doesn't want anyone in need to feel obligated, but anyone can shop here."

"We do accept financial donations," added John, the future businessman. "If everybody keeps contributing, we can be a self-supporting enterprise and have some left over to help the Gentlemen's Club."

"When will you open?" I asked.

"Next weekend!" said Sherry as John resumed his tasks.

"So…you're really going to Tulsa?" said Sherry tilting her head.

She knew the answer full well.

Still seated on the counter, she reached out her hands, inviting me to come near. Her blue eyes searched my face for a response.

"I was really hoping you would go with John and me to Oklahoma State. I hear they've got a great golf team and Stillwater is a fun town; three generation of Solomon's can't be wrong."

As Sherry placed one hand on my shoulder and used the other to fondle my hair, I was captivated by her beauty and charm. I drew closer, placing my hands on her waist as the door suddenly opened to interrupt the moment.

"Becks!" I exclaimed as I released Sherry and moved away.

"Wha...wha...what's goin' on?"

Becky took a deep breath and just stared at me. She placed the large cardboard box she was carrying next to Sherry.

"What ya got there, Miss Becky?" asked the blond of the younger pony-tailed redhead inconspicuously.

"Some stuff for the mission my mom sent over," Becky replied, still staring at me with loathing.

"Got anymore? Need some help?"

My question sounded more like a plea.

"No and no!" Becky rejected my offer as she stomped out the door.

"Gee...what got into her?" I asked Sherry, pretending not to know.

Sherry jumped down from the counter and giggled, pushing me on the chest. Then she chided me in playground style.

"Timber gots a girlfriend! Timber gots a girlfriend!"

On Monday after school, I gave TJ and Becky a ride to work for their evening shift at Oak's Corner. Becky sat in the middle, placing her school books between us to create a visible divide. She had refused to talk to me at church yesterday and now she just looked the other direction and only visited with TJ.

"You got a birthday coming up, don't you?" TJ asked Becky, obviously trying to break the tension.

"Thursday. Thanks for remembering, TJ."

"Sweet sixteen, huh?" I added.

Becky pretended not to hear me. Instead, she continued her flirt with our friend.

"So, is your gift a new car?" asked TJ.

"Hardly!" answered Becky, shoving an elbow into TJ's ribs. "But Mom is getting me contact lenses. Finally I can get rid of these stupid glasses!"

At the store, Dad, Paul and the Deacon were conferencing in their accustomed meeting booth. Becky marched into the deli, making sure to greet everyone, and still pretending like I didn't exist. Ms. Martha hugged her as the two chatted about school.

"You look a little aggravated, Timber," said the Deacon. "What's on your mind?"

"Women!" I replied, shaking my head.

All three men laughed as the Deacon pounded the table nearly spilling Paul's Cherry Coke.

"Welcome to the club, son," said my father.

I was embarrassed. I looked quickly over at Becky to see her enjoying my frustration. She had an appearance of mission accomplished.

"Are you happy now?" I mouthed in her direction.

"Are you?" she shot back.

Paul had a meeting arranged that afternoon with the Bearkillers and the reunited Sampson family at the Gentlemen's Club. He had asked me, rather ordered me, to join in. Silas was waiting for us in the back of my pickup as we left the store.

"So Tim, having a little trouble with relationships?" asked Paul, pulling shut the cab door.

"Becks. She's always been like a little sister to us. That seems to be changing. She's puttin' conditions on this relationship stuff."

"Becky is just trying to get your attention, son," Paul surmised. "She's becoming a young woman and is not that interested in being a little sister. You should be thrilled that such a special young lady admires you so much."

I stopped the car in the parking lot of the Gentlemen's Club. Paul looked straight at me putting a hand on my right knee.

"The most important part of my profession is dealing with relationships. Whether it's our relationship with Christ or with others, they are all personal. Relationships are a continuous on-going thing that always require gentle encouragement."

I knew Paul was giving me a lesson; a tutorial for my future as-signment. Although I could not totally comprehend the message, I knew it was important.

"Stay humble, Timothy. This is your greatest attribute. It is a gift from God. Let the Holy Spirit guide you and give God thanks in any situation."

Jack Bearkiller met us at the door of the Gentlemen's club. Silas woofed and rushed to greet Sandy, who was sitting by his older brother on a couch in the new lounge. Donna sat across from them next to Phoebe. All stood as Paul entered the large old courtroom.

"Silas is starting to make himself at home around here," Jack said as the overgrown dog lay on the couch almost smothering the Sampson boys.

Sam was dressed in new jeans and a western shirt. His hair had been cut like that of his younger brother. Phoebe wore a new yellow pantsuit. Her long silver-blond hair had been slightly trimmed and reshaped around her face.

Mother and son appeared healthier. The color had returned to their faces. Their once sunken eyes from last Thursday were now gone.

"Can I get you anything, Colonel? How about you, Timber?" asked Donna.

"We're fine, Donna. Thank you," said Paul. "Let's all sit down over here."

We gathered at one of the long study tables. Sandy turned off the stereo that was playing my Creedence tape.

"Nice touch," I told Sandy.

"Well, I heard you were coming," he said proudly.

"So, how's it going with everybody?" asked Paul.

"Sandy and I took Sam down to see Emmitt this morning," Jack said. "We got him spruced up a little bit. Then Sam and Phoebe were the first customers of the new mission."

"Jackie Solomon was so wonderful!" Phoebe said appreciatively. "Just like everyone around here has been. Colonel, I can't thank everyone enough.

I just can't believe how far Sandy has come. He's become quite a young man. He plays his guitar for me and shares Bible verses."

"Sandy is also starting our new youth Sunday school class at church," added Donna.

Phoebe's optimism had revived her once lost beauty. Hope had restored her soul. Sam remained distant with his arms crossed.

"We got another idea I think you will like, Colonel," continued Jack. "Phoebe's background is in food service. What do you think about her taking over our kitchen duties while she's here? It's a way she can help contribute."

"It's your call, Jack. Sounds good to me," Paul said. "What do you boys think of this place?"

Sandy looked over at his older brother. Sam smirked.

"I think it's great," replied Sandy. "I think Sam will get used to it."

"Colonel," said Phoebe, "you know it's just a matter of time before Demas gets all liquored up and comes lookin' for us. I'm afraid of what might happen."

Paul reached across the table and held both of Phoebe's hands in his. He spoke to her with the utmost sincerity.

"We're all concerned about your safety. Do not go anywhere alone. God is on our side."

"Thank you, Colonel. Thank you!" said Phoebe, noticeably relieved.

"And Sandy, let's get your mother and Sam to church Sunday."

December

Ms. Martha put together a little birthday celebration for Becky after school on Thursday. When TJ and I got to the store, Silas greeted us on the drive wearing one of those silly pointed birthday party hats that fastens with a rubber band.

Martha and Mom had crafted a strawberry birthday cake with Becky's name on it. Sandy was on hand with guitar. The rest of our gang, along with Paul, waited in the deli for the guest of honor while Joyce ran the checkout counter.

When Becky and her mother arrived we blew the party whistles as Sandy led us in a chorus of Happy Birthday. The sixteen candles were blown out and the cake and ice cream was served. A few customers were treated to a party plate.

Several small gifts and some cards were opened. My parents gave her a necklace and Paul presented her with a new Bible.

Becky was still playing hard-to-get with me. I'd searched the evening before for the perfect present. I stumbled on the perfect gift at the Archer's Grove jewelry store.

I saved my present for last. I slid the small gift wrapped package across the booth table. Becky peeked up at me with a quizzical glance as she slowly unwrapped my gift. Everyone was curious.

It was a small jewelry box. Ohhhs and ahhs were heard as Becky opened up the small blue container. A little light came on and a music box style melody played the Creedence Clearwater tune… 'Long as I Can See the Light'.

"Thank you, Timber. That's sweet," said Becky as she examined my gift, swaying side to side.

"Tomorrow Becky gets her contact lenses and then I'm taking her shopping," said Sarah, hugging her daughter.

"I'm so excited!" said Becky.

Somehow I felt left out of Becky's enthusiasm. I sat down by Paul and whispered for only him to hear.

"I know, stay humble."

During the previous week the Corinthia Falls city maintenance crew had strung traditional Christmas lights across Main Street and up and down the street light poles. Extra attention was given to the Gentlemen's Club and the new mission.

Saturday morning, the 5th of December was the grand opening and ribbon cutting ceremony for the new Corinthia Falls Mission. The whole town showed up, along with many struggling families anxious to try out the complimentary shopping.

It was jacket weather. A large baby-blue ribbon was held up waist-high by all the notables crowding to get into the photo taken by the county newspaper. Mayor Emmitt Sharp was in the middle along with John and Jackie Solomon. They were flanked by Paul, Ms. Martha and the Deacon, Benny and Doc Pyle. Ant, TJ, Sherry and I stood off to the side when Jackie Solomon called out to her daughter.

"Sherry, have you seen your brother?"

At that moment John Jr. wheeled into a parking space across the street in his red Camaro. John, dressed in slacks and a matching black sports jacket, hopped out of his sports car and rushed to open the passenger door on the other side.

A beautiful young girl stepped out gracefully. Layered auburn hair circled her face. She was dressed in Jordache jeans with short heels and an oversized yellow body sweater.

"Hurry! Hurry! Hurry!" urged John, guiding her hand-in-hand as they rushed to cross Main Street and get in the picture.

"Looks like Johnny gots another one of those country club babes from Muskogee," suggested Ant to our small group.

"Better look again, boys," said Sherry.

"John?" came the first sound from the attractive girl, as if suggesting that he slow down.

"Oh...my...gosh!" said TJ.

TJ leaned slightly downward putting both hands on each of my shoulders rocking me back and forth. Ant and I caught on at the same time. We could tell by the sound of the girl's voice it was Becky.

The funny glasses were gone. A touch of makeup revealed just a hint of her formerly freckled tomboy face. Our little friend had blossomed.

"No way!" said Ant in disbelief.

"Yes, way," Sherry confirmed.

I had no words. I tried to talk but nothing would come out. I am sure my blank expression gave away that for the first time in my life I felt jealousy as John and Becky held hands, crowding in on the far end of the ribbon cutting formation.

"Come on, Timber," said Sherry, grabbing my arm. "Let's get in the picture."

"Come along, boys," Sherry added, looking back at a still flabbergasted Ant and TJ.

"Okay, everyone is present now," Jackie Solomon informed the photographers.

Paul dedicated the Corinthia Falls mission with prayer.

"Wait a sec!" shouted Benny. "Where's Silas?"

Paul let out a shrill whistle. Silas made his way through the crowd to the front of the ceremony.

"Sit!" ordered Paul.

Silas set on his haunches and posed in the front of the lineup. As cameras flashed, a large pair of scissors were passed down the line, with everyone involved taking a snip out of the ribbon. The final cut was made by Becky as she slightly held her breath while John held the blue ribbon for her.

As soon as the ceremony was over, the doors to the mission were opened. Most of us stayed to assist the Solomons on their first day. The volunteers seemed as eager as the shoppers.

While helping replace the quickly emptying shelves with Christmas toys and household appliances from the backroom, I met up with Becky.

"You look incredible, Becks."

"Well, thanks Timber," she replied showing little interest in me.

"Need a ride to work tomorrow after church?"

"No, John's taking me."

Sherry Solomon met me in the hallway at church the next morning. She asked if we could sit together. I could see her twin brother assisting Becky in the nursery, supposedly to give Sarah a day off to attend the worship service.

The ladies' group had the church decorated for the Christmas Advent season. Fresh branches of cedar adorned the pulpit area and the still-blocked-off balcony and its banisters. Poinsettias were strategically placed throughout the sanctuary. The holiday spirit filled the old church with the first sounds of traditional worship carols.

Sandy was finishing his first Sunday school class held in the back of the sanctuary. His group was small and attended mostly by junior high students.

The Bearkillers brought Phoebe and a reluctant Sam Sampson to church for the first time. The congregation went out of their way to make them feel welcome.

Sherry sat by me, holding my upper arm and leaning her head on my shoulder in her regular fashion. TJ sat to my other side.

"Cheer up, bro," TJ whispered to me trying to sound encouraging. "I wish I had the troubles with my love life that you're having."

Ant leaned over from behind us, anxious to add his advice.

"Women. Can't live without 'em. But you sure can't live with 'em either."

"How the heck would you know?" said TJ.

Appropriately, the Colonel's sermon was titled "The Differences Between Men and Women."

The following three weeks leading up to Christmas were very active for our town as well as the church. Store fronts, including Oak's Corner, were decorated for the season. The community was energized with the opening of the mission and the official state licensing for the Gentlemen's Club.

By the middle of the month, the local court system had appointed three teenage boys to full time residency. Like Sam Samuels, they would be entering the Corinthia Falls school system at the beginning of the next semester in January.

At the suggestion of Paul and the urging of Sherry, I spent my free afternoons and Saturdays volunteering time at the mission. It was decided that while I or any other approved adult was there that the boys from the club could help out. This would give them a sense of belonging and responsibility. The five young men, except for Sam, were very enthusiastic and helpful during the holiday rush.

My relationship with Sherry was enhanced as we spent more time together at school and working at the mission. I took her Christmas shopping in Archer's Grove. She even joined me driving her father's golf cart at Cherokee Creek while I practiced. She was as encouraging as she was gorgeous.

Becky was enjoying the attention of Sherry's brother. They were always together. She mostly disregarded me at school. When I saw her at the store, her attitude was the same. I missed her, but was fortunate to have Sherry to minimize my torn heart.

School let out for Christmas break on Wednesday, the 23rd. Sherry and I along with the Gentlemen's Club boys and Jackie Solomon ran the mission. The pace was frantic with the demand for last minute gifts to help less fortunate families.

"Timber?" said Sherry at the end of our shift. "Let's go together for Christmas Eve communion tomorrow night at the church. Then you can come over to the house for my father's annual eggnog party. There'll be some people there you know…. please!"

I knew I really did not have a choice. I also knew that a couple of the people I knew at the Solomon's Christmas Eve party would be John and Becky.

"Sure."

"Oh, great!" said the sparkling Sherry. "We close at six tomorrow. We can leave from here."

Our family's plan for Christmas would be similar to that of the past years. My parents would work Christmas Eve evening, giving the other employees an early start to enjoy the holiday. The store would close on Christmas Day.

Presents under the tree would be opened early on Christmas morning, followed by a large meal together. In the afternoon we planned to attend the Gentlemen Club's special open-house reception, knowing that there would be plenty of time for football in between.

The hopes for a White Christmas faded as the weather turned unusually warm for December in Oklahoma. The wind blew and it was clammy.

The bell tower on the church chimed 'O Holy Night.' The damp hay spread at the base of the church nativity scene gave a musty odor. Sherry and I were welcomed by Silas at the front doors wearing a unique red and green Christmas collar with a silver bell.

Inside the foyer was Ms. Martha serving as the greeter for the communion service. She gave us the hugs that she was famous for and led us to the sanctuary.

The church was dimly lit with Advent candles in the altar area where Paul and the Deacon received various families at the communion table. Ann Sharp played the piano softly in the background as different groups took turns receiving the holy sacraments.

The tradition at the Christmas Eve service was for folks to come and go at their leisure. Matthew and Clara Cox were kneeling at the communion table as Sherry and I sat down. During our time of quiet meditation, Jack and Donna Bearkiller quietly entered the church with Ant and his older sister, who was home from college. They were joined by Phoebe and her sons and the three new boys from the Gentlemen's Club.

I held hands with Sherry as we knelt. The moment was holy and personal. Paul administered prayer and offered us the bread of life. The Deacon did the same, serving us the wine representing the blood of Christ.

As we were leaving the sanctuary I felt very spiritual and sensed renewed confidence. I acknowledged my friend Ant with a wink and patted Sam Samuels on the shoulder. We passed Doc Pyle and Benny in the hallway. Sherry snuggled next to me as we exited the church.

My thoughts were turning to eggnog when we were startled by the old green familiar pick up that had pulled up on the church lawn. Sherry gasped with horror as Demas Samuels stepped out.

His bib overalls covered a stained white t-shirt and mud covered boots. A camouflage hunting cap sat crooked on his head. His partially grey beard covered the bottom half of his face. In the front pouch of his faded denims the wood-grain handle of a pistol was exposed.

The smell of moonshine wafted through the warm, humid night air. Demas swaggered from side to side, trying to keep his balance while searching us with his calculating eyes.

"You're that kid that came out with the preacher man that kidnapped my boys!"

I had seen drunks before. I had seen people angry and confused. But as I looked down the steps of the church into his steel-green eyes, it was the first time I'd looked into the face of evil.

I nudged Sherry to the side with one arm, though there was no place for her to escape. I tried to hide my nervousness and remain calm. My heart was beating like a bass drum. I knew I could physically overcome the small intoxicated madman, but did not want to entice him to pull out his gun.

"Step aside, sonny!" ordered Demas placing his right hand on the revolver. "I came for my family. I saw 'em go in there."

"Sir, I'm afraid I can't do that," I told him, watching his hand on the gun as Sherry crouched in fear. "I'm sure we can arrange for you to see your family."

I held my trembling hands out in a calming gesture.

"Let's just settle down."

As I was looking down the steps at the determined Demas Samuels, I could hear the jingle of a small bell from the shrubs to my lower left, next to the church down below. Across the street I could see Emmitt Sharp cautiously bringing his car to a slow stop, aware of the circumstance.

The opening of Emmitt's car door startled Demas. He pulled his handgun. As he took his first step toward us, Silas sprang from the bushes and flew through the air overwhelming the demonic man.

As Silas landed on Demas pinning him to the ground with his bulk, the gun went off.

I dashed down the steps to secure the gun while Emmitt pulled off his belt and tied Demas hands behind his back.

The church emptied at the sound of the muffled gunshot. The scene they saw was self explanatory. Sandy and his mother were pushed back into the church by Jack Bearkiller. Sam walked down the steps and stared at his unconscious father.

Paul rushed to the aid of his best friend and partner as Silas lay on his left side in a pool of blood on the sidewalk. The wounded, oversized dog looked up at his master with sad brown eyes. His large black tongue touched the sidewalk as he gave a couple wags of his bushy tail.

Sherry rushed to my arms in tears. As Paul tried to comfort Silas stroking his huge head, Doc Pyle pressed his ear down on the dog's big black chest.

"He's got a good heart beat but it's losin' a lot of blood. Nobody move him. Call an ambulance!"

More church members arriving for communion were greeted with the heartbreaking scene of Paul kneeling by Silas. The congregation gathered inside the church to console the Sampson family and pray for our much beloved furry friend.

Deputy Jimmy arrived a short time later followed by the Quanapah County ambulance. The paramedics rushed with a stretcher to place Demas in the ambulance.

"Not him! The deputy can take in that guy," ordered Doc. "Him!" Doc pointed at Silas.

"That's just a big ol' dog," said the attendant.

"Young man, that's not just a big ol' dog," replied Doc. "That's a hero!"

There was no eggnog party that Christmas Eve nor was there a reception at the Gentlemen's Club on Christmas Day. At the suggestion of the Deacon a vigil was held at the church that Christmas Friday. Continuous prayers were offered for Silas and the Colonel as well as the Sampson family.

Demas was put in the Quanapah County jail on multiple charges awaiting a hearing. Sherry and I would have to go to Archer's Grove Monday to be interviewed by the district attorney.

The music at the Christmas service the following Sunday lacked its usual joy. The congregation remained in grief for their big canine friend and town mascot that had become a part of our everyday lives.

Mr. Solomon addressed the large gathering of worshipers on Silas's condition. The bleeding was under control but a .38 caliber slug remained lodged underneath his heart.

The benevolent banker said Silas was resting well though somewhat confused at the animal clinic in Archer' Grove. The Colonel had not left his side for the last two days.

The local DVM requested no visitors since Silas was sedated.

She was concerned that too much excitement might cause more damage.

John went on further to announce that every expense would be covered and every avenue pursued to continue Silas's life. The next day a special team from the Oklahoma State Veterinary Hospital would examine Silas.

Paul walked through the side door of the church as John Solomon was finishing his comments. He entered the center circle of the congregation and gave John a big-man hug.

Still dressed in his normal black attire, the Colonel's eyes displayed the underlying circles of a couple sleepless nights. The chain that held his silver crucifix around his neck chest high was now dangling together with Silas's silver Christmas bell and dog tags.

We were all anxious for some words of comfort. Sherry squeezed my hand. Paul gazed out at the congregation, turning slowly to ease us with his soothing smile. Without music or song, he powerfully voiced the words of his revised Doxology with special emphasis.

"Praise God, from Whom all blessings flow!

Praise Him, all creatures; people and animals here below!

Praise Him above, ye heavenly host!

Praise Father, Son, and Holy Ghost!"

A scattering of amens and nods of approval swept his captive audience. Paul continued.

"When I think of the wisdom and depth of God's plan during this Christmas season, I fall to my knees to the Creator of all things and creatures in heaven and here on earth.

"I pray that from his unlimited resources He will give us the powerful strength of His Holy Spirit. I also pray that we will be more and more comforted as we learn to trust Him. May we have the understanding of how deep God's love really is though we will never fully understand it.

Now Glory be to the Father! By His mighty power of work in us and even in a big, black dog, He is able to accomplish more than we could ever ask or hope. Amen."

During the rest of the Christmas break from school, I spent my time helping at the store and working with Sherry and John at the mission. Paul borrowed a car from the Solomon's to drive back and forth every day to be with Silas.

The special team of veterinarians decided that surgery was too risky for him. His prognosis was improving but he had lost a lot of weight. Silas would have to live with the bullet wedged in his chest; another affliction of the flesh with which his master was so familiar.

Joyce talked my father into ordering several hundred small silver bells to pass out at Oak's corner. They showed up all over Corinthia Falls on necklaces and bracelets, car rearview mirrors and mail boxes, pets and small children in support of our ailing town hero.

On New Year's Eve all the town's high school students brought in 1982 at the Solomon mansion. The accommodation of the Solomon's den was exceptional as a couple dozen of us partied through the evening.

Sandy entertained us with his guitar. He played as we sang along, even doing some of the old CCR standards at my insistence. TJ introduced us to some new dance moves that no one could duplicate.

As the final countdown to midnight began, several couples including John, Becky, Sherry, and I positioned ourselves together for the traditional New Year's kiss at the urging of the others.

Becky looked beautiful and happy. I made sure she could not sense my envy as I kissed John's sister. Becky made sure I could see her as she put a big lip smack on John.

The party roared with approval as it turned into a competition of who could kiss the longest. I gave up. John raised his fist in triumph several moments later.

"Beat ya, sis!"

January

On New Year's Day the next Friday, TJ and I met up with Ant at the Gentlemen Club's rescheduled open house. Two more boys had been added to the residence, bringing the total to seven including Sam and Sandy.

The young men acted as greeters and hosts for the all-afternoon affair. Their new social skills were evident. The Bearkiller's efforts were effective and contagious.

We were served punch and Phoebe's homemade snacks as we were given tours of the whole facility. The boy's rooms were personalized with sports posters and personal keepsakes.

The kitchen was immaculate and well stocked. The old courtroom was comfortable and well kept. A new large framed picture of the mission's grand opening with Silas in the center was added to the wall of portraits.

Ant showed off his family's new living quarters. His job was tutoring and getting the boys prepped for school at Corinthia Falls.

One of the old offices was now a private study where the young men could receive private instruction from Ant or any of the many other volunteers.

One of the new boys, a slender 16-year-old African American from Tulsa named Cyrene, was mesmerized with TJ. 'Cy' and TJ bonded quickly. Whether it was their common skin color or their shared love for basketball, Cy put the future Georgia athlete on celebrity status.

In the coming months, Cy became like an adopted little brother to TJ: a second son for the Johnson family. On Wednesday afternoons TJ finally had someone to work out with in the old gym.

By mid-afternoon many of the people from the church had gathered. The lounge was full of people admiring the New Gentlemen's Club and the progress the Bearkillers had made.

The guys and I were watching college bowl games on the console TV when Paul made his entrance. Many rushed to greet him with questions about Silas.

Sam Samuels was more attentive than he had been in the past few weeks, but his mannerisms were anxious and fidgety.

"I have something I need to say to all of you and especially to you, Colonel," announced Sam nervously from the center of the lounge.

Sam, dressed handsomely in slacks and a nice dress shirt, was joined by his mother and younger brother. He stood in between them as Phoebe held his arm and Sandy put his arm around his shoulders. The family stood in unity and support.

Most of the gathering found a seat on one of the couches or the chairs, giving their full attention to the once dreaded and feared Samuel's boy. Jack Bearkiller quietly turned off the television as Paul remained standing just several strides away, facing the Samuels family.

"I know in the past I have not been one of your favorite people. My behavior has been misguided by a man that was my father in name only.

My conduct and crazy antics directed at this town were the result of jealousy. You see Sandy and I wanted to be a family but didn't know how. I had felt uncared for all my life until the day Timber and Colonel Armstrong came to visit us at the farm."

Tears filled the Sampson family's eyes. Sam's voice cracked as he continued.

"I just want to say I'm sorry and thank all of you for giving us another chance. I always wanted to be like Timber Oaks and have the family and respect he had. I always wanted a father like the Colonel. And like that big bear of a dog that probably saved several lives the other night, I always wanted to be a hero."

Emmitt was the first to stand and applaud his former antagonist. Paul stepped forward and hugged Sam and his family while others waited their turn in line.

"Sam," said Paul assuredly, looking him square in the eye, "You are a hero!"

School resumed the following week. On Tuesday morning, TJ and I were called to Principal Cox's office. Waiting for us was Mr. Cox, accompanied by an attractive young woman in her early twenties. She had ash blond hair pulled up neatly in the back. She wore a mid-length, purple skirted business suit. Her manner was professional and serious.

I thought at first she must be with the district attorney's office. She had the same demeanor as those Sherry and I had spent much time with the past week reviewing the Demas Sampson incident.

"Boys, this is Priscilla Luke. You might be familiar with her from the sport pages of the Tulsa World," Matthew said.

"This must be Timothy," said Ms. Luke extending her hand.

"Timber," I said politely. "Nice to meet you."

"And you must be Thomas Johnson," she said, turning and looking up to my friend with the same businesslike handshake.

"Just say, TJ," he suggested.

"Better watch out for that one, Ms. Luke." said the principal referring to TJ. "He's a celebrity in training."

"Anyway, Priscilla is here to do a story on the two of you. It seems having two future university athletes coming from our small school has stirred some interest," said Matthew, as he reached for the door knob to leave the three of us alone in his office.

"Well alrighty then!" said TJ feeling in his element.

"Thomas, try to behave," warned Matthew.

Ms. Luke sat at Matthew's desk while TJ and I faced her on the couch in the small office. The reporter pulled a yellow legal pad out of her brief case and slid on a pair of small reading glasses. She turned on a small cassette tape recorder.

TJ turned on the charm. His goal seemed to be entertainment and he tried to break Ms. Luke from her stern attitude. By the end of the interview he had succeeded.

The following article headlined the sports page the next day under our picture posed in front of the school:

LARGE THINGS COME IN SMALL PACKAGES!
Two Small Town Athletes make it to the Big Time
by Priscilla Luke, Tulsa World..................January 6, 1982

The small lakeside town of Corinthia Falls is the unlikely residence of two future Division I scholarship athletes. The nearly defunct school system with a total enrollment of less than seventy students and no athletic program is bubbling with excitement for hometown locals, Thomas Johnson and Timothy Oaks.

Corinthia Falls, the small community in Quanapah County is best known for its proximity to Lake Corinth and being the host of the ever-more-popular Quanapah Challenge, held annually on

Memorial Day weekend.

Johnson or TJ, as he is better known, is a projected 6' 5" forward for the Georgia Bulldogs. He practices at the old Corinthia Falls gym which boasts only one basketball goal.

Oaks, a 6' 1" future golfer for the University of Tulsa Golden Hurricane goes by the nickname Timber. He works out on the local driving range. There is not a course near the town and, like Johnson, he has never received formal coaching or instruction.

Both young men are charming and intelligent with a quick wit. I sat down for a brief conversation with them yesterday.

> Luke: So, the obvious question. How did two young men from the same school system without a sports program or facility attract the attention of college recruiters?
>
> Johnson: Talent!
>
> Luke: Seriously?
>
> Oaks: That would have to be Colonel Armstrong. He's a missionary who's been working with our church for the last several months. Through some of his contacts we were given a shot. God played a part.
>
> Luke: You mentioned God. Does faith play a big part in your lives?
>
> Oaks: Yes. TJ's father pastors at our church.
>
> Johnson: Yep, I'm a preacher's kid. Don't I look like a preacher's kid? I bet people have warned you about preacher's kids.
>
> Luke: What kind of influence has living in a small town had on you?
>
> Oaks: Everything. It's who we are. Everyone has been very supportive of both of us.
>
> Luke: TJ, what's it like being from the only black family in Corinthia Falls?

Johnson: I'm black? Oh my gosh, I am! Timber, why didn't you tell me?

Luke: (with boys laughing) I guess I asked for that.

Johnson: Actually, my parents and I feel very honored to be here.

Oaks: And he likes standing out.

Luke: The two of you seem very close. What kind of a relationship do you have?

Johnson: Relationship? Well, Timber's my second cousin. Can't you see the family resemblance?

Oaks: (more laughter) We're very close and will be for life. TJ is like a brother and I know he feels the same way. It's part of growing up in a small town. Relationships are what life's all about.

Johnson: No matter what happens, we will always be there for each other and Corinthia Falls will always be there for us.

Luke: Corinthia Falls recently made headlines when it was reported that several citizens with the help of a large dog thwarted an attack from a drunken man. Was either of you involved?

Oaks: Everyone was involved.

Johnson: Timber had a gun pointed at him, but Silas saved the day.

Luke: Silas?

Oaks: The big dog. He's the Colonel's buddy. He saved my life and maybe several others.

Johnson: Silas is a team player.

Luke: It was reported he was shot. How's he doing?

Johnson: As well as can be for having a bullet stuck in his chest.

Oaks: It's a miracle Silas is alive. He's coming along fine.

Luke: From what I've learned, miracles are common around Corinthia Falls. What's your future hold?

Oaks and Johnson: (in unison) Destiny!

By the end of the week the article in the newspaper featuring TJ and me hung on the bulletin boards at the church, at school, at the Gentlemen's Club and of course at Oak's Corner. TJ gave out copies while he worked the front counter, practicing his autograph on each one.

On Saturday morning I drove Paul to Archer's Grove to visit Silas. The town hero was starting to eat again. We would use my Saint Hauler pickup to deliver a load of high protein dog food from the farmer's co-op in Archer's Grove.

The night before, Quanapah County received its first snow of the season. The fluffy light snow covered the grass and dormant woodlands through the winding hills but the highway was just wet.

I was looking forward to visiting with Paul on the way to see my good friend, Silas. I would be the first from town outside of Paul and Mr. Solomon to see Silas since he had been wounded.

"So what's been on your mind, Tim?" asked Paul as we began our short winter trip. Paul sensed I was deep in thought as I drove.

"What's on my mind? Well there's school, graduation, Silas, golf, college not to even mention my future leadership of a ministry I know little about."

"Is that all?" asked Paul sarcastically. "There's got to be more."

I took my eyes off the road just long enough to look at Paul. I felt as if he could read my mind so I came clean.

"Girls…"

"But of course." said Paul. "Women…can't live with 'em, can't live without 'em, but you *sure* can't live with 'em."

"You been talkin' to Ant?" I asked

Paul laughed as he slapped my dashboard.

"Well Tim, school, graduation, your education and even golf will take care of itself. Just remember to stay focused and concentrate just as you are while driving on this wet pavement.

Silas is coming along. You will be able to see that for yourself here pretty soon. Now about your love life…"

I'm sure my face was turning a little red. It was time for my mentor, a man who had been single all his life, to advise me.

"It's Becks," I blurted out. "every time I see her with Johnny Solomon I want to die."

"You can't die yet. God has plans for you, Tim."

"Yes and I'm kind of at a loss about those plans, Paul."

"The question is, son," continued Paul, "what have you learned from all of this?"

"Not to take anyone for granted," I started. "Everyone is special even though you might not recognize it at first. It's like you said, 'It's all about relationships.'"

"Excellent, Tim! You have just learned the first rule in missionary work. God's teaching you through your experiences."

"And that God is always in control even if I'm not?" I added.

"Yes, He is," said Paul. "That's rule number two. What about Sherry? I see the two of you together quite often."

"I like Sherry. She's been a good friend, but I don't see it ever being more than that. I have learned that rich people can be pretty cool."

"Yes, they can be," said Paul. "John and Jackie Solomon are good stewards and are teaching their practices to their children.

God has blessed them for their giving. Even Jesus used wealthy people to promote His ministry. Our work is to serve the poor, but don't ever try getting a job from someone that's broke."

Paul continued his counseling till we got to the co-op in Archer's Grove. I jumped in the back of my truck and scooted out what was left of the melting snow by hand, wearing a spare golf glove. Paul went into the store to pay for the dog food with a collection taken up by the church.

An employee came out of the co-op using a dolly supporting ten forty-pound bags of Silas's favorite chow. As we were loading the large bags into my truck I asked Paul if he thought this would be enough.

"Only if he gets well soon!"

On the way across town to the animal clinic Paul informed me that he would soon be leaving Corinthia Falls. I had been expecting this for some time.

"How soon?" I asked.

"In probably about a month, Tim. There are several loose ends to tie up, but the vet says Silas should be able to travel by then.

My work in Corinthia Falls is done for now. We have made a lot of progress and I know I'm leaving things in good hands."

"Where to this time, Paul?"

"Colossi, Arkansas; small town in the southeastern part of the state. So, I won't be too far away. It's only about five hours from here.

I hope to stop back by toward the end of May. Silas and I would really like to see that Quanapah Challenge. Then it's off to India."

"Small town?" I asked.

"Several," Paul replied solemnly.

"Tim, I'll keep in touch with you," said Paul with a hand on my shoulder as I continued driving. "Save all my letters and any correspondence from the Association or the Circle of Care. You will need them in the future."

We were met at the front counter of the Archer's Grove Animal Clinic by the head veterinarian. She hugged Paul like an old friend.

As soon as Paul asked her how his friend was doing, a familiar loud deep repeating bark came from the rear of the building.

"Sounds like he wants to tell you all about it himself," she said.

Silas was standing against the iron bars of his large private cubicle. His eyes sparkled. The barking turned into whimpers of joy as the vet unlocked his cell and we entered. His massive paws landed on my shoulders and forced me to my knees as he proceeded to greet me with a ceremonial face washing.

I could tell he had lost some weight. A large cloth bandage encircled his back and chest. He was frisky and pranced excitedly.

Three dog beds nestled together in a corner supplied a spot for him to sleep off the cool concrete flooring. It was obvious he had been well kept and looked after.

As Silas repeated the same greeting ritual with Paul, I noticed the many post cards, pictures, children's Crayola drawings and hand written notes plastered neatly on the walls of his cage. They were from all of Paul's churches throughout the Grace in Fellowship Association.

The get-well messages that lined his canine stall featured hand written letters with pictures of people of all ages, races and color in front of their churches, clinics, missions and foster homes. Some were from the southern United States and some from other countries. Many of the images had Silas posing with them. All expressed their love.

As I stood there, I realized I was in the presence of, not one, but two great missionary evangelists. The Circle of Care was not only Paul's call to ministry. It was also Silas'.

O ver the next couple of weeks different members of the church accompanied Paul on his trips to Archer's Grove to visit Silas. My parents took him a bag full of beef bones from the Oak's Corner meat department. The Bearkillers took Ant to see his pal. Benny and Doc joined Paul once and so did the Johnson's. It was even arranged for the Sampson's to visit the dog that helped change the direction of their lives. All were relieved to see the progress he was making.

A special surprise birthday party was planned to be held at the Gentlemen's Club for Ant and TJ's eighteenth birthday. Both were born on the same day, January 23rd. When we were younger we used to celebrate all three of our birthdays together. That tradition faded through the years. My birthday on Valentine's Day was just too far removed.

The Deacon and Martha along with Ant's parents assigned good ol' Benny to procure the perfect presents for their sons. Our local skilled entrepreneur took to the task eagerly, not to mention his handsome commission. Benny worked long nights in his garage behind the car lot on the project. I was called in as a consultant but was sworn to secrecy.

Oklahoma weather is always changing and unpredictable, and so it was during the third week of January. The tranquil winter we had enjoyed turned quickly with the ominous forecast of the two words rural people in the southern regions of the country dread the most…Ice Storm!

Temperatures hovered just below freezing as a light rain began to fall on Thursday. All of northeast Oklahoma was predicted to receive major icing with Quanapah County being ground zero.

School was cancelled for Friday. That day Oak's Corner was busy as the locals bought supplies and topped off gas tanks for the impending ice accumulation.

The other two places that were just as full of activity were the local hardware store and the mission. I helped the Solomons hand out blankets, battery powered heaters, and other provisions deemed necessary.

By Friday evening over an inch of ice covered the power lines and trees as the icing accelerated. Power outages were numerous. The sound of timber cracking and utility transformers bursting filled the night.

By Saturday morning Corinthia Falls was without electric power. A row of downed utility poles lay dangerously across the northbound highway. Trees and all vegetation were bent by the weight of the ice and kissed the frozen ground. Ice covered vehicles crept and slid on the nearly impassable roadways.

Oak's Corner had enough backup generation to power the freezers and interior lights. The rest of the town was closed down, eerie and gray.

Most of the propane heated houses common in our rural area were useless without electric power circulating air. Ironically, older and more modest dwellings with wood stoves or fireplaces fared much better.

The Gentlemen's Club was turned into an oasis of refuge. Powered by three borrowed welding generators, the building provided warmth, light and sanctuary from the effects of the winter storm.

By Saturday afternoon families moved in with sleeping bags and groceries. Many lay on a bed of overcoats and blankets. The boys turned over their bedrooms to the elderly. The wait was on for Quanapah Electric to restore power and the ruthless weather to end.

My parents remained at the store, seeing to it that as little damage as possible was caused to the business by the ice. I moved into the Gentlemen's Club, along with most of the town.

The leaders of the church assisted the Bearkillers in running the temporary safe haven securely and efficiently. The women worked the kitchen as the men saw to it each family was as comfortable as possible with their own corner of space.

The Solomon's, along with the rest of the neighborhood from Cherokee Creek, joined us. Whether it was because of the cold in their totally electric homes or their desire to serve, all lived and worked together with a sense of community.

Dinner was served to almost two hundred. Although all were thankful, a sense of despair filled the old courthouse. Small groups gathered together for prayer and hugs of concern.

My two buddies and I worked together clearing tables and passing trash bags around, gathering napkins and paper plates and generally just cleaning up after dinner.

"So, how's your birthday going?" asked TJ to Ant.

"Memorable, I'm afraid," answered Ant, glum and uninspired.

Suddenly, Benny and the Corinthia Falls Jazz Band took over. Accompanied by Mr. Cox, John Solomon, Nate Anderson, Sandy and Mr. Hummingbird on tambourine, Benny and the boys strutted into the lounge from the kitchen with instruments in hand and broke out in uplifting music and song: a little joy to replace the anxiety.

The toe tapping began. The band's resonance was elevated by Ms. Martha's soul-felt vocals. The uplifting rhythms temporarily erased the discouraging situation that had left our town devastated.

TJ was the first to get in to the swing of things. If basketball was his first love, then dancing was his mistress. The animated and vibrant show off took to the center floor with skillful gyrations, displaying his agile talent.

Sherry was next to join TJ in the spontaneous dance. They were then joined by Ant. John Jr. pulled Becky into the mix followed by the rest of the teenagers and the foster boys in residence. Before long even the smaller children and toddlers got into the act.

The adults supported the entourage, keeping time by clapping hands to the beat. The widow Fullbright, not to be left out, grabbed an unsuspecting Colonel. The odd couple jitterbugged to the end of the song to the delight of all.

After Martha and the band finished the tune, TJ, Sherry, Paul and the widow took their appropriate bows. Instantly, the familiar chorus of Happy Birthday began as two small cakes lit with candles were brought out of the kitchen by Joyce and Donna.

An elated Ant seized the moment to vault himself again on TJ's shoulders. The two friends twirled around as Ant conducted the music. Both of my pals basked in the attention.

As soon as the boys blew out their candles, Benny made an announcement.

"Folks, if you'd like to join us, there is something waiting for Thomas and Anthony out in the parking lot. Everyone be careful and watch your step. The rain has changed to sleet and it's very slippery out there."

Out front Emmitt was holding a large battery-powered flood light that illuminated two reconditioned 1969 Chevrolet pickups, the same model as my Saint Hauler.

One was Georgia Bulldog red with mag wheels and a refurbished black interior. A red personalized tag on the front read TJ.

The other was bright canary yellow with oversized tires and a chrome stepping rail. The inside had been customized with extended foot pedals. The matching front plate in Cherokee design said simply 'BEAR.'

Both trucks were immaculate and appeared show room new. Only the falling sleet covered the polished craftsmanship of Benny's talent.

I positioned myself down in the parking lot just to see the look on the boys' faces. I was very excited for my two best friends. The secret gifts I had known about for some time were finally theirs.

TJ's eyes looked like baseballs. A big, white smile engulfed his dark face. He slipped and fell to the ground in his excitement. His new pal, Cy, helped him up. TJ jumped into the driver's seat and Cy joined him on the other side.

Ant was just as animated. My small friend encircled his new transportation taking in all the details. I opened the driver's side door pointing out the stepping rail for easy entrance and customized interior that enabled a small guy to handle a pickup.

It was great to see the guys so thrilled with their new rides. I knew the Bearkillers could afford it, but I suspected the Johnson's got a little help from my parents.

The people gathered around the trucks to touch and admire. Some applauded while others congratulated. Ant honked on his horn while TJ started his engine and revved the accelerator.

"No, no, no!" shouted Benny, his frozen breath rising in puffs. "No driving in this weather! I worked too hard on these things. They'll be just fine here till the weather breaks."

As the celebration continued out in the frigid parking lot, I noticed Paul motioning for me from the entrance door to the Gentlemen's Club. I joined him inside where only several folks remained. We sat together on one of the couches.

"Tim, what have you experienced through the last couple of days?"

I thought about my answer. I knew I was getting another lesson.

"Well, the town is now prepared to come through in a time of crisis. I've experienced the benefits of a church that is involved in the community. I've seen how much joy can overcome."

"Not bad," said Paul. "The Circle of Care we promote has to start out as a small circle. Before the small circles can be connected to other circles and the larger all-encompassing circle each must become as self sufficient as possible.

"What...?"

"I will explain. The projects your church has taken on need to strive to support themselves. If the mission or this foster home was always reliant on outside help for funding, how would they be able to reach out and help other small communities struggling to develop their own care circles?

For instance, with the help of the Solomons, the new mission may actually be profitable. Last Wednesday the board of directors of the Gentlemen's Club voted to give half of the proceeds from the Quanapah Challenge to the continued funding of this foster home.

"What about the government helping out?" I asked.

"Governments, although many times well intentioned, must tax their own people to secure funding for social projects, often taking away money from those in the best situation to help sponsor positive causes.

When governments intercede with financing, they usually make the rules. Those rules sometimes interfere with the promotion of the gospel message we have in Jesus Christ, which is our first goal.

We are just many small circles connected together, dependent only on each other and God with Christian compassion for one another and the world."

Many of the people were beginning to reenter the building from the cold outside. A line was forming for birthday cake. Paul wrapped up my lesson.

"When the Association builds a new church or, say, a foster home or maybe a clinic or an adoption agency or school, passing the plate is not enough. If we are to change the world by making Disciples of Christ we should follow what the scriptures teach us. 'Build your house on a solid foundation.'"

Families cuddled together on the floor and furniture with makeshift bedding in the courthouse, trying for sleep. Babies cried and men snored. I huddled down in the hallway with TJ and Ant. Both were too excited about their birthday gifts to ever stop talking. I think I got about two hours of sleep.

The next morning, Sunday services were held right there in the Gentlemen's Club. After breakfast, Sandy led a large group of the teens in his ever-more-popular Sunday school class. All of us attended, even Sam.

Paul preached from the judge's bench as Ms. Martha and the choir occupied the jury box. Paul used his message to inform the congregation of his intent of leaving soon for Colossi, Arkansas and his hope to return for the Quanapah Challenge. He added some words of comfort and praise.

"My goal at Corinthia Falls is that you will support each other and continue to work within our Circle of Care with the power of love. I want you to have full confidence and understanding of God's plan which is Christ himself. In Him is all the wealth of wisdom and understanding.

Although I will be away from you, my heart is with you. I am filled with joy. You are living positively as you should, with faith in our Lord."

After one more restless night at the Gentlemen's Club, power was finally restored to the town. Monday morning's welcome sunshine reflected brightly on the ice-covered trees and shrubs. All of nature glistened, revealing the natural beauty of the winter scenery as well as the destruction.

For the next week the sound of chain saws and hammers could be heard throughout town as the removal of downed tree limbs and rubbish began. The restoration effort was aided by the boys from the Gentlemen's Club. Yards were cleared, phone lines reattached and roofs repaired.

The gang's trio of pickups was put to use hauling away the debris. TJ and Ant used a layer of visqueen plastic to protect the beds of their new assets.

Phoebe allowed us to pile the brush on the old Sampson place. On the first Friday night in February we celebrated with a bonfire.

The few remaining animals on the farm had been cared for by the men of the church. The sheriff's department had dismantled and removed Demas's moonshine still for evidence. The dispensation of the property was waiting on the Sampson's pending divorce and the outcome of Demas's trial.

Sam and Sandy did not attend our end-of-the-ice-storm party, nor did their mother. Their memories were still fresh and haunting. I wondered if they would ever return.

February

The night of the big Valentine's dance sponsored by the Gentlemen's Club was held on Saturday the 13th. The community, church, and school were all invited. It was a most anticipated evening to dress up and bring a sweetheart to dance the night away.

I picked up Sherry at her house. John was leaving to get Becky. His Camaro was spotless. Several long-stemmed red roses lay in the passenger seat.

"See ya a little later, Timber!"

I was afraid of that, I thought to myself. The thought of watching him sharing the evening with Becky, their arms around each other, gave me that queasy feeling down inside.

Sherry was beautiful as I expected. The pink party style dress she wore was perfect. Upon her instructions, I was dressed in a white suit and pink shirt so we would match. She sat close to me on the ride into town.

"Timber, this is going to be so much fun! Oh, and by the way, happy birthday, you cute little Valentine."

A disc jockey from a popular Tulsa radio station was hired to play music with his elaborate sound system. The Gentlemen's Club lounge floor was cleared to make a dancing area. A large crystal ball reflected over the center of the dance floor in the dimmed lights. Hearts and cupids dangled from the ceiling.

We got there just in time to see TJ make his grand entrance. He looked like a black version of John Travolta dressed in a flashy black suit with a bright red dress shirt, escorting three girls on each arm.

In 1982 rural Oklahoma it was still awkward for kids of different races to date. Earlier in the week, TJ overcame any tensions by announcing he would take all of the girls in high school without a date to the dance. I don't know how he got all six girls into the cab of his truck.

"Group date," said TJ to Sherry and me as he strutted by us flamboyantly with his entourage.

TJ, as usual, was first on the dance floor breaking the ice. He was encircled by his young lady friends for the first dance. The loud speakers blared out Jessie's Girl while other couples joined in the gaiety.

Ant worked with the boys in residence, hosting and serving punch and refreshments. The young men were well dressed and looked eager to attract some attention from TJ's girls.

The town had really gotten into the sweetheart theme. The Colonel brought Becky's mom. Interestingly, Benny and Phoebe were coupled up. To the humor of everyone, Doc Pyle escorted the widow Fullbright.

The Andersons volunteered to work the store that night, freeing up the Johnson's and my parents to join in the fun, along with most all the married couples from church.

As the night wore on I tried not to look interested in Becky. She was wearing the perfect little black dress with a reddish-orange corsage that complemented her hair. She was having a wonderful time dancing to every song with John.

I had to admire Ant. He was not shy about asking any of the girls to dance. On the slower numbers his short stature put him only chest high to his partners, making it almost impossible to find a place to rest his head.

"And now a special request," announced the DJ in a soft voice, "for Mr. Timber Oaks, celebrating his eighteenth birthday tomorrow, here's an old standard from the boys of CCR called 'Long as I Can See the Light'."

As the crowd applauded, Sherry and I were urged toward the center of the floor for the special dance. John Fogerty's gruff vocal style matched the slow and slightly melancholy rhythm as Sherry laid her head on my chest. I closed my eyes and took in the first part of my favorite song as we slowly danced.

John and Becky were first to join us on the floor. As the saxophone solo played in the middle part of the tune, other couples took to the floor, Sherry caught John's attention.

"Switch!" she said.

Before I knew it Sherry was dancing with her twin brother and I was left holding Becky. I was startled. We danced barely touching. I felt like I was some sort of consolation prize.

I just looked at how beautiful Becky was while I tried to search for words. The once little blue-eyed freckled girl in glasses had broken my heart. She looked up at me tilting her head with a soft, probing smile as the music came to an end.

As we walked off the dance floor together, Becky seemed to be leading me to one of the side rooms—the one Ant used to tutor the boys. The remodeled class room was dark with only a little light protruding through the open doorway. We walked in together for a chat away from all the noise.

"So, you guys havin' fun?" I asked finally finding something to say.

"Sure Timber, aren't you?"

"I guess so. Looks like things are going well with you and John."

"John's cool," replied Becky as she slowly measured me, confidently in control of the conversation.

"What's it like dating the most popular girl in school?"

"Well, Sherry's just great. She good lookin', talented, smart and fun to be with…but to me she'll always be second best."

"Oh?" said Becky.

I knew the words I needed to say. It was the truth and it came from my heart.

"It's hard to get serious about Sherry Solomon when there is someone else."

"Someone else?" asked Becky, prying out my confession as she paced in front of me.

"Becks, I've missed you. I miss everything about you. I missed all the fun and good times we had together. Ever since we were little I thought of myself as big brother; now I wish I was something more.

And now you're drop-dead beautiful. I guess you always were. I don't only miss what used to be but what will never be."

"I wouldn't be so sure of that, Timber Oaks."

Becky reached over and turned on the light switch. She leaned up against the big green chalkboard on the wall in front of the classroom. Here face lit up and her eyes sparkled. Written out on the board with pink colored chalk was a message that must have been written earlier.

I LOVE YOU, TIMBER!
WILL YOU BE MY VALENTINE?
HAPPY BIRTHDAY!
BECKS

Becky held her breath with her fingertips over her lips. As we fixed on each other, our smiles broke out into laughter. We held on to each other with that sensation of true love, first love and only forever and ever love.

"It's always been you, Timber! From that first day years ago I watched you mowing Mom's front yard, I knew it was you. It's just hard to get your attention."

We continued our embrace, our foreheads touching. Our giggles and moment of enchantment were interrupted by the appearance of the Solomon twins standing in the doorway. Sherry had her arms crossed in an act of frustration. John took a step forward to scold us.

"Why you dirty little two-timers!"

Instantly, Sherry busted out laughing. John bent over, hooting with glee. Becky joined in with Sherry as the two girls hugged and cackled. I finally put it all together.

"So the three of you were in this altogether?"

"Four," said John still chuckling up a storm, pointing to Paul just outside the door.

I'm sure my embarrassment was evident. Over the last couple of months these guys had played me well.

"Looks like our job is done here, twin brother," said Sherry proudly. "We really do love you guys!"

Paul winked at me then turned and conveyed his young accomplices back toward the dance floor. As the music started again, Becky and I shared our second-ever kiss.

You can't find something till you have lost it. For the rest of my life, I would never lose Becky again.

The following week my daily routine had changed. Gone now were the days of chauffeuring TJ and Ant. The guys were enjoying the new found freedom of owning their own transportation.

Becky was now my constant passenger. We found ourselves together on the way to school and after. Like most new young lovers, we were together most of the time.

On Thursday evening Paul and I were invited over to dinner at the Hooper's. Becky and Sarah fixed a nice pork chop dinner. The small two-bedroom home was humble but tidy and nicely decorated.

After dinner Sarah gave us a quick tour. I was well familiar with the living room that was adorned with pictures of Becky starting in infancy. They brought back many memories of the freckled-face tomboy all the way up to her transformation to a beautiful young woman.

For the first time, I got to see Becky's bedroom. It was baby-blue, of course, with a matching bed set. On the walls were pictures of me through the years along with newspaper clippings of my golf tournaments and the recent articles on TJ and me. Next to her bed stand was her Bible and the little music box I gave her for her birthday.

"That's about long enough for the two of you in there," Sarah told Becky and me. Her warning was light-hearted but effectual.

We gathered together in the living room. Sitting on the sofa, Paul and Sarah enjoyed a cup of coffee. Becky and I relaxed in the two passenger loveseat.

"It's not that I don't trust you, Timber," continued the school teacher. "But this is my house and some rules must be observed."

"Mom!" chided Becky, embarrassed as she leaned over against me.

"Words from the wise," added Paul setting down his mug of java. "Sarah's rules are for your own protection."

"So Becky, what's in your future?" asked Paul.

"Hopefully Timber, but I want to teach. I like kids."

"It's in the blood," commented Sarah. "And by the way, young lady, you are still a kid yourself and so is Timber."

"Teaching will serve you well," said Paul. "You know, Becky, most young people in love believe that they will spend the rest of their lives together. They have not taken the time in the courtship to learn all about each other. Often they find out too late, leading to unsuccessful relationships and failed marriages.

"I have to admit that Timber and you are somewhat of an exception. You've grown up together. You share common values as well as your faith. These are very important, but remember you are both still very young."

"Alright already," Becky sighed. "Will everybody quit telling me how immature I am?"

Paul and Sarah laughed. I consoled Becky. Paul continued.

"I'm not questioning either of your maturity. As a matter of fact, you are both way ahead in the game. With Timber leaving for college soon, I think you will find that you will learn more about each other when you are apart.

"Ladies, Timber has accepted a long range assignment in my ministry. It is not to be of your concern right now, but it is important that Timber and Becky listen carefully to me."

I was surprised at what Paul had revealed. Becky looked at me curiously. Sarah nodded her head in approval.

"Follow God's example in everything you do. Live your lives filled with love for others. Keep yourself pure. Do not give in to lust. You can be sure that any immorality, impurity or greed and self-indulgence will be used against you by those wanting you to stumble.

Learn how to live simple lives uncomplicated by the demands and temptations of this world. God has a plan for you. Be faithful and remember that the love of Christ is your greatest possession.

The last day in February was on a Sunday. The church was overflowing with well wishers gathering for Paul's farewell. So many visitors were on hand that Paul and the Deacon were forced to open the balcony.

Paul's garage apartment had been cleaned out. His bags and few belongings were packed in the trunk of Benny's Coup de Ville. Benny would drive him to Colossi, Arkansas after the church service.

As the service started, Ms. Martha led us in a rousing rendition of *He's Got the Whole World in His Hands*. As the second verse began, Silas came prancing through the foyer to the center circle of the sanctuary followed by Becky and Sarah with all the children from the nursery.

The congregation erupted with shouts of joy and tears of jubilation as the hymn continued. Everyone clapped to the beat while those up front reached out to pet and touch Silas.

The giant dog looked healthy and happy. His ears were up and his tail wagged high in the air almost keeping time to the music. Silas' eyes glistened as he enjoyed his triumphant return.

Laughter filled the church that day. Different people of our community took turns thanking Paul with heartfelt humor. From the ladies group to Sandy's Sunday school class, from the nursery and the choir and from the Mission to the Gentlemen's Club each group shared their gratification with kind words, hugs and cards.

As the worship service continued I marveled at how one man of God and his canine companion had made such a difference to Corinthia Falls in just several months. I could not help but wonder how I would ever replace a man of his stature—an old soldier that was changing the world one town at a time.

Paul finally got to take some parting shots. Everyone enjoyed his taking Benny and Emmitt to task, warning them to do their scuffling outside of the church. He then asked for prayers for the widow Fulbright who had taken very ill.

Paul went on complimenting the Deacon, suggesting he should have full-time status as our pastor. With that I looked over at my father, knowing replacing his key employee may cause some hardship. He smiled and nodded approvingly.

"And here's a little something for you, Deacon," said Paul, reaching inside the collar of his black dress shirt and pulling out his whistle on a chain. "This is handy in getting their attention."

Then Paul left the church with these words.

"May our Lord Jesus and God our Father, who loves us and grants us everlasting life, comfort you and give you strength and hope. Remember, we can achieve anything with the power of Christ."

It took Paul and Silas nearly an hour to make it to Benny's car after the service. Groups of people waited in line in the cool February air to bid their farewells.

Paul took some deliberate time with Sam Samuels. They met together with Emmitt. Though no one could hear what was being said, it appeared to be a soldier to soldier thing. As Paul patted Sam on the back and shook Emmitt's hand, it was obvious Emmitt was being appointed a mentor.

Benny and Silas were waiting in the car as I opened the front passenger door for Paul out of respect and a chance for any last minute instructions. Paul motioned for TJ and Ant to join us.

"Now the three of you remember what I have taught. Depend on each other and the Holy Spirit to guide you. Be responsible and continue your loyalty to God's mission."

March

The widow Fullbright's condition had taken a turn for the worse. Now ninety years old, she had developed pneumonia while trying to recuperate from a fall. The Deacon and Ms. Martha along with Doc Pyle made several trips to the hospital in Archer's Grove to be with her in her last days.

I had always known the widow to be a spry old lady who always did her best to embarrass me when the opportunity arose. I knew her roots went deep in Corinthia Falls' history. School was dismissed and most businesses closed on Friday the 12th. At the funeral, a crowded church learned of her amazing past.

In loving memory:
Margaret Mathea Fullbright

Born............January 6, 1892 Pisidia, Missouri
Died.........March 9, 1982 Corinthia Falls, Oklahoma

Preceding Margaret in death were her husband Sinclair
and their son James

Pallbearers:
Dr. Robert Pyle, Emmitt Sharp, Jack Bearkiller, William Oaks,
John Solomon and Benny Larson

Interment:

Lake Corinth Cemetery

Doc Pyle began the eulogy. He pointed out that most of Margaret's friends had passed, leaving him, her personal physician, one of the lifelong citizens of Corinthia Falls with knowledge of her past.

Maggie, as Doc referred to her, came to Corinthia Falls from northern Missouri around the turn of the century with her parents in a horse-drawn wagon. They were farmers by trade looking for a new start.

She married Sinclair Fullbright in 1911. Sinclair was hard working and ambitious. He was dedicated to building Corinthia Falls into a prosperous town.

By the 1920's he was the largest property owner in the county. Sinclair became the majority stockholder in the Quanapah Bank. Doc pointed out that it was Sinclair that gave John Solomon's father a start in the business.

In 1922 when Maggie was thirty, the couple lost their only son, James. He was eight years old. They never had any more children. Instead, Maggie served on the school board and volunteered as a helper to the teaching staff.

Sinclair continued to deal in real estate development. As the original town father, he helped establish the current water system and was influential enough with the local and federal politicians in the 1940's to implement construction of the Corinth Dam that produced Lake Corinth.

Sinclair died in 1965. The town missed his leadership. Without Sinclair, the bustling town stopped growing. Most of the commercial development went to Archer's Grove.

Maggie remained and stayed active in the church, school, and community. She had lost a son and a remarkable husband, but she still loved Corinthia Falls.

The Deacon read us a letter that Maggie had dictated to him on her death bed. It was addressed to the town and church of Corinthia Falls. I could hear her crackling voice and the wit in her words.

'My dear friends, by the time you are hearing this I will be in a much better place than you are. But if I couldn't be where I am now, I would wish to be with you.

Corinthia Falls has been my whole life. The experiences and relationships I had living in our small town all my life gave me happiness and joy. The town, the school, and the church gave me courage and the desire to live so long.

The most precious thing I got a hold of in Corinthia Falls was my faith. It came when I was young. It nourished me through the hard times and secured me in my old age. Faith is the only possession I am taking with me.

Please keep encouraging each other in this faith just as Col. Armstrong did for you. He revitalized old Corithia Falls with his passion for Christ. My only regret is my husband Sinclair did not live to see it.

I have one last request. I love so much what you did with the Gentlemen's Club. If we could do it for young men, we could do it for young ladies, too! I am leaving some money to our Circle of Care to help establish a foster home for girls. Sinclair would have wanted it that way.

And now I bid thee sweet farewell till we meet again. It's time for me to go marching in.

Margaret

P.S. Mr. Timber Oaks, my first name is not Widow!'

I could feel everyone in the church looking at me as Margaret got her last gibe in at me. Over the polite laughter, Becky squeezed my hand and reminded me that: "It was only because she liked you so much, Timber."

After the Deacon said the last words over Margaret at the cemetery, the banker Solomon approached my father and signaled for the Deacon and several others to join in. John requested a meeting of our Circle of Care directors at the Gentlemen's Club the following Saturday morning with the Bearkillers. It had to do with Margaret's final request.

The next morning, I accompanied my father to the meeting. As I remember, the others present were the Bearkillers, Doc, Benny, the Deacon and Ms. Martha, Mayor Emmitt and of course John Solomon. After several reflections on Margaret Fullbright's life, we all stood around the table in the kitchen as the banker started the impromptu meeting.

"As most of you probably suspect, the Fullbrights accumulated some wealth through the years. Maggie was the church's biggest benefactor. She was very generous. The only property she is leaving behind is the old Fullbright residence on the east side of town.

The Fullbrights have no living heirs. As her banker, I wanted all of you to be aware that our Circle of Care and the Corinthia Falls Church will be her only beneficiaries. There are some legal issues to settle, but the distributions for her financial estate will be quite substantial.

"How substantial?" asked Dad.

"Well, Bill, I can't give you an exact figure yet, but…"

John leaned over and whispered into my father's ear.

"Oh my, my, my, my…" said Dad sitting down at the table with both hands on top of his head while staring into space.

"How many my's was that?" asked Benny curiously.

"I counted four—four my's," answered Doc.

You sure it wasn't five?" asked Emmitt. "I think it might have been, 'Oh my, my, my, my, my'. Bill was fading at the end."

"Oh my, my, my, my…," repeated Dad.

"Yes, my, my," confirmed John.

All of us joined my father, sitting down at the large table to a chorus of echoing mys. It would be a couple of months until we found out what all the mys added up to, but Margaret was loaded.

The Deacon looked soberly around the table and suggested prayer. He began by praying aloud.

"Dear Lord, oh my…"

The first signs of spring in Corinthia Falls are the white blossoms of the fruitless pear trees and the dogwoods imbedded in the budding woodlands. The next sign was the beginning preparations for the Quanapah Challenge. The last couple of weeks of March, 1982, were no different. Spring fever was replaced with QC fever.

Store fronts and windows were painted with lettering welcoming visitors to the Quanapah Challenge. Two large signs were placed at the opposite ends of town greeting tourists to the home of the QC to be held Memorial weekend, May 29th. Posters were hung, flyers distributed and press releases were showing up in the local and state newspapers.

An ABC network crew worked with Doc Pyle and other QC organizers and sponsors. Strategic positions were established for the camera crews to provide the live broadcast on Wide World of Sports. Since the Gentlemen's Club would be the focal point of the relay as well as the finish line, ABC would construct a temporary platform on the lawn out front to serve as a stage for the event.

Wiring and sound systems were placed in the different tactical locations. Several colorful banners were hung building to building across Main Street. By the first of April everything was in place for the grandest Quanapah Challenge event ever staged.

April

It has often been said of Oklahoma in springtime, you can experience all four seasons in one week. The end of March and the beginning of April was no exception. Very cool weather gave way to a warming trend. By Friday, April 2nd, Corinthia Falls and northeast Oklahoma was enjoying an early glimpse of summer with temperatures in the mid-eighties.

We all knew it would not last. Unseasonable weather mixed with strong winds from the south means something has to change. An approaching cold front from the north led the weather service to issue a tornado watch with possible severe storms for late that afternoon.

As soon as school was out, Becky and I headed for Cherokee Creek. I did not want to miss a chance to practice in the warm, windy conditions. Besides, I was doing my final tune up for the high school spring golf season.

We had left TJ and Cy working out in the old gym. The new dynamic duo had put together several half court basketball scrimmages on Wednesdays and Fridays made up of some of the boys from the Gentlemen's Club. TJ said the young men were very aggressive and eager, but would probably be more suited for football.

Ant was working at Oak's Corner that afternoon. With Deacon now appointed full-time pastor, my father decided to give a few of the Gentlemen's Club boys a chance at employment. Each took turns on weekends and afternoons under the strict supervision of Ant.

We got to the neighborhood driving range and helped ourselves to the Solomon's fancy golf cart as usual. Becky liked to drive. As I began hitting balls from the longer distance, our conversation turned to the weather.

"Think it's going to storm, Timber?"

"I imagine. That radio guy said a storm line is forming on the other side of Tulsa. It's starting to look a little dark out there." I pointed my three wood to the west.

"Hey Becks, you heard about Demas?"

"Only a little. I heard my mom and Mr. Cox talking some about it at school. What's going on?" Becky fought with her auburn hair in the wind.

"Well, from what Dad says, Demas will be spending a long time in prison down at McAlister. Sounds like Phoebe's divorce went through and she will get the Sampson place.

"Good for her. Timber, that man almost killed you!"

"We don't have to worry about that now. The thing is for Phoebe and the boys to get a fresh start."

"Will they be moving back to the farm?"

"I don't know, Becks. Lots of bad memories out there."

It was not long before the sky turned an ominous color of gray. The wind switched to the northwest, ushering in a sudden drop in temperature. As soon as we saw the lightning, we were off the driving range and on our way back to town.

By the time we got back, the Corinthia Falls tornado warning siren was sounding from city hall. Becky held tight to my right arm as we drove through the blinding downpour. I knew instinctively to get to the store.

One of the safest places to be during a tornado is inside a walk-in cooler or freezer in a grocery or convenience store. Many times my father had shown me pictures from trade magazines with stores demolished and the walk-ins still standing intact on an otherwise vacant foundation.

Dad was waiting for us at the front door of Oak's Corner. Already inside our large secure walk-in was Ant, a couple boys from the club, Mom, Ms. Martha and several stranded customers. Although the cooling fans were temporarily turned off, the refrigerated air chilled Becky and me through our wet clothes.

My father stood guard just outside the cooler door watching over his dominion. The electric power went off briefly several times. Then we could hear a roar that sounded like a locomotive was running over the roof of the store.

What seemed like an eternity was only ten minutes. My father opened the door. We were greatly relieved to find everything undamaged. I walked out of the store with Dad in a lightly falling rain to inspect the premises.

Trash cans were turned over. Fresh green leaves marking the beginning of spring speckled our driveway and the highway. The Quanapah Challenge banner that hung over Main Street two blocks down was now tangled on the store canopy.

"Another close call," said Dad after our quick assessment.

Living in Oklahoma in the springtime, one becomes used to close calls. This was the closest I ever experienced.

The excitement was all over and the sun began peeking through the clouds to the west when Benny pulled up to the store in his El Camino. Stopping on the drive next to Dad and me, Benny rolled down his window and announced excitedly, "Looks like it hit the old Sampson place!"

Benny sped out of the drive and headed west on the highway.

Mom and Martha were left to run the store as Dad, Becky, and I pursued Benny in my truck.

Our trip was slowed by the rain-slicked dirt roads that had now turned to mud. By the time we got to the Sampson farm, a crowd had gathered.

We witnessed first-hand the power of nature. The old farm house had been demolished, leaving only a concrete foundation. The sheets of metal siding that had once made up the barn were scattered like bits of trash across the fields.

The familiar green truck lay upside down nearly a hundred yards from its usual parking place. The rusty windmill was shredded to pieces. The tractor was the only thing remaining in one piece. The animals still lurking in the fields were frightened and confused.

Most of the town was now showing up on the property to see the destruction. Little was said as there were no words for what we saw.

Becky and I walked over the area that used to be the barn, searching for anything worth salvaging for Sam and Sandy. I bent over, uncovering some hay that concealed the black handled knife that the Colonel used to teach the boys about sin. As I fiddled with it in my hands, I turned to Becky.

"Becks, does all this answer your question about them moving back here?"

"Timber, I think God answered that question."

The following Sunday morning at church all the talk was about the tornado. Prayers were given for the Sampson family as well as praises to God for sparing Corinthia Falls.

At the end of the service, Doc Pyle announced a meeting of

the Gentlemen's Club board of directors and all committee members of our new Circle of Care to be held that afternoon. Doc informed "all the usual suspects" to gather at the Club at 3:00.

I knew my father had been working on something. He had been out of the store most of the day before. I figured it had something to do with Maggie Fullbright's endowment.

"So, what we got goin'?" I asked Dad on our ride to the meeting.

"Got to get a mite creative," he said.

The lounge of the Gentlemen's Club was full of Doc's 'usual suspects.' The Bearkillers were setting next to Phoebe and her boys. Doc, appearing in control of the meeting, was huddled with Emmitt, Benny, and John Solomon. Mr. Cox and the Deacon were working the crowd.

"Well, the Oak's boys are here. Are we ready to get started?" announced Doc.

The town doctor opened the meeting by appointing Becky's mom to take the minutes. Doc talked about how many of us held various positions at the church, the Gentlemen's Club and the Circle of Care. So it is in a small community. He said all three entities would have to work together on the upcoming proposals.

"Are you ready, Bill?" asked Doc, looking over to my father.

"Sure."

Dad stood and addressed the meeting from in front of the judge's bench. He put on his reading glasses and found his place in a spiraled notebook. This had to be important. Corinthia Falls had always trusted my father. When Bill Oaks talked, people listened.

"Folks, we need to think outside of the box. We have before us an excellent opportunity to do God's will. I know we have seen a lot of God's plan unfold before us in the last year, but just like the Colonel told us, 'He's not through with us yet.'"

Most of you should know by now that Margaret Fulbright blessed us by leaving us her entire estate. John Solomon has been working hard with the attorneys on the transfer of these assets. Although it is substantial, we must remember as people of faith the importance of being good stewards. Mrs. Sampson, will you join me?"

Phoebe quietly walked up and stood next to my father. She held a Kleenex in her hand to wipe the tears.

"As you know, Phoebe and her family have been through quite a lot, not to mention last Friday's tornado that devastated their farm. There was no insurance and the Sampsons have no means to ever rebuild nor do they desire to do so.

So like I said, it's time to think outside the box. Follow me close here, because we have come up with a proposal. Mrs. Fullbright's estate was in liquid assets except for her home. When all the legal work is finished, we propose to deed the Fullbright home to Phoebe, giving her family a place to live. This would give them independence and a fresh start. In return, Phoebe would deed her acreage to our Circle of Care. We feel this is a win-win situation.

As you should be aware from the letter read at Maggie's funeral and also from the stipulation on use of the monies in her will, it is to be used for a girl's home similar to what we have done for the boys at the Gentlemen's Club.

Rather than build a girl's home on the former Sampson property, we brainstormed a bit. What if we rebuilt the farm? We could have lodging and put together the real life workings of a modern farm. We would move the boys from town to the farm. They would help take responsibility for the animals, have chores and assignments and assist in raising cattle. These profits could go toward the financing of the facility. It was also suggested they might put on an annual rodeo."

"But what about a place for girls?" asked Clara Cox.

"Yes, Clara, what about the girls?" Dad continued. "With the boys moving out to the farm, this building, according to Jack Bearkiller, would be perfect for a girls' home.

Construction will take some time on building a farm and lodging for the boys, but it's doable. Then we can start working on the girl's home."

Jack and Donna nodded their heads in agreement. It was suddenly like a light came on as everyone got the big picture. I heard a couple of amens which was followed by applause. My father's common sense approach and small business savvy was brilliant.

The motion passed unanimously. It was also agreed upon to change the future name of the Gentlemen's Club to the Corinthia Falls Lady's Home.

"So, will we still call the new farm the Gentlemen's Club?" asked Sarah.

"Better not!" said Doc. "You put a sign out in the country that says Gentlemen's Club and it might be mistaken for a bordello."

Doc's comment got a lot of laughs but also carried with it some logic. I stood and made a suggestion.

"Why don't we just call it the Corinthia Falls Boys' Ranch?"

I started my senior year of high school golf the second Saturday of April. There were many opportunities for tournaments and match play in the small school division for eastern Oklahoma. Since I was the Corinthia Falls golf team, I was only allowed to play for medalist honors. In other words, each team of five members would add up their total combined strokes. The winning team had the lowest combined score.

I could compete only as an individual. My goal was simply

to win the 18-hole tournaments with the lowest all around score. The only team work involved was finding an adult representative of our school to accompany me as was required.

Sandy's Sunday school class surprised me the Sunday before with six new baby-blue golf shirts with a white descending dove over the front pocket and a new baby-blue golf bag with Saints etched in white letters across the top. Along with my white golf shoes and white slacks, I was dressed to make a run at the state small school championship to be held the following month.

April 10th - Checotah
Finished third with a 79. Guest coach - Matthew Cox. Lots of wind. Mr. Cox did give me some pointers on what type of degree to go for at Tulsa.

April 17th – Stillwell
Second place trophy. Shot a 78 thanks to a good putter. Guest coach – Mr. Hummingbird. It was a fun ride. He likes Creedence, too.

April 24th – Poteau
Finished with a 77, tied for first. Lost on the first playoff hole. Guest coach – Doc Pyle. He was not an actual representative of the school, but we didn't tell the officials. Walking 18 holes just about exhausted Doc.

May 1st – Eufaula
Eastern District tournament. My best performance of the spring with a 75. Another second place. Qualified for state tournament. Guest Coach – Sarah Hopper along with Becky. My game was looking good; Becky was looking better.

Every week I received a letter from the Colonel. He gave me encouragement on golf, but each letter was also filled with life lessons and more details on his ministry. The letters would continue off and on through my college days.

Paul suggested, rather ordered, that I save all the letters together for future reference. I kept them in safe keeping in a binder that I still have to this day.

May

The school held a pep rally for me the following Wednesday. Sherry led the cheers while Benny and the band stirred up the assembly. The Oklahoma State Small School Golf Tournament would be held in Oklahoma City that Friday and Saturday.

I was determined to win. I had played the year before at the same course when I finished runner up. I felt confident and my game was improving. My scholarship was in place; my future was secure. It was time to bring back a State Championship for Corinthia Falls.

On Thursday a group of well wishers gathered at Oak's Corner to see off the caravan of my supporters and me that would make the three-hour trip down Interstate 40.

My parents, Sarah, Becky and I rode in our family car. Benny loaded up a used Suburban off his used car lot with Ant, TJ, Principal Cox who was my 'guest coach', his wife Clara and Sam and Sandy Samuels.

The two day thirty-six hole tournament was hosted by the Oklahoma Park Golf and Country Club. Once again I could challenge the beautiful course. Gone were the humble rocky fairways and acorn covered greens of the eastern part of the state.

Coach Apollos met us as we arrived at our motel. Crazy George wasted no time reminding me about destiny. For the first time in my life I had a real golf coach. He worked with me both mornings on the practice tees.

"It's not just about golf, Timber, it's about destiny!"

I spent most of my free time by myself when I wasn't with Becky. My thoughts were on golf as the others--especially TJ, Ant and the Samuels boys--enjoyed the indoor pool and the other amenities of the luxury motel.

The weather was perfect for golf that weekend. The temperature hovered around eighty as the usually gusty Oklahoma spring winds had settled to a light breeze. On Friday morning it was time for some destiny.

Friday – 1st Round

My best round of golf that year. I carded an even par 72, three strokes ahead of the field of over sixty competitors except for that one guy. Last year's state champion from a private school with a scholarship to Oklahoma State came in with a 71. I was not worried about the rest of the pack. It was the slick, country-club-bred dude with all his coaching and grooming that I had to catch.

Saturday – Final Round

Being the leaders of the state tournament, Andrew Reuben and I teed off last. We both brought our best game with us. I chased Andy all day. We were both under par when I birdied the 17th hole, leaving us tied at 3 under par.

A crowd of spectators and the field of high school golfers gathered around the par four 18th hole for the finish. I had the honors.

I drove the ball just slightly to the right and ended up behind a precariously placed oak tree just off the fairway. After punching out a second shot to get out from behind the tree, the best I could do was bogey.

Andy's drive was straight and in the middle of the fairway. He went on to par the hole and win the tournament. Another second place trophy for the Corinthia Falls' trophy case; disappointment and questions to myself about this destiny stuff.

At the presentation on the final hole when I received the second place trophy for the second year in a row, my little group of supporters sang our Saints Go Marching in theme song. It was to be the first of many occasions in which I would hear it on a golf course.

Becky and the rest consoled me with comforting words and embraces. Crazy Coach George congratulated me on an excellent round of golf: a round of 70, my best effort ever.

"It's not about the golf, Timber," said Coach.

"Just think, bro," added TJ. "If there would been one of those satellite dish shaped receivers somewhere 'round that big tree, you would have been state champion!"

The following Thursday, after school, the Solomon family had arranged a little pool party in their backyard for the graduating seniors. It would be just the five of us with the twins' parents and Becky. Sherry insisted on Becky being there.

When I picked up Becky at her house, I could tell she was nervous. It did not take long to figure out why. Becky was wearing a swimsuit. It was a paisley one-piece and she wore a matching yellow cover-up. Still, this was the first time I ever remember seeing Becky dressed for swimming.

On the ride over I kept looking at her and grinning. I could not help but appreciating the view although she was very self conscious and, besides that, she didn't swim.

"Stop it, Timber. Just keep your eyes on the road. You know this is hard on me. It's my first time in a bathing suit since third grade!"

"Becks, relax!" You look great. I mean really great."

"As great as Sherry?" she asked, tilting her head with questioning eyes.

Sherry and Becky had become great friends, but I could sense a little glamour competition going on in the swimsuit division. To me Becky was the most beautiful thing God ever created. I tried to convince her of that.

"Becks, you are drop-dead gorgeous. I'm sorry I can't take my eyes off of you."

"You didn't answer the question, Oaks!"

"Sherry's good lookin,' but you are really lookin' good. I'm in love with you. To me you are the most beautiful girl in the world."

"I love you, too," she replied.

I escaped the estrogen trap. Praise God.

It was a nice afternoon for a pool party. The early May weather was around eighty degrees. We were the last to arrive at the Solomon's Cherokee Creek mansion.

TJ was sitting in the hot tub wearing sunglasses. John Jr. and Ant were in the heated pool. They were joined by the two little tan Pomeranians floating on a small foam raft. John Sr. was starting up the gas grill on the patio. Sherry met us at the back gate.

"Becky, you look darling!" exclaimed Sherry wearing her traditional white two-piece.

I was interested in the guys' reaction to Becky's attire. TJ took notice by rising up slowly and peeking over his shades. The boys in the pool stopped their game with the drifting yapping pups to check out Becky.

"And to think I lost her to Timber…" panned John.

Becky flashed her familiar red blush. She knew she had passed the test. The girls retreated to the lounge chairs to put on suntan lotion. We all pretended not to notice.

Jackie Solomon came out on the covered patio with a pitcher of some fancy tropical punch and plastic mugs.

"Hi Timber! Hey there, Becky! How about something cool and refreshing: Seven Fruit Punch?"

TJ was the first one there. John and Ant boosted themselves up and sat on the side of the pool. I helped Jackie distribute the drinks.

"I can't believe that the five of you will be graduating in just ten days," said Jackie. "Where has all the time gone?"

"Well, it's been quite a year, ma'am," said Ant.

"Amen, brother!" underlined TJ.

"I don't know if there will be a whole lot of times together much more like this; not for awhile anyway," said John.

I went over to the fence, gazing out at the Cherokee Creek driving range. So much of my time was spent there; so many memories made.

"Timber, why so quiet today?" asked Sherry, noticing my despondency.

"He's still trying to bring that championship home to Corinthia Falls," TJ answered, half-reading my mind.

"You three need to give it up," urged John. "You're champions enough."

"That's right, son," confirmed John's dad overhearing the conversation. "They have done the town proud; all of you have."

I smiled and took it all in. There was one more thing to try and little time left.

"I know that look, Timb," prodded Ant. "You might as well

tell them what you've been visiting with Doc about."

"I don't think now's…" I started.

"Timber wants to enter a local team in the Quanapah Challenge," interrupted Ant.

"Say what?" questioned TJ. "Timber, until they add basketball and golf to that relay we're stuck on the sidelines. Dude, these teams are loaded with some bad cats."

The girls looked up from the tanning session and took interest. Becky was puzzled.

"Timber, you can't be serious!"

I waded into the corner of the shallow end of the pool swirling my punch and sat on the top step. I listened to the entire rebuttal as Mr. Solomon began tossing hamburger patties on the grill.

"Buddy, if I didn't know you better, I'd think you had been smokin' somethin'," said John. "World class runners and swimmers, experienced rock climbers, professional jockeys and who knows what kind of livestock?"

"I guess you guys are right. I was just trying to think outside the box," I replied quoting my father's familiar phrase.

"Better get back into the box, bro," warned TJ.

The subject, at least for now needed changing. TJ walked over to Mr. Solomon to give him some unneeded pointers in the art of grilling. I turned to Ant.

"So, Mr. Valedictorian. How's the speech coming?"

"My preparation has been thorough," began the scholar.

"We would expect nothing less," replied Sherry.

"I will vocalize a monologue filled with proper eloquence and charm. A verbal dissertation filled with anticipation, optimism and expectations: a tribute to our history, an accolade to our present precedent and homage to our potential prospects."

As we looked at Ant trying to figure out what he'd just said, TJ strolled over from the patio nodding his head affirmatively.

"My thoughts exactly."

Corinthia Falls was full of activity in the middle of May. School was winding down and the Quanapah Challenge was winding upward. Oak's Corner was busy with the influx of Lake Corinth tourists and campers.

Volunteers from the church worked with the Gentlemen's Club prepping the Fullbight home and moving the Sampson family to their new residence. Our Circle of Care was gaining momentum. The Solomon's added a line of used window air conditioners and gardening supplies to the mission.

The Gentlemen's Club was up to fifteen boys in residence. A new committee led by Joyce Anderson was formed for the change-over of the Gentlemen's Club to a girls' home. Joyce insisted that Becky serve on the transition team.

Out west of town, near the old Sampson spread, a new proud billboard was put in place. It read: Future Home of Corinthia Falls Boys' Ranch.

Sunday afternoon, May 16th was Graduation Day. The church was full earlier that morning with relatives and friends of the five graduating seniors of Corinthia Falls.

We wore our baby-blue caps and gowns as the Deacon delivered a special sermon message from Luke 11: Don't Hide Your Candle…Be a Beacon unto the World.

As the Deacon charismatically articulated the words of Christ, I could hear Creedence Clearwater in my inner ear singing about lighting a candle in the window.

It was muggy in the old gym that afternoon. The place was packed for the commencement, with people fanning themselves with graduation bulletins. Several large fans in place of a worn out air conditioning system helped stir the sultry air.

The five of us entered the gym from the rear doors and marched to the stage as Mrs. Sharp on piano played Pomp and Circumstance. As we took our seats on the right side of the stage facing our audience, the podium was set up on the left.

I looked out at all the familiar faces that had been an integral part of my life—our lives: my parents, the Deacon and Ms. Martha, Ant's mom and dad Jack and Donna, Doc and Benny, Mayor Sharp, Principal Cox and Clara, John and Jackie Solomon, Nate Anderson (who came alone so Joyce could faithfully run the store), the Hummingbirds, Chet and more recently Sandy, Sam, and Phoebe and, of course, sitting on the front row were Becky and Sarah.

They had all had a hand in molding our lives. We had all had a hand in molding each other.

After the Deacon's benediction, Mr. Cox made his speech. Next was Ant's Valedictorian address. From where we were seated on stage, we could tell it was going to be special. It was hard not to laugh when we could see behind the side curtains. Sam and Sandy Samuels made some unusual preparations to assist Ant.

"And now it's my honor to introduce Anthony Bearkiller, our Corinthia Falls valedictorian," announced Mr. Cox.

With the aid of a small wooden box so he could see over the podium, Ant adjusted the microphone downward. At the same time he began to speak, a recognizable pair snuck into the back of the gym unbeknownst to the assembly except for those on stage.

The Colonel stood quietly putting a finger to his lips urging those that could see him not give the surprise away. Dressed in his customary black with sleeves rolled up to his elbows, Paul held Silas tight on a short leash.

It was hard to concentrate on Ant's speech. I was sitting by TJ and afraid his big grin and suppressed laughter would give things away. I just knew it was a good speech that was well arranged and delivered.

As Ant came to the end of his address, he began to talk about the obstacles in life. Those yet to come and those obstacles we had overcome.

"We have survived the curse of a goat!"

With those words Sam Samuels released the repainted red billy goat from back stage. The goat ran wildly around the stage. Hysterical laughter ensued. The goat finally came to stand next to Sherry and started chewing on her graduation gown. John and I lost our caps as we tried to separate the goat from Sherry. TJ and the audience bent over with laughter.

"We have endured the wrath of wild fowl!"

Sandy let go of the pair of infamous geese. One flew into TJ's arms. TJ wrestled off the goose as feathers flew. The other goose waddled out to the edge of the stage and scolded the whole audience.

The barnyard frolic continued with bleats and quacks as everyone in the gym was now on their feet cheering on the animals and the graduating class.

"And we have overcome the intimidation of a bear!"

As usual, Silas was on cue. As the melee continued on stage, the Colonel unleashed Silas. The giant dog ran down the center aisle of the gym and charged the stage.

Ant stepped down from his perch to greet his friend. Silas sprang through the air and burst onto the stage, knocking down both Ant and the podium. Two terrified birds and a red goat headed for protection off stage.

Ant was pinned under Silas, so the twins, TJ and I helped

Ant to his feet. To the delight of the audience, we huddled around Silas, receiving a group face washing.

Ant recovered the reverbing microphone from off the stage floor. He approached center stage and finished his speech.

"And we can do anything with the help of Christ who gives us power!"

Paul and Silas moved into the Gentlemen's Club. Their stay would be temporary, just long enough to experience the Quanapah Challenge that was less than two weeks away. Then they would return to Colossi for most of the summer.

I spent most of the first two days with Paul. I helped bring him up to date with what had been going on with the church and the Circle of Care along with the other community leaders.

Paul tutored me privately on my future. The Colonel emphasized the importance of a business degree while I attended Tulsa University.

"You are going to be managing a large and diverse ministry, Timothy. Problem solving skills, organizing, and administrating will be essential."

I finally got up enough nerve to share with Paul my silly ambition of entering a team in the QC. Consistent with the Colonel's nature, he did not find it silly at all; as a matter of fact he suggested we visit with Doc.

We met with Doc Pyle at his office on late Tuesday afternoon after business hours. It was just ten days to the QC. For many years, Doc had been the presiding Gentlemen's Club officer heading up the annual Memorial Day event.

At first Doc was amused. But when he heard my ideas on how to approach the contest, my research and the 'thinking outside the box', he began to take an interest.

Paul came up with a brilliant idea that made the whole thing come together. Doc clarified some rules and added his suggestions. We decided to call a meeting with my friends at the Gentlemen's Club for the following evening.

It took all of my efforts to convince the others to attend the meeting, especially when they found out what it was all about. Everyone seemed to have obligations at the store or somewhere else. There was very little interest. With Paul's insistence, we finally got everyone together.

We met in the Gentlemen's Club kitchen at the large meeting table. In attendance were Paul and Silas, Doc Pyle, the five graduated seniors, a reluctant Becky and the Sampson boys. Doc got things started.

"I guess you all know why you're here?"

"Yep, and we've been through it all before," said TJ.

"I think the idea is wonderful, but there is no way for a local team to compete. It comes down to talent," added Ant. "You better have a ringer or two."

"That we do," confirmed Paul, turning things back over to Doc. "And we also have home field advantage."

Sherry and John Solomon looked on curiously.

"Let's look at this from a different angle," said Doc. "The last leg of the relay is the two mile run from the State Park to town. These college types are some you might see competing in the 1984 Olympics.

They will run this thing in about eight and a half minutes. Timber, the best runner we've got in Corinthia Falls can run it in about ten minutes; not bad for a golfer. So by the time we get to the run, we need to have at least a minute and a half lead to give us a chance."

"There you go. Meeting dismissed!" proclaimed TJ.

"Thomas, quit your doubting and listen," scolded the Colonel.

"The third leg just before the run is climbing Eagle Cliff," Doc continued.

Doc handed out several photographs around the table of last year's competition at Rock Hill. The twins and TJ studied them carefully.

"Look on the far right of the hill that the climbers are avoiding. These climbers are very gymnastic and agile. They're just looking for a grip to pull themselves upward. They stay away from the projecting rock formation on the right side.

"See how they look like small cliffs all arranged from about nine to eleven feet apart, one overhanging the other? In between these overhangs, the structure is very concave, that is, curved inward. This makes it very difficult for a traditional climber.

Now if TJ could jump from one cliff to another hoisting himself upward like he's demonstrated he can do on a basketball goal..."

"You say somthin' to me, Doc?" asked TJ, already defiant.

"Look, Teej," I said standing up, "We're only asking that you give it a try. There's still time to practice."

"There ya go," added John. "And if you slip and fall you simply get a bath in the lake."

TJ walked around the table nervously. Everyone was waiting for an answer.

"Do I look like a mountain climber? Black folks don't climb mountains!"

"I wouldn't be too sure about that," shot back Ant in his knowledgeable manner. "The guides that lead climbers up Mt. Kilimanjaro are Tanzanian; native Africans."

TJ and I went eye to eye. He then did the same with the Colonel.

"Okay! I'll give it a try," said TJ, giving in. "But I want to see the rest of this plan. I still haven't spotted your ringer."

"That's where the Colonel comes in," said Doc. "Paul?"

Paul approached the table from the corner of the room. TJ and I took our seats.

"As we continue taking this relay in reverse order, the second stage is Rock Hill. This stone covered hill is so steep that the animals, mostly mules, donkeys some horses, maybe a bull and whatever else may show up, cannot ascend it directly. The riders have to move upward from side to side to retain balance. This takes time.

"Now this will be the first time for me to witness this personally, but I've seen a few clips on TV. I always had an idea for the perfect animal. One that was nimble enough to run a straight line to the top of the hill and strong enough to support a mount."

Paul stepped back and looked down at his large canine companion resting between Sam and Sandy partially underneath the table.

"Up boy!" urged Paul.

Silas as usual took the opportunity to be on center stage. He sprang up landing his front paws on the kitchen table. The impact nearly knocked the table over. We all stood to keep from getting hurt. I watched as a common light bulb went off in the other's heads.

"Ringer!" exclaimed Ant.

"Dead on, ringer!" echoed TJ.

Sherry broke into her cheerleading mode.

"Silas! Silas! Silas!"

The rest of us joined her in the cheer. We pounded on the

table to the rhythm of our chant. TJ went into one of his dance routines as the massive dog remained leaning on the table with his long black tongue hanging out, enjoying the attention.

The moment was exciting. Finally the gang was catching on that all this was within our capability.

"I think Silas can cover the hill in about a minute. This will take about four minutes off the average time," estimated Paul.

"Brilliant!" Ant deducted. "So, all we got to do is get one of those race horse jockeys from the track down in Sallisaw to ride Silas…"

"No, that will not work Anthony," said Paul. "First of all, Sallisaw is not local and this is a local team. Second, it would best if Silas' rider was someone with whom he was well acquainted and comfortable."

Everyone's eyes in the room, including Silas,' turned and stared at Ant. It was obvious he was the perfect size and fit. Ant knew he had no choice.

"Okay, it's you and me big boy," said Ant, scratching Silas between the ears.

"The thing is you will have time to practice. I figure we can place one of those Oak's Corner cheeseburgers at the top of the hill and Silas will get the idea. You just have to find a way to hold on."

TJ began high-fiveing Doc. The others became more eager and encouraged. Paul looked over at me and raised his eyebrows, signaling that it was now my turn.

This was going to be the hardest sell. That's why Paul, Doc, and I saved it for last. I remained standing and nervously addressed the others.

"We still need someone for the first leg; the swimming part. Someone who can make the half mile across the lake in around fifteen minutes. That's how fast the big boys and girls do it."

"Timber, John's a good swimmer," suggested Sherry. "He swims at home and at the lake all the time."

"Thanks sis, but we're talking world class swimmers here. I can swim, but not like that."

"Well, that's where Sam and Sandy can help us," I offered. "Remember, we've got home field advantage. Listen to Sam."

Sam was eager to share his information. He used his hands as a prop to share his knowledge.

"Well uh, you guys know where that race begins with the swimmers down on that Boulder Ridge Marina gas dock? Well, ya see, just several feet away is an old cable stretchin' from one side of the lake to the other.

"The Corps of Engineers left it in their back when they flooded the old river to make Corinth Lake. It was used way back then by a ferryboat to get big loads across the river since there wasn't a road.

"At nights, Sandy and I used to dive down and attach our jug lines to it and fish all night out of our rubber raft. That there cable is only about fifteen feet or so deep and it's easy to find!"

"Isn't jug fishing illegal on the lake?" asked John.

Both Samuel boys laughed.

"Just about everything we did was illegal," said Sandy.

"So Timb, what's this got to do with swimming across the lake," asked Ant curiously.

"Get the big picture," I said. "Since we don't have a world class swimmer like John said, what if someone could dive down there and grab hold of that cable. Using their arms, they could pull themselves through the water."

"Okay, I get it," said Ant. "Our swimmer uses the cable to propel their body through the water giving them leverage against the other swimmers. They would have to be athletic, a light weight, but, most of all, they would have to be able to hold their breath for long periods of time…oh, I see where you're going…"

Becky pushed herself back from the table. She had been more reserved than the rest of us throughout the discussion. She looked up at me with searching and fearful blue eyes. I felt guilty, as if I had just betrayed her.

No one dared look at Becky except me. The others were watching for how I would engage her. Becky stood up, held her breath as was her custom and turned to face the corner of the room in a private moment.

"Becks, I'm sorry to ask you this way, but you're the only one that can do it."

"Timber Oaks, look how you have backed me into a corner!"

Becky turned and looked deep into my eyes. We both had tears that were beginning to fall as I reached out and held her at arm's length.

"I just got brave enough to wear a swimsuit for the first time in eight years. I don't care for the water and the only reason I'd swim is to keep from drowning. Now, you got all our friends hopes so high and it all depends on me just because I can hold my breath!"

"It doesn't all just depend on you, Becks. Look around. We are all one team and we always will be."

The others seemed to feel that it was time to add some support. TJ went first.

"Girl, I wouldn't worry about drownin.' If you don't do it the rest of us will kill you first."

Becky forced a smile.

Sandy cut in. "Sam and I will be there to help. You will need some of those eye goggles. We can start out nice and slow."

Becky nodded her head slowly. I looked over at Paul for his

approval. He smiled, as if once again he could read my mind... this was the perfect girl for me.

"All right then, ever'body in here!" said TJ reaching his long arms across the center of the table holding his hand open. "You too, Silas!"

We huddled across the kitchen table to clench hands and Doc, Paul and even Silas, with a little help from Ant, joined in.

"On three, ready? 1-2-3... Saints!"

With a short time to prepare, our practice sessions began the next day. One thing we had going for us was that home field advantage Paul mentioned. It allowed us to use the actual course of the Quanapah Challenge to craft our techniques.

John Solomon was our all around back up. If anyone got hurt or could not perform on the day of the relays, he would take their place. He took part in all practices, even adding some suggestions.

Sam and Sandy worked exclusively with Becky. They used the Solomon family ski boat patiently helping her locate the under-water cable and demonstrating the technique necessary to propel her through the water.

Sherry used her God given gift of encouragement. She spent most of her time on the boat with the boys giving Becky that much needed confidence.

Doc worked some with TJ. About all the doctor could do was help him locate a route of projecting rocks from the base of the Eagle Cliffs all the way to the top. Since Doc did not climb, he stood at the base of the cliffs and could be heard shouting his instructions to TJ from across the lake.

Naturally, Paul worked with Ant and Silas. Silas caught on

quick when he learned of his meaty reward waiting for him at the top of the hill. The problem was for him to learn that Ant had to go along for the ride.

Ant took a lot of tumbles on Rock Hill and accumulated a body full of scrapes and bruises. The difficulty for Ant was finding a grip. After two days of trial runs, Ant and Silas still could not get to the top together.

There was little for me to do but run. I broke in a new pair of running shoes. I ran the two miles from the State Park down the highway across the dam and into town four times a day. I was getting very close to doing it in my ten minute goal.

Throughout the town, Quanapah Fever had merged with Saint's Hysteria. The word was out that we had put a team together to compete in the QC. The little town that had seen so many miracles over the past year expected nothing less than one more.

All the signs promoting and welcoming spectators and visitors in windows and on the roadside for the Memorial Day event were coupled with posters proclaiming 'Go Saints' and 'Baby-blue!' For the first time in many years, Corinthia Falls had a sports team... their own team.

At church that Sunday, most of the church members were wearing baby-blue. Silk screened t-shirts had made their way around town. Some promoted the Quanapah Challenge but more supported the Corinthia Falls QC team with a 'GO Saints' logo.

Our team sat around the inside circle of the church. Although Ant, TJ, Silas, Becky and I were the main participants, we included the twins and the Sampson brothers as an extension of the team.

Church was late getting started as we all answered questions about the race. We shook hands and received pats and yes, a head pet or two, as the enthused congregation added encouragement.

"We know you can do it!"

"You make us so proud!"

"We believe in you!"

We all knew now what this was all about. We were carrying the banner for Corinthia Falls; a banner of pride and self respect. This was our town, this was our faith and this was our time.

After the Deacon settled down the congregation, the service finally began. After the opening hymn, he turned the announcements over to Doc.

Doc reviewed the final details in preparation for next Saturday's QC. He emphasized that with the television coverage of ABC Sports, this would be the biggest crowd ever in Corinthia Falls.

Doc estimated that the number of people attending would be at least twice as large as last year.

The church, along with the Gentlemen's Club and the newly formed Circle of Care, would handle parking, assist vendors, operate fund raisers and direct traffic.

Paul was to deliver the sermon that day. It would be his last time to address the Church of Corinthia Falls. The church was eager for his final instructions.

The Colonel, dressed in his traditional black, approached the center circle of the congregation. He then unbuttoned his dress shirt revealing his own baby-blue Saint's t-shirt. The impression Paul made was so euphoric that Benny, Ms. Martha and the praise band broke into our Saints Marching In theme. The ecstatic congregation stood, clapped and joined in.

Paul spent little time talking about himself, where he had been or where he was going next. Instead, he delivered a pep talk to the church and to our QC team.

"I urge you to dedicate your bodies to Christ. Let them be the kind of living sacrifice He would acknowledge. When you think of all He has done for this church and town, is that too much to request?

"Let God change you to a new way of thinking and believing. He will show you what to do through His Holy Spirit. Then you can experience His wonderful force in your lives.

"Remain humble. Appraise your worth by the faith God has given you. Our bodies have many components and so it is with this church. Since we are all parts of one body, we all may work differently but in unison through Christ.

If you can preach the Good News, then speak out! If you can serve others, than serve them well! If you can teach, then be a good teacher. If you are good in business, be generous with your money. If you are a leader, lead wisely. If you can encourage others and show kindness, then just do it!

"If you can swim across large lakes, do it to glorify God. If you can climb mountains and scale hills, do it for His name sake. And if you can run, run and win the race God has given you! Our war will continue till Christ returns, but a battlefield is in place before us. People of Corinthia Falls: Prepare your army!"

Sunday afternoon I drove Paul and Silas out to the old Sampson acreage. Paul was anxious to see the place again after the tornado leveled the farm and barn.

Silas had a nice run of the land, even taking a dip in the cattle pond. Paul and I walked the grounds. We envisioned together the future Boys' Ranch. Paul was very pleased with the way the Circle of Care was investing Mrs. Fullbright's endowment.

"Timothy, I want you to stay involved with everything the Circle of Care does here at Corinthia Falls. Here you have a model of how small communities and towns should operate. Developing other Circle of Cares throughout the world depends on your ability to organize and encourage.

"As the future administrator of the Grace in Fellowship Association, you will have struggles and challenges. When you come home from college to visit, listen to your people's difficulties and frustrations.

Just like Corinthia Falls, everywhere you go you will be working volunteers in the body of Christ. Remember the Senator's words, 'Those that know how work for those that know why.' Stay focused on the why."

Our QC team resumed practice sessions on Monday just five days before the big competition. We worked out at different times, due to volunteer and work schedules. I joined Becky and the Sampson boys that morning to see how things were going at the marina.

Becky was very dedicated and up to the task, as were Sam and Sandy in assisting her. She looked cute in her one piece suit with eye goggles on and her red hair gathered back in a pony tail reminiscent of her tomboy days.

By now Becky was able to locate the underwater cable without the use of the boat. She could dive into the lake from the marina dock and position herself over the old ferry cable. Taking a deep breath she would find the cable and pull herself along.

It was the first time she would attempt to cross the half mile lake. Sam, Sandy, and I escorted her across the lake in the Solomon family ski boat. Sherry cheered her on from the dock.

We could track her progress from bubbles reaching the surface. Sam was prepared to go in after her if there were any problems. Sandy used a stop watch to keep track of her time.

As planned, Becky only came up for air five times which was quite remarkable. She managed to pull herself through the lake underwater in just over seventeen minutes. This was just two minutes slower than the faster swimmers could make it across Lake Corinth.

When we helped Becky into the boat after completing the swim, she was entirely exhausted and very cold. She reminded us that the water temperature at fifteen feet below was much colder than the surface.

Sandy anchored the boat at the bottom of Rock Hill where the swimming competition would end and the animal and rider leg of the relay began. The Colonel, Silas and a frustrated Ant had just arrived to take another shot at the hill.

Paul's cheeseburger award idea was working well, but Silas could not figure out that Ant must stay aboard. The Colonel stood at the top of Rock Hill. Yelling at us with his hands cupped around his mouth, he announced, "We're going to try something different."

"Great!" said Ant, waiting with us at the bottom of the hill with Silas.

Ant was prepared with elbow and knee pads. Silas was eager for lunch. Ant mounted Silas and clutched on the new leather collar with hand grips Paul had designed.

Before Paul gave the shout to begin, he held up what looked to be two of Oak's Corner cheeseburgers. This made Silas just more excited and ready to go.

At Paul's command, they were off. Silas headed straight up the steep and rocky hill. Ant sat far back on Silas' torso. He stretched his small body out, streamlining his body atop Silas, using the new collar for balance.

The boys and I cheered them on. We could hear Sherry doing the same from across the lake. All was going well till Ant took a tumble two-thirds of the way up. It was close but yet so far.

Silas kept on going riderless to the top of the hill. When he got there Paul did not reward him. Instead, he tossed one cheeseburger down the hill to Ant.

"Now eat it and make sure Silas can see you doing it."

Ant brushed himself off, pulled the wax paper wrapper off the cheeseburger and began eating. Ant used exaggerated sounds and gestures. Silas stood atop the hill and drooled.

It took a good half hour to get both dog and rider back to the bottom of the hill for another try. Again, Paul waved two cheeseburgers for Silas to see. Again, they began the near vertical ascent.

Paul knew Silas well. I don't know what clicked inside the big bear-dog's head, but somehow he got it. Ant's ride was smoother as Silas slowed down and was more deliberate. When they reached the spot of the previous mishap, Silas came to a stop, giving Ant time to readjust.

For the first time in many attempts, both dog and rider made it to the top together. The boys and I and even Becky exchanged high-fives in the boat with Sherry screaming her appreciation from across the lake, Ant went into his Rocky Balboa impersonation thrusting his fists in the air. Silas got his one-burger reward.

"Did you get a clock on that?" I asked Sandy enthused.

"One minute and thirty-seven seconds flat!"

"Yes!" cried Sam, clenching both fists.

At lunch I met up with Doc and TJ at the store. TJ was working the morning shift so he could work under Doc's instruction in the after-hours. Their report was good.

"TJ's taken a few spills into the lake," said Doc. "It happens when some of those smaller projecting rocks break off when he tries to pull himself up."

"Yep, some of the rocks just crack off in my hands," added TJ.

"It's messin' with my style."

"The good thing about it is he now has a trail to follow, knowin' what rocks will support him," said Doc. "That's something we wouldn't be able to discover without that home field advantage. Our reach and pull-up strategy is working so good that TJ might want to change sports."

"Sounds like you've been eating watermelon again, Doctor," said TJ.

Later that afternoon it was my turn to work on the two mile run. John Solomon drove us down to the State Park in his Camaro. After the run we planned to take my pickup to retrieve his car.

The plan was for me to run hard for the next three days, then take off Thursday and Friday to get my legs back under me and be well rested.

John was being a real trooper. As our official relief pitcher, he tried climbing the cliffs with TJ, he swam across the lake several times and now he would run with me.

John was not a bad athlete, but neither was he exceptional. As hard as he tried he could not keep up with me on the run. By the time we crossed the dam at the halfway point, he was a couple city blocks behind.

I remember looking back to check on him. John was struggling and gasping for air. I yelled out encouragement. I didn't see the rock lying on the asphalt highway. My right foot came down squarely on the misplaced stone.

I immediately went down, taking a tumble off the side of the road. I tried to get up but couldn't put any weight on my right foot. The pain I felt in my ankle was not nearly as rough as the pain I felt in my heart. I knew it was a sprain.

I sat with my legs stretched out before me clutching my injury. John soon caught up with me. Bending over and gasping for air,

John examined the situation. He could see the problem just as well as I could feel it.

"Oh man, Timber...dang! Can you walk?"

"Nope."

Fortunately, the barber shop was closed on Mondays. Emmitt Sharp passed by in his car. He stopped as soon as he recognized us. Sam Samuels stepped out of the passenger side. Sam and his new mentor approached John and me with inquisitive reactions.

"What in tarnation, Timber?" said Emmitt scratching his head.

"Messed up ankle," replied John for me.

Sam stood motionless except for the sad shaking of his head.

"Okay, let's help him into the back seat and get him to Doc Pyle's," ordered Emmitt.

The old doctor joined the four of us in the examination room. I was laid out on the table with my naked ankle exposed. As soon as Doc saw the swelling, he let go with some cursing that would make a sailor blush.

It was not a major injury; a grade one ankle sprain. But the hopes of competing in the Quanapah Challenge and bringing a championship to Corinthia Falls were fading. Obviously, I felt like I had let everyone down.

"How long, Doc?" asked Emmitt.

It was only five days till the QC. We all knew what he was asking.

"Usually a sprain of this type takes a good week or so. I got some crutches you can use, but I would prefer you to lie on the couch. Put no weight on it at all. Ice it down for thirty minutes every four hours."

Doc sat down in his swivel chair. He sighed and looked at me sternly.

"Timber, there's no way you'll be able to run by Saturday."

Emmitt and Sam turned away, moaning in unison.

"I'll do the best I can, dude. But I'm a lot slower than you on that run," said John, discouraged.

"But Doc, is there any possible way?" asked Sam trying to spark some hope.

Doc just simply shook his head.

"Not in any type of medicine I practice."

Bad news spreads quickly through a small town. The gang joined me at our house that evening as I lay on my mother's couch in the living room with my right foot elevated.

Becky sat next to me trying to console. Ant and the Samuel boys spent most of the time pacing the floor. Sherry tried her best to lift our spirits to no avail. TJ sat in the easy chair and pouted.

The Colonel and Silas showed up after Paul got the news. While Silas licked on my ice-packed ankle, Paul suggested prayer.

"I'll pray alright!" announced TJ in a scorn voice.

"Dear Lord, we have a swimmer afraid of the water, a dog with a bullet lodged in his chest and a runner on crutches. Please grant us healing! Amen."

The Quanapah Challenge

I woke up Saturday morning the day of the Challenge to the sound of Silas munching on a frozen bag of corn that my mother had placed on my ankle before my parents left earlier to open the store. I could smell the breakfast being prepared in the kitchen.

The night before was spent on the couch with the window open just enough to hear the sounds of music coming from downtown. A concert of local bands and music groups performed on the stage in front of the Gentlemen's Club for those gathering for the QC. I heard rock and roll, gospel, and bluegrass. Benny and our local band even tried a little CCR. That was a nice touch.

The swelling on my ankle had gone down. As Silas came to my bed to greet me, I sat upright on the side of my bed. I put my hands on top of his back for leverage to raise myself up. I walked to the kitchen in my boxer shorts to see who was cooking. It was the first time I'd walked on my own in five days.

"I got us some breakfast going," said Paul.

I was stunned to see the man in black dressed in a baby-blue golf shirt with the dove embroidered over the pocket, white slacks and white tennis shoes.

"You going for a new look?" I asked, sitting down at the kitchen table.

"The whole town is, Tim."

The Colonel carried two plates of buckwheat pancakes and sausage links to the table. A pitcher of fresh squeezed orange juice and a carafe of maple syrup were set before us. Silas leaned his head over the table to examine the homemade meal.

Paul offered a short blessing. Then we sat quietly enjoying our breakfast. We left just enough for Silas to finish off.

"It's going to be a big day," said Paul.

I could hear just the hint of a question in his voice. I knew where this was leading.

"Paul, I can walk. At least I made it this far on my own."

"Let's try it out a little more," suggested Paul.

I got up from the table and followed Paul gingerly into the living room. On the couch was laid out a pair of white gym shorts and a light blue tank top jersey with Saints across the chest. Placed across the uniform was the Moses' rod golf club, Destiny.

"Coach Apollos is here?"

"And so is Coach Aquila. They spent last night with us at the Club. George said the old eight iron makes a good walking cane. Whether you run or not, might as well dress for the occasion. We're going to have to get going. It's almost 8:30 and this thing starts at 11:00."

I shook my head in agreement. I was well aware of the time. I picked up Destiny and examined it once again. As I walked around the living room floor testing the ankle, I used the golf club as a crutch, holding the head of the Moses' rod in my hand.

"So far, so good!" cheered Paul.

"So far…" I repeated.

"Timothy, listen to me. You have a big decision to make regarding whether to compete or not. You are the captain of this team and its inspiration. As a leader, you will be faced with many more difficult choices in the future.

Sometimes we need to back off a little. We get so close to the problem that it's hard to come to a conclusion. We have to remove ourselves temporarily from the equation and weigh the long term results."

I studied Paul's words as he handed me the clothes from the couch.

"It's not about me—it's about the team?"

"And the final effect on that team or mission no matter the outcome," said Paul.

"So, I should just let John run in my place?"

"That's up to you," continued Paul. "John's a good soldier, but he is not an athlete the caliber of Timothy Oaks. John will give you his best, but it will cost you valuable time.

"You have an excellent game plan. If the team puts John in a position to win and he fails, he will blame himself. That could affect him for a long time. If you run and fail, it will be because of a freak injury."

"Time to suit up, Tim. We'll talk some more on our way to town. We're going to have to make a walk of it. There are no parking places left."

Paul, Silas and I walked through the neighborhood toward town. A pair of army issued field glasses hung from the Colonel's neck. The front lawns were all adorned with small yard signs supporting the Saints. I was gaining more confidence in my ankle but I kept old Destiny handy.

The late May weather was typical for eastern Oklahoma. The temperature would be rising to the low 80s with a slight chance of rain for late in the afternoon. These conditions would not affect the QC.

Main Street from Oak's Corner to the school turn-off had been closed down. The downtown area was filled with food and souvenir vendors. A swelling of spectators gathered in the streets and sidewalks. Network cameras, reporters and even local politicians were working the crowd while patriotic music played loudly over the public address system from the stage at the Gentlemen's Club.

Our first stop was at the store. Oak's Corner's driveway was roped off till after the competition but that did not stop the walk-in traffic. It was nearly elbow to elbow in the store while the lake holiday traffic merged with QC attenders and competitors.

Oak's Corner was Team Corinthia headquarters. TJ and Ant, dressed in their baby-blue jerseys and white shorts, helped Cy and Joyce at the front counter. Becky was busy in the deli helping Mom and Ms. Martha prepare and distribute as many cheeseburgers and fries as possible.

The local town people cheered as I walked in with Paul and Silas.

"Timber! Look, he's ready to go. Yes!"

I was somewhat taken aback and not quite ready for the reception. Those unfamiliar with the town and me looked on curiously.

"I told ya he'd make it!" shouted TJ over the noisy crowd of customers.

We made it to the deli area. Coach Apollos and Coach Aquila were seated in the back booth with Emmit and Sam Samuels. The three had Sam's total concentration as they shared war stories. All four stood almost at attention as the Colonel joined them.

Becky made eye contact with me from behind the deli counter with a questioning smile. She was dressed in the same shorts and jersey as the rest of us barely revealing a one-piece baby-blue swimsuit underneath. I returned a grin.

"Timber! I see you've got Destiny in your hands!" said Coach Apollos, the fireplug of a golf coach.

I shook hands and greeted both coaches.

"I'll let you have this back now, coach. I think I can get around without it."

George Apollos reached up and put his hand on my shoulder while taking back the golf club.

"Son, you can never abandon destiny, but I'll hold on to the eight iron."

John Solomon came charging through the crowded market to the back of the store followed by Doc Pyle. John was anxious and dressed out to run. Doc wore a bright yellow open-collar shirt worn by all the judges to make them easy to identify.

"So, what do ya think?" asked John, nervous and uneasy.

I looked over at Doc who had his eye on my ankle. I lifted up my right foot and swung it around a couple times. I almost felt like apologizing to John.

"If it's alright with you, I'd like to give it a try."

"Alright with me? You bet it's alright!" replied John joyfully.

"Let's take a look at that ankle," said Doc dryly.

I could see Doc wasn't in favor of all this. I removed my shoe and sock and set my foot on the bench of the deli booth while Paul, Sam, the coaches and the others looked on anxiously. Doc felt the ankle and made a shrug of futility.

"Just because the swelling went down doesn't mean you're cured. When you go to running you'll find that out. We'll have some crutches waiting for you. You might end up crawling to the finish line."

My parents had nudged their way forward and heard Doc's stern words. My mother was worried. I searched both their faces for encouragement. I assured Mom that I would be fine, though I did not know if I would.

Doc reached into his baggy pants pocket and pulled out an

Ace bandage. He securely wrapped the ankle while the others watched.

"I figured it would come to this," muttered Doc. "It's time you kids get going. It's just an hour and a half till race time."

Becky held hands with me as we all walked together down the street: Ant and Silas, TJ, the two college coaches, the Colonel who was toting a bag of cheeseburgers, along with the Samuel brothers and John. We headed for the final registration at the Club.

As the local folks yelled out words of support, we heard the shouting of a familiar attractive blond reporter trying to catch up with us.

"Timber, Thomas, wait up!"

It was the same young lady that interviewed TJ and me in Mr. Cox's office the previous winter: Priscilla Luke. It was obvious that, like the rest of the media, she was trying to get a storyline on the QC.

"Ms. Luke," said TJ always eager for a headline, "I guess you can't get enough of this place."

TJ continued to flatter Priscilla while introducing her to our group. The aggressive young journalist handed out business cards to Coach Aquila and Coach Apollos as well as to Paul.

"Boys, your story is the hottest item going around here," said Priscilla as she walked with us, switching on her miniature tape recorder.

"Boys and girl and dog," I corrected pointing out Silas and Becky.

"Okay then, now as I understand it, Timber you are running, TJ is climbing and Becky is swimming?"

"And Ant is riding Silas," I added.

"Isn't this the dog that became the hometown hero last Christmas?"

"Yep," answered TJ, "still got the bullet in his chest."

"Do you think you can pull this off? There are lots of talented athletes involved and Timber, I hear you are injured?" she said, glancing down at my wrapped ankle.

"Well, we have home field advantage. Check with us after the race," I suggested.

"Mmhm, when we're hoisting that big trophy up there," said TJ confidently pointing at the large first place prize resting on a stand atop the Gentlemen's Club outdoor stage.

"I'll do that. Good luck!"

Naturally, Benny Larson was the announcer and voice for the Quanapah Challenge, not to mention one of the biggest advertisers along with Coca-Cola, Pepsi and the Archer's Grove Bank.

The backside of the stage was laced with advertisements for Larson Motors and Pawn. Two large screen televisions sat at opposite corners of the decking facing the street to provide live coverage of the QC from ABC Sports. Inside the Gentlemen's Club the network had set up the main control.

While we were checking in at the registration, Benny approached the standing microphone.

"Last call for all teams to register. All team members and animals must be at their locations by ten fifteen."

Benny then went into a string of commercials for local businesses, adding his gift of persuasion and salesmanship to each one. He then reminded everyone to get their Quanapah t-shirts and souvenirs from the young men of the Gentlemen's Club operating their booth in front of the barbershop.

"I need to take that guy with me on a recruiting trip," commented Coach Aquila.

We were the last of the thirty teams registered to check in.

Postmaster Chester and Mr. Hummingbird handled the registration booth.

"Looks like we've got a formal protest here," said Chet.

"Seems last year's champs, Arkansas U., think Silas is a bear, which is against the rules."

Chet handed the official written complaint to Paul.

"I figured that might happen," said Paul. "This is Silas's breed and registration papers from the state of South Carolina, along with dog tags from five states."

"Works for me!" said Chet as we all breathed a sigh of relief. "Becky, you need to catch a ride in that red van heading for the marina with a load of swimmers. The rest of you take that one over there to the State Park."

"Is it okay for some of the rest of us to tag along?" asked Paul.

"One escort per competitor," Chet informed us. "And good luck kids!"

It was decided that Sandy would accompany Becky to get her lined up at the marina dock. Paul would be with Silas and Ant, cheeseburgers and all. Our future college coaches teamed up with TJ and me.

We gathered in a small huddle together in the middle of Main Street for some last minute inspiration and prayer. Before we could bow our heads we were interrupted by the emotional clamor coming from Sherry Solomon and her two little baton-twirling girl friends.

Sherry dressed in the same white shorts and blue jersey top as the rest of the Saints and waving her baby-blue and white pompoms, ran out to greet us followed by the little girls looping their wands in the air. Together, they performed a planned routine.

"We are the Saints,
White and baby-blue!

We're ready to win,

How about you?"

Sherry finally got to be the head cheerleader as she'd always dreamed. She played the part perfectly and had the young twirlers in synch. As they finished, all three of the cheering group ran and hugged Becky.

TJ adjusted his sunglasses, noting how well Sherry fit in her jersey and shorts. A quick elbow in the ribs from Paul recaptured his attention.

Our huddle of prayer grew as the girls and others dressed in our school colors joined us. With Silas on a leash held by Ant in the middle of our circle, Paul suggested Coach Aquila was more accustomed to praying before competitions. Coach delivered.

"Father of mercy and grace,

We know that for those of us that are in Christ Jesus, you have no condemnation. You have freed us and through that freedom we have nothing to fear; we have nothing to lose. Grant us this day the joy of competition, knowing that through you all things are possible!

Amen."

I watched Becky walk toward the van with Sandy. She looked over her shoulder at me all the way to her ride. It was the look of hope. It was the look of love.

Shortly after we started our two-mile trip to the State Park, Coach Apollos asked to be dropped off before we even got to the dam. I was confused but knew he had his reasons. Coach still carried his eight iron.

"Timber, Destiny and I will wait here."

The Corinth State Park was filled with lake goers lining up to get in on the action and empty horse trailers that had been filled with mules, donkeys, horses and one longhorn steer from the

Dallas Athletic Club.

With Silas in his new hand grip collar, Ant led him down the side path from the park to the base of Rock Hill. The other livestock was already gathered there, still unmounted, by what looked to be mostly small, professional type riders.

Using Paul's binoculars from the edge of the State Park overlook, we could see across the lake to Boulder Ridge Marina where the race would begin. I spotted Becky in her baby-blue swimsuit being assisted by Sandy.

Coach Aquilla, with his stop watch in hand, stood together with Paul and me. TJ, still in his sunglasses, made his way down the old road on our left that led to the climbers starting spot on Eagle Bluff. Needless to say, TJ looked very out of place, as did Becky, Ant and Silas.

From our vantage point where the running part of the relay would begin, we could witness the first three stages of the Quanapah Challenge. Spectators crowded near the overlook viewing area. Network camera operators were in position on the lake and the marina as well as under the hill and the cliffs and all along the route.

Teams made up of swimmers, riders, climbers and runners in matching colors represented major universities like Arkansas, Oklahoma, Oklahoma State and Missouri. Smaller colleges throughout the area were represented as were several athletic clubs and gyms and one bar from Muskogee.

They came from as far away as south Texas and Alabama and from Kansas to Colorado, each possessing uniquely skilled athletes and beasts—each team desiring the title of Champion of the Quanapah Challenge.

The talented, world class distance runners had gathered just several yards away from us at the top of Eagle Bluff where they would await the tag from the climbers. Each athlete went into a special session of stretching and preparation with which I was not familiar.

"Might as well join them, Tim," suggested Paul. "But be careful. Some of those exercises look kind of tricky. Jorell and I will keep an eye on things."

I felt good and ready as ever to run. I stretched out next to the other runners trying not to be intimidated by their thin, flexible bodies shaped perfectly for distance running.

The runner next to me stretched his calves. "Hey, school boy!" he said in very proper English diction. "You look a little overdeveloped for running. Pick up a scholarship anywhere?"

I recognized the very popular and talented Kiano Omondi, African born distance runner for Arkansas and record holder in the 5000 meters.

"Tulsa," I replied.

"Tulsa doesn't have a track team." He laughed.

"No," I agreed, "but, Kiano, you ought to check out the debating team."

As the time grew nearer to the start of the QC, the sound of the loud speakers coming from the campgrounds featured the audio of the live broadcast.

"Spanning the globe to bring you the constant variety of sport... the thrill of victory... and the agony of defeat... the human drama of athletic competition... This is *ABC's Wide World of Sports!*"

The voice of the famous sports announcer, Jim McKay, broadcasted to the nation from the stage in front of the Gentlemen's Club in Corinthia Falls, Oklahoma.

McKay's introduction continued with the background of the race and the legend of Chief Quanapah. He talked about the

272 ∽ KIM HUTSON

history of the Quanapah Challenge and of Corinthia Falls. He pointed out the diversity in the skilled athletes and animals. He discussed the layout of Lake Corinth and the course. He then concluded.

"And this year for the first time in the history of the Quanapah Challenge, the host town of Corinthia Falls has entered their own team. A group of underdogs and an actual dog take on the best in the world at the Quanapah Challenge!"

Lake Corinth was marked off with a series of buoys on either side of the swimmers' path across the half mile stretch of slightly rippling water. Boats filled with camera people, judges and life guards idled just outside the marks.

The local lake patrol trolled just outside the navigational buoys, protecting the participants from any unaware or wayward vessels. A paramedic unit floated near the middle of the lake prepared for any emergency.

I rejoined Paul and Coach Aquila, anxiously awaiting the start of the QC. The Colonel went into his military mode, taking charge of the situation.

"Timothy, one last look then I want you to be as calm as possible. You don't want to run your race before you even begin it."

Through Paul's binoculars I could see the race about to begin as the swimmers took their positions on the edge of the dock just in front of the gas pumps of the Boulder Ridge Marina. They were mostly young men with shaven or low cropped hair. The few ladies involved wore tight fitting swimming caps. All looked experienced with lean bodies molded for their sport.

And then there was Becky. She was much smaller than the males and even the other girls. Her auburn hair contrasted her light blue swimsuit. She wore eye goggles similar to the other swimmers.

As the competitors crouched next to each other in a diving position with toes overhanging the wooden dock, Becky was alone on the south side, aiming for the hidden cable five yards below the water. She looked beautiful as she concentrated on her mission.

The sound of a ship's bell could be heard across the lake. The water athletes formed one big splash as they dove into the sparkling water of Lake Corinth. Bunched together, they resembled torpedoes kicking up white water, heading for the same determined destination.

Becky dove deep under the water in search of the ferry cable. Jorell started his stop watch as I handed the binoculars back to Paul.

The spectators lining the overlook cheered for their favorite teams. The three of us were oblivious to McKay's commentating of the race except for the mention that Becky Hooper from Corinthia Falls was apparently swimming underwater.

Minutes went by as the swimmers come to about the one-third phase of the swim, still all clustered together. There was no sign of Becky who had yet to surface for air.

"How long she been under, coach?" I asked, as Jorell looked on intently.

"My gosh, it's almost been four and a half minutes!" said the worried basketball coach.

Concern about Becky's wellbeing was evident from the officials monitoring the waters. It was also heard in McKay's apprehensive voice. Pointed to a spot by the skipper of the paramedic boat, two lifeguard types dived into the lake on a rescue mission.

I was confident in Becky and figured she was farther along than what they expected, but I knew it was past time for her to surface.

"That's five minutes!" cried out Jorell.

"Becks!" I exclaimed, pointing to the little redhead piercing the surface of the water just to the left and slightly behind the throng of her competition.

The crowd around us let go with a sigh of relief and began to cheer.

"Girl has a set of lungs!" said the admiring coach, as Paul rested his binoculars on his chest and began to applaud.

Becky treaded water while she caught her breath. Replenished with air, she resumed her underwater pull and thrust on the old cable.

Down below us, the equine teams were mounting and posturing for position. A lot of room was given to the steer that looked determined to charge the hill with or without a rider. Ant kept Silas on leash as the big dog kept his eyes on his master atop the hill and he had surely resolved not to let anyone beat him to his prize.

As the swimmers reached the halfway point across the lake, first to last was only separated by ten yards. Becky again resurfaced, another twenty yards back. Catching her breath, she dove down for more.

Coach Aquila again checked his stop watch and estimated Becky was fading and would probably come in at least a couple minutes behind.

"That's good enough," said Paul.

I agreed. All was going according to plan. The first swimmer hit the rocky beach in a record time of 14 minutes and 46 seconds. The freestyle swimmer from the Arkansas Razorbacks ran through the last several feet of water and tagged the jockey of the team mule.

The other exhausted swimmers followed in turn. The Quanapah Challenge had reached the second phase: the race up

Rock Hill. The team from Dallas was in the middle of the pack.

The restless longhorn steer bulled his way straight up the rocky hill through the cascading livestock, shocking the other animals. In all the confusion the steer threw the cowboy trying desperately to hold on. As cowboy and steer headed back to the beach to start over, disorder continued.

Frustrated horses, mules and donkeys objected to the steer. Several animals lost their mounts and also had to start over. Silas and Ant would have to be patient to avoid the near-stampede.

Becky rose up from the lake about fifty yards out. Too worn out from the vigorous swim to catch her breath, she swam the rest of the way on top of the water. Dragging herself to the shoreline and avoiding barnyard obstacles, she tagged Ant.

"Just over seventeen minutes," announced Coach.

Ant was straddling Silas with one foot touching the ground. He was doing his best to restrain the huge dog from attacking their chosen and well rehearsed practice pathway till they could find their path through the quagmire of livestock.

By then Silas was almost foaming at the mouth. When the course of choice was clear, the Colonel and Ant yelled in unison.

"Now!"

Ant steadied Silas using the hand grips on his collar. As Silas and Ant charged Rock Hill, the loudspeakers in the park announced that Corinthia Falls had taken the lead. Once again, Silas and his little rider readjusted halfway up and continued the attack.

"Come on, big boy!" shouted Paul.

"Hometown hero!" echoed Coach.

"Home field advantage," I cried out.

After the duo of boy and dog reached the hill's crest, Silas ran straight for Paul and his cheeseburger. The official in charge cleared Ant to dismount which allowed him to run on his own down the road to the bottom of Eagle Bluff to tag TJ.

The crowd from all around the park was now cheering for Corinthia Falls. We had home field advantage and now home field support.

"Were counting on that two minute advantage we'll need for your run, Tim!" shouted Paul while fending off Silas and motioning for me to get into position for my run.

From where I stood, I could not see TJ. I did see his pair of designer sunglasses go flying out into the lake.

I hurried over to the starting area for the run. As I watched the Arkansas mule and rider make it to the top of the hill followed closely by several other tandems, I had to rely on Jim McKay's description of the Eagle Bluff climb.

"This is young Thomas Johnson trying to maintain the lead for the hometown favorite, Corinthia Falls. Thomas will be starting his college career next year playing basketball for the University of Georgia Bulldogs. Not an experienced climber, Thomas is using a leaping technique chinning himself up from cliff to cliff.

"Oh no! Thomas just lost his grip. He's now sliding about twenty feet downhill and into Lake Corinth. Let's see if Thomas can regroup. He looks scraped up.

"He's digging in now and resuming his plan of leaping and pulling himself to the top of Eagle Bluff where his teammate Timothy Oaks awaits his tag to start the two mile run to downtown Corinthia Falls."

I felt my heart pounding in my chest as adrenaline took over. I had no thoughts of a bad ankle. I just wanted to see TJ's grinning face come over that last cliff and give me a tag. McKay continued:

"Other climbers, much more experienced than Thomas are

now starting their ascent of Eagle Bluff led by Arkansas and followed closely by Missouri University. The skillful surges of mountain climbers are making up valuable time on Thomas and Corinthia Falls."

The sounds of the speaker system faded from my mind. The cheering for Team Corinthia had drowned out the voice of Jim McKay. I waited anxiously, standing in the midst of big time distance runners for TJ to appear.

In the near distance I spotted Paul and Jorell. From their angle they could see most of Eagle Bluffs. The coach was watching his stop watch while shouting out support to his future pupil and appeared to be giving another time estimate to the Colonel. Paul cupped his hands to his mouth and yelled at me over the noise.

"Timothy! We are going to need a nine minute and thirty second run!"

I knew what that meant. Our lead was down to around one minute. I had done the research. I would have to run two miles in what would be an unofficial Oklahoma high school record.

I thought of how close we were. I thought of my teammates and friends and the effort they had given to fulfill my vision of a championship for Corinthia Falls. I thought about Becky. I thought about our church and prayed for one more miracle.

The crowded Corinth State Park erupted as a large dark, bloodied hand emerged over the large boulder at the top of Eagle Cliff. TJ let out a violent groan, pulling his weakened body to the top.

His jersey was torn open and shredded. His chest and knees were bleeding and bruised.

As I stood reaching out my hand for his tag from just behind the starting line, he limped over with his last ounce of strength. As he collapsed to his knees, we touched hands.

"Finish it, Timber!"

Although this was a two-mile race, I took off in a near sprint, having little ability to pace myself with one of the world's greatest runners chasing after me. The road to the highway that meandered and wound through the State Park was lined with spectators calling out for Corinthia Falls.

As I ran through the entrance gates of the park heading onto the highway, I could see off to my side in the distance Kiano beginning his chase in his red and white uniform after tagging the Arkansas climber.

From the starting point to the park entrance was just over a quarter mile. That made Paul and Coach Aquila's estimate of a one minute lead a little generous.

The slightly downhill one mile trek to the Lake Corinth Dam was starting to put some pressure on my bad ankle. I could feel the beginning of some pain in my right calf. A small convertible sports car with a mounted camera filmed the race, staying just a short distance in front of me.

I could almost feel the crowd of milling people on both sides of the highway as some even reached out to touch me and the lead camera car. I knew it was the fastest I had ever run. The pain up my leg increased sharply.

I knew better than to look back but could not resist when I got to the half-mile long dam that had been kept clear of spectators. I looked over my shoulder to see Kiano effortlessly gaining on me, less than 300 yards back and closing fast.

I felt myself slowing down. Between fatigue and the overwhelming pain from ankle to waist, I began to doubt. I tried to block out the stinging of each step as I continued across the dam, concentrating on victory.

As I plodded my way to the end of the dam, I could see the

sides of the highway which was also Main Street, lined with cheering people for the final quarter mile. Not far away was the fanatic QC crowd that bulged over the sidewalks of Corinthia Falls.

I could hear the speakers announcing from the Gentlemen's Club that Timber Oaks of Corinthia Falls led Kiano Omondi of Arkansas by 200 yards. I could see the finish line; a large blue ribbon stretched across Main Street, parallel to the stage. I could sense the excitement and the hope of another Corinthia Falls miracle.

With the dam well behind me, I was still fighting back the pain. The next thing I knew I was lying on my side upon the hot Oklahoma asphalt. The desire of the spirit gave way to the limitation of the flesh. My ankle just gave out.

The cheering sounds of the crowd faded in to one massive sigh; onedeep groan of despair. I tried to recover. Pushing myself up, I could only stand on my left leg. I looked back to see Kiano crossing the dam.

"It's about destiny, Timber!"

There he was standing next to me on the shoulder of the highway: Coach Crazy George Apollos. He was right where we let him off the bus. With the golf club still in his hand and using it as a pointer for emphasis, my future drill sergeant of a golf coach began to evangelize.

"Just look up there at that town! You have nothing to lose. Destiny awaits you!"

I looked through the pouring sweat in the direction Coach pointed with the Moses Rod. There was my home town and the finish line just two city blocks away.

"Son! You Can Achieve…"

I steadied myself on both feet as I joined Coach, reciting the inspirational words of Colonel.

"…Anything with the Power of Christ!"

I started out hopping on my left leg and then began gingerly putting my other foot down. With my arms balancing my crippled body, I erased the pain and concentrated on my goal.

The familiar faces of town folks were coming into focus, encouraging me with their hand gestures yelling at the top of their lungs while others were folding hands as if in prayer. As I started to pick up my pace, I could see the Deacon lead Ms. Martha to the open microphone stand on the Gentlemen's Club stage.

Ms. Martha appeared worried while the Deacon placed one hand across her back, offering support. Her deep and striking voice resonated throughout Main Street and Corinthia Falls. She slowly and deliberately began to sing.

"Oh – when – the – Saints, Go Marchin' in…"

The Deacon stood next to her waving both hands above his head urging the crowd to join in the sing-a-long as Sherry, Sam and Benny climbed on the stage to lend their voices.

"Oh – when - the – Saints Go Marchin' in…"

I pounded the pavement to the beat of the song with my good leg while dragging my right foot and picking up my pace. Coach Apollos ran beside me just off the road pointing, no, almost gouging me, with the old eight iron.

"Find your Destiny, Timber Oaks!" barked Coach.

"Lord – I – want – to – be –in that number…" continued the chorus.

What sounded like all of Corinthia Falls accompanied by a heavenly choir began to sing louder and louder, picking up the tempo with each line of our town's hymn. My hobble went from jog to trot from run to dash.

"When the Saints go Marchin' in!"

Just a block away from destiny, the singing became so

loud that even the famous sports announcer's broadcasting voice became muffled by the hysterical voices influencing my determination.

It's a peculiar gift that God gave the world with time. Time… the measuring rod for our lives. Often time moves so quickly and then it can move so slowly. Although time is constant and unvarying, it has a way of stopping long enough to print images on our souls—a snap shot for eternity.

So was that frozen moment when my hands outreached Kiano's, breaking the finishing line ribbon and falling into my father's outstretched arms. A jubilant cheer burst from the crowd, mixed with thunderous applause that must have been joined by a host of angel wings.

The celebrating throng lifted me onto the stage. Though I could hardly stand and would not walk on my own again for three weeks, there was no need for crutches that day. The arms of the town's support crowding the stage sufficed.

I can barely remember the interview with Mr. McKay. Overwhelming joy filled my mind and spirit as cameras flashed and questions were asked. I thanked God for making all things possible.

By the time Priscilla Luke pushed her way through the mob, attempting her interview, my teammates had joined me. Becky, TJ and I rode on the shoulders of our community. Ant mounted Silas for a victory lap while hoisting the Quanapah Challenge trophy.

With the visiting spectators beginning to disperse back to the lake to resume their weekend of recreation, the town folks paraded us down Main Street, carrying us to the water tower just outside town. The celebration went on there till dark. Somehow, the old rusty tower looked more respectful. It must have been the new freshly painted sign:

Home of the Quanapah Challenge
1982 Champions
The Corinthia Falls Saints!

Thirty Years Later

Priscilla's Story

"On the green light, Ms. Luke," instructed the young camera man filming my wrap up of the Lone Star Open with the back drop of the eighteenth hole and the historic club house.

"One, two, three and we're rolling…"

"It was another flawless performance for the world's number one rated golfer, Maleko Kalani, here in Austin at the Lone Star Open. The thirty year-old Island Liona, finished six strokes ahead of the field carding a sixty-five in today's final round to come in at seventeen under par.

This weekend's warm up for next week's PGA Championship to be held in Tulsa left the fashionable Hawaiian as front runner and favorite to complete golf's legendary grand slam after already winning the Masters, U.S and British Open earlier this summer.

"Timber Oaks, still looking for his first tour victory in his over twenty year career thrilled the gallery at Austin, finishing fourth coming in at nine under. The forty-eight year-old Oaks, part time golfer and full time Christian missionary, has been playing the best golf of his career as he heads back to Tulsa to play his home course, Whispering Waters, host of the 2012 PGA.

"So next week it will be interesting to see how the world's best golfer in pursuit of history matches up against what may be the world's most popular never to win.

From Austin for the United Sports Network, Priscilla Luke reporting."

I have always covered sports. Since my early days in Oklahoma as a beat reporter till working for USN, I have tried to show and tell the story beneath the story—the personal side of the athlete and the struggle.

I have gone from journalist to side line babe, from syndication to national network, from obscure to infamous. I have reported from locker rooms, interviewed the loved and the notorious, graced magazine covers and even danced with the Stars.

My zeal for career cost me a marriage in the beginning. Now fifty-two, still naturally blond and happily married for almost twenty years, I am about to cover the story that I have pursued for so long.

I first met Timothy 'Timber' Oaks in Corinthia Falls, Oklahoma along with his friend TJ, now known better as Tom Johnson, the coach of last year's NCAA's National Championship Men's Basketball team, the Georgia Bulldogs.

The story behind their lakeside town was as remarkable as it was miraculous: a town without an athletic team that produced a professional golfer and humanitarian, as well as an NBA player and college coach. It is the story of a community and a legendary apostle that established a foundation for one of the world's great Christian ministries, the Circle of Care.

Tomorrow, I am off to Tulsa as the guest of Timber and Becky Oaks. I will have full access to my friend and, I must add, mentor.

You will hear the story beneath the story: the struggle, the family, the ministry and, of course, the golf of Timber Oaks.

The short Monday afternoon plane ride from Austin to Tulsa gives me time to reflect on the life and times of Timber and Becky Oaks: their life, their times and their ministry. I open my laptop to my traditional starting page on the web, Faith Fellowship's Circle of Care.

The intricate website allows churches and individuals a vast network of communication and information regarding the activities of one of the most recognized and successful Christian ministries in the world today.

Over on the right side of the home page is listed the Board of Directors of the Executive Committee.

Col. Pavlos Lincoln Armstrong, Founder
Timothy Oaks – Chairman - Broken Arrow, Oklahoma
Thomas Johnson - Athens, Georgia
Dr. Anthony Bearkiller - St. Louis, Missouri
Jorell Aquila – Dallas, Texas

I remember the first time I met Jorell covering the Quanapah Challenge in Corinthia Falls long ago. Our acquaintance was brief because of all the drama that played out on that day. I remembered how handsome and poised was Tom Johnson's tutor and future basketball coach.

I always followed TJ's athletic career from Corinthia Falls, to the Georgia Bulldog's basketball, then on to a three year stint with the New York Knicks and on into coaching. It was on a trip to Athens to do a story on TJ that Jorell granted me an interview.

The assistant coach was very engaging and sincere.

During TJ's senior year at Georgia, Jorell became head coach. TJ went on to become an All-American while Jorell remained coaching the Bulldogs through the 1992 season.

Our paths continued to cross. Jorell took a job for USN, commentating and covering college basketball in 1993. Shortly thereafter, his wife died in a car accident, leaving him with two children: a daughter, Jalissa, and a son, Jorell Jr.

We started dating whenever our schedules permitted. I fell in love with Jorell's children first, then with him. We have been married since 1994 and live in Dallas, locating us close to the USN headquarters where we both are employed.

I have two beautiful grown stepchildren that do not share the color of my skin but we are one in heart. Jorell and I dedicate our time to our three passions; our family, covering sports, and the Circle of Care.

The ever charismatic Thomas Johnson was hired by Jorell as assistant coach at Georgia after his three years in the NBA. Today, TJ still refers to my husband as The Coach. TJ became the head coach of the Bulldogs in the 1993 season after Jorell retired from coaching.

After eighteen years of coaching, TJ, with the help of his old Corinthia Falls protégé, Cyrene, put together a team that won last year's NCAA Championship in Denver, defeating the University of Kansas in the Finals.

It was hard for Jorell to do the color commentary for USN, broadcasting to an international audience while keeping his emotions in check. Timber, Becky, Anthony Bearkiller and I sat with TJ's family and mother, Ms. Martha, during the Final Four tournament.

Who could ever forget the end of the game celebration and

interview at mid-court, with Jorell hugging his one-time pupil and successor while TJ thanked his mentor? With tears rolling down his cheeks, TJ also expressed gratitude to his best friend, Timber Oaks, and his late father, the Deacon.

TJ is active in the Circle of Care, serving along with Jorell and Anthony as directors. He gives motivational speeches and conducts sports clinics focusing on small communities.

I will never forget the small Native American teenager riding up Rock Hill at Lake Corinth on what must have been the world's largest canine. Silas and Anthony made the most auspicious pairing.

Anthony Bearkiller, MD, PhD, FRCS and with a host of other initials following his name graduated from the University of Oklahoma Medical School and went on to study oncology at Chicago University.

Today, as small as Anthony is in stature, he is a giant in the medical community in the diagnosis and treatment of many forms of cancer. His research has led to cutting edge surgical procedures as well as preventive indemnification.

Dr. Bearkiller practices out of Saint James Cancer Institute, located in St. Louis, Missouri. He is married with three children and I understand he has just welcomed a new member to the family, a very rare and huge breed of dog.

Anthony serves as the Circle of Care Director of Medicine, consulting and conducting cancer screening clinics throughout the United States and abroad. He has also worked with the mission creating clinics and rural hospitals that provide primary care.

And then there is Timber and Becky Oaks. Timber played golf for Tulsa University for four years under the direction of the unorthodox George Apollos. Although the golf team never contended for a national championship, Timber was selected as a second team All-American his senior year.

Becky graduated from high school two years after Timber, and she joined him at Tulsa to pursue her teaching degree. They were married the following summer. It was the event of the year for Corinthia Falls.

Anthony and TJ escorted Becky down the aisle. Colonel Armstrong, in what would be his last appearance at Corinthia Falls, served as best man. Sherry Solomon, now better known as Sherry Sands, the daytime talk show host, was the maid of honor. Ms. Martha sang and Deacon Johnson performed the wedding. Once again Silas stole the show, acting as ring bearer.

Timber and Becky lived in a small apartment in south Tulsa. In 1986 Timber finished his education and golf experience at Tulsa with a business degree in marketing and management. This was at the advice of Colonel Armstrong to help give Timber the training for his future position directing the Circle of Care.

Over the next couple of years, Timber qualified for the PGA tour and worked with the Colonel and others on mission trips to small communities promoting the Circle of Care. Becky graduated in 1988 with a degree in education.

Colonel Armstrong kept in close contact with Timber throughout college and beyond. Although they could seldom be together in person, the phone calls and especially the letters kept coming. The letters were lessons in leading and organizing, preparation for life and ministry, testimonial and prophetic writings that formed the apostle's epistles, several personal and some to be shared.

As most of the followers of Pavlos Lincoln Armstrong's ministry know, the Colonel went missing along with his companion Silas on a missionary trip to the Philippines somewhere north of Manila in the summer of 1990.

The Grace in Fellowship movement was stunned but not

disheartened. Following the precise direction and the agenda that the Colonel left in place, Timber was propelled into the leadership of the Circle of Care at the tender age of 26.

Golf was what Timber did for fun and for income, but the Circle of Care ministry is his passion. As the Colonel advised, he quickly surrounded himself with the people he knew and trusted. Through the use of the evolving technology of computers and cellular communications, Timber Oaks led the Circle of Care to a well organized and connected network of churches worldwide that continued to support each other spiritually, physically and financially.

New churches were built. Clinics in deprived areas were established. Communities of faith became stronger. Foster homes and adoption groups were instituted. The hungry were fed and the poor were supported by creating more self efficient and self reliant Christ-based local societies.

With a foundation of faith in Jesus Christ and with missionaries throughout the world, the Circle of Care continues to grow and thrive. The young golfer from Corinthia Falls and his adorable wife continue Colonel Armstrong's vision of connecting small communities and churches throughout the world, providing devotion, optimism and assistance.

Today, the Grace in Fellowship's Circle of Care has become one of the most beloved and recognized ministries around the globe and Timber Oaks, the humble, hand-picked man of God who never attended a seminary or pastored a local church is one of the most respected Christian evangelists of our time.

In 1992 with just enough success on the PGA tour, the Oaks' moved into their current home in Broken Arrow, Oklahoma, a thriving small city just south of Tulsa. The next year, Becky gave birth to their son, Pauly.

Pauly was diagnosed with Autism early in childhood. He was not able to talk till he was almost five. In view of his trouble communicating with others, the Oaks decided to home school Pauly.

It was not that Pauly could not learn—as a matter of fact, far from it. Pauly's disorder is better known as Asperger's syndrome; an obsessive interest in a single subject is a major symptom of AS. Some children with AS have become experts on unique and particular subjects. Their expertise, high level of vocabulary and formal speech patterns make them seem like little professors.

Becky continuously worked with her son and his symptoms: poor communication skills, obsessive or repetitive routines, and physical clumsiness. As Timber often would say, "God just wired him different."

Becky has devoted her knowledge and expertise on Autism, using her teaching skills throughout the Circle of Care. It is estimated that one out of every one hundred children are born with some sort of the disorder that trouble families and can often result in divorce.

Timber continued to play golf. Though never winning an event, he was competitive. It has often been reported by those that cover the game that Timber enjoyed himself too much on the fairways and didn't take golf seriously enough to win big.

And then the whistling began. Timber recalls it started at the 1996 Byron Nelson in Dallas. On the final hole that Sunday, with Timber finishing in the middle of the pack, his second shot approach landed in easy birdie distance on the green.

Feeling carefree and full of joy, Timber mimicked his former mentor, the Colonel. Using a golf club for a baton, he marched and high stepped to the green with the cadence of a drum major while whistling Saints Go Marching In.

What started out as a display of bliss caught on with the

public and turned into what we all know now as a golf tradition. Weekend sports show's highlight the familiar routine of Timber Oak's approach shot on the eighteenth hole on Sundays. Networks covering the tour would see their ratings improve as Timber played the last hole of a tournament.

It is a shared celebration of life and golf. The gallery would whistle and sing Timber's theme song after his approach. Caddies would pull the golf bag in front of their bodies horizontally and pound out a rhythm as if playing a drum while joining in on the march.

Often, Timber's playing partners would join in on the fun while Timber twirled a golf club and entertained the gallery. The carnival atmosphere Timber created and his reputation as a spiritual leader on and off the course along with his history from Corinthia Falls earned him the nickname of 'The Saint'.

Golf has a Golden Bear, a Shark, a Tiger and now an Island Lion and a Saint.

I'm very familiar with Tulsa International. The medium-sized airport this Monday has sparse traffic. Travelers, myself included, are dressed in shorts and light clothing, trying to endure the hot and humid Oklahoma August.

Making my way to the baggage claim where luggage from my flight is already entering onto the carousel, I manage to go unnoticed. Not so for Timber Oaks, who is chatting and signing autographs for a small group of admirers.

"Priscilla!" shouts Becky Oaks, still stunning as ever, though her short hair is now more brown than red and her freckles have faded.

As Becky hurries to greet me, I adjust my carry on and

computer case for the upcoming embrace. Becky squeezes me tightly as if someone in desperate need of a hug.

I pull myself away from her to a short arm's length while holding both her hands. A small tear runs down Becky's face.

"What's wrong, hon?" I ask.

"Not now. It's just good to see you and we have you for a whole week!"

"Now remember, girl, this is pleasure but also business," I caution her.

"Hey, Ms. Priss!" yells out Timber from the other side of the baggage claim area while politely excusing himself from his fans.

Timber is dressed in sandals and jean shorts with his customary light blue golf shirt and a large white canvas floppy hat. At forty-eight years young, he still is naturally handsome and not five pounds heavier than when we first met thirty years ago. Timber joins Becky and me in a group hug.

"I'll get your bags. Which ones are yours?" says Timber, motioning toward the carousel of rotating luggage.

"Easy to spot," I say. "There are five of them all matching pink."

"Five! Becks, she's movin' in!"

"That would be just fine with me," replies Becky, helping me out with my load by carrying my computer case.

Timber grabs the first two pink suitcases and loads them into the back of their minivan parked just outside the revolving doors of the departure area. Becky and I catch up on the latest family news.

"We might have to wait just a little. We have a surprise guest this weekend," says Timber to me with a wink while retrieving my last three bags.

I look at Becky curiously.

"Mark should be arriving anytime. He's flying in with his people on a private charter," says Becky with bright eyes and a wide smile.

My investigative journalist mind goes to work. I knew nothing of another invite to the Oak's home for the week. Let's see... private charter, sounds like this Mark has an entourage and is showing up during PGA week in Tulsa.

"Does this Mark play golf?" I question Timber and Becky with a tilt of my head.

"His close friends call him Mark and yes, he's pretty good at golf," Timber teases.

"Mark?" I ask, so excited I am about to burst. "Mark as in Maleko? Maleko Kalani is staying at your house with us for the week?"

"Timber and Mark have been planning on this for over a year and a half," Becky says, keeping her hands on my shoulders as if to keep me from erupting.

"They did not want the press to find out where he was staying, so Prissy, try and keep it quiet," Becky pleads.

Storylines are running through my head as I envision having the Island Liona and the Saint all to myself during PGA week. Timber almost bursts my bubble.

"Mark knows that you will be here to do a story on Becky and me and the Circle of Care. Respect his time and privacy. He's trying to win a golf tournament."

"And you are not trying to win?" I shoot back with some defiance.

Timber carries the rest of my load out to the minivan as the locals continue to visit with him and offer assistance.

"You're Priscilla Luke!" cries out a middle-aged woman, obviously attired for this week's big golf classic.

"Honey, its Priscilla Luke! That sports gal that can also dance!" she hollers out to her husband who's trying to get Timber's attention.

With my cover blown I exchange the typical polite commentary that is so common in this situation. The lady is more interested in my dancing technique than my reporting savvy. I sign her PGA Tournament brochure right under where she already has Timber's autograph.

My new acquaintance's attention turns to the arched corridor that leads to the baggage terminal. Airport personnel flee their offices and positions while travelers and tourists flock to the entryway with enthusiastic eagerness. An almost electric energy emerges.

Shouts of "Maleko! Maleko! It's the Lion!" ring throughout the energized crowd flocking after Maleko Kalani and his entourage.

The world's best golfer is a little shorter than Timber but thicker in the chest and biceps. A pair of sunglasses rest on his mop-top black hair. His specially designed island-style blue shirt, knee length shorts, sandals and perfect physique give more the appearance of a Polynesian beach boy than that of a golfing champion.

Maleko is accompanied by his easily recognized caddie and his companion, Chico, the short and older mustached Argentinean.

Three gentlemen casually dressed surround Maleko and Chico separating them from the swarming throng of autograph hounds and fans. An airport concierge trails them with a baggage cart full of luggage, golf bags and other golf related gear.

"Girls, in the van!" orders Timber loudly while he holds the double glass doors for us.

Becky and I rush to the backseat of the van that still has the engine running.

"Mark! Chico! Over here," Timber yells as he waves to get their attention.

Steadily working his way toward the exit, Maleko flashes his famous smile and obliges his fans while signing pamphlets, t-shirts and babies. The struggling bodyguards gingerly create a path for him.

"Chico, toss his stuff in the back of my van."

"Si. Muchas gracious, Senor Timber!"

Chico places two matching leather suitcases in the hatchback of the open van on top of my luggage. Maleko's escorts shove him into the front passenger seat as Timber maneuvers us through the crowd of cell phone photographers.

"Well, what's the plan?" asks Maleko as he exchanges fist thumps with Timber.

"We'll be home in about twenty minutes. I think you know Priscilla?"

I am unaware of the close camaraderie between the two athletes. Maleko turns in his seat and acknowledges me.

"We've met briefly a couple times. I've seen her out there and answered some of her questions in the press room."

Maleko reaches back with a courteous handshake.

"Hey, my wife really loved that dancing gig. She says you should have won."

"How is Susan?" asks Becky.

"Susan is Susan. She's eight months pregnant with number three. I'm giving her this weekend off. That reminds me. I better check in."

Maleko pulls out his iPhone. After a brief conversation with his wife he passes the phone around to Timber and Becky. Both inquire on how she is coming along.

Maleko's phone continues to ring. He conducts business with

what sounds like agents and then Chico. I take the cue and check my own messages. Becky does the same. Timber is amused at the simultaneous talking.

After all the concurrent telecommunication business ceases, I attempt to engage Maleko.

"Maleko?"

"Call me Mark," he replies.

Encouraged that we are already on a first name basis, I continue.

"So, what's up with your arranging to spend what may be one of the biggest weeks of your life with Timber and Becky? I realize you're friends but you're going for the grand slam of golf."

"On the other hand, maybe you should stick with Maleko," Mark suggests.

Timber laughs aloud and gently pounds the steering wheel at Mark's sarcasm. While turning on to the Broken Arrow Expressway, Timber shakes his finger at me in the rearview mirror.

I realize my first attempt at digging for information out of the great young golfer has been thwarted. Mark and Becky smile at Timber's warning gesture.

"Prissy is doing a story or I guess she's going to do a book on the Circle of Care ministry," Timber says, giving me some grace.

"It's more about you, Timber, than anything else. The world is ready for your story and it's about time. I have only been prodding you for ten years."

"Sounds like best seller material?" suggests Mark.

"Timber has personally contributed over two hundred pages on just his senior year in high school. It's good enough that he should just continue and make it an autobiography," I announce.

"It's your turn, girl," Timber replies, knowing that was our agreement.

"Let me tell you what Mark. If you really want to know and

understand your friend here, you should read this. Is that okay, Timber? I've got several copies."

I reached into my purse and pulled out a small red flash drive and offered it to Mark if Timber would permit the proposal. Timber shrugs his shoulders with a why not gesture. Mark returns his shades to the top of his head and examines the small device.

"Sounds like a good way to relax tonight," says Mark slipping the flash drive into his shorts' pocket.

"Bout there," Becky tells Mark and me as we turn into a nice, quiet suburban neighborhood.

"Great!" replies Mark. "I always wanted to see how a saint lives."

We slowly meander through the well kept and pleasant middleclass suburban area till we reach a cul-de-sac. The double garage door opens on the middle house. The one story native-stone home is well kept and neatly landscaped with an American flag in the middle of the front yard on a small flag pole. The garage is well organized but vacant of any other vehicle.

"Here we are," says Becky, "Nothin' fancy, but it's paid for."

Always the gentleman, Timber courteously opens the back door of the van for me. Becky leads Mark and me into her home through the garage entrance past the washing machine and dryer and on into the kitchen while Timber handles our luggage.

We admire the open setting of the kitchen that lends itself to the cozy living room area separated only by a dining bar and three upright stools. I feel a cold, wet sensation that chills my exposed legs.

"Nicklaus! Be nice," scolds Becky gently.

Mark is the first to make the acquaintance of the Oaks' family pet, bending over and petting the head and rubbing the ears of the beautiful chocolate colored Labrador Retriever. Nicklaus then turns his attention to me to make sure both guest are properly greeted.

Timber comes through the back entrance carrying Mark's two pieces of luggage. I finish my introduction with Nicklaus but not before receiving a wet tongue across my face.

"Nicklaus, huh?" asks Mark, grinning at Timber. "How original."

"Becks is putting you in the guest room," Timber says and leads us down the hallway. "And Prissy, you're in Pauly's room."

"Where is Pauly?" I ask.

"He'll be here shortly. Pauly's out measuring the course," reports Timber. "He's gonna be on my bag this week."

Mark and I exchange a glance at each other with raised eyebrows at this announcement. Timber tosses Mark's bags on the queen-sized bed that complements the neat and efficient quarters.

"Will this work for ya?" asks Timber as Mark looks into the bathroom that is connected to what must be Pauly's room by separate doors.

"Do you prefer the toilet seat up or down, Miss Luke?" asks the quick-witted islander.

Timber is more amused than I am. Becky meets us back in the center of the hallway, toting three pieces of my luggage.

"You're in here, girl," she says.

"Becky, I can get my stuff."

Timber hurries out the back before I can beat him to it. Becky rests the load on the floor of a typical teenage boy's room, although obviously just cleaned. Mark follows us and looks through the doorway.

Pauly's room has a golf theme. The young man is understandably infatuated by the sport. The walls are covered with framed pictures and sports magazine covers, most of them autographed by the most popular players on the PGA tour. On his nightstand next to his stereo, there is a picture of his dad blasting out of a sand trap. Above the headboard of his bed is a large poster of Maleko in full swing with the inscription across the bottom 'Ailana Liona'.

"Nice décor," offers Mark, admiring Pauly's taste.

Timber returns from the garage with the rest of my luggage.

"Make yourselves right at home. Help yourself to anything you need," announces Becky hospitably. "Timber is going to throw some burgers on the grill in a little while."

"Burgers on the backyard grill?" inquires Mark. "That's better than motel food. Gots a real Oklahoma feel to it."

"Buddy, in Oklahoma if you can't grill it or fry it you don't eat it," Timber says.

"What did you expect, a luau?" I add.

"That reminds me. I got something for Timber," says Mark, heading back to his room.

Timber settles down on the dark leather couch, sinks in and relaxes. He flips on the remote to the large television screen to USN while tossing his floppy hat onto the coffee table.

While I follow Becky into the kitchen to be of assistance, I notice that Timber's close-cropped hair style has returned to the shaggy look of his youth. A large, beige adhesive bandage is slightly exposed through the now longer locks that cover his neck. I decide for now not to comment.

Mark reenters the living room area with a half-dozen island shirts on separate hangers, very similar to the ones he has made famous. Mark not only wears them while playing but also promotes the distinctive, one-of-a-kind apparel. Mark proudly offers them to Timber.

Timber stands up, takes a shirt from Mark, and holds it up

against his upper torso. All of Mark's shirts are in golf course galleries, pro shops, and sporting good stores; they include an array of themes and many are custom designed.

Timber's shirts are all the same with the baby-blue background covered with a paisley Hawaiian array of white descending doves. Timber seems impressed.

"What ya think, Becks?" asks Timber, still displaying his guest gift in front of his chest.

"I like it! Nice job, Mark," says Becky. I nod my head.

"The trick is the special stretch material in the inseam of the shoulder area allowing no restriction for a full backswing," Mark points out to Timber like a proud promoter.

"And the profits from these shirts go to support your foundation?" I ask, already knowing the answer.

"Yes, ma'am! The Ailana Liona Foundation, but you knew that."

"And the proceeds go to at-risk youth?" I continue.

"We concentrate on childhood disorders. As we grow the foundation, we're looking into ways we can be more effective here and all over the world. That's why I'm interested in talking with Becky about her work with Autism."

"So…a possible merger of some type with the Ailana Liona Foundation and the Circle of Care?" I ask, addressing all three.

Timber takes the rest of his new golf shirts back to his master bedroom and winks at me over his shoulder. Mark joins Becky and me in the kitchen and searches through the refrigerator.

"What ya looking for?" ask Becky.

"Well, a cold beer would be nice, but I forgot where I was at."

"I could have Timber run down to the corner store and get you some. It would just take a sec," Becky offers.

"No, that's alright."

Mark settles for a diet cola and walks out back through the sliding glass doors that lead to the patio and the backyard. I follow him out with a bottle of water.

The backyard setting is pristine, serene, and beautiful. A concrete patio is covered by an extended overhead cover matching the home. It is comfortably furnished with outdoor wicker-style furniture made for relaxing or entertaining, with a circular table that seats six for outdoor dining. A ceiling fan circulates a breeze.

A small spa hot tub is off to the left side and a large charcoal grill is located on the right. Soft music comes from a couple speakers located under the roof. The neatly manicured yard is landscaped with begonias and impatiens that thrive under the shadows of the native hardwood trees.

By design the homes in the area have no fencing. Seven other backyard areas in the neighborhood along with the Oak's surround a three-acre deep blue-green pond.

A small island in the center of the pond features a fountain that forms an umbrella like spray with water from the pond that gently trickles back to its source. The natural setting is complete with several swans, playful squirrels and merrily whistling song birds.

Mark sips his diet cola taking in the tranquil ambiance.

"This is not what I had envisioned," he says, acknowledging my presence.

"So you expected to find nothing in Oklahoma but cowboys, Indians and wheat fields?" I jest.

Timber joins us outside with his companion, Nicklaus.

"Nice atmosphere, huh?" asks Timber as he readies the grill and lights the charcoal.

Mark and I sit down in a pair of comfy chairs, petting Nicklaus while Timber continues to meddle with his fire.

"Everyone around here gets along as well as it appears?" inquires Mark. He's clearly used to more privacy.

"It's very harmonious, my friend. I think it's Hound Dog Island out in the middle of the pond that helps keep all the neighbors integrated."

"Hound Dog Island?" I question.

"You'll see what I mean before the evening is over."

Becky comes out to the terrace with a platter of fresh ground beef patties complemented with onions, peppers and cheese. Timber takes the gourmet-fashioned burgers and hand tosses them on the sizzling grill.

The sound of the garage door rising in the front of the house alerts us that Pauly is home in time for dinner. Nicklaus rushes around the south side of the house, greeting Pauly with a happy bark.

Pauly runs to the backyard followed by his dog. The two run around and play with Nicklaus jumping up on Pauly in a simulated dance routine. The playful scuffle ends when Pauly notices us.

Except for his red hair and freckles, the young man of eighteen looks just like his father when I first met Timber at Corinthia Falls. Pauly hurries to the covered patio and shakes hands with Mark and gives me a hug. Pauly had met Mark before but not in such a personable setting. I had not seen Pauly in almost a year.

"Easy to tell who you belong to," says Mark.

"Spittin' image of his parents!" I add.

"Well Pauly, is Whispering Waters ready for these two?" I ask.

"Oh, it's ready alright!" announces Pauly excitedly.

Pauly goes into a long dissertation using hand gestures in deep detail on the layout of the course. Mark and I listen curiously, charmed by the boy's chatter. After about ten minutes, Pauly stops for a breather.

"You got all that written down?" asks Mark.

"No sir, Mr. Kalani," replies Pauly.

"It's Mark. Mr. Kalani is my grandfather."

"Pauly doesn't use notes," adds Timber. "He knows everything about Whispering Waters or as it's known around here…Water World. Go ahead, try him, Mark. We know you are more familiar with the course than you let on. You've been spotted sneaking in and out of Tulsa several times this summer."

Mark sits back deep in his chair and grins his famous smile. Looking squarely up at the rookie caddy, Mark gives him a test.

"Number eleven, the long par four, left side bunker, distance from the middle of the trap to the center of the green?"

Pauly does not hesitate.

"One hundred ninety-nine yards from center to center. It plays like two hundred twelve, uphill at 8 degrees. The green plays from northeast to southwest with usually a south breeze in your face this time of year. If you can get a good stance, the perfect shot is to strike the ball with a slight fade…a six iron for you, Mark; Dad would need a four with some sizzle."

Mark looks at me in astonishment as we both begin to laugh along with Timber.

"This your first time out with your Dad?" asks Mark of Pauly's caddying debut.

"Yes sir!" says Pauly.

"Son, help your mom. These burgers are 'bout ready."

"You've got to be proud of him, Timber," I comment.

"We are," replies Timber with a smile. "He's just wired differently. He loves golf but is a little too uncoordinated to compete. So, he's a student of the game."

"I'll say!" adds Mark. "Maybe he can teach Chico some things."

"Or the other way around," suggests Timber knowing that Chico is one of the most respected caddies in the business.

As the delicious-smelling burgers come off the grill, Becky and her son bring out buns, coleslaw, fried sweet potato wedges and a pitcher of iced tea mixed with lemonade. Timber dishes out the burgers around the thoughtfully set table then leads us in a blessing.

The conversation over the outdoor dinner table turns to stories of shared acquaintances and experiences in the world of golf. Mark gives us a short geography lesson on the Hawaiian Islands and Timber and Becky reminisce about the night they spent in the Lincoln Bedroom of the White House at the President's invitation.

After finishing helpings of Becky's blackberry cobbler, Mark asks to be excused.

"I'm still adjusting to the Central Time Zone. If you don't mind, I'm going to retire early. I think I'll plug in the computer and read that story Timber wrote."

"Read, but no downloading!" I ordered.

"Excellent meal, guys," says Mark. "What time in the morning, Timber?"

"Say, 7:30, so we can get in a practice round," Timber responds. "You got that, Prissy?"

"Got it, boss."

"Aloha ahiahi." Mark bids us a good evening.

I help Becky clear the table and tidy up in the kitchen. As the sun is going down, Becky and I rejoin father and son on the patio. The conversation is apparently on golf strategy for the PGA Tournament. The surrounding houses' evening lights start to shine, as well as the accent lighting on Hound Dog Island.

Nicklaus approaches Timber with a baseball sized, hard rubber ball in his mouth. The brown Lab again dances with anticipation.

"Looks like a little fetch is in order?" I deduce.

"Something like that," says Pauly.

I notice in the dim twilight, many different breeds of dog are perched in the middle of their particular back lawns, giving their full attention to Timber and Nicklaus and particularly to Hound Dog Island.

There is a pair of miniature Dachshunds next door hurrying toward the edge of the pond. Across the way, a small white Poodle is joining up with a tan Cocker Spaniel in the adjacent yard. Straight across the pond, I could make out a Dalmatian. On around the bend is a slick Golden Retriever, then a tiny, yapping Chihuahua and, completing the circle, is some sort of Bulldog, surely the result of some sort of fantasy breeding.

Neighbors stand at their backdoors. Some wave toward Timber while others encourage their pets. Pauly hands Timber what looks to be a pitching wedge that was lying up against the house. Nicklaus relinquishes the slobbery rubber ball to Timber as he heads toward pond's edge.

A chorus of expectant barking rings all through the area. Timber drops the ball in the center of the Oak's backyard and delivers a perfect thirty-yard lob shot that lands squarely in the small, island fountain. The race is on!

Splashing into the placid waters using tails for rudders, competition to be the first dog to get the ball explodes. Nicklaus is first to reach over and retrieve the ball from the concrete, glowing fountain. All the other wet dogs peruse him in his gleeful victory lap around the island.

The running, howling and snarling continues as the bigger

dogs seem to be playing keep away from the smaller pooches. I am witnessing a ritual that seems more like a canine revival. I cannot stop laughing as I think of the good story this would be to catch on film.

Mark suddenly appears out on the patio to witness the commotion, dressed in only boxer shorts and an undershirt. He shakes his head positively.

"Now this is more what I expected out of Oklahoma!"

Tuesday

I am an early riser, but not as early as the Oak's family. I slip on a robe that Becky left for me at the foot of my bed and stagger toward the kitchen.

A fresh pot of hot coffee is sitting on the counter, surrounded by large mugs and various flavored creamers. A pitcher of grapefruit juice and a fruit plate rest on the serving bar, along with bagels and raisin bread.

Looking out the kitchen window, the August sunrise sparkles off the heavy overnight dew. The swans in the pond seem to be greeting the new day. As I drink my first cup of inspiration, Nicklaus paws on the back door, asking to be let inside after finishing his breakfast.

The bright-eyed family pet briefly greets me, then scampers to the first closed bedroom door. I softly knock, then peek in the room. Nicklaus bolts through the small opening.

Inside the Oak's family home office, Timber, Becky and Pauly are busy at individual desks each studying their personal networked computer screens. Timber turns around in his swivel chair and greets me with a welcoming expression while carrying on what sounds like a counseling session on his cell phone.

Becky looks up from her computer and motions for me to join them. Nicklaus rests his head on her lap while she reviews her email.

I continue to the center of the office that must be the brain trust and central headquarters for the Circle of Care. Standing in the midst of all the Oaks, I can observe how diligently and attentive they are to the ministry. Even Pauly seems involved in some sort of Christian youth chat room.

As I continue to sip my morning coffee. Careful not to disturb, I survey the many pictures and portraits hanging on the wood paneled walls. The history of Timber and Becky's life's mission is encapsulated through these images.

The large picture of the Colonel and Silas stands out the most. There are portraits of TJ's and Anthony's families, Jorell's and my clan hang, along with the entire Solomon family.

Older snapshots of the people from Corinthia Falls that were such a major part of the couple's youth are spread throughout. I particularly admire the one of the Deacon and Ms. Martha.

Most of the pictures are of people, families, and church groups that I do not recognize but probably heard about through mission reports; a collection of souls with smiling faces throughout small towns and villages all over the world that have been touched and spiritually enhanced by the Circle of Care.

Curiously, there is only one golf picture—a photo of Timber and his idol, Jack Nicklaus. There are three different shots with Timber and Becky with former presidents Bush, Clinton, and Bush.

I love the picture of Timber's parents in front of the old Oak's Corner Store. Then there is the handsome shot of Reverend Alex 'Sandy' Sampson standing at the pulpit in his Northside Tulsa Church.

The most humorous pictures are the ones of Dr. Pyle of Corinthia Falls' fame standing beside a wagon load of watermelons accompanied by a red goat and another of Timber and John

Fogerty, both with guitars, in a make-believe duet.

Timber finishes his conversation and stands as Becky sends her final email. Timber puts his arm around me as Becky gives me a morning hug. They both look fresh, as if they've been awake for hours.

"How'd you sleep?" asks Timber.

"I dreamed of an ocean full of dogs," I confessed.

"Let's get some breakfast," Becky says, escorting me back to the kitchen.

Becky pulls an egg casserole dish out of the oven. Timber retrieves some more plates and silverware from the cabinets.

Pauly is hungry and anxious.

Mark is dressed in another of his Ailana Liona tropical shirts, this one several shades of orange. With his white slacks, he looks dashing, as usual.

"Aloha kakahiaka!" he says, which must be Hawaiian for good morning.

"Aloha kakahiaka, hoaloha," replies Timber tipping his coffee cup toward Mark and surprising his friend with his command of the Hawaiian language.

"Not bad Timber, but you need to work on that Okie accent," suggests Mark.

As soon as plates are filled, Becky blesses our morning meal. Pauly heads to the sofa with his plate and juice. Setting down his breakfast on the coffee table, he reaches for the remote and picks up USN on the large screen. A preview of the PGA and Whispering Waters is showing.

I join Pauly in front of the television as we both watch intensely.

Becky sits between Mark and Timber at the dining bar with their backs to us, all pretending not to notice the broadcast.

"That's quite a story I read about your home town last night," begins Mark.

I try to divide my attention between golf and the conversation, very interested in both.

"Tom Johnson...wow! I know you guys are great friends and go way back, but I didn't understand the relationship till now. He works in your ministry, right?"

"Yep. TJ does motivational speaking and runs sports clinics in the off-season for us. He's also a member of our national board of directors, along with Ant and Jorell."

"And your parents?" asks Mark.

"Timber's folks live in Bella Vista, Arkansas at a Christian retirement community," Becky answers for Timber who is working on his second glass of grapefruit juice. "They're getting up there, but take good care of each other."

"Benny Larson ended up becoming my father-in-law. He hasn't changed!' declares Timber shaking his head with a big smile.

"They still live in Corinthia," adds Becky

"Let's see...the Deacon, Doc Pyle, the Sharps, Joyce and Nate and many of the others have passed on. They are the true Saints of Corinthia Falls.

"Crazy George died just a while back," remembers Mark.

"Two years ago," confirms Timber. "Coach willed me his Moses Rod!"

"How 'bout the Sam's?" Mark asks.

I am amazed at Mark's interest. I stand and approach the threesome, turning my attention to the morning dialogue. Timber, Becky and I exchange serious glances after Mark's question. Timber looks off to the serenity of the backyard, reaches down to pets Nicklaus, then answers.

"Sam Samuels followed the Colonel's lead and became a

Green Beret. He died a hero in Iraq."

With that information Mark slumps his shoulders and seems to lose his appetite. Timber continues.

"Sandy is a pastor in Tulsa doing a great job. We get together quite often."

While helping Becky clear the breakfast dishes, Timber remains upbeat.

"How 'bout them Solomon twins?"

"You mean your old girlfriend?" taunts Mark.

Becky shares a smile with Timber.

"She's that gal on daytime TV, right? My wife watches her all the time."

"Sherry Sands," says Becky. "She one of my best friends, along with Prissy, of course."

"What happened to her twin brother, Becky's old flame?

"You mean Jonathon Bartholomew Solomon, III?" proudly asks Becky with a twinkle in her eye.

"Mark, I'm sure you're familiar with Solomon and Guild?" says Timber while putting plates in the dishwasher.

"Sure, the big-time banking guys. They're one of the major sponsors this week."

"The main sponsor," corrects Timber.

"They contacted my agent to do some ads," Mark reveals. "You don't mean this John dude is...?"

"CEO!" Timber cuts off Mark. "The family is one of the key benefactors of the Circle of Care. He's presenting the Wanamaker trophy this year."

"Hu'ihu'i! Uh, that means cool," translates Mark. "I've just got to know...what was in the tap water at this Corinthia Falls?"

With breakfast over, I did not have much time to get myself ready for my first visit to Whispering Waters. Spending so much time on the road living out of a suitcase, I'm well prepped in the art of five minute makeovers. A quick shower, a curling iron, a fresh face and I am ready.

A glance in the full length mirror and I remember to put my hair up for the summer heat. I find the sunglasses that match my pink golf shirt and slacks. I grab my matching bag already packed from last night with sunscreen and technologically sophisticated reporter gadgets.

"Not coming today?" I ask Becky while passing through the kitchen to meet up with the guys that are waiting for me in the garage.

"Not today. I'm waiting till the weekend."

Becky's answer seems to bring her out of an almost prayerful reverie.

"Girl, you're going to have to share what's eating at you."

"We will. Now be off."

Out in the garage, Timber is dressed in his usual baby-blue and white with his newly acquired floppy hat. He and Pauly are introducing Mark to the Saint Hauler; the unspoiled and per-fectly conditioned baby-blue and white 1969 Chevy pickup from Timber's youth.

Mark is walking around the prized vehicle, lightly touching the perfectly shined chrome and admiring its form. Pauly lifts open the hood for Mark to check out the engine.

"It's perfect! It's just like the one in your story," says Mark.

"It is the one in the story," explains Timber. "We take good care of him. Had a few nicks taken out, but he's an original. Pauly gets to drive him around town."

"You talk about it like it's alive, Timber."

Timber and Mark smile. I am captivated by how the two popular sportsmen deflect their concentration to an over forty-year-old relic on the eve of the golf tournament of the year.

"Are we taking it today?" urges Mark. "Prissy can ride in the back."

I give Mark a you-can't-be-serious stare and climb into the minivan that is already pulled out of the garage onto the driveway waiting for us. I get in the backseat with Pauly. Timber and Mark are still talking cars.

Our short drive to Whispering Waters down the Creek Turnpike turns more serious. Timber drives with Creedence playing on the CD player while Mark and I review our messages and return texts.

The Richard Lloyd Jones, Jr. Airport was a public airport located five miles south of Tulsa just west of the Arkansas River. It served as the reliever airport for Tulsa International. In one of the largest tornado outbreaks to ever hit northeast Oklahoma, the facility was obliterated in 1998.

The City decided to rebuild the airport in another location and use the old airport site for a state of the art public golf course. The investors were determined to rival the famed private Southern Hills Club. Opened to the public in 2006, Tulsa more than succeeded in their goal.

Featuring a layout that runs alongside the Arkansas to various streams and ponds from the major river, Whispering Waters is unique as it is beautiful, with networking creeks and natural pools flowing throughout the course.

The scenery is inviting, but the aqua environment can provoke a serious golfer either professional or amateur. Whispering Waters does not speak softly. The degree of difficulty it presents resonates with a roar, so to speak.

Tulsa's achievement of crafting a destination course with full amenities ranks it as one of the 100 best golf courses in the world. This achievement was rewarded by PGA officials with this year's Championship. Timber Oaks, who does not belong to a private course, is Whispering Water's most popular commodity.

Turning into the parking lot designated for players and staff only, the attendant does not even ask for Timber's pass. We are waved on through as Mark looks the other way so as not to be recognized as riding with Timber, which could result in a loss of privacy.

As soon as we exit the van, we are recognized by a bevy of my fellow reporters.

"Here they come," warns Mark.

"Do not be transformed by the world…"Timber quotes scripture to his young friend.

I pull my recorder out of my pink bag to pick up on the minuscule interviews. I pity the others who are not as blessed as I am to have access to Maleko Kalani and Timber Oaks for the entire week.

As expected, the redundant questions come for Mark. 'What do you think of the course?' 'Do you feel any extra pressure as you aim for golf's Grand Slam?' 'What did you do to prepare.' 'Is it this hot in Hawaii?'

Mark, as always, is calm but precise. Although a bit overly charismatic in the limelight, he is always a courteous gentleman.

After several minutes of rolling cameras and quick quips, Mark excuses himself to the locker room.

Timber is not as fortunate to make a quick getaway. The local press has swarmed its hometown hero and favorite missionary. The questions to Timber are more on a personal level.

'Is it true your son is caddying for you this week?' 'Where's your next mission trip?' 'What's with the silly hat, Timber?' 'Can we expect Tom Johnson to show up?' 'How's Becky?'

Timber takes his time to answer each inquiry individually. He reaches out to touch most of the reporters as many are long time acquaintances. It's obvious that Timber carries on a special relationship with these people just as he does with almost everyone.

The day is very routine for a major championship. Players work on the driving range and get a good taste of the course. Pauly is with Timber, constantly making suggestions and observations. I continue to follow the father/son team throughout the day, remaining true to my assignment. Besides, 'The Liona Legion' all dressed in island shirts and leis are dreadfully hard to penetrate.

We finish in the late afternoon, having a real taste of the Oklahoma August heat. The guys do several more interviews and promos. I even consent to a couple myself with more exasperating questions on my dancing.

We all are exhausted on the ride home. I wonder to myself how these players can put up with five more days of a hundred-degree-plus weather. The van air conditioner blows full blast. I break the silence.

"What's it going to take to win this thing?"

"A golf ball that floats!" Mark snaps, referring to all the water hazards.

"Seriously," I ask in my sports journalist tone.

I seem to be ignored by the two professionals up front. Interestingly, Pauly steps in, getting Mark's and Timber's full attention.

"Gotta keep the ball dry! I'd say if you want to be in the hunt on Sunday, par or slightly under will do it."

The degree of difficulty presented by Whispering Waters is confirmed by the glance that Mark and Timber exchange with each other. We all take note of Pauly's prediction.

Becky is waiting for us as we enter through the kitchen. A fresh pitcher of lemonade awaits us on the counter. Becky hands Timber a sheet of paper that looks to be filled with handwritten notes. Timber reads while he makes a direct path to the family office.

"Something wrong?" I ask Becky as Mark and Pauly help themselves to the fresh, cold refreshment.

"There was a major earthquake in Kenya this morning. The Circle has an outreach mission there near Nairobi that was hit hard."

With that news, Pauly quickly joins his father in the office and shuts the door behind them. I immediately call Jorell on my cell to get him updated on the situation. I hand the phone to Becky so she can fill in the details. Mark and I listen intently to Becky's description of the circumstances to my husband.

The sound on the living room TV is turned down. The news channel is showing clips of the damage in Kenya. Becky hands my phone back to me. I finish up with Jorell. The three of us end up standing together, studying the natural disaster on the screen.

"So, what's going on now?" asks Mark.

"They'll be in there for a while, most of the evening I imagine," says Becky.

Being involved before with the Oaks in this type of situation, Jorell and I know the routine well. I help Becky answer Mark's questions.

"This is what Timber is best at...organizing and deploying. Timber will first be briefed by our local mission there in Kenya... then a board of director's conference call with TJ, Anthony, Jorell and some others... the assessment of the situation will be appraised...then a proper line of action will be established."

Mark finishes his second glass of lemonade while Becky takes up where I leave off.

"The Circle is well suited in times of crisis to respond to this sort of thing. We have the resources to react quickly which is important. Timing is everything.

"The first thing will be a mission team of first responders. They will network with other Christian groups serving the area. We will follow up shortly with more relief help after we have a better handle on what supplies and services are needed. We can act faster and more efficiently than governments by cutting out a lot of red tape."

Our conversation takes us back to the kitchen as we gaze out at the backyard. Mark swirls the ice cubes in his empty glass.

"Will your husbands be going to Kenya?" asks Mark.

Becky and I look at each other with reassuring smiles. I answer for both of us.

"I expect them both there by the middle of next week. They will probably head up the second supply group."

Mark shakes his head in amazement.

"And Timber is organizing all of this from that little room back there?" he asks Becky directly.

"And Pauly," she replies, "and Jorell, Ant, TJ and our whole world-wide organization."

"But you're right, Mark," I say, "Timber is the man."

"No wonder he can't win a golf tournament," concludes Mark. "He's too busy saving the world!"

After changing into some more comfortable clothes, I join Mark, Becky and Nicklaus on the backyard patio. Timber and Pauly remain on lock-down in the office.

Mark has stripped down to a pair of shorts and relaxes in the backyard spa. The circular fan spins overhead; the water is at a refreshingly cool temperature.

Becky has taken over for the involved Timber as backyard chef. She begins to place large pieces of marinated chicken on the hot grill. Nicklaus offers any assistance she may need with a wet nose that seems to be sucking in the entire sweet-smoky aroma that drifts through the light but still-warm breeze.

Becky and I sit down at the patio table, helping ourselves to some tortilla chips and homemade salsa.

Becky and I begin a conversation on her most passionate topic...Autism. From the hot tub, Mark listens in.

After taking note of our discussion, Mark gives a summation.

"It always comes down to money, doesn't it? There's something I'm curious about and so are many others. I'm beginning to realize how this Circle of Care works. You network your resources through membership to expand and provide services just as you are doing now for this earthquake.

Why doesn't Timber use the marketplace to supplement your funding? I mean, just think of how marketable he is? He's popular with everyone, has a great story, and relates well to the public. So many large corporations would pay some big bucks for his endorsement. Just looking around I'd say he'd be a natural spokesman for dog food and charcoal. They could have Saint this and Saint that..."

I knew the answer to this one. Timber and Becky had addressed this many times before. Coming from the world's best golfer who makes more money from his advertising endorsements than he does on the tour, it is a reasonable question.

"Those that represent God and Christian principles in the public arena," states Becky, "whether as members of the clergy, disciples or missionaries, it's an unusual position to be in. An endorsement through the media may be misconstrued as having

God's support or a divine backing of one product over another."

Mark steps out of the spa and begins to dry off with a large towel. Nicklaus helps out by licking the droplets off his toes. Becky tends to the grill turning the chicken pieces.

"So, that's why the Saint doesn't wear or display any logos on the golf course? Man, that's leaving a lot of money on the table."

"You should know, Mark," I answer.

"Dealing with the secular world with one foot in and one foot out can be very delicate," Becky continues. "It was one of the Colonel's first lessons he taught Timber. Timber does do some local public service spots, but our promoting centers on our ministry…the Circle."

"Then you're sayin' making money through advertisement is unchristian?" challenges Mark.

"Of course not," says Becky. "We believe in honest and free enterprise and an entrepreneurial spirit. Endorsements are just not right for Timber."

Mark puts on the island shirt that he left draped over the dining chair and puts it on. He sits down with Becky and me and samples the salsa. He then speaks to the heart of the matter.

"Becky, I know this week is partly about an attempt to do some merging with the Ailana Liona Foundation with the Circle of Care's Autism program. How's that going to work? My charity is not necessarily Christian-based."

"But you are a non-competing non-profit organization," Becky says. "The Ailana Liona Foundation proceeds are not the result of a public business but rely on private contributions in return for a commodity that is not for personal income. Timber is very impressed with what you've put together."

"Mark, do you think you need to work on the Christian part?" I ask, recognizing a good chance for evangelism when I hear one.

"Well, it's not like I'm a bad person or anything. I believe in God and try to live by the Golden Rule. My family while I was growing up attended the First United Methodist Church of Honolulu. That's where I was baptized and conformed."

Becky and I almost choke on our chips and lemonade. Grinning broadly, I correct Mark.

"I think you mean confirmed."

"Yeah, that's it…confirmed," says Mark.

"Still attending church?" asks Becky.

"Always around Christmas. I make my living on Sundays you know. The wife and kids handle the church stuff."

Becky looks at me with a tell-tale grin. We both realize Mark is a lukewarm Christian by his reference of church as stuff. Becky gives the world's best golfer some advice.

"Don't be surprised if Timber talks to you about that church stuff."

"I've been expecting that. Other guys on the tour come to him with their personal problems. Timber always gives them his time and listens. I don't know much of what they're talking about but it usually ends up in prayer either in the club house or on the course. Everyone trusts him."

Becky reached out across the table and clutches Mark's hand and does the same with me.

"Speaking of prayer," she says, "let's have grace before supper."

As we bow, she also prays for the earthquake victims and asks God for discernment for her Autism project. Before the amens, she requests healing for Timber.

She softly squeezes both of our hands as she finishes and begins to remove the chicken onto a platter off the grill. Mark looks over at me with a puzzled expression. I shrug my shoulders to show my ignorance.

We go inside to eat where it's cooler. I help Becky prepare five plates of grilled chicken, potato salad and barbeque beans. Becky delivers two full plates to the office for Timber and Pauly.

After dinner we retire to the living room, flipping the television channels between the earthquake and USN coverage of the PGA Championship.

Most of the sports clips are of Mark, the Ailana Liona. The interviews that feature Mark break the solemnity of the evening.

"You handled most of that pretty well, Lion," I kid Mark.

"Hey, I'm a pro," says Mark with a grin.

Timber and Pauly come out of the office about sundown. Placing their dishes in the sink, both head to the tranquility of the backyard as Becky, Mark, and I follow. Timber lies back in the synthetic lounge chair. Pauly helps Nicklaus find his favorite toy.

"So when do you leave?" asks Becky.

Timber is ready for the question.

"Jorell and I fly out of DFW Tuesday morning. We got things put together. We're taking Pauly with us."

"How bad is it?" asks Mark.

"It's worse," Timber announces solemnly. "Those folks really got jacked up."

"The Barclay's is just two weeks away. You passin' that up?" asks Mark. "Man, you still got plenty of points for the Fed-Ex!"

"I'm finishing out my season this Sunday, Mark. That decision was made before all this happened."

"What? What's wrong with you?" He turns. "Prissy, you're the reporter. Let me in on this!"

I am as stunned as Mark. Something must be wrong…very wrong. Becky looks out toward the pond, wiping an eye. Pauly and Nicklaus prepare for the evening canine race to the island pond.

All the participants are in place in their respective backyards for the scramble. Pauly, who has pretended not to hear the adult's conversation, has the rubber ball in place and holds out the pitching wedge for his father. Mark still shaking his head in surprise walks to the center of the lawn with Timber.

"I've got to check this out," says Mark.

"Wait a sec, Timber!" I shout out as I hurry to the backyard table to retrieve my cell phone to film the unusual event.

Timber winks at Mark, swings and hits his fountain target again. Mark cheers for Nicklaus to be the first swimming dog to get the ball. As Nicklaus wins the race, Mark lifts his fist in triumph and shouts.

"Mr. Nicklaus is the Poi Ilio!"

"Huh?" asks Pauly.

"Hawaiian Water Dog."

"Mark, you better hope Whispering Waters doesn't turn you into the Water Dog this week!" warns Pauly.

Wednesday

The morning ride to Whispering Waters for the last day of preparation begins with Mark riding shotgun next to Timber again.

We had just enjoyed another hearty breakfast with the early-rising Oaks family. The Hawaiian Lion fidgets with his iPhone. He has some questions for the Saint after reading his story the last few nights.

"That Colonel Armstrong guy was quite the fella?"

"That he was!" replies Timber. "No one has had a bigger impact on my life. He embodied the meaning of evangelist."

"Evangelist?" asks Mark in a tone that sounded like Timber's description of the Colonel was somewhat understated.

"Well, many people confuse evangelism with excited, charismatic preaching and teaching. The Colonel could do that. But actually a true evangelist is itinerant, always on the move, sharing the Gospel and preparing the way for the Lord's work."

"So you're an evangelist?" suggests Mark.

Timber takes his right hand off the steering wheel and reaches over and shakes Mark's arm as if to congratulate him on his logic.

"That I am! And so is Prissy and Pauly and…actually that's what our Circle of Care is all about…evangelism."

"Then with a car load of evangelists we should be going to a revival rather than a golf tournament," Mark muses.

Timber looks in the review mirror at Pauly and me in the backseat, giving us that unique Timber wink.

"Maybe we are my friend, maybe we are."

Whispering Waters is bustling more today than yesterday. I check in with my credentials at the media center. After comparing notes with the local reporters and checking out some of my favorite sports blogs on my cell, I wait for Timber and Mark at the driving range.

Pauly, along with Chico, Mark's prominent South American caddy, have their respective golfer's bags perched with several baskets of driving range balls ready, both wearing their required green Whispering Waters caddy pullovers and dressed similar to their particular pro.

The two have formed a personal bond even with the contrast in age, character and culture. From the roped off area separating the spectators from the driving area, I listen in on their attempt at conversation.

"I never see you wearing the same island shirt," says Pauly. "What do you do with them after you wear them?"

Chico explains in his best English.

"Senor Maleko and me, we both put our name on them, like you say…autograph? Dey is worth more money dat way."

"eBay?" asks Pauly.

"Si, mi amigo. Dey pay."

Pauly and I, along with every golfer and caddy within hearing range unite in hysterical laughter over Chico's mistranslation. I quickly recover and jot down the faux pas, knowing that it will fit into my story.

As with most driving ranges, the fairway is marked with flag pins at various distances. Both men start out hitting balls with wedges at the closer targets. They progress to the mid irons, taking aim at the middle distance pins with accuracy reserved only for the best in the game. Mark starts up a conversation while both continue striking balls.

"So Timber, will there be golf courses in Heaven?"

"You know, I've often thought about that myself," replies Timber while working on his back swing. "I wonder how beautiful the course would be and the layout. Whatever it would look like, it would be perfect. That's God's standard."

"The perfect round of golf…what would that be like?" wonders Mark aloud while lining up for another swing.

"Perfection, that's what separates us from God," Timber explains. "Tell me, Mr. World's Best Golfer, what would be the perfect round for you?"

Being a reporter, I wish I would have asked that question. Mark and Timber stop and face each other while Pauly, Chico, me and some of the other golfers listen in. Those that are familiar with Timber know a teaching moment when it comes around.

"I know what you're getting at. Winning is the ultimate goal in any outing, but if you're talking about scoring…" Mark takes a few seconds to consider the question.

"I'd say perfection would be to birdie all the par threes and fours and eagle the par fives. That's about as perfect as it could get."

"No aces?" remarks Timber. "Well, on this course you would card a fifty. That's never been done before on any course—not even close. But still, it's short of God's standard for perfection."

"So what would be a perfect round for God?" asks Mark, a little defiantly.

"Eighteen holes…eighteen strokes," states Timber with a matter of fact expression, looking the Hawaiian Lion eye to eye.

"Impossible!" declares Mark.

"Nothin' is impossible for God, my friend," the Saint persists. "What you got in your hand there, a seven iron?"

Mark nods.

"That'll work fine. See the one hundred and fifty yard flag out there? Let's see you hit the shaft pin in the air. Not the flag or the base but the pin itself."

"What would that prove, dude?"

"Go ahead and try for it. It would take a perfect shot."

The rest of the golfers on the range have stopped their practice to witness the challenge. Spectators and fans creep closer. Chico hands Mark a brand new ball from his bag. Using the deep concentration that he's noted for, he dries his hands and takes a couple of practice swings, then takes dead aim. His sweet swing delivers a high lifted shot that looks almost ideal.

"Be right!" demands Mark of his ball in flight with the same determination as if he was competing in tournament play.

The ball comes down with the right height and distance but misses the pin by less than a foot. Everyone watching sighs at the close attempt. Mark, golf's fiercest competitor, grimaces with disgust.

"Nice shot!" says Timber. "That was very good, but that's the problem…good isn't perfect. What you just did is commit a 'sin.' By definition, you missed the mark."

"Just like your Colonel with the knife in the barn?" Mark says, remembering Timber's account of Colonel Armstrong describing sin to the Sams in the barn.

"Exactly! It does not matter how good that shot was, the fact is it wasn't perfect. Like I said, God's standard for us is perfection. Not just in one golf shot but every shot. In other words, everything we do in life, every action or even thought, God expects perfection. The only way we can have an eternal relationship with God is to always hit the mark; to be sinless."

"Everyone knows you have a relationship with God," Mark counters. "But you can't be sinless. No one can!"

"Mark, we all miss the target God has set for us and fall short of His glory. God by His own nature can only be righteous. He is the perfect judge; the perfect referee and He hands out penalty strokes."

"Then everyone loses. That's not fair," reflects Mark.

"But being perfect means God must be fair. He's so fair that he created a way for our sins to be forgiven."

"Preach it, Timber," I think to myself.

"Isn't this where Jesus comes in?" asks Mark.

"Yes, it is. God never gives up on us even when we do ourselves. He humbly made himself human to come down and play the perfect game of golf; to live the perfect life without sin or penalty strokes. He never hit a bad shot."

"So, what you're saying is that Jesus had to be perfect to prove that it could be done or God couldn't expect us to live sinless lives either," Mark says.

"And because He loves us," adds Timber.

Mark asks the inevitable question.

"Then why did Jesus have to die?"

Timber looks around at the other golfers nearby. Even a few fans and media types hear the conversation and draw closer. The driving range is dead silent. Timber smiles and delivers.

"Because the penalty stroke for every missed shot, every sin is death. A judge who pardons law-breakers isn't a righteous judge at all. Ignoring sin would make God unjust. Death is God's justifiable consequence for sin... 'For the wages of sin is death.'"

It is amazing to watch Timber as God works through him. Timber...the golfer, the Saint, the evangelist...preaches on.

"Jesus took on all the sin, all the bad shots of mankind and made the perfect sacrifice. He paid for our sins—our bogeys, double bogeys and errant tee shots with His blood because nothing else would do. He paid our penalty with His death.

"And then to prove He had the power over death, something none of us can manage on our own, He rose from among the dead. For if He could not conquer death, then how could we?"

Mark looks on with an expression of comprehension as do others in Timber's swelling audience. Most seem eager on this hot summer morning for more Good News as Timber reaches for a club from his bag.

"Is that what I think it is?" asks Mark as he and Chico examine closely the antiqued eight iron in Timber's hands that looks like it came from a junk pile.

"That's the Moses Rod. We refer to it as Destiny," says Timber, showing off the legendary piece of scrap iron.

Timber motions to his son who tosses him a fresh golf ball. He drops the ball on the ground where Mark attempted to hit the 150 yard pin. Timber finishes his message.

"When we accept God's offer of eternal grace in our hearts and with our voices, He sends to us the perfect swing coach; the ultimate caddy to help navigate the most demanding shots."

"The Holy Spirit," says Pauly, as if on cue.

Timber beams at his son's affirmation. He starts to line up the shot using Destiny, taking aim at the same target Mark barely missed.

"He gives us counsel on length, distance and wind that we may avoid sin and hit God's target; His will for our life."

Timber takes a practice swing. Everyone watching is motionless. It is a God moment.

Timber swings Destiny. When the old club makes contact

with the ball there is an unrecognizable clang. The ball in flight is less direct and hits lower than Mark's effort and appears to be far to the right of the objective.

But at the halfway point, it begins hooking to the left, then strikes the shaft of the pin just under the flag, sounding a loud clang that echoes through the driving range.

Everyone including Mark stare at the ball lying next to the base of the pin. Mouths are open and chins nearly hit the ground.

"Hallelujah," I feel my heart whisper.

While witnesses of the miraculous golf shot are still focused on what they've just seen, Timber turns back toward Mark, turns his eyes toward the heavens and pulls the white floppy hat lower over his forehead. I can read his lips as he offers up a prayer.

"Thank you," is all he says.

After following Timber and Pauly around Whispering Waters on their second practice round, I cool off in the media center and take part in the interview sessions.

A long table displaying the huge Wanamaker Trophy, the famed prize of the PGA Championship, is covered with microphones enveloped by a mass of reporters with sometimes agonizing questions. Cameras roll, snapshots flash, as the leading golfers get their turns deflecting hypotheticals.

Mark, about the tenth golfer in front of the mics addresses a horde of inquiries. I finally get my chance to ask a question. I address him like the other journalists, not wanting to reflect a close friendship.

"Maleko, in your quest for golf's grand slam, who do you think will be your stiffest competition this week?"

"Ms. Luke, as always the golf course is my competition."

Timber is the last to address the packed room. Again the questioning is more soft and personable. Not expected to ever make the leader board but loved by the press, the Saint chums it up with his self-effacing humor. A writer asks of his goal for the PGA Championship. Timber humbly replies.

"To stay hydrated and make the cut so I can hang with you guys on the weekend."

The director of the media announces a surprise for Timber. Walking around the corner after a quick introduction is John Solomon, Timber's longtime friend, associate and CEO of Solomon and Guild, sponsor of this year's PGA Championship.

John is well recognized from the national commercials in which he appears for his banking corporation. He is tanned, silver headed, and still handsome, dressed appropriately in white slacks and a baby-blue sports jacket. The financial mogul hugs his old pal.

Questions are asked about their relationship and what it was like growing up in Corinthia Falls with Thomas Johnson. Both men take some friendly digs at each other. It is obvious they are very close and involved together.

John is asked who he is pulling for to win the PGA, as if that was not a for-drawn conclusion.

"Our corporate headquarters are in Chicago. Rooting for Timber is kind of like being a Cubs fan. Loyalty and patience become a required virtue."

I visit outside on the parking lot with John while we wait for Timber and Mark to finish signing autographs. Pauly pulls up the van for an attempted getaway. Before Timber gets in the van, he shares a few words with John while Mark and I take notice from the backseat.

"How's the Circle's relief effort going in Kenya?" John asks him softly, showing concern.

"Jorell and I leave Tuesday. We'll keep the website updated."

John reaches into his blazer and pulls out what appears to be a check.

"Then you might want to take this with you," offers the business tycoon.

Timber unfolds the personalized check, scans it and puts it in his back pocket.

"Thanks, my friend. We can always count on you."

The two men embrace. Pauly has the car moving before his father can get his passenger door shut.

"How much?" I ask.

"Much, very much," replies the grateful missionary.

Becky has refreshments waiting for us as we return to Camp Oaks. Two half-gallon pitchers of something that looks tropical sits on the kitchen counter with five iced-down glasses.

"Watcha got there, Miss Becky?" I ask.

"Something I thought might help Mark feel a little more at home. It's a mixture of guava, pineapple and lime juice."

The guys are the first to fill up their glasses. Timber takes time to hug his wife as she whispers into his ear and hands him her daily notes. Timber heads to the office, taking time to relieve himself of the silly hat, tossing it toward the living room couch. Pauly follows his father to assist in another session of work on the Kenya assistance endeavor.

"Becky, if you don't mind, I'm going to try out your chill tub again," says Mark.

"Good idea. Think I'll join you," I concur.

The Oak's backyard is once again our oasis of retreat. Soft music is playing on the patio. A brisket is smoking on the grill. Mark and I get a refill of island juice and ease into the refreshing waters of the spa.

"So, what do you think?" I ask as we both peer out toward the pond.

"Think about what, Ms. Luke," asks the great golfer.

Mark is not an easy nut to crack. He never forgets my occupation.

I have him in a relaxed situation, yet he won't relinquish.

"Off the record?" he asks.

I reluctantly concede with a head nod.

"Timber talks about God's standard for perfection," Mark appears to be wondering aloud. "But this family seems to be as close to perfect as it can get. They never lose their tempers; they never say anything bad about anybody and go around doing all these good things."

I stop to reflect on my reply as now the questioner is being challenged.

"What you heard on the driving range, Mr. Kalani, is about God's grace. It's best not to compare ourselves with one another regarding who is better or closer to being perfect. God loves us so much, He gave His only Son…and I think you know the rest?

"Timber and his family are not perfect. No one is. They too have fallen short of God's glory, but they are saved through faith alone, not through all the good things they do…so they reflect humility and have no need for arrogance."

"So it's all about faith; faith alone," concludes Mark, taking a swig of juice. "Where does faith like yours and Timber's come from?"

"Faith comes from God." I know the importance of my answer. I silently call on God for assistance.

"God develops our faith by revealing his love for us through the promises in his Word."

"You mean the Bible?"

"That is where you find his Word, Mark. You know one thing that I learned from my husband is that everyone is fighting their own wars. What battles are you wrestling with?"

Pauly comes out to the patio and joins us in the spa, saving Mark from my inquiry. Maybe this is best that he ponders that thought.

"Hear you're paired up with Tiger for the first two rounds," says Pauly settling down into the cool, bubbly water. "That'll be good. The Lion versus the Tiger!"

Timber follows his son out to the backyard and checks on the grill. Mark comes out of a self-induced trance. Timber joins in on the golf talk.

"Lions and tigers and bears…oh my!"

Becky comes out with a handful of bath towels just in time to sing along with me a rendition of Off to See the Wizard.

"Be afraid…be very afraid!" mocks Mark.

"Who you guys got?" asks Mark, directing his question more toward Pauly.

"Chipper Anderson," says Pauly always on top of everything golf. "Second year guy from Alabama."

"He's a good, young talent," I chip in trying to be part of the flow.

"You going to be preaching to him, Timber?" asks Mark playfully.

"I doubt it; his father is a Presbyterian minister. Pauly and I visited with him in the lounge. Looks like good Circle of Care material though."

"Mom, Dad's got the eight twenty tee time tomorrow and then one thirty five on Friday," announces Pauly as we begin to exit the spa. "Mark goes off at seven fifty and one oh five."

"So you're all expecting an early breakfast?" asks his mother.

"I'll be glad to help, girl," I promise her while drying off.

"Well, you can help me now with this brisket dinner."

After we enjoy the sliced brisket with an incredible Polynesian sauce that Becky found on the internet, the three guys retire to the couch, switching between coverage on the cable news of the PGA and the Kenya earthquake. Pauly jumps off the sofa as if he just remembered something.

"Mom, is it okay if Chico comes over for dinner tomorrow night? He said I'd have to check it out with the 'la jefe.' Don't know if he was talking about you or Mark."

Becky looks up from loading the dishwasher. While waiting for Mark to answer, she confirms that it's fine with her.

"What do say, man?" asks Pauly of Mark, obviously enthused. "He also asked if he could cook."

"We should be back early enough with the early tee times tomorrow. It could be very entertaining," suggested Mark. "He has his own syndicated food show back in Argentina; a man of many talents."

"Yes!" Pauly says excitedly, pumping his fist forward.

Becky and I finish up our kitchen details. The phone rings and Becky quickly dries her hands and answers. After a short visit she motions for Timber to take the call in the office.

"It's your husband," she informs me. "The guys are putting together another conference call. You can sit in on it if you like."

"I'll wait till they get through with the good ol' boy stuff. That usually takes up the first ten to fifteen minutes."

Becky agrees as she pours us a glass of sweetened iced tea. Mark and Pauly sink into the couch. Mark is digging for more information out of Pauly on Whispering Waters. Pauly obliges and is thrilled with holding the attention of the great Ailana Liona.

Becky and I make our way to the family office. The door is

open and the speakerphone is on. We walked into the middle of a male bonding and ribbing ritual.

"Hi, Honey! Hey fellas!" I greet the gang, letting them know that Becky and I are now present.

After an exchange of informal pleasantries with Jorell, Anthony, and TJ, the conference call turns to the serious business of the Kenyan disaster. I am proud of Jorell for taking charge of the relief effort since Timber's consumed with his last golfing outing of the year.

As the Circle's executive session winds down, Mark walks down the hallway and peers into the open office door. I realize it's the first time he's seen inside. Timber encourages him to join us.

"Hey guys, the Island Lion has just walked in!" announces Timber.

Cackles, hoots and crowing fill the office with the announcement of Mark's presence. They sound like a bunch of over-awed school boys.

"Watch out for the Saint!" TJ warns. "He's overdue."

Mark joins Timber and the rest in laughter.

"Has Pauly fixed your swing?" asks Anthony playfully.

"Maleko, how's things going in Oklahoma?" asks Jorell.

"Pauly has me swinging like an Okie," replies Mark in good fun, "and when I get bored I just take a swim out to Dog Island."

Familiar with Oak's household, TJ laughs hysterically. The bantering goes on till Mark signs off with an aloha. He remains in the office studying the wall pictures and artifacts while the counsel finishes up.

The well-worn New Revised King James Bible lies open on a small table underneath a reading lamp. It catches Mark's eye. I watch Mark examine his new discovery.

He picks up the leather Bible and thumbs through some of

the many hand written side notes and the underlined, highlighted verses. Mark inspects the frayed cover and touches the golden engraved name of the original owner...*Pavlos Lincoln Armstrong.*

Becky nods her head, affirming Mark's question before he can ask. Timber gets up from his desk after closing out his meeting and approaches Mark.

"It makes for good readin'," Timber says. "Start with the Book of John."

Timber assists Mark in finding the Gospel According to St. John.

"And since you like to read before bed, you might enjoy this."

Timber walks over to his book shelf and retrieves a blue school- type binder. He offers it to Mark while opening it to the front. He fans through the pages of poly-protected manuscripts, some hand written and some typed, all addressed to Timber and simply signed ...Pavlos.

"This is the collection of the letters the Colonel sent to me through the years before his departure. It's kind of a counseling that I share with our churches. Consider it his manifesto."

Mark takes the Bible and binder and heads for his bedroom without saying a word. Suddenly, we hear Nicklaus pawing at the door.

"It must be about that time?" I say aloud.

Not to be left out of the evening finale, Mark closes the Colonel's compilation and lays both books on the guest room bed. He joins Becky, Timber, and I to the backyard.

Pauly has things all set up: rubber ball, pitching wedge and a procession of dogs surrounding the pond ready for take off. Timber links up with his son, taking hold of the ball launcher while Nicklaus takes his mark at the pond's edge.

Before Timber can finish his swing, Pauly reaches out with an arm across his father's chest.

"Hold on, Dad. Here comes Goliath!"

A very huge, hefty dog of mixed breed enters the fray between the yards of the Poodle and Cocker Spaniel. In the twilight I can make out that one ear is missing, his face is scarred and his personality is defiant. With his head lowered and tongue hanging near to the ground over a full jaw of teeth, the ominous four–legged creature proudly makes his way to Dog Island's bank placing one paw in the water.

The intruder receives a rebellious reception. The Chihuahua runs in circles with unending yapping. The Cocker yelps in objection. The larger dogs howl in a formal protest. Nicklaus looks back at Timber in apprehension. The little white poodle runs back to the security of its master's arms on the porch. Individual neighbors lurk outside their backdoors with concern.

"What in the…" begins Mark stepping from the patio out onto the yard to get a closer look.

"Call the city pound. Get a dog catcher!" I plead.

Timber raises his right hand and waves to the pet owners across the way signaling that he has things under control.

"Wiener Dog Brigade?" Pauly suggests to his father.

Timber nods his head while seriously surveying the situation. Pauly runs through the garage backdoor holding a yellow regular-sized golf ball. He tosses the ball to Timber.

The twin-size Dachshunds, bold and territorial, know no fear. Timber launches the yellow sphere with a perfect lob over the pond just several feet past Goliath. The mammoth dog goes for the ball with the Wiener Dog Brigade in hot pursuit.

Goliath picks up the ball in his mouth and makes a run for it while the two small warriors determinedly nip at his tail and posterior parts. Working in unison with skilled precision, the duo chases the uninvited bully from their private playground surroundings.

After a couple of moments, the dynamic diminutive soldiers return in triumph to our applause and cheers from backdoor spectators. The poodle safely returns to the water's edge.

With things back to normal, the evening's informal procedure resumes. With swimming, frolicking and playing, Hound Dog Island is back to normal.

"They whipped the Great Kahuna," exclaims Mark.

"Wiener Dog Brigade!" replies Pauly proudly. "David and Cinderella."

"Great names for little underdogs," says Mark.

While we enjoy watching the spectacle going on out on the pond island, I smile.

"So is Timber."

Thursday

It's an early rising time for the first day of the PGA Championship. The 4:30 wake-up time was delivered by Timber knocking on my bedroom door. Do these people ever sleep?

I remember I promised Becky to help with breakfast. As I throw on my robe I can hear Mark doing some kind of stretching routine behind his closed door.

Becky has everything ready; an old-fashioned breakfast of ham and scrambled eggs along with blueberry muffins. I apologize to her while filling up my coffee cup.

Timber is taking a multitude of pills from different bottles of all shapes and sizes, chasing them down with what looks to be a glass of rich, gray syrupy liquid. He turns away from me as if hiding the process.

"Loading up on vitamins?" I ask.

"Somethin' like that," he says while rinsing out the glass in the sink.

Mark and Pauly join us almost simultaneously. Pauly is dressed identical to his father in baby-blue and white with the exception of different head gear that they both are already wearing.

The Ailana Liona will go with khaki pants and a dazzling purple island shirt for the first round. Both golfers are easily identified by their familiar wardrobes. All three gentlemen appear restless and ready to get started.

I excuse myself before they sit down for breakfast, opting for a muffin that I take back to my room. I am behind again and do not want to miss the ride to Whispering Waters.

I quickly make myself ready. Loading up my journalistic gear and strapping it all over my shoulders, I scamper to the kitchen where the Oak's family has circled for prayer. Holding hands together, Mark reluctantly joins them, knowing no one is going anywhere till prayer time was over.

"Hurry and join us, Prissy!" urges Becky.

I break into the tight encirclement between Timber and Pauly.

"Anything anyone would like to mention?" asks Timber cheerfully.

We all search each other's faces for the first volunteer. I suggest the obvious.

"Let's pray for the people of Kenya and the relief effort."

"And for healing," adds Becky taking a deep breath, the old habit she cannot seem to break.

"Very well then," says Timber, closing his eyes. "Let's bow our hearts."

This morning Pauly takes the wheel of the family minivan. I sit up front with him, leaving the two competitors in the backseat. Both are plugged into their iPods appearing very relaxed. I wonder what CCR song Timber is listening to as I review my emails and messages.

Traffic has picked up on the turnpike although it is still dark out. Many golf enthusiasts are up early, anxious to get to Whispering Waters. A car load of fans traveling beside us notice Timber. It probably is that silly hat that gives him away.

Their windows are rolled down, trying to get Timber's attention. Mark slumps in his seat trying not to be noticed while Timber obliges his admirers with a thumbs up.

"You never get tired of it, do you?" says Mark, unplugging his earphones.

Timber just smiles contently.

"Get in some reading?"

"Well, it's not like I never read some Bible before, but last night the words seem to be jumping off the page," Mark admits.

"I looked through some of the letters that Colonel wrote you…he was a fascinating man."

Timber nods encouragingly.

He says, "Prissy, can I borrow a pen and a small piece of paper?"

I reach into my pink bag of tricks to fulfill Timber's request.

Although he's reading upside down, I can tell Timber is writing down Bible verses with a notation…Matthew 19:16-30 (The Rich Young Man).

"Let me know what you think," says Timber, offering the note to Mark.

Chico is waiting to escort Mark to the locker room as we walk through the back entrance gate just off the parking lot. Both caddies and players hurry to prepare for the early start.

The first glimpse of daylight reveals what looks to be a Hawaiian carnival. Almost half the crowd is wearing Ailana Liona shirts. For those that don't have one there are several purveyors handy.

Vendors are offering pineapple juice for $8 a cup, frozen pina coladas for $20, beer for $10 with the exception of the dark-blue labeled Hawaiian Primo brand which is $15. Water is the most in demand at a bargain of $5 a bottle. I got my stash of bottled H20 out of the Oak's family fridge.

After checking in at the media center, I contact my superiors at USN for any updates. They have more questions for me than

I have for them. Rumors are evidently swirling around back in Dallas of my close contact with Maleko during the week.

Forging my way to the first tee to watch the early pairings is not an easy task. Amid a crowd asking me for autographs and annotations, I have to infiltrate a mass of Tiger and Kalani fans, all eagerly and aggressively pursuing their heroes.

Just inside the roped off area separating the spectators and me from the initiating tee box, Danny Tertius is all miked up ready to do his live television fairway coverage for USN. Dan, a former PGA touring member, is best known for his unique style of quick wit and anecdotes while reporting.

Dan and I are old friends from several years back. He is always effervescent and amusingly cordial. My slightly graying, forty-year-old USN colleague from Australia spots me on the other side of the corded barrier.

"G'Day, Ms. Priss! You look the spunky in pink."

"Are you up to all this heat?" I ask.

"I've done the Outback; this'll be like a spring stroll through the park. The heat is on you, girl. The buzz is you got the insidey with Maleko this week. How's that doin' for ya?"

"Nice try, Danny boy," I say, "but the word from me is mum."

Our little flirtation is being interrupted as the first two golfers approach for the 7:00 tee time. Before Dan backs off to the side, he asks a favor.

"We'd like to get you in for a few words here and there, especially on the weekend. Can you give it a go?"

"If it's on camera I'll need a little heads up," I reply, protecting my vanity.

The army of supporters wait almost impatiently by golf standards for the 7:50 tee time of Tiger Woods and the Island Lion: two golfing greats starting out head-to-head. Both affable yet serious, the two talented champions drive long, lofting shots well past the middle of the fairway of the par four opening hole.

Tiger's militia and the even more numerous Liona Legion, depart to track their conquerors. The first tee now seems nearly vacant and void while a few locals and I linger for Timber Oak's 7:50 tee time just three pairs back.

It already feels ominously warm as the eastern sun glares down on Whispering Waters. Creeks, ponds, and pools twinkle in the fresh morning daylight.

The next few pairings start their rounds in ten minute intervals. Perspiration and inspiration speckle the faces of golfers and gallery alike. Water, hand towels, sunglasses and energy drinks reign.

If it were not for the heat I would feel immodestly dressed for my age. I went with the pink shorts and matching sleeveless top that Jorell bought for me in our last mission trip to Mexico. The pink visor clusters my blond tresses. The matching tennies may be too much, but I am true to form.

The local Oklahoma media types as well as Timber Oaks' homegrown allies have begun to gather, waiting for the Saint's arrival. Warm applause and appreciative cheers greet Timber and his son, amid shouts of "You da man, Timber!" and "Keep on Marchin', Saint!" Timber responds with his charismatic and magnetic charm, slapping palms and exchanging pleasantries with the familiar faces. Timber removes his droopy cap, revealing his already damp bushy hair, tips the cap to his fans while acknowledging his playing partner of the first two rounds.

"How 'bout a little love for my pal, Chipper here?" Timber urges the small crowd.

The Saint's congregation responds in kind. Timber puts a hand on the young Alabaman's shoulder and whispers encouragement.

After the first two drives, Chipper's slightly farther down than Timber due to his youthful strength, I cannot help but admire and feel blessed at the sight of Pauly walking alongside his father, sharing in a major tournament—the boy born with autism that I had watched grow into a compelling young man.

As I follow Timber and Pauly down the side of the fairway with a small group of partisans, I jot down a quick note of my thoughts.

Could the man that has seen and been a part of so many supernatural phenomenons experience one more? Does God have another miracle in store for Timber Oaks? What a story that would be!

Timber is his typical self. He loves golf and his environment, acting more like a child at play than a professional golfer. He confers with the gallery throughout the round, enjoying the camaraderie and circumstance. Pauly remains serious, instructing his father on each shot, oblivious to Timber's amusing antics.

Even though animated and gregarious, Team Oaks plays it conservatively. Knowing their home course well, they avoid the temptation of going for risky shots that Whispering Waters often rewards with a wet golf ball. Timber is playing it safe.

I keep up with the rest of the field via cell phone. The live feed provided by USN features, not only live performance, but individual player scorecards and updates. All morning the sighs reverberating throughout Whispering Waters far outnumber the cheers from the rabble of fans throughout the gallery following the likes of Tiger and Maleko, Phil and Westwood, Kaymer and Furyk.

The Island Lion's aggressive style of play suits his moniker. Attacking on every opportunity to score, he does not disappoint the Liona Legion with his serious insistent manner but yet

somewhat dissatisfies them with his opening tally. Frequent birdies are followed by a few more bogies for a first round score of 74,
two over for the day.

The Saint playing in his traditional mode fails on all birdie
attempts and comes up short of par on four different holes, the
victim of the notoriously fast Bermuda greens. The two leaders
after Thursday's opening round post even par. Starting out with
a 76 on the perfidious Whispering Waters leaves Timber in his
proverbial spot in the middle of the pack.

Pauly leaves the Country Club earlier than we with his new
friend, driving Chico's rental car. We are promised a gourmet
Argentine meal after they run by the supermarket.

Mark is sequestered to the media center for his reflections.
Timber is spared the agony. That's the difference between number
one and average; the distinction between good and great.

Mark is distraught on the ride back to Fort Oaks. Even after I
inform him after all was said and done, he is just two off the pace.
It is clear that by Ailana Liona standards, his performance was
unacceptable.

Timber seems unfazed. After all, his goal of making the cut
appears to be in reach. But it is fair to summarize that Whispering
Falls won the opening round.

Becky and Nicklaus greet us in their individual fashion with
the dog prancing for attention and the Saint's wife providing a
couple decanters of cool liquid refreshment. Two fatigued competitors and one exhausted reporter pet the canine and graciously
accept the thirst quencher.

The living room television is still tuned to my favorite
sports network. The volume is loud enough that Becky can hear
it throughout the house and I assume particularly in the home
office. USN is doing the wrap up coverage featuring clips and

commentary of the day's first round. There is much ado about Mark and little if anything on Timber.

Becky embraces her husband and commends him while handing him his daily list of messages. Mark is subdued, still displeased with himself.

"You did good out there today, Honey," Becky praises Timber. "And Mark, you were awesome as always."

Mark manages an unimpressive smile while we help ourselves to seconds of iced tea and lemonade.

"Becky girl, I was so proud of Pauly!" I tell her. "I think he's found a career!"

"Yes, Timber and I are both proud."

I try to change Mark's somber mood with a zesty suggestion.

"Who's all for an Oak's backyard cool splash while we wait for our celebrity chefs?"

"Not for me," pouts Mark. "I've seen enough water today."

Mark takes his refilled glass back to his assigned quarters for what we all hope is a practice in attitude adjustment.

"Got a little work to catch up on," says Timber, flashing Becky's to do list.

"I need to wait for Chico and Pauly. This could be fun!" says Becky, the courteous domestic supervisor.

As the group disperses, all that remains with me is the sociable brown Labrador, reminding me with a damp nose nudge that he is still at my disposal.

"Looks like just you and me, Nicklaus boy."

Lying back in the refreshing tranquility of the soothing water, I mentally preview tomorrow's agenda. Nicklaus' bushy upright tail moves back and forth just above the rim of the spa to remind me of his loyal attendance.

I awake from my semiconscious state to the backyard entrance of Chico Dominquez, patronizing and flamboyant as he extols his escort. Becky is showered with adjectives on her backyard surroundings with words like 'preciosa' and 'hermoso'.

After pleasantly greeting Nicklaus and me, Chico assures us in his fusion of English and Spanish that Pauly and he have everything under control. Before reentering the house to join his young assistant in preparing our evening meal, he stops to examine the treasured Oak's outdoor grill with the declaration of 'perfecto!'

Becky and I giggle together like school girls at Chico's antics as we are finally left alone. She surprises me by stepping out of her yellow summer dress and sandals, revealing a black one-piece swimsuit and joining me.

It is time for a much-needed girl talk. As we discuss and catch up on everything from families, friends and relationships to earthquakes, golf and God, I cannot break into Becky's secret anxiety. My female journalistic intuition tells me it is a health problem, but all three Oaks appear to be in perfect physical form.

Chico brings Pauly out to the patio and gives precise instructions on how he wants the fire in the grill arranged. Their conversation is mostly in Spanish. Holding a fresh bag of charcoal, Pauly carefully listens to his South American tutor and converses with ease in the foreign language.

"Have you ever taught Pauly Spanish?" I ask his mother.

"No, I have a background in French." She smiles as we watch Pauly tending to the grill.

"Then doesn't this surprise you?"

"Not when he's focused," Becky admits. "Nothing really surprises us with Pauly anymore."

After wrapping towels around us and going back into the house for a quick change, we get to observe the bustle going on in Becky's kitchen. Chico is busy at a chopping block mincing shallots, parsley and garlic for the food processor. Three thick-cut sirloin steaks are airing out, waiting for marinating.

Pauly is working on a fruit salad of apples, mandarins, peaches, bananas, oranges and papaya with most of the peelings missing the disposal and hitting the floor. Listening keenly to Chico's commands, he attends a sauce pan simmering with milk and sugar. The aroma of fresh lemons and oregano saturate my imagination.

While everyone gathers at the patio table with anticipation, Mark joins us, notably recuperated from his self pity after the self-imposed quarantine. The outdoor table top is covered with a white table cloth and a center piece of fresh-cut burgundy geraniums. Becky's finest chinaware adorns six place settings. The crystal wine glasses are filled with chilled apple cider.

Chico removes the sizzling basted sirloins from the grill carefully arranging them on a platter. Pauly delivers fruit salad and fresh toasted baguettes and proudly announces the main course.

"Steak Gaucho with Argentinean Chimichurri Sauce and Fruit Salad with dulce de leche!"

"Bon appetit!" adds Chico as both caddies take a bow.

"Bueno trabajo, Chico and Pauly," says Mark to the chefs, lifting his glass in a cider toast. All join in tilting their goblets toward Chico and Mark and follow with a round of applause.

With Pauly's help in translation, Chico instructs us on the proper method to enjoy the gourmet cuisine. The meat is served on the baguettes and eaten together. Timber suggests that Chico lead us in prayer. Chico being Catholic crosses himself then obliges. This is a classic dinner with friends to be treasured.

After enjoying the delectable banquet, Timber pushes back from the table and suggests that Mark help him clear the table and do the dishes. Mark, not used to such an offer, especially in the middle of a major tournament, finally gives in and helps.

Chico remains with Becky, Pauly and me. I cannot help but peek through the glass doors to witness the Saint and the Lion performing the trifling chore.

"What I would give for a picture of that," I say out loud. "If I tried for it, Mark might confiscate my cell phone."

Pauly jumps up from the table silently gesturing for my phone.

"It's in my room on the dresser...or I guess it is actually your room."

The eager teenager pulls the door open just enough for him and Nicklaus to shimmy through. Pauly uses my iPod to take pictures of his father and Mark with Nicklaus nearby, hoping that some scraps fall on the floor.

Mark looks agitated when he sees Pauly. Timber notices what is going on and comforts his friend with an arm around his shoulder. Mark forces a smile. They turn together in front of the kitchen sink and pose for the perfect portrait.

"Bueno! Dey is good for teach other," declares the Ailana Liona's famed sidekick.

"How do you mean?" I ask him.

Becky looks on with interest too. The well traveled sage is known to be more than Mark's golf adviser. He also plays the part of philosopher and psychiatrist. Using hand motions to help with his paraphrasing, Chico enlightens us.

"Senor Madera...Timber, need Maleko's agresividad...how you say...aggressive? I mean say at golf. La Leon need Timber zumbido."

Pauly comes back out just in time to translate.

"He's saying that Mark needs to be humble like Dad."

Nicklaus follows Pauly back outside in anticipation of Hound Dog Island time. Pauly hands me my cell. I review his stream of freshly captured digital images with Becky looking on over my shoulder. Chico gets up and stands between us to appraise Pauly's camera work.

The outside speakers resonate with some instrumental Latin salsa, compliments of Timber. Chico is pleasantly surprised and cha-chas with an imaginary partner.

"Looks like it's that time again!" says Mark as the kitchen duo joins us for the evening encore with a fresh pitcher of cider.

Mark interrupts Chico's dance routine and points out to him the dogs gathering in adjacent yards. They walk out toward the pond with Timber where Pauly and Nicklaus, await.

"You're going to love this Chic's. It's a dog fiesta."

Chico catches on quick as Timber initiates the game, lofting the ball into the island fountain. The enthused South American urges on his favorite canine competitive swimmer.

"Go el pequeno perro! Vivo el Chihuahua!"

Friday

It's a good morning to sleep in. I awake to the glow of sunshine illuminating my room. The staggered tee times for the Saint and the Lion—Mark at 1:05 and Timber at 1:35— make for a relaxed morning.

The Oaks family is occupied in the Circle of Care administrative center. The sound of keyboard typing and low toned conversation is audible in the hallway behind a closed door.

The aroma of hot coffee and freshly cooked sausage links guide me to Becky's kitchen. A waffle maker sits on the counter next to some ready-to-pour batter. Maple syrup simmers on the stove. It looks like a help yourself kind of morning.

Holding off on breakfast, I help myself to a mug of desire and nibble at one of the sausages wrapped in a napkin. I set up shop in the living room still comfy in my robe.

Turning the TV to mute so I can keep tabs on the early coverage of the second round, I arrange my laptop and note pad on the coffee table and settle into the sofa to catch up on some work.

Timber comes out of the office for a refill of java. He is fresh and already dressed for a day of golf.

"Sleep well, Ms. Priss?" he asks from the kitchen, replenishing his cup.

"Very."

Mark wobbles into the kitchen, dressed in only a pair of green long-legged pajama pants. Squinting in the early daybreak's radiance, he inspects the layout and pours some coffee.

The Lion tips cups with the Saint to salute the morning. Again, I pretend not to listen in by acting occupied with my business.

"So I read the story in the Bible last night," says the Lion, "'bout the rich guy…sounds like you were directing that at me?"

"Ya think?" says Timber. "In fact, God directs that story to all who seek eternal life."

"So I'm too rich to get to Heaven? I need to sell off everything I've worked hard for?" Mark shakes his head. "You know, I read one of the letters to you from Colonel Armstrong that talks 'bout wealthy people and how God can use them…"

Timber puts his coffee cup down on the counter. I know Timber well enough. He got the reaction he planned and expected out of Mark.

"Remember when we talked about sin?" Timber says. "Jesus was pointing out the rich young man's sin. He used the Ten Commandments like a mirror. This was an honorable guy. He didn't cheat, lie or steal, but the reflection he saw in the mirror was not what he had perceived. He was not keeping God's law as he pretended to be."

"So his sin was his wealth?" asks Mark, still sipping his morning coffee.

"No, not at all!" says Timber.

"This fella was in pretty good shape till Jesus held up that mirror.

Do you remember the Tenth Commandment? It's the one that gets us all."

"Uhmm…not really, not sure. Is it…"

"It states not to covet—to not get attached to possessions or desire the possessions of others. In other words, desire only God and do not worship stuff. Love God and one another, not material things.

"It doesn't mean you can't have lots of stuff or that you must sell everything you own. Christ showed the rich young man his sin so he could repent and follow Him. He went away sadly because he realized that he loved his possessions more than God and couldn't part with them.

"If God asks you to give up anything, you should be prepared, Mark. It's a mind-set that keeps us from being selfish with wealth so that nothing will become between you and God."

"So rich guys can go to Heaven as long as they don't covet?" sighs Mark with relief while refilling his cup. "Thought I was in trouble there for a minute."

"…and you're one of the richest people I know and I know a lot of them. Let's see, I think you own three nice homes: Hawaii, Palm Springs and Florida. There's the yacht, luxury cars, a pricey art collection, various successful business enterprises…I hear you're going to purchase your own private jet soon?"

I continue to appear busy while I am in reality transcribing the dialogue on my laptop. Mark stares at Timber face to face and does not comment on the jet.

"You know, I don't think you really covet any of those things. Admit it. Sometimes it all just gets in the way. What do you really covet, Maleko Kalani?"

Mark turns his back to Timber and walks over to the glass doorway. Deep in thought, he gazes out at Hound Dog Island and the peaceful scene of the geese gliding on the pond. He rotates back toward Timber and stares at the floor.

"It's the trophies, isn't it?" Timber says, sounding very Colonel-esque. "It's all those championships and titles. That's what you really covet. Soon you may have more major titles than Jack or

Tiger, making you the greatest of all time.

"That's what you put first in your life…being the best and that is what makes you such a fierce competitor. All your talent comes from God, Mark. You just nourished and polished that talent.

"There is nothing wrong with competing, winning or being the best, but in reality, God who made you deserves the glory, not the Ailana Liona. Sooner or later you're gonna have to decide if you can lay down those trophies before God."

Timber reaches out with a consoling hand on Mark's shoulder. Mark, knowing his pride has been revealed, looks up to the older and wiser man.

"Mark, let me know when you are ready to lay down those trophies."

The morning begins to wane. Timber and Mark have taken their discussion to the patio table out of ear range. Pauly and his mother come out of the office. Becky smiles and asks if she can get me anything then assists her son with his breakfast.

I finally catch up with my reports and research. It's time to shut things down. Becky refills my mug while Pauly joins me on the couch with a plate full of waffles covered with peanut butter and syrup, an extra heaping helping of sausage and a tall glass of milk. Pauly grabs the remote.

"Mind?" he asks me while turning up the volume.

"Not at all. I'm all caught up for once."

Pauly eats while studying the television. The live commentary from the USN announcers is mostly about Mark and how tough Whispering Waters is playing. The young caddie consumes breakfast as well as the golf coverage. I try to get into his thoughts.

"So what's your prognosis for today on our two golfers?"

With his eyes remaining on the TV screen, Pauly wipes his lips with a cloth napkin.

"Chico said last night that he needs to get Mark to play within himself and quit going for impracticable shots. He also said that Dad needs to do just the opposite…play outside of his normal game."

"Wonder why?" I thought aloud.

"Well, Chico agrees with me," says Pauly proudly. "Coming in with anything under par could win this thing. With the way things are going, Mark might be the only one capable of that.

"But since Dad is familiar with the course, he should be more aggressive. You know, try to establish some momentum."

"How you going to get that accomplished?"

"First, we gotta make the cut. Chico's predicting it at plus seven or eight. That's kinda high for a major, but all the guys are strugglin'. Dad just needs a repeat of yesterday's round for that."

It is almost 11:00 by the time Pauly pulls the van into Whispering Waters for the second round of the PGA. More reporters are on hand to greet us than before. I fear they are catching on to the Saint and Lion arrangement.

Mark acknowledges them but hurries on through security. I know Timber and Pauly are anxious to get to the practice green to work on the Saint's putting that was a bit sub-par yesterday. Still, Timber manages to give them some time.

Every day seems hotter. The Ailana Liona and Tiger start out just after 1:00. Mark went green today in one of his flashy shirts with matching green golf shoes and trousers in contrast to the always-refined Tiger Woods.

Chico, faithfully on Mark's bag, waves to me and blows me a kiss. I wait for the crowd following two of the world's best golfers to recede. Good old Danny follows with them, but not before informing me that the network would like to get me on the air somewhere around the sixth hole.

"Thanks for the warning!" I shout, now many yards away.

Dan turns back toward me from the middle of the fairway and yells in his familiar Aussie twang.

"Least I could, missy."

The grueling 100 degree weather was taking its toll on the players. As the day grew hotter, Timber continued to struggle with the putter. Midway through the sixth fairway with my nose freshly powdered and trying to look presentable in my pink ensemble, Danny caught up with me for the quick interview.

"I got standing here beside me Ms. Priscilla Luke, USN personality fresh from her dancing fame. Prissy, I see you're following your old buddy Timber Oaks this weekend. How's it doin' with the Saint?"

I go into my professional broadcasting routine trying to be relevant and informative while looking pleasantly into the camera lens.

"Well, Dan, as you know, Timber is the hometown favorite. He is respected and loved for his ministry throughout the world. In the Tulsa area Timber and his wife, Becky, are adored for their community outreach. This week it's a family thing as his son, Pauly, is caddying for him for the first time. Timber Oaks and his family are a great story in this year's PGA."

"But Priscilla, the Saint is getting' a little long of tooth. At forty-eight, do you give him a chance to ever win? Somethin' he's failed to ever do."

"I hope so Dan. He's a man of miracles."

"Thank you missy, and back to you mates up in the booth..."

I keep a close eye on my hand-held scorer. By the time Timber and Pauly get to the eighteenth tee, Mark has finished, obviously taking Chico's advice of a more conservative approach.

The Lion concluded the second round with one birdie, one

bogie and put together a string of pars for an even par round of 72, several strokes ahead of Tiger. That is good enough for a share of the lead remaining at two over par.

Chipper and Timber are playing in the final pairing of the day. The score of the young upstart from Alabama has ballooned today, leaving him out of this weekend's competition. His manner is still good-natured, obviously enjoying his time spent with the Saint.

Timber's round is typical of him. After 35 holes and looking at one of the toughest finishing holes in golf, Timber's tally is a disappointing plus nine. The USN commentators are projecting a plus eight for the cut.

This adds to the dramatics of live television. Everyone's Mr. Nice Guy would need a birdie on the demanding par four eighteenth to qualify for weekend play. So far in two rounds, Timber has not managed any hole under par.

With the rest of the field already in the clubhouse, the remaining crowd gathers around the final hole to see if Timber Oaks will join a privileged assembly of seventy to challenge for the title.

Number 18 is nicknamed the Tree of Tragedy. The 480 yard par four features an enormous—beautiful but ominous—oak tree just to the right of the fairway beyond the halfway point.

Surrounding the front of the small green is another one of Whispering Waters' menacing hazards: a rock-lined creek that serves as a moat providing a line of defense for the small oval-shaped green.

Chipper has the honors and leads off with a drive that ricochets off the tree into the deep wooded rough on the right. He looks over at Timber and simply shrugs.

Timber removes his floppy cap that's dripping with sweat. He takes a hand towel from Pauly and wipes his hands, face, and soaked hair while examining the task before him.

The Saint would normally play it safe and use a fairway iron to avoid the oak tree to the left. Then he would lay up in front of the creek on his second shot hoping to put the ball in position for a short approach shot that could land close enough for his par four.

However, this is no time for pars and meritocracy. Pauly removes the baby-blue head cover of Timber's driver and presents it to his father with some guidance.

"We need a three, Dad."

I stood next to Dan behind the tee box. He whispered into his microphone describing the degree of difficulty facing Timber. A hush fell over the gallery. Timber smashed his longest drive of the day to the left and beyond the oak tree, settling just off the fairway in the short-cut rough.

The homeland hero is cheered as hope lingers. While Chipper struggles to pound his way out of the woods, Dan and I, along with anxious golf fans, hurry to put ourselves in location for Timber's approach.

"His lie is good just off the fairway and standin' up," says Dan to the USN audience. "Mr. Saint is starin' at 180 yards, over the creek and onto the racin' green. Looks like his boy, Pauly, is handin' 'em a five iron. He's gonna give it a go!"

Timber's smooth swing picks up the ball cleanly but the shot appears short looming perilously toward the creek. The ball finally lands on the upper rocks off the far side of the dangerous stream. It then takes a lively bounce on up to the green, trickling through the grass and stopping just two feet from the pin.

The partisan gallery erupts. The cheering and applause break into a spontaneous glee club whistling rendition of Timber Oak's theme song. There is no bigger smile than Pauly's as the Saint marches on to his tap in.

As Timber finishes off the short putt for his birdie three, many of his fellow professionals have gathered around the green to watch and congratulate their friend and companion. The first to greet him is Maleko Kalani.

As Pauly wheels the family van into the double drive, the garage overhead door is open. Mark and Timber are trying to recover from the scorching day.

"Ohhh, no," moans Timber, burying his forehead on my shoulder.

"Ohh, yes!" Pauly gives an opposite reaction.

Inside the garage, parked next to Timber's Sainthauler is a sports car that looks fresh from a photo shoot of some futuristic hotrod magazine. It has a dark blue and white racing stripe running right down the middle. Mark leans forward to see what the Oaks boy's reaction is all about.

"Whose is that?" I ask Timber.

"Never seen it before, but there is only one person I know that would be driving it."

"Benny!" Pauly shouts gleefully.

As the excited teenager jumps out of the van and runs through the garage, Mark puts it all together.

"The guy from your story about your home town? Isn't he your father-in-law?"

"Sorry about this, Mark. It's just bad timing," says Timber. "Benny will shoot you some sort of a deal. It's just his nature. Let me know when you have had enough."

"Take it easy, Timber," I say as the three of us exit the van. "Benny's a good guy. Besides, I haven't seen Sarah in a long time. I've only been able to keep up with her on Facebook."

"There they are. The world's greatest!" says Ben Larson flatteringly, joining us in the garage with Pauly under an arm.

Benny, seventy, gray and still well fit and vibrant introduces himself to Mark and then gives me a bear hug.

"So, what you got here, Ben," asks Timber, knowing full well that a Benny promotion is imminent.

"Fellas, what we got here is a pure American muscle machine— a two-thousand twelve Boss three-oh-two Laguna Mustang with four hundred and forty horses under the hood. It's all about power and handling."

Pauly slips into the driver's seat as Mark and I make a closer inspection.

"It's boss alright!" says Pauly, firmly gripping the padded steering wheel, pretending that he's racing down a freeway.

"Is this another one for the collection?" asks Timber.

"You know me, son," says Benny. "We'll wait and see."

"Yep, I know you for sure."

Becky is with her mother as we enter the kitchen. Sarah is in her mid-sixties and a little plumper than when I last saw her. But she still has the distinguishing auburn hair. We embrace, exchanging pleasantries.

"As soon as we saw you birdie that final hole on television, Timber, I told Sarah 'we need to get over to Broken Arrow.' So we loaded up some southern fried and a couple melons and got here soon as we could."

Benny points out the array of fried chicken and all the fixings on the counter in tub-like containers, along with two dark-green watermelons. Mark warmly makes acquaintance with Sarah then steps across the kitchen and begins rolling the huge melons along the counter as if to examine them.

"I've heard about you people and watermelons," says Mark. "I wouldn't want to take any chances."

Benny lets out a horse laugh. Seizing the moment, he pulls

Mark outside to pitch business. Mark is more interested in talking about Corinthia Falls. Timber joins them to offer protection to Mark.

Pauly digs into his first serving of chicken and heads for the big screen to catch the highlights of the tournament with Nicklaus trailing him. This leaves us girls alone in the kitchen to do some chatting.

"Becky, how's Timber holding up?" the retired school teacher asks her daughter.

Becky shakes her head negatively as if to suggest that now was not the time. I feel like I'm intruding on something private. I excuse myself from the conversation and join the guys out back.

The backyard grill gets a needed rest. After an evening of grazing on extra crispy and watermelon, the raucous attack on Hound Dog island gives place to old stories about Corinthia Falls, and numerous financial transactions are proposed. Benny and Sarah go on back home to Corinthia Falls, but not before promising to be at Whispering Waters the next day with Becky.

Mark has gone back to his room with another reading assignment from Timber. I help Becky tidy up in the kitchen.

Pauly has remained fixated on the television the whole time. He pauses the screen on a local Tulsa station's weather report. Stopping his father before he can retire for the night, the diligent novice caddie beckons.

"Dad, you might want to take a look at this."

Timber walks over and stands next to his son as both study the morning forecast.

"Looks like more of the same hot weather, son."

"Yes, but take a look at the dew point in the morning... seventy-eight. That's extremely high. We are in the very first pairing tomorrow. They will be watering the course all night, which should be followed by very heavy dew on the ground,"The course will play much softer on, say, the front nine anyway... you know, a little more forgiving. It's time to be aggressive. Like you say 'Once saved, what's to lose?' Let's attack!"

Timber cocks his head sideways considering his son's reasoning. With an assured smile and a well-done pat on the back, Timber concurs. "Very well then, we attack."

Saturday

Pauly, Timber and I leave well before dawn to make the 7:30 tee time. Sharing the tournament lead, Mark would be in the final pairing for a 1:40 start. It is agreed that he will ride in later with Benny and Sarah in the flashy new Mustang.

The course conditions Pauly spoke of the night before prove to be accurate. Whispering Waters is saturated from the overnight watering and a very heavy dew. The humid-balmy air is thick enough to slice.

The early rising crowd, many adorned in Ailana Liona attire, gathers around the first tee box to watch the Saint and Gary Santos, a qualifying club pro from Arizona, get the third round initiated.

Just six strokes separate the field. As usual, Timber finds himself chasing the field. Sixty-nine golfers and Whispering Waters separate Timber from the lead.

Timber swaps greetings with his usual cast of supporters in the early morning haze. The Saint is somewhat less gregarious, appearing more focused on his game and less on camaraderie.

Pauly hands him his driver and Timber delivers. His faultless first shot on the short par four opening hole leaves him with a short approach. Timber gets it up and down for a birdie thanks to the slower play and softer, saturated green.

The six hundred yard par five seems no match for the Saint.

But two perfect drives and a thirty foot putt smack the center of the hole for a rare eagle three.

Dan catches up with me on the green of the par three third hole. Like any good correspondent, Dan wants to be in on the story and the action. This morning the story is Timber Oaks. Timber rolls in a short birdie putt to make him four under for the day in just three holes. The Saint's following swells.

Benny, Sarah, and Becky catch up with me on the fifth hole par five, all three panting to get closer to Timber's assault. Benny is supercharged as he yanks the girls through the ignited gallery for a closer view.

"That's what I'm talkin' about!" shouts Benny loudly, almost hyperventilating. "The Saints da man!"

Becky and her mother retreat away to a more comfortable distance. They remain close together throughout the round trying not to distract Timber's concentration. With their eyes shut on each stroke Timber makes, I can sense their silent prayers.

At the par four ninth hole, Benny plays head cheerleader for the ecstatic crowd as the Saint rolls in another birdie putt. Dan begins to run out of Aussie jargon superlatives for Timber's front nine performance.

The Saint goes out on the front nine carding a six under par 30 leaving Team Oaks plus two for the tournament and tied for the lead with Kalani and Mickelson, the final pairing still a couple of hours from starting their round.

As the latter morning heat intensifies, the formidable course begins to return to her unsympathetic state. But on this day there would be no playing it safe as is the usual custom of the Saint; no laying up short or hitting for the fat part of the green. With his son at the helm, the Saint of golf and leader of the prominent Circle of Care are in the zone.

On the twelfth hole par three Timber's tee shot stops inches from the pin, and the engorged following usually reserved for the likes of Maleko, Tiger, and Phil can hold back no longer as the whistling begins. At first it is soft, as if a light harmonic breeze is filtering through the trees. By the time Timber completes his swing on his final approach shot from the middle of the eighteenth fairway, the sound of the Saint's Marching theme vibrates throughout the course.

It is a moment to capture on the final green. I snap every picture I can with my cell phone: images of Becky holding her breath in the foreground, Pauly hushing the melodious supporting throng to stillness, Timber lining up his putt from various angles soaked with perspiration. Hundreds of cameras prepare to flicker.

The Saint drops in another birdie three on the final hole for the second day in a row to the thunderous approval of his golfing congregation. Removing his sweat stained floppy cap, Timber shakes hands with his playing partner who has suffered a tough day at Water World, waves to the crowd that is now singing his song in full accord, hugs his beaming son and family, then marches into the scorers' tent to sign his score card. It is a Whistling Waters course record of 64, putting the Saint at even par for 54 holes with the lead in the clubhouse.

I wait in the packed media room full of journalists that have left the course temporarily as we await Timber's arrival. I check my cell for updates. USN is leading off the afternoon coverage with a highlight segment on Timber's round of 64.

The field of participating challengers for the revered championship are retreating to the perils of Whispering Waters. All are falling off the pace with the exception of the Ailana Liona.

Finally, Timber enters the media center to a warm reception of complimentary reporters and twinkling lenses. He is accompanied by Pauly. It is evident that the day is a special shared achievement between father and son.

Before Timber and Pauly can sit down to address the anxious swarm, an enlivened John Solomon enters to embrace the Oaks boys. After a quick inaudible exchange with Timber, the tournament's sponsoring executive makes a speedy exit, but not before responding to a reporter's shouted question.

"Where ya goin', John?"

"To polish off the Wanamaker Trophy for the Saint!"

"That might be a little premature," commented Timber.

Timber first gives thanks to God and family. He expresses gratitude for all the enthused support. Answering the array of questions with typical golfing clichés, Timber praises his son on his direction of the record breaking round.

When it is time for my question, I cannot resist asking Pauly, "What's your advice for your dad tomorrow? It appears it might be a position with which he is unfamiliar."

"Intimidation!" a pokerfaced Pauly counters to laughter of his father and everyone in the room.

Timber Oaks has never been and cannot be intimidating.

Becky left for home with Benny and her mother after Timber's round was complete. The euphoric entrepreneur of Corinthia Falls was anxious to drop off his daughter-in-law and get back home to replay Timber's round he had TiBo'd.

Becky and I laughed off his threat to bring his saxophone to play at the final hole tomorrow when Timber does his traditional marching routine. We wondered who he would have to bribe to get his sax through security.

Timber and Pauly retreat to the cooler confines of the clubhouse to convalesce from the heat and watch the rest of the afternoon's tournament. I try to freshen up and follow Mark through the back nine.

Mark plays brilliantly as the Liona Legion urges on their leader. With the rest of the world's best assortment of golfers succumbing to Water World, Mark, with his diligent concentration and keen ball striking, dissects Whispering Waters.

By the time 54 holes of the PGA Championship is finished, Mark tallies a two under for the day's round, leaving him at even par for the tournament and tied with Timber Oaks for the lead. The closest grouping is four strokes back. The USN network gets what they were promoting all day. Golf fans and followers of theatrics get their dream match up: the Saint, the world's favorite underdog and conscience of the game versus the Ailana Liona, the sport's most dominant player and standard bearer.

Mark fields questions from a quarry of reporters in the media room while downing two bottles of water. His wet matted-down black hair and flushed Hawaiian complexion reveal his exhaustion.

Dan picks up on my earlier question of Pauly, asking Maleko if he feels any intimidation from Timber Oaks. After another round of laughter, the Lion comments thoughtfully.

"I have no room for intimidation in my game. But look, the guy at forty-eight years of age shoots a sixty four on one of the toughest courses with the hardest conditions I have ever played. He knows Whispering Waters and is playing the best golf of his life."

Mark is escorted to the minivan by Chico and his private security team where Timber is in the backseat and Pauly and me upfront. Mark opens the side passenger door and offers an excuse for not joining us.

"Things are starting to get awkward. They're catching on to where I'm staying. Think it would be better to stay with Chics and the guys at the hotel?"

"Don't be ridiculous, Mark!" I object. "Besides, Becky has a surprise for you fellas."

"...and all your stuff is at our place," adds Timber. "One more night won't hurt."

With a slight reluctance, Mark slides in the back seat but not before Chico gives Pauly the well-done sign. As the beaming young redhead maneuvers our way out of the parking lot, Mark slaps Timber on the knee.

"Man! What got into you today?"

Timber leans back against the corner of the backseat interior relaxed and content, shutting his eyes as if in a dream state.

"Golf," he replies.

The shiny new red Cadillac Escalade parked in the front drive of the Oak's abode gives away the secret Becky has planned. Timber and Pauly rush inside excitedly without saying a word.

"What's this all about?" asks Mark,.

"TJ's here!"

"Thomas Johnson? Cool!"

The welcoming party is already in full swing out on the patio as Mark and I make it through the house to the backyard. Timber and Pauly are trading simulated boxing punches with TJ. The masculine bonding routine is accented with the aroma of hickory smoke that permeates the late afternoon air.

TJ wears a red Georgia Bulldog golf shirt with white athletic shorts and leather sandals. He is heavier and broader than in his playing days with a shaved head, a graying goatee and gold rimmed glasses. He looks like a modern day, larger version of his father.

No one can lighten up a room or even the great outdoors more than Thomas Johnson. His personality is infectious. The playful scuffling winds down as the bigger-than-life coaching great hugs his godson and best friend simultaneously.

"Looky out now, don't want to hurt ya. You boys got a championship to win!"

TJ moves on to me. Rather than an embrace, he holds me in ballroom dancing posture performing dips and swirls while gliding me across the patio to the rhythm of the soft jazz melody playing on the outside amplifiers.

"Ahhh, the famous ballerina in pink!"

I cannot help but blush as TJ bows at his waist to me after the brief, impromptu dance. Pauly, Timber and Mark offer a round of applause.

"Maleko! Tom Johnson." TJ extends a hand and clasps his other around Mark's shoulder.

"Mark," offers the new acquaintance.

Both smile and shake hands, showing the mutual respect I have often witnessed when champions meet. TJ flatters his new friend.

"The Ailana Liona; the man and the legend…"

Mark gets in on the fun.

"Thomas Johnson; the great rock climber of Corinthia Falls!"

"Don't know what all these people have been tellin' you, Mark, but rock climbin' is not on my résumé."

"What do you have cooking, chef?" I ask.

The overused Oak's family grill is shut, billowing blue smoke through the vents. Next to it is an upright homemade looking contraption the TJ brought along. A large bag of hickory nuts, a fresh bag of charcoal, a large pair of tongs and a mop type baster are his only accessories.

"Hickory smoked pork ribs with Georgia mop sauce; an exceptional culinary delight from the South. You're gonna love it. Nicklaus and I have been working on this since this mornin', right fella?"

TJ bends down and scratches his friendly canine assistant's head. Becky joins us on the patio with a pitcher of her lemonade tea and five ice filled tumblers.

"What ya got planned to go along with the ribs, Teej?" she asks.

TJ pretends to be insulted with the question.

"Sauce, Ms. Becky. My Georgia mop sauce is all you need."

Becky shakes her head, amused with TJ's conceit. She fills Timber a glass of tea and informs him.

"Honey, you have a million emails and phone messages in the office waiting for you. Your parents called. Talk to them first. Sherry left a message… Jorell's been trying to get through. Everyone is excited for you but there's some updates on Kenya."

"I need to take care of a little business myself," adds Mark.

As both sportsmen excuse themselves, TJ checks on his work. Retrieving a simmering sauce pan from the kitchen, he opens both grills and mops the ribs.

While Pauly, Becky and I enjoy our refreshment, the talk turns to the day's events. The topic is championships and the witty Thomas Johnson is holding class.

"Ya know, sports imitate life…" he began.

"Seems I've heard that before," I interrupted at the mundane cliché.

Thomas keeps right on with the lecture, mopping the ribs and pretending not to hear me.

"It just don't matter what game you're playin'… football, basketball, golf or, man…even Chinese checkers. Just like in life, a championship is always defined by just a few special moments; after all the strugglin', the competition between resisting forces, it comes down to the special moments: a football recovered in the end zone, a point guard steals the ball at mid court for the winning lay-up, holing out from off the green or saving a lost soul. It's those unforeseen unique occasions when work, patience and preparation, fate and destiny identify what will be remembered. And just like the game of life, tomorrow will be no different."

TJ carves the racks of ribs in the kitchen on a cutting board. The meat is so tender it falls from the bone. He serves it up with extra sauce and a handful of paper towels. Mark is the first to rejoin the rest of us, refreshed from a shower. Soon after, Timber returns from his office labor to get in on the finger-licking barbeque.

The large screen is muted promoting tomorrow's broadcast pitting the Saint versus the Lion. The ribs are perfect. As we sit throughout the living room at self-appointed dining spots, we focus on the one course meal and try to ignore the golf.

I help Becky gather the discarded ribs into one massive bone pile. TJ finds some dish towels in the sink cabinet, wets them and wrings them out.

Y'all gonna need one of these," he says while distributing relief for sticky fingers and lips.

While I pass back through the kitchen, Timber's iPhone rings. He placed it there while eating. I pick it up to hand it to him but not before noticing: A.BEARKILLER, MD illuminated on the screen.

"Timber, its Anthony!"

Putting him on the speakerphone seems like a great idea.

"Hi, Anthony!" I answer, surprising him.

"That you, Priscilla? Thought I was calling Timber."

"You're on the speaker, Doctor. Watch what you say."

"What's going on down there, guys?" asks Anthony. "You still have Maleko with you?"

"Aloha, Doc," Mark answers, identifying himself.

"Great golf today, guys. I got to watch most of it. Mark, I hope you understand that I'm a little prejudiced on how this all turns out."

"Don't worry Ant, I'm coachin' up Timber," TJ chimes in.

"Oh, so you got the big oaf there?" Anthony gets in the first verbal jab.

"Well, you deranged minuscule form of Dr. Jekyll!" playfully retorts TJ. "Where you get off callin' me an oaf?"

"Here we go, again," says Becky rolling her eyes.

"Okay, okay…I just wanted to call and congratulate Timber and Pauly and let them know we would be pulling for them tomorrow."

"Thanks, Uncle Ant," acknowledges Pauly.

"It's more like Atom Ant," TJ says.

Everyone laughs and begins to talk all at once, but Timber rises from the sofa and makes a calming motion with his hands.

"Thanks, little buddy. How's the new dog?"

Well, he's still a pup—just about a hundred pounds or so. I've spent thirty years looking for another Silas. Found him on that last mission trip to Thailand. I'll post a picture on the Circle's webpage."

"Got any results from the last test?" asks Timber.

Becky ambles closer to the iPhone with a concerned and serious air. Pauly slowly rises from the recliner. Even TJ's wide smile vanishes. Mark looks across at me from the living room to the kitchen with a silent questioning glare. I return a clueless expression.

"Timber, I think maybe we should review that on Monday. It's a big day tomorrow," Anthony suggests, obviously delaying.

"No, it's okay, Ant. Trust me. This is a good time."

"All right, if you're sure…" sighs Anthony. "The result from the blood work we did last week shows no positive improvement from the last round of biological therapy we implemented. Your vitamin regimen is keeping you strong but in fact the cancer is progressing."

Pauly bolts out the backdoor and trots down to the pond. TJ looks somberly at Timber as if waiting for orders. With a silent motion of his head toward the backyard, Timber sends his best friend off to console his son.

"What in the world are you talking about, Anthony?" I ask, trying to make sense of the doctor's words.

"Should I go on?" asks Anthony.

"Yes," Timber replies firmly.

"Prissy, Timber has stage-four metastatic melanoma. It has reached his lymphatic system. Timber has been receiving palliative care with the goal being to help him feel better both physically and emotionally. It's a type of treatment intended to control pain and other symptoms and to relieve the side effects of the rest of the regimen his body has been going through after surgery and radiation. We're faced now with quality of life rather than extension of life."

Timber picks up his iPhone turning the speaker off and retreats to visit with Anthony in the privacy of the master bedroom. Mark is dumbfounded. Becky places her hands over her eyes and sobs, leaning against the counter.

I rush to embrace my friend. With all my womanly instincts, I find no words to placate her. She slowly looks up into my face. We look together through the kitchen window down to the pond. Pauly is wildly skipping rocks on the water in the dusk while TJ attempts to counsel.

"His mind just can't handle it, Prissy. He can't handle the fact that his father is being taken away from him. That's why this weekend is so important."

"Surely there is something that can be done!" I plead. "God works miracles. He can save Timber."

Becky's beautiful blue eyes look deep into my soul and she wipes her tears with the corners of her fist.

"God has already saved my family, Prissy. One day, one way or another, we will all be cured."

Her statement of faith touches my spirit. In typical Oaks' fashion, the one most deserving of comfort provides the comforting, restoring my faith.

Timber softly lumbers into the kitchen after finishing up with Anthony. He holds his palms outward, as if there was little else to say. He connects with Becky and me in a threesome embrace. Mark looks on dazed and disoriented, not knowing how to fit in or what to say.

"So that is what the bandaged neck is about," I murmur, "… that silly hat, the longer hair, the massive amount of pills…"

"Yeah, skin cancer," says Timber. "I got a little too much sun and what we thought was a blister was much more. Don't forget to use your sunscreen."

"But who all knows?" I ask Timber, still holding hands with Becky. "Why did you keep it so quiet? Why didn't you tell me?"

Timber, appearing calm as always, reaches down, putting his right hand on my shoulder.

"Prissy, we didn't tell you because we wanted you to do your story unbiased and without pity. We will make an announcement after we get this Kenya thing under control. Only a few know 'bout it…TJ, some of our staff and Jorell."

"My husband knows and didn't tell me!"

"Hey girl!" Becky clutches my hands while explaining. "Jorell was honoring Timber's request. Don't you think it hurt him not to share it with you?"

I walk away to a lonely side of the kitchen with my eyes closed, thinking about Jorell and the anguish he must feel—the grief that we need to share.

With hands resting on his hips, Mark walks across the kitchen and confronts Timber, looking just slightly up at the taller man.

"Timber Oaks, you're the bravest...no, the greatest man I've ever met."

Mark's hard, dark eyes begin to water. I think to myself, has anyone ever seen the great Ailana Liona weep? Timber studies the emotionally stunned Hawaiian's face.

"If I'd a known..." begins Mark.

"You would of what?" Timber says. "Brought me flowers or thrown a major championship? I don't want your pity, Maleko Kalani, I want your heart. I'm chasing your soul. I want your best and so does God; in golf and in life!"

Timber slaps Mark's upper arm a couple of times, leaving the champ with his thoughts. Timber exits to the backyard to unite with TJ and his son. His downhill gait to the pond is deliberate, as is his mission.

I do not know what they are talking about as Mark and I gaze out at the trio in silhouette through the closed glass doors. Whatever is happening, it's working.

First, Timber holds Pauly tightly while the boy's body shakes with sobs. They stare death in the face as father and son. Then, perhaps, Timber skillfully switches the subject to golf and the opportunity that awaits father and son tomorrow. The jesting and encouragement is effective. Both men's arms criss-cross Pauly's shoulders as he walks up the backyard slope between them, chuckling and forming an optimistic bond.

Becky steps out to meet them making sure her son's emotions are secure. TJ leaves the family together on the patio and joins

Mark and me in the kitchen. Nicklaus, alone in the middle of the yard with ball in mouth, drops the toy, canceling the evening assault on Hound Dog Island to the disappointment of his comrades across the pond.

Pauly leads Nicklaus into the house while his parents remain alone. Boy and dog curl up on the living room sofa together in the sleeping consignment they have shared for the past week. Pauly clicks off the television.

I turn off the lights over Pauly. Mark and I hide in the dark shadows gazing out at Becky and Timber. They are alone together under the illuminated veranda.

TJ fiddles with an old CD lying on top of the stereo located underneath the kitchen cabinet. He inserts the disk and toggles it to his chosen selection.

The old, slow pulsating Creedence Clearwater melody about lighting a candle in the window envelops the moment. Timber slow-dances with his bride to the song that began their romance so many years before. They both close their eyes and gently sway, clutching each other close and closer.

"Undying love?" Mark whispers.

"…and devotion." I add.

TJ moseys up behind us as we all three monitor the ultimate dance of dedication. As usual, TJ's conclusion is deeply felt.

"God's timing."

Sunday

My night is restless and filled with anxiety. I long for Jorell's calming caress, and I struggle with Timber's physical condition and the plight of his family.

Upon waking, the first thing I notice is a pink, paisley Island Liona shirt draped across the chair next to my bed. Mark must have specially ordered it for me and put it on overnight delivery. My guess is last night just was not the time for it so Becky left the designer top out for me to lift my spirits.

The house is eerily quiet for a Sunday morning that should be so promising—two friendly competitors competing for one of golf's major championships. I skip the coffee pot for later, shower and prepare for the day.

Wishing I had packed an outfit in baby-blue, I try on my Ailana Liona, ensembling the shirt with another pair of pink shorts. Not bad, but not Timber-ish.

The front page of the Tulsa World is laid out on the serving bar with headlines exalting the Saint and dual pictures of Timber and Mark. The world of golf, as well as all of sports, will be focused on Tulsa, Oklahoma this afternoon.

Homemade cinnamon rolls and orange muffins encircle a steaming pot of coffee. With Danish wrapped in a paper towel and a cup of caffeine, I study the sunrise penetrating the trees reflected in the pond. It is as if nothing had changed, but so much has.

I open the door to the Oak's family office not announcing myself first. Timber stands and grins widely at my island attire. Ironically, Timber and Pauly are wearing the same custom made Island Liona golf shirts that Mark had presented last week. The Oaks boys' fashion show is refreshing.

"Looks like all three of you are going on a cruise!" Becky suggests with a giggle.

"You guys are wearing that stuff on the course?" I ask.

"Absolutely!" affirms Timber, still posturing. "To the course and to church. We want to be dressed for the occasion."

"Church?" I question.

"It's Sunday morning, isn't it?" replies Timber matter of factly. "Somebody needs to wake up the Lion!"

Pauly stops the Saint Hauler pickup on the side of the road just outside of the Broken Arrow neighborhood. He uses the esteemed old vehicle in a covert operation to elude the press that had camped out the night before in front of the Oak's home. The secret was out: the Ailana Liona had been lodging with the Saint.

I get out and help Pauly pull off the canvas mat covering Mark and Timber who hide in the truck bed. Timber has an expression of mission accomplished. Mark is not amused at sinking to such depths.

The four of us cram into the cab. Mark had reluctantly agreed to attend church. It was early and out of routine for a championship day. But after last night's revelations, how could he refuse Timber's request?

"Northside, Dad?" asks Pauly at the wheel.

"Yep, Northside. We can make the 9:00 service and have plenty of time for golf."

I know the story behind Northside Gospel Church, though I had never been there. Of all the Circle of Care churches in the area that the Oaks frequented, none were held more fondly than Northside. It was a great choice, but I doubt it was coincidental.

Pauly skirts through downtown Tulsa. As with most city business districts on Sunday morning, the traffic is light. We enter a meager neighborhood in the north section of town—known for modest and poor housing.

The small white steepled church is old but well kept. Some windows are stained glass—others clear replacements. The lawn has been recently mowed around swing set and other playground apparatus.

Down the graveled parking area alongside of the church, about twenty older cars and trucks are parked. Pauly parks the pickup at the end of the row.

The simple white bordered marquee out front reads:

Northside Gospel Church
Sunday Morning Service:
Breakfast 7:30
Worship 9:00
Sandy Sampson, Pastor

Timber leads us up the three steps to the church entrance. Just outside the door he is greeted by a bald, undersized gentleman dressed in a white dress shirt, blue jeans and cowboy boots. His elderly eyes has pleasant laugh wrinkles.

"Timber! Well it's so nice to have you this mornin'," he says, giving Timber a hug. "Watched ya some on TV yesterday…gonna be a big day!"

"God bless you, Demas," replies Timber, reaching down to embrace the smaller man, then entering the church.

Demas welcomes Pauly. They obviously are well acquainted.

Then it is my turn.

"I have heard a lot about you, Mr. Sampson," I say. "It's nice to finally meet you."

"You are even purtier than you are on TV...you sure can kick a leg, too. And this must be the Hawaii Lion? Son, you sure can swing a stick!"

"Thank you, sir." Mark shakes Demas' hand graciously but somewhat dumbfounded.

As we walk through the entrance, Mark tugs on my shoulder.

"Is that the guy that almost killed Timber?"

"In the flesh. He served his sentence and now does time for the Lord, helping out his son."

"Then what about the mother?"

"No, they are not together. Phoebe runs a mission for the Circle in central Mexico."

The inside of the church is anything but traditional. There are no customary pews in the hardwood floored sanctuary. Pillows, cushions and mats are spread out, encircling the center of the worship area. Toys, little trinkets, stuffed animals and dolls are scattered about. The hearty scent of fresh breakfast saturates the church.

"Mr. Timber! Pauly!" shouts a little boy of preschool age.

The youngster is followed by a small stampede of small children exiting the kitchen dining area from the back of the church.

Timber and Pauly are engulfed by a clinging brood of kids of different colors and sizes—some healthy, some noticeably physically or mentally challenged.

Mothers and older adults pursue the procession. The grown-ups, mostly women, wait their turn to greet Timber while Pauly is wrestled to the floor by the enthusiastic youth.

In the midst of the excitement, Timber attempts to introduce

Mark and me. Many of the ladies appear star-struck at the presence of Mark and they remember me from my celebrity dancing. Hesitant and awkward, Mark and I try to fit in.

The beaming Sandy Sampson, dressed in knee length shorts and open collar white shirt, is followed by his cute wife with her pixie-cut brown hair. Kimmie is also in shorts. Both are covered with red 'Jesus Loves You' aprons.

Sandy embraces his old friend and mentor. The perky pastor's wife is next in line. Timber continues with the introductions.

"Well Pastor, I know you know Prissy, but I'm not sure about your bride?"

"Honey," began Sandy, "meet Priscilla Luke; sportscaster, dancer and evangelist. Prissy, this is Kimmie. Been married six years now."

"I've heard all about you," says Kimmie, reaching out both hands and clenching mine. "So nice for you to join us."

"And I doubt this guy needs any introduction," Timber maintains.

"Wow! Maleko Kalani! A wide-eyed Kimmie bursts out. "Don't you fellas have some golf to play today?"

"Hey kids!" Timber gets the kids' attention allowing Pauly some relief. "Ever meet an Hawaiian Lion?"

Several of the children creep closer to study Mark. His Polynesian features are strikingly different from anything to which they're accustomed. A hyper little girl, apparently autistic, angrily protests that Mark is not a lion.

Another boy asks Mark if he would like to play. Hand-in-hand, they go off together to inspect the array of toys.

"Looks like ya'll brought your Caribbean roots with you," comments Sandy referring to our island shirts. "Get you guys somethin' to eat before we start the service? There's plenty left. The food pantry brought a whole load of groceries over last week."

"I think we're good. How 'bout you, Prissy?" asks Timber.

"Still full of cinnamon rolls, but thanks," I offer, as two small girls drag me away to check out their doll house.

No one is a stranger around this church. That is a uniqueness at Northside Gospel. The personality of the pastor and his wife is reflected in her people. This is a respite of love, refuge and hope for young mothers and their children who suffer from pitiable domestic circumstances; a safety net for those who may otherwise fall through the spiritual cracks.

The worship service starts late. It takes some time to hustle up thirty children. Pauly calculates thirty three, but counting is useless.

Demas stands in the hallway like a shepherd protecting his flock. Ironically, the man who once attacked the church is now guarding it.

Sandy with guitar in hand begins playing upbeat contemporary worship music from the center of the sanctuary, surrounded by his congregation. All remain standing: singing, clapping and dancing as Kimmie accompanies her pastor husband on tambourine.

Timber and Pauly know the routine well. The songs of praise are familiar to both and also to me. We engage ourselves with the children. Mark claps his hands slightly off-beat while trying to decipher what he's experiencing.

After three high energy numbers, Kimmie leads us in prayer—simple yet poignant. Everyone is seated on the floor on a cushion or soft pad. Cuddling is allowed. Babies, toddlers, and squirmy children are encouraged to relax.

Tiny whispers, the overhead fan, and the hum of two overworked window air-conditioners are the only sound. Sandy retrieves a stool from the corner. With guitar resting on his lap, he sits down in the middle of the circle. Kimmie dims the lights.

Sandy plays and sings a beautiful acoustic arrangement of an enduring hymn about an old rugged cross and a laying down of trophies. I tap Timber on the knee and motion with my eyes toward Mark. The Lion has a flushed look on his face. His dark eyes begin to water as a disabled boy rests his head on his lap.

Timber's wink assures me he is aware of the situation. As the soft melody lingers, Mark becomes more engrossed. Though Timber makes no sound, I can read his lips.

"Holy Spirit, move."

Reverend Sampson's message for the day is a reenactment of David and Goliath. Pauly is drafted to play the role of the giant. A small boy in leg braces is cast as David. Sandy's style and direction is humorous and simple enough for the children to understand yet effective communication for the adults.

After another song, Sandy asks Timber to say a few words. The missionary father figure is comfortable in this environment. Golf is his subject. Timber pulls a stuffed envelope out of his pants pocket.

"Anyone want to see David slay Goliath today?"

Children react with anticipation to Timber's invitation.

"I have afternoon passes here to Whispering Waters for everyone!"

The ride from North Tulsa, south to Whispering Waters in the packed cab of the Saint Hauler is quiet and reserved. Mark leans against the inside of the passenger door with his game face on. Whether concentrating on golf or reflecting on the morning worship service, I do not know. I suspect a little of both.

The blistering heat is back by 11:00 a.m. as we pull into the private parking. We are not recognized by security in the antique pickup.

Fortunately, the host of media types waiting for the Saint's and Lion's arrival did not spot us either. We escape, barely noticed.

We hurry off to our positions: golfers to the locker room, Pauly to the caddy tent, and me to the media center to check in. The digital leader board in the clubhouse reflects the difficulties of a field of golfers on the course trying to catch Mark and Timber.

Maybe they're being over-aggressive on the unforgiving course or maybe it's the heat. The Lion's and the Saint's tally of even par going in is now good for a six-stroke lead.

I catch up with Chico and Pauly at the driving range. Both are intense as they assist their pros. Mark and Timber warm up, peppering golf balls. They are mostly oblivious to spectators lined up, waiting eagerly for the classic duel for eighteen holes.

The Liona Legion exudes a party-like atmosphere, dressed in their traditional island apparel with the sounds of tropical music coming from various small portable hand-held gadgets. This meshes with 'Saint's Sanctuary' with their baby-blue shirts and floppy caps as they hum and whistle in unison the 'Marching In' hymn.

The animated crowd follows the two golfers to the practice green as tee time approaches. Cameras and reporters track each move they make.

"Nice shirt, Timber!" shouts out a member of the Liona Legion.

"Thanks," says Timber. "Got it from a friend."

Mark looks up at the exchange and points his putter at Timber in a mock salute. Everyone laughs approvingly.

A waving Coach Thomas Johnson catches my attention and almost everyone else's in attendance. TJ, dressed in baby-blue slacks coordinated golf shirt and visor along with blue tinted sunglasses, is joined by Becky, Benny and Sarah.

The tall, well recognized sports icon makes his way through the crowd down near the practice green, leading his old companions, while obliging autograph hounds. As we five gather, the entire congregation of the Northside Gospel Church appears up on the entrance gate veranda.

Excited and frolicking children dressed for the hot weather are herded together by mothers and chaperones. Pastor Sandy, Kimmie, and Demas look confused, trying to get their bearings. Sandy spots the easily conspicuous TJ. We all assemble around TJ halfway up the hillside.

Becky is thrilled by the children. She picks up a small autistic boy and holds him in her arms while other little ones vie for her attention. The liability of assisting with the small church flock will distract her and ease her tension this afternoon.

TJ is excused to huddle with his best friend just off the practice green. Both look flamboyant: Timber in his new island-style attire and TJ in his flashy baby-blue Corinthia Falls outfit. TJ removes his shades and appears to be giving Timber an enthusiastic pep talk.

Like a scene from a halftime inspirational speech, the colorful coach inaudible from my distance, gesticulates as Timber takes it all in. After a couple of back slaps, TJ motions for Pauly to join them and Timber's personal support group of family, friends, and children.

John Solomon has linked up with our last minute devotional, looking very prominent in his descending dove, light blue golf shirt. TJ places Timber in the middle of our circle while small hands and larger ones are laid upon him.

Mark and Chico stop respectfully to observe our impromptu ceremony from the nearby putting surface. A dozen or so spectators gather with us.

"Your turn, Pastor," says TJ queuing Sandy.

"This is the day the Lord has made…" announces Pastor Samuels.

"…let us rejoice and be glad in it!" the joyous united group of believers exclaim.

The 1:40 projected tee time for the Lion and the Saint is rapidly approaching. I stand next to Benny, Sarah and TJ just behind the segregated off tee area of the first hole as we wait the announcement of the final pairing.

"No saxophone, Ben?" I ask, breaking the tension.

"It's around," he declares.

Impossible as it is to subdue my emotions and remain calm and neutral, I try to be professional. With my pink bag full of widgets, I prepare to cover the final round of the PGA Championship.

Timber and Mark are cheered as they enter the tee box, along with Pauly and Chico. All four exchange handshakes and greet the crowd of supporters.

I wonder what is going on in Timber's mind: the struggle with his health, his preoccupation with his ministry, the tragedy in Kenya or the opportunity of the long sought-after championship and the $1,350,000 in prize money? Even the $810,000 second place payoff would make a nice life insurance policy.

The tournament gallery announcer introduces both golfers in customary and traditional style.

"In our final pair, the two-time PGA Champion from Honolulu, Hawaii…Maleko Kalani."

Mark acknowledges the reception from the gallery, lines up his first shot and takes one practice swing. Seeming a little self-hurried and lacking his usual keen concentration, Mark duck-hooks his tee shot deep into the trees on the left of the fairway and buries his ball in the rough. The Liona Legion moans.

"And from Corinthia Falls, Oklahoma…Mr. Timothy Oaks."

Timber tips the goofy, floppy hat to his well-wishers. Pauly hands him his driver from the bag. Uncharacteristically dressed in his Ailana Liona golf shirt, Timber places the perfect shot down the center of the fairway of the par four hole. TJ and Benny pump their fists into the air. Becky breathes again. The whistling has already begun.

Mark has to scramble from beneath the trees and settles for a bogie. Timber taps in for a routine par. For the first time in his life, Timber Oaks is leading in the final round of a major championship.

Danny catches up with me on the second tee. The USN field announcer, my colleague, is ecstatic.

"Prissy girl, our telly audience is goin' through the bloody roof! The guys back in Dallas tell us were approachin' Super Bowl ratings with this one. Jest look at the crowd!"

"I know, Dan. It's great."

"Anyhow's girl, the boys upstairs want some voice commentary from ya on this tee off. Nothin' on screen, jest vocals?"

"I got ya covered, mate," I answer in my best Aussie accent.

As Dan and I prepare for the interview, I notice Mark looking despondent. Chico is troubled with the Lion's lack of focus.

Both are confused.

Timber has the honors. The Saint duplicates his previous effort, driving another well placed ball faultlessly to perfect position. Dan starts our on-air discourse.

"I'm here again with my gal, Priscilla Luke. I hear you have had quite the time hangin' out with these two blokes all week?"

I try to keep from smirking at Dan. I feel the questioning is not appropriate. Before I can answer, I notice Mark and Timber in dialogue. The Hawaiian Lion is anxious. He refuses his driver from Chico.

"Sorry, just a second, Dan."

I edge closer to make things out.

"I'm ready!" Mark keeps repeating to Timber.

"Okay, ready for what?" Timber asks trying to steady him.

"You know, to lay down my trophies. I don't need what I got. I need what you have!"

Oh my sweet lord, I think to myself, a confession of faith right here and right now? How will Timber handle this?

Dan pursues me with his microphone. I reach back an open hand almost pushing him away.

Timber waves to TJ nearby in the gallery. Catching his attention, Timber now points toward several others, motioning for them to join him. Benny and Sarah, Becky, Sandy and Kimmie along with TJ and I gather with Timber, Mark, Chico and Pauly. We are separated by the roped-off second tee box, but are close enough to touch and to hear.

The Ailana Liona takes a knee and closes his dark eyes, which are suddenly brimming with tears. We cluster together placing our hands on Mark. Other believers reach out. Curious spectators creep closer, growing quiet. Dan holds his live mic deep into the tightly bunched grouping. USN cameras keep rolling.

The significance of this situation is much more compelling than the result of any golf tournament. After a pause for silence, Timber begins.

"Maleko Kalani, do you confess publicly that you have sinned against God and that your sins separate Him from you?"

"I do, yes," answers Mark, looking up at Timber then farther beyond as if into heaven.

"Are you truly sorry? Do you want to turn away from your past and turn to God for forgiveness?"

"I do."

"Then repeat after me with your lips and from your heart: Please forgive me, and help me turn away from my sin."

Mark patiently echoes Timbers words sentence after sentence.

"I believe that your Son, Jesus Christ, died for my sins, that He was raised from the dead, is alive, and hears this prayer…I invite Jesus to become my Savior and the Lord of my life, to rule and reign in my heart from this day forward… Please send your Holy Spirit to help me…I pledge to grow in grace and knowledge of you…My greatest purpose in life is to follow your example and do Your will for the rest of my life. In Jesus' name I pray, Amen"

"Amen."

As tears fall, Mark is welcomed into the family of God. First by Timber, then by all his new brothers and sisters that can get to him. An expression of relief and liberation glows on Mark's bronzed face.

Dan is speechless for the first time in his career, astonished by what he has just witnessed; by what he has just transmitted unknowingly to an international live television audience that would later be estimated at over half a billion people. It was the profession of a sinner. It was the Ailana Liona laying down his trophies before Christ.

A PGA official warns Mark and Timber that they are on the clock and must keep things moving along. As all disassemble, Timber takes Mark's driver from Chico. Handing it to his opponent, Timber cannot help but quip to the tournament official.

"Sorry, sir, we just paused for a Word from our Sponsor."

"What's next?" asks the newborn golfing superstar.

"You'll have plenty of time for what's next," assures Timber. "For right now there is joy…and there is golf. Let's have some fun!"

Mark is rejuvenated. Gone is the worried look of torment. Refreshed and bright eyed, the converted rich young man's effort-less and silky-smooth drive lands twenty yards past Timber's, far down the middle of the second hole fairway.

The Liona Legion erupts. The Hawaiian Lion's game is back. Timber nods commendably at Mark, adding confidence to his opponent. As Pauly straps Timber's bag over his shoulder, I can barely hear him comment to his father.

"Now look what you did!"

"Son, it's what Jesus did."

If Mark's drive was excellent, his approach shot is better. The birdie he makes after Timber takes par puts both at even par.

The high level of play continues. Both golfers assault a now-defenseless Whispering Waters. The Liona Legion and the Saint's Sanctuary of supporters, along with the entire golfing world are being treated to a dazzling performance.

Timber and Mark walk as one down the fairways. The Lion is now the Saint's new found protégé, asking questions between holes. Both are enlivened with the exchange.

The two island-shirted warriors push each other toward ex-cellence on the course both whole-heartedly encouraging each other in a rare display of sportsmanship. They applaud, congratu-late and even high-five one another after each brilliant shot while their respective caddies and a stimulated gallery celebrate the demonstration.

Mark continues with his thunderous, accurate drives eagling the par five seventh hole. Timber again displays his finesse around the greens birdying number eight from the sand trap. The island mantras persist. The whistling and singing for the 'Saint marching in' increases in volume.

As the unrelenting pair make the turn at number nine after

rolling in two birdie putts, the leader board reflects their success:

Kalani -5

Oaks -5

Both remained deadlocked; five under for the first round and, astonishingly, five under for the championship.

The children from Northside with little concept of the game of golf, know only that their hero is doing well. Mothers— Sandy and Kimmie—along with Becky and Sarah keep them in the fold. Becky's attention is split between children and golf while trying to keep her overflowing emotions at bay.

Benny is packaged energy for his age. He virtually runs to be in position for each shot Timber makes, sometimes crouching down to all fours for a bird's eye view, then leading the cheers after Timber's every swing.

Dan runs down TJ and me on the edge of the tenth fairway. TJ has been my escort most of the afternoon. The prominent basketball coach banters with the crowd as he supports and yells out encouragement to his brother in arms as if tutoring from a hardwood sideline.

Dan asks to put TJ on the air to reminisce about his and Timber's special relationship. Reluctantly, TJ obliges. As the impromptu live interview comes to an end, Dan poses one more question.

"Does your mate have da stuff to hold off a lion?"

"Well, he is the Saint," confirms TJ. "With Timber, miracles are commonplace."

I try to stay centered on my storyline. I feel my writing skill is not a worthy narrative of this inconceivable affair. In my frustration, I vent.

"Teej, I cannot cover these last nine holes adequately! It deserves the eloquence of a poet, not the fluency of a sports journalist."

TJ smiles down at me, wiping the sweat from his brow.

"Sounds like you're waxin' poetic to me."

I pay special attention to chronicle my personal thoughts. The followers of golf are mindful of Timber's accomplishments. Millions know of his ambassadorship for the game and his ministry to humanity, creating disciples of Christ for the transformation of the world. Almost none witnessing this demonstration, however, are conscious of the physical challenge that may abbreviate his life.

As the mid-afternoon August sun bears down on Whispering Waters punishing both Mark and Timber, I wonder if the Saint can maintain the pace of the younger and well-conditioned Liona.

I speculate in my narrative whether Timber would be able to enhance his legacy; to finish out as a champion. How undeserving of a thought. Timber Oaks is already a champion to all that know him or are touched by his life.

The final back nine holes of the PGA Championship will belong to the Lion and the Saint. The rest of the field of golf's best has succumbed to the course known as Water World. Timber and Mark's lead is insurmountable.

The anomalous duo persists with their pursuit of excellence. Acting more like carefree teenagers in a game of 'Try and Top This,' they seem to work as a team, encouraging and pressing each other's talents.

TJ and I check my iPhone to catch the USN network coverage as the commentators run out of superlatives and adjectives to describe the performance. It is a friendly but emotional game of David versus Goliath, the Yankees and the Cubs, Rocky battling Apollo Creed; the world's dearest loved underdog against one its most prosperous, agile champions in a timeless display of sportsmanship and grit.

At the fifteenth hole, Becky can no longer restrain herself. She finds refuge with TJ and me. Our tall, dark friend, well experienced in the trauma of athletic competition, offers comforting words.

"It will all be over soon, Becks. Benefit from the thrill of the moment. It's somethin' most never get to experience. This is life at the fullest. Sooner or later, destiny will play its part separating the victor from the opponent."

Becky holds on with both hands to TJ's arm for emotional support and will not let go. Prayers go out as hope endures.

The crowd swells behind the final twosome, nearly rupturing the fairways and almost inundating the greens. The tournament officials frantically hold back the gallery from overwhelming the course.

As Mark and Timber skillfully match each other hole per hole, their record pace continues. It is a treat for the sport's enthusiasts that I'm sure most hope will never end. The delirious throng of the Liona Legion and the Saint's Sanctuary unite as one in tropical songs and the whistling of the old hymn.

As both golfers and caddies reach the eighteenth tee box to a thunderous ovation, the leader board tells an amazing story.

Kalani -11

Oaks -11

It has been an earth shattering, record setting performance

at Whispering Waters: ten under for the championship and ten under par for the day!

The foursome of Mark and Chico, along with Timber and Pauly, pause together for a brief respite. They all come together, smiling profusely and slapping palms, congratulating each other on what has already been an astonishing afternoon.

Chico hands Mark the last bottle of Aqua Fina from his golf bag. The islander drenches his dark mop-top with most of the water and quaffs down what remains.

Timber removes his saturated floppy hat. His abundant perspiration and damp brown mane has washed away the bandage on the back of his neck, partially revealing the inflamed lesion. Pauly hands him a towel to dry his face and hands.

Mark has the honors. He declines the driver that Chico has offered reaching instead for a fairway wood. It is an uncustomary strategy for the Ailana Liona; sacrificing his superior strength and driving distance—playing a safer shot to avoid the notorious, ominous Oak tree in the right-center of the fairway.

Officials raise outstretched hands for quiet. With a smooth cautious swing, Mark's ball lands safely in the fairway short and left of the Tree of Tragedy.

The towering shots that Timber launched from here the previous two rounds on his way to birdies are fresh on everyone's mind. Could this be the opportunity long awaited? Was it the moment of destiny about which TJ preached?

Pauly hands his father the driver. Timber nods his head in agreement. The gallery becomes silent with anticipation. Timber holds nothing back.

As TJ, Becky, and I clutch each other from behind the tee box, the Saint's shot looks like a replicate of yesterday. Pauly crouches down low, watching the trajectory of the ball as it reaches the tall Oak tree.

I look down at my iPhone to follow the camera angle. Immediately, there is the all-familiar sound of a golf ball finding lumber. What briefly appears to be the perfect drive lacks the elevation. Our optimism begins to disappear at the sight and reverberation of Timber's ball ricocheting throughout the branches of the mighty Oak.

The reaction of the spectators lining the jam-packed eighteenth fairway tells the tale. The uniform moaning and disheartened gasps are followed by an eerie hush spreading through the gallery of fans. Timber's ball rests closely next to the massive tree trunk and on the near side, blocking his next shot toward the final green.

TJ hangs his head and sighs. Becky briefly closes her eyes, refusing to look. Benny is nowhere to be found. The tournament officials allow the gallery to follow behind the final twosome onto the fairway, creating an encirclement from the Oak tree area all the way to the final green.

Mark is further away and will go first. He has a clear shot to the green fronted only by the creek. The olive-colored flag marking the target in the back of the green hangs limp. Many familiar professionals have gathered here with the multitude to witness the finish.

Chico advises Mark on the shot. It is easy for them to discern that Timber will have to punch his ball out from the tree that is blocking his approach leaving the Saint at a huge disadvantage.

This situation would normally dictate a safe shot that would lay-up just short of the creek in excellent position for a par four placing all the pressure on Timber, but not today, not for the world's greatest golfer— certainly not for Maleko Kalani. Instinctively, the

Lion will go for the kill.

Chico and Mark decide on a two-iron for the 260-yard approach. Timber and his fans' last hope is for Mark's over aggressiveness to cause a mistake, but there is no mistake.

The Ailana Liona's shot clears the creek and bounds onto the green. His perfectly launched ball treks toward the hole as if it had eyes. The coaxing of the ball by the Liona Legion erupts as the dimpled little white sphere halts less than two feet from the hole. A birdie three is imminent.

The Lion and his caddie celebrate the shot of the tournament. It is the moment. It is the instant in time that TJ had predicted when destiny blended with talent to define a championship.

Timber, standing just short of the Oak tree twenty yards from Mark, reacts in typical fashion. Grinning and shaking his head in concession, he smiles broadly, pointing the index fingers of both his hands toward his friendly adversary.

Becky has seen enough golf over the years to know this one is over. Timber's brilliant charge over the last two days has come up one Oak tree short. She breaks away from TJ and me to find her mother. Sarah is waiting for her with the children, shaded by the trees and brush, just right of the fairway.

Timber walks up to his misplayed ball nestled three feet in front of the Oak. There is barely room to take his stance. His only choice seems to be punching the ball out to the right. Without any other option remaining, Timber shrugs his shoulders in a gesture of rationalization. Pauly hands him his pitching wedge.

I take notes for my report, keeping my eyes on Timber, then glancing over at Becky and back toward Pauly. I realize it is not a golf story I am writing. It is rather a testimonial to the forty-eight-year-old golfer/evangelist, his family, his mission and his influence.

I recognize the melody playing on a harmonica emanating faintly through the nearby woods. Sandy stands among his gathered congregation of Timber supporters playing the Corinthia Falls anthem. He plays the Saints Marching In reverently and unhurried. The children, led by Kimmie, begin to sing along to the hymn they know by heart.

The singing becomes contagious as the Whispering Waters golfing audience of both the Liona Legion and the Saint's Sanctuary join together in harmony to pay homage and respect to Timber Oaks. Becky's blue eyes begin to fill. She holds in her breath while admiring her husband and the moment. Pauly, standing next to his father with the old baby-blue golf bag, buries his freckled face in his hands and weeps.

Chico and Mark join Timber in consoling his son. As the accolade comes to an end, the gallery gives Timber a compassionate ovation. I dry my eyes to watch Timber salute the appreciative crowd with the doffing of his floppy hat.

TJ does not partake in the sing-along. Rather, he seems preoccupied with a brightly painted local Tulsa television van that has nudged closer, in all probability to pick up on the Timber tribute. The technology laden van is equipped with an overhead semi-oval satellite transmitter/receiver. It parks parallel, directly outside of the out-of-bounds markers, just inside the right fairway tree line just behind us.

TJ seems to be talking to himself. It is almost annoying. Maybe this is a coach thing; a way to deal with his emotions.

"Are you sure? Okay, yep, that's it then!" TJ asks and answers to himself or some force unseen.

As Timber prepares to punch his ball out toward us from the confines of the smothering tree, TJ waves both his long arms in the air, frantically trying to get his old pal's attention. Timber cannot help but notice him. Thinking it is another goodwill gesture, Timber smiles and waves back to his longtime friend.

"No! Wait! Wait!" yells TJ, turning and pointing at the television van where a local reporter is attempting a live remote.

Timber eyes TJ and then the van, visibly confused.

"The transmitter on the truck!" shouts TJ at the top of his lungs now standing partially out on the fairway. "Think back, man, Cherokee Creek!"

Timber stares at the van with the dish-shaped transmitter. He tilts his head sideways as if a light bulb has flashed in his memory, then looks questioningly back at TJ.

"Think outside of the box, Timb," says TJ. "What's to lose? I've seen you do it before!"

Timber walks back to the far side of his ball, studying the angle of a shot from ball to van transmitter to green. He takes several steps back to calculate the geometry of the imaginative golf shot. He glances around the tree toward his target, well over 200 yards away.

I remember Timber's story about the driving range in Corinthia Falls and how he dented up the Solomon's satellite receiver. The idea of duplication is ludicrous. I challenge TJ.

"Teej! You two cannot be serious? What if he misses the whole van and takes a ten for the hole? Second place is worth a lot of money!"

"More serious than ever, Prissy. Now stand back and take notes!"

Timber gets assistance from a fairway official after informing him the direction he will be hitting. With the help of TJ, the official directs the people on the crowded sideline to clear a path. The gallery moves in back of the tree line, exposing the van. The transmitter remains ideally positioned outward toward Timber and slightly upward some thirty paces away.

Mark and Chico look on, very bewildered. The announcing team of USN audible from my hand held is just as baffled. I feel a tug on my shoulder. It is Dan in a quandary.

"Prissy, what in the…"

"Never mind, Danny Boy, you would not believe me anyway."

Timber stands directly over his ball looking up at the large Oak tree. He stares at a lower limb where a mourning dove is perched.

Pauly has no advice. He rests the base of the golf bag on the ground and tilts it in the direction of his father for his selection.

Timber points to the Moses Rod.

Pauly pulls out the antiquated eight iron, wipes down the old withered, leather grip and presents it to his father. Timber looks down the shaft of Crazy George's old but influential weapon and takes a couple of practice swings.

Becky returns and snuggles in between TJ and me with finger tips covering her nose and mouth. TJ notes Timber's club selection.

"Just look, girls! Timber has Destiny in his hands!"

Timber digs his golf shoes into the ground firming up his stance with his backside nestled against the broad tree trunk. Staring out at the transmitter, he takes direct aim.

Concentrating down on the golf ball, Timber softly utters some words we cannot hear. It does not matter. TJ recites the scripture with him word for word.

"We-Can-Do-Anything-With-The-Help-Of-Christ-Who-Gives-Us-Power!"

With a heartfelt swing of the golfing relic, Timber propels his ball into the round, cupped transmitter. The tiny orb strikes the fiberglass shroud whirling alongside the hollow space. The centrifugal force routes the ball into a low trajectory flight toward the green as if carried by angelic wings.

It is frequently affirmed that sport does imitate life. The metaphor is so proper in the challenging and frantic eve of fulfilling an insurmountable goal or achieving a far reaching dream. Working hard, planning well and staying loyal to the task—no matter the overwhelming obstacles encountered—competitiveness can keep an individual or team in the game for at least one last opportunity.

Just as a last-second desperation pass into the end zone, a lengthy heave crosscourt at a basketball goal with time expiring, a business concept facing a far reaching hurdle or a lifelong dream just out of reach, having a chance at that final last-gasp attempt requires talent, passion, effort, dedication, and destiny. All of these qualities are multiplied and enhanced by one essential component…faith.

In the days and weeks to come, Timber Oak's final swing as a PGA professional sent golf reporters, writers and sports show announcers scrambling for description and poetic narrative. Bold headlines would read 'The Immaculate Redemption' and 'St. Timber's Clincher.' Film clips of 'The Saint Parting Whispering Waters' began every national sports program.

It is faith that brought Timber to this moment. It is faith that will march him finally home.

The golf ball continues its scorching flight toward destiny. Coming to earth just short of the green and looking doomed to the stone skirted creek, Timber's ball deflects off a border rock and bounces up, high enough to elevate it to the green's surface.

As everyone in attendance witnesses the miraculous, TJ and I watch the ball rolling upward toward the pin on my phone screen as we continue to prop up Becky. The gallery volume crescendos with approval and enthusiasm, urging the ball closer and closer. The swelling applause increases as the Saint's ball kisses off the Liona's, adjusting its path and coming to rest on the lip of the cup.

Some said it was the touch of a warm Tulsa breeze or the vibration of the antics and gyrations of the engrossed audience at the green. But I know better. It was the hand of God that tipped Timber's ball into the cup and rattled the pin.

TJ joins with the entire gallery throwing double clenched fists into the air. The noise is deafening. Timber's first take, standing just to the right of the tree is one of disbelief. Pauly falls to his knees. The Ailana Liona bows with both hands extended forward in a flattering salute.

As Timber realizes what he has just accomplished, TJ rushes the fairway to greet him with an in the air hip-to-hip bump. Timber looks for Becky. I help her through the rushing throng. Timber, still with the Destiny eight iron in hand, embraces his companion and twirls her off her feet, losing his hat.

I realize, of course, that there are many PGA Tournament Champions, but Timber has joined an elite group of professionals to record an eighteen hole total of 59. Pauly makes his way through the celebrating melee to show his parents the scorecard.

With the help of Kimmie and Sarah, Sandy and Demas corral the youth of the Northside Gospel Church around the Oaks family. With TJ and me also in place, Sandy huffs vigorously on his harmonica. It is time for the Saint to make his last, yet finally triumphal march.

Mark and Chico gather with us. Timber starts the victory procession twirling and pumping the Moses Rod as a drum major leading his band in a style that would make Pavlos Lincoln Armstrong proud. Becky marches beside Timber as a featured majorette. Pauly and Chico follow closely behind in stride, with golf bags situated lengthways across their waists making up the drum line.

Everyone wants to be a part of this parade either in formation behind it or waiting for its arrival. The gallery converges on Timber and his convoy rejoicing as angels welcoming a new soul to Heaven, clapping and singing to the sacred refrain. A jubilant John Solomon brandishes the huge Wanamaker Trophy at the center of the eighteenth green. Not to be left out of the celebration, Benny stands on top of the clubhouse roof playing his saxophone in accompaniment.

Nine Months Later

Priscilla's Conclusion

J orell and I took Mark to visit Corinthia Falls the following May at his request. The Ailana Liona had recently accepted a special position on the Circle of Care's Board of Directors. His new title includes assisting Becky Oaks in the ministry of Childhood Disorders and Development.

Early that morning, we went first to the Boy's Ranch, where all three of us got a lesson in horseback riding. The residents proclaimed Mark the Hawaiian Cowboy.

Next, we toured the new Thomas Johnson Gymnasium next to the high school. Jorell recounted to Mark the day he recruited TJ in the aged half-court gym.

Jorell stopped the car so Mark could pay his respects to the monument on the lawn at City Hall. The marble shrine is dedicated to Corinthia Falls' fallen hero…Sgt. Samuel Sampson.

Mark insisted we stop by the recently established Anthony Bearkiller Health Services Clinic. There, Mark was able to witness first-hand the progress the Circle of Care has made in treating and caring for the disadvantaged.

It was a must to check out the old Corinthia Falls Church.

Mark took pictures of the life-size bronze statues out front of the Colonel and Silas. The pastor regaled us with the history of the congregation while we sat in the sanctuary's encircling pews.

As the bell tower of the Church of Corinthia Falls signaled twelve noon with the chiming of the town's self-proclaimed hymn, it was time for lunch. We were treated at the old Gentlemen's Club, now known as the Sherry-Becks Young Ladies' Center, to a meal of sandwiches and some fine fellowship.

Before our last stop, we took in the Corinthia Falls' Mission. It was going strong. Adult volunteers assisted by young people from the Ladies' Center and the Boy's Ranch carry on the vision of the Solomon clan, providing essentials to families in need. Mark donated a shipment of Ailana Liona golf shirts.

We found the best place to observe the beauty and tranquility of Corinthia Falls, from the elevated summit of the Lake Corinth Cemetery. From here you can see a panoramic view of the serene clear-blue waters down below surrounded by the rock formations of the lake and the peaceful town to the south: the dwelling place that nurtured a group of youth who inherited a ministry and changed the world.

As you saunter through the marbled memorials to the Saints of Corinthia Falls, you will come upon an old Oak tree in the far northwest corner shading a modest baby-blue headstone. It is where the Mourning Doves like to play. Etched in white lettering it reads simply:

Timothy 'Timber' Oaks

1964 – 2013

The Saint Went Marchin' In!

We are traveling in the footsteps
Of those who've gone before,
But we'll all be reunited
On a new and sunlit shore!

Oh, when the Saints go marching in
When the Saints go marching in!
Oh, Lord I want to be in that number
When the Saints go marching in!

For more information on the <u>Oklahoma United Methodist Circle of Care</u> please visit the author's website at <u>kimhutson.com</u>

CPSIA information can be obtained at www.ICGtesting.com
224372LV00001B/1/P